D0193059

REMEMBER LOVE

Also by Mary Balogh

The Westcott Series

SOMEONE TO LOVE
SOMEONE TO HOLD
SOMEONE TO WED
SOMEONE TO CARE
SOMEONE TO TRUST
SOMEONE TO HONOR
SOMEONE TO REMEMBER
SOMEONE TO ROMANCE
SOMEONE TO CHERISH
SOMEONE PERFECT

The Survivors' Club Series

THE PROPOSAL
THE ARRANGEMENT
THE ESCAPE
ONLY ENCHANTING
ONLY A PROMISE
ONLY A KISS
ONLY BELOVED

The Horsemen Trilogy

INDISCREET
UNFORGIVEN
IRRESISTIBLE

The Huxtable Series

FIRST COMES MARRIAGE
THEN COMES SEDUCTION
AT LAST COMES LOVE
SEDUCING AN ANGEL
A SECRET AFFAIR

The Simply Series

SIMPLY UNFORGETTABLE
SIMPLY LOVE
SIMPLY MAGIC
SIMPLY PERFECT

The Bedwyn Saga

SLIGHTLY MARRIED
SLIGHTLY WICKED
SLIGHTLY SCANDALOUS
SLIGHTLY TEMPTED
SLIGHTLY SINFUL
SLIGHTLY DANGEROUS

The Bedwyn Prequels

ONE NIGHT FOR LOVE
A SUMMER TO REMEMBER

The Mistress Trilogy

MORE THAN A MISTRESS
NO MAN'S MISTRESS
THE SECRET MISTRESS

The Web Series

THE GILDED WEB
WEB OF LOVE
THE DEVIL'S WEB

Classics

THE IDEAL WIFE
THE SECRET PEARL
A PRECIOUS JEWEL
A CHRISTMAS PROMISE
DARK ANGEL /
LORD CAREW'S BRIDE
A MATTER OF CLASS
THE TEMPORARY WIFE /
A PROMISE OF SPRING
THE FAMOUS HEROINE /
THE PLUMED BONNET

A CHRISTMAS BRIDE /
CHRISTMAS BEAU
A COUNTERFEIT BETROTHAL /
THE NOTORIOUS RAKE
UNDER THE MISTLETOE
BEYOND THE SUNRISE
LONGING
HEARTLESS
SILENT MELODY

REMEMBER LOVE

A RAVENSWOOD NOVEL

MARY BALOGH

Berkley
New York

BERKLEY
An imprint of Penguin Random House LLC
penguinrandomhouse.com

Copyright © 2022 by Mary Balogh
Penguin Random House supports copyright. Copyright fuels creativity, encourages diverse voices,
promotes free speech, and creates a vibrant culture. Thank you for buying an authorized edition of
this book and for complying with copyright laws by not reproducing, scanning, or distributing
any part of it in any form without permission. You are supporting writers and allowing
Penguin Random House to continue to publish books for every reader.

BERKLEY and the BERKLEY & B colophon are registered trademarks of
Penguin Random House LLC.

Library of Congress Cataloging-in-Publication Data

Names: Balogh, Mary, author.
Title: Remember love : a Ravenswood novel / Mary Balogh.
Description: New York : Berkley, [2022] | Series: A Ravenswood novel ; 1
Identifiers: LCCN 2021049538 (print) | LCCN 2021049539 (ebook) |
ISBN 9780593438121 (hardcover) | ISBN 9780593438138 (ebook)
Subjects: BISAC: FICTION / Romance / Regency. |
LCGFT: Romance fiction. | Historical fiction. | Novels.
Classification: LCC PR6052.A465 Re 2022 (print) |
LCC PR6052.A465 (ebook) | DDC 823/.914--dc23
LC record available at https://lccn.loc.gov/2021049538
LC ebook record available at https://lccn.loc.gov/2021049539

Printed in the United States of America
1   3   5   7   9   10   8   6   4   2

Book design by George Towne

This is a work of fiction. Names, characters, places, and incidents either are the product of the
author's imagination or are used fictitiously, and any resemblance to actual persons, living or
dead, business establishments, events, or locales is entirely coincidental.

REMEMBER LOVE

THE WARE FAMILY OF
RAVENSWOOD

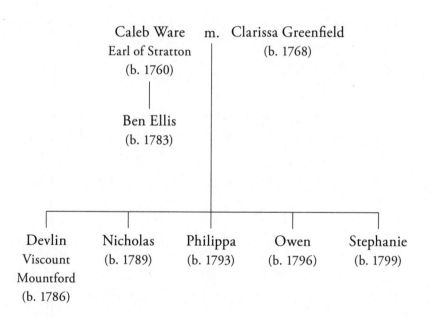

Caleb Ware   m.   Clarissa Greenfield
Earl of Stratton   (b. 1768)
(b. 1760)

Ben Ellis
(b. 1783)

Devlin   Nicholas   Philippa   Owen   Stephanie
Viscount   (b. 1789)   (b. 1793)   (b. 1796)   (b. 1799)
Mountford
(b. 1786)

PART ONE

⤫

1808

CHAPTER ONE

R avenswood Hall in Hampshire, home and principal seat for a number of generations of Barons and Earls of Stratton, was the center of the universe to most of the people who lived within five miles or so of its imposing splendor.

The current earl, the sixth, was Caleb Ware, a handsome, vigorous, genial man in his late forties who was well liked by all who knew him, and even loved by many. He had done his duty to family, title, and community early in life by marrying the lovely and charming Clarissa Greenfield, daughter of a neighboring landowner of some substance, when both were very young. They had produced a family of three sons and two daughters before he reached the age of forty. The fact that his lordship had also fathered a son prior to his marriage, shocking though it was when it was first disclosed, was not ultimately held against him, for he had had the decency to acknowledge the child and bring him into his own home when the mother died three years after giving birth to him. The earl and his countess had raised the boy in almost every way as one of their own, and he enjoyed the affection of both.

Ben Ellis, the earl's natural son, now twenty-five years old, was the steward of his father's vast estates, having chosen to stay home and learn all the intricacies of the profession from his elderly predecessor when he might have gone off to study at Cambridge and pursue some other career. The position had been his when the older man retired. His father had even insisted upon paying him the same handsome salary and upon increasing it a year later.

Devlin Ware, Viscount Mountford, the earl's eldest legitimate child, was twenty-two. He had completed his studies at Oxford the year before and returned home to assume his responsibilities as his father's heir. Fortunately, he and his older half brother, who had arrived in their home a scant three weeks after Devlin's birth, had always been close friends and worked well together.

Nicholas Ware, aged nineteen, a handsome, fair-haired, sunny-natured young man who closely resembled his father in both looks and disposition, was about to begin the career as an officer in a cavalry regiment that had been intended for him from birth. He was looking forward to it immensely, especially since he was likely to see plenty of action, with hostilities heating up between Britain and France under the ambitious leadership of Napoleon Bonaparte.

Lady Philippa Ware—Pippa to her family and close friends—was fifteen and rapidly turning from a pretty girl into a lovely young woman, to her mother's great regret. She was slender and dainty and blond haired and lively, and she was yearning for beaux and balls and a come-out Season in London in three years' time, as soon as she turned eighteen. An eternity away, in her opinion. Just around the very next corner, in her mother's.

Owen Ware was twelve. His mother sometimes described him as one-quarter pure sweetness and three-quarters undiluted mischief. He was intended for the church when he grew up, but both his parents agreed that the church might very well heave a collective sigh of relief if he eventually insisted upon another career—as a pirate upon the high seas, for example, or as the inventor of some mechanical horror, such as a hot-air balloon that would carry him off all the way to America and turn his mother's hair white long before he got there.

Lady Stephanie Ware was nine years old and everyone's favorite, though she sometimes felt that it was a real nuisance to be the youngest in the family, and the youngest by a long way when one thought of Ben and Devlin and Nicholas. Even Pippa. But what irked her more than anything else was the constant assurance by everyone around her—mother, father, siblings, governess, and nurse, to name a few—that any day now she would lose her baby fat and grow into a tall and slender beauty. Was she still a baby at the age of *nine*? When exactly was this miracle going to occur? And did her family love her so dearly just because she was fat and ugly and they felt sorry for her? But she tried hard not to be a complainer or whiner, for none of the rest of her family were either of those things, even Ben, who was not quite their brother and did not have the courtesy title even though he was older than Devlin. Stephanie wanted to be a worthy member of her family. She loved them all dearly. Especially her papa. And especially—never mind logic— Devlin. *Not* especially Owen, who was a pest of the first order and was always trying to frighten her in silly ways, like putting frogs in her rainy-day boots—as though she would not hear them croaking to be let out!—and long-legged spiders in her bed, which she simply picked up in her bare hand and transferred to *his* room. He was such a *child*.

Ravenswood Hall had been built and refashioned and added to and repaired and even almost totally pulled down and rebuilt once in the dim, distant past. The new hall, as it was still sometimes called, had in turn been altered numerous times since then, with the result that now, in these early years of the nineteenth century, though it was an imposing structure of gray stone, it could not be described by any distinct architectural name. It still had elements of its medieval predecessor. It was almost but not quite classical. And it had touches of almost everything between those two extremes. It was not particularly beautiful, though most people who were familiar with it might be surprised to hear that. To them it was simply Ravenswood, the grand house about which their lives revolved.

It was a familiar sight even to those who did not live within its walls, for it was clearly visible across the river that separated it from the village of Boscombe. Many grand homes were hidden for privacy within high walls and behind thick woodland. Not so Ravenswood. Grassland, dotted with a few ancient trees and liberally strewn with crocuses and daffodils in early spring, bluebells a little later, and assorted wildflowers through the summer and autumn, sloped gradually upward from the wrought iron gates and the low, moss-covered stone wall on the Ravenswood side of the river to the ha-ha, the steplike device that was invisible from the house but prevented grazing sheep from wandering too close to it and titillating their appetites with the cultivated flowers in their beds there and fouling the closely cropped lawns with their droppings.

The middle of the central, south-facing block of the house was one story higher than the rest of it and was approached by a steep flight of marble steps leading up to a pillared porchway with a carved stone frieze and peaked roof above and to a set of high double doors opening onto the grand entrance hall beyond. The massive east and west wings on either side of the central block and jutting forward from it were topped at the front rather incongruously with octagonal turret rooms. A visitor to the house had once compared them to onions—it had not been a compliment—and remarked that they completely ruined any claim to classical beauty the housefront might otherwise have presented to the world. The world did not appear to agree. Young people who lived at the hall or visited it frequently invariably loved those rooms. They had windows facing in every direction and were bright with natural light and warmed by the sun. They made wonderful playrooms and reading nooks and romantic retreats, though they did not necessarily perform all three of those functions at once.

The central block housed the family rooms and their bedchambers above. The west wing contained the more formal rooms, including the portrait gallery, the ballroom, the grand dining room, and reception rooms of varying sizes. The east wing had offices on the lower floor, guest chambers above them, and the nursery and schoolroom at the top, though the countess occasionally asked rhetorically of no one in particular whose idea *that* had been. There was a north wing, making of the house a great hollow square. That wing housed the family carriages, with the servants' quarters above.

A courtyard filled the hollow at the center of the house. It was approached by doors in each wing and by two magnificently carved stone archways and wide tunnels on either side of the marble steps in the southern wing. The courtyard was always lovely, with its neat, flower-bordered lawns and a rose arbor and fountain at the center. There were covered, cobbled cloisters about the perimeter.

The land north of the house was largely taken up by stables and paddocks on one side, kitchen gardens with extensive displays of flowers, vegetables, and herbs on the other.

The park stretched for a few miles to the east and west and consisted largely of rolling land with lawns and the occasional flower bed or copse of trees, walking and bridle paths, and driving lanes. There had once been a formal parterre garden before the house, its graveled paths constructed with geometric precision, its beds bright and fragrant with flowers and herbs of carefully coordinated colors and aromas and bordered with low, carefully clipped box hedges. It had been removed during the previous century, however, by the current earl's grandfather, who had preferred to look out of the drawing room windows and those of his bedchamber above upon a less dramatic, more rural scene. It was he who had had the ha-ha built and sheep introduced to the meadow below. Flat lawns and a few flower beds and artfully placed trees had replaced the parterres.

On the highest of the grassy rises to the west of the hall, within a short walking distance of the house, there was a pavilion built to resemble a Greek temple. It was an open structure with comfortable chairs and love seats within. The pillars that supported the roof formed a pleasing frame for the views in every direction: the river and the village, the rolling land of the park—which invariably brought stillness and peace to the soul—and the long lake to the west. Upon an island not far from the near shore of the lake there was another stone pavilion, not unlike the one on the hill but of smaller size. It was put to a variety of uses. Most often it sheltered the musicians the countess was fond of bringing in during the summer to entertain select gatherings of guests who were rowed across to the island to enjoy the music and the champagne and dainties both savory and sweet that always accompanied it. Sometimes more sizable orchestras played for larger audiences as they picnicked upon the shore, but on those occasions the music was a mere background to conversation and laughter as guests enjoyed one another's company and the beauty of their surroundings.

To the east of the hall there was more rolling land and what was known as the poplar walk—some people made a pun of the words *poplar* and *popular*, as though they were saying something everyone had not heard several dozen times before. A long, straight alley of lovingly cultivated grass was bordered on either side with poplar trees standing to attention like soldiers on parade. Benches were set at intervals along its edges for the relaxation of those who were in no hurry to reach the end of the walk. But at its end was an imposing glass summerhouse, a secluded retreat in which to sit on a summer day, or on a rainy day if one did not mind getting wet on the way there and back. A long line of hills lay some distance behind the summerhouse, separating the earl's land from that of Sir Ifor Rhys. A well-defined path over the crests of those hills was used by walkers wanting some vigorous exercise and by riders. Sometimes even a gig or curricle driver braved the narrowness of the trail and the steepness of the drops on either side for the sheer adventure of it and for the views, which were nothing short of awe-inspiring in a number of places.

Considered all in all, Ravenswood was surely one of the loveliest of the great estates in England. Or so those who lived within its influence believed quite firmly, most of them not having seen many or even any of the others.

And it was a happy place.

The earl and his family did not hoard either the house or the park for their exclusive use and pleasure. They did not keep it even just for members of the Ware family who lived nearby or for the countess's family, the Greenfields. No. The Wares of Ravenswood Hall were generous on a far wider scale with what was theirs. There were public days, two each week, often more during the summer, when the gates stood open and anyone was welcome to cross the bridge over the river and enjoy all the park had to offer, though it was understood without ever having to be stated or written down and posted on a board outside the gates that the family ought to be accorded some privacy close to the house.

However, the family did share even the house and its immedi-

ate environs on numerous occasions, some of them annual events.
There was always a party for the children of the neighborhood on
the afternoon of Christmas Eve, for example, and a supper and ball
for the adults on Boxing Day. There was a picnic by the lake following
a wildly popular treasure hunt on Valentine's Day, weather permit-
ting. The weather did not always permit in the middle of February,
of course, but even when it did not the festivities were not canceled.
Rather, they were moved indoors, where all four wings of the hall
were called into use for the treasure hunt, and everyone was herded
into a couple of adjoining reception rooms in the west wing afterward for tea.

Village assemblies were often held in the ballroom, since the
assembly rooms above the village inn could become so crowded
when everyone attended—as everyone often did—that it was virtually impossible to dance. School events such as plays and achievement days were frequently held at the hall, since the schoolroom
was not large enough to accommodate unlimited numbers of parents, grandparents, aunts, uncles, and cousins in any great comfort.

The event that was always most eagerly anticipated each year,
however, was the grand fete that was held on the last Saturday of
July. It was a daylong affair. It began in the middle of the morning
with a prayer by the vicar, songs by the young people's choir, and
dances about the maypole performed by a group of young persons
who gathered together once a fortnight all year long to learn new
formations and to practice the steps. The maypole was always
hoisted for the occasion on the lake side of the front lawn.

The opening ceremonies were followed by an outdoor luncheon
and an afternoon of activities for everyone. There were contests for
people of all ages and interests, from lace making for the women to
log splitting for the men to races for the children, to name but a
few. There were stalls at which one could spend one's hard-earned

money upon garish frivolities and sweetmeats, or on a faint chance to win a prize by hurling balls or darts at supposedly fixed objects, which had an annoying habit of moving or bending as soon as they were touched. There were always a fortune-teller, a portrait painter, and one or two new attractions each year. Last year there had been a juggler, who had not dropped any of his colored batons or whirling plates or flaming torches even once. There was the presentation of prize ribbons to the winners by the countess and a hearty shake of the hand by the earl. And then there was the lavish picnic meal by the lake while an orchestra played spirited tunes from the island pavilion and everyone declared they were still full from luncheon—and then devoured everything in sight because anything made by the Ravenswood cook really was too delicious to be resisted.

And that was not even the end of the day's festivities.

After eating their fill, those who lived close by dashed home to wash and change into evening finery, while those who did not retired to guest chambers assigned to them in order for them to get ready for the evening ball and—yes—a late supper. Those who had young children and no one at home to look after them were not doomed to miss all the fun. Nurses and maids who had volunteered for the task—and a generous monetary reward for their services—looked after the children in the nursery and put the babies and infants to sleep, sometimes two or even three to a bed or cot, while their parents frolicked.

Eager anticipation of the fete always grew for weeks beforehand. Many kept an anxious eye upon the western sky for days in advance, as though it were possible to will the arrival of good weather for the occasion. And perhaps it *was* possible, for almost no one could remember a time when the whole thing had been washed out by rain—a remarkable record when one considered the notorious unpredictability of English summers.

———

T he anticipation had begun this year. The Countess of Stratton, who was always exclusively in charge of the fete, was
already busy planning it with her large staff of helpers—which included her children but not her husband. The Earl of Stratton generally stayed well out of his wife's way, since the organizing of social
events was a woman's work—or so she reminded him whenever he
did interfere. For instance, this year he had suggested impulsively
to some of his neighbors at the village tavern one evening that they
introduce something new to the fete in the form of a few boxing
matches for the men to watch and even compete in.

Although his suggestion had been loudly cheered and toasted
with mugs of ale, the countess was not at all enthusiastic about it
when her husband arrived home and broached the subject with her.
She vetoed the idea without any discussion. There would almost
certainly be *blood*, she pointed out to him, and that was not something anyone would want to cope with on a fete day. Besides, a
boxing contest would draw away all the men and leave all the
women to entertain themselves and their children.

The women would *not* be amused.

"Really, Caleb," she said, shaking her head, though she smiled
at his exaggeratedly chastened expression. "Please leave everything
concerning the fete to me."

Which he did happily enough, though there were going to be a
few disappointed men in and about the village. He could watch
boxing matches to his heart's content throughout the spring months
each year, of course. Many of the other men could not.

The Earl of Stratton went to London each spring for the parlia-
mentary session—something that coincided with the social Season,
for which large segments of the *ton* flocked to town to mingle with

their peers and enjoy themselves for the few months following Easter with a frenzy of parties and balls, routs and concerts and soirees, and too many other social entertainments to name. The countess was not often of their number. She preferred to remain at Ravenswood with her children and neighbors and friends except for one or two brief dashes up to town to attend some special event that had arisen and to look in upon all the shops on Bond Street and Oxford Street to view the newest fashions while her husband was in attendance at the House of Lords.

It was an arrangement that somehow suited them both and aroused little adverse comment among their neighbors. The earl was admired for doing his duty without complaint, while the countess was commended for keeping her children in the country, where they had far more fresh air and freedom than they would find in town. Despite the enforced separation of a few months each year, the earl and his countess were widely believed to be a close couple, warm and charming, with a happy family.

While the countess was busy with preparations for the fete, the earl spent his time inspecting his farms, which Ben Ellis and Devlin ran flawlessly between them, and calling upon his neighbors to catch up on all their news, which in most cases was in short supply, though the tellers generally made the most of what little there was. He enjoyed listening to their stories and eating the cakes that were offered him and drinking ale, and even cups of tea when there was no other beverage on hand. And he called upon everyone, regardless of age or social status. He called upon his family members and upon Sir Ifor and Lady Rhys. He called upon the blacksmith at his smithy and the blacksmith's wife and mother-in-law in their home. He called upon the doctor, a single man he had known from boyhood, and upon his old nurse, now retired and living in the village with her great-niece. He even called upon the widowed Mrs. Shaw, a recent newcomer to the village, whom most of her neighbors treated with some reserve since they did not know her or anything about her except that her husband, an officer with the East India Company, had been killed in action during the Indian wars, poor man.

And the earl assured everyone, as he did each year, that this summer's fete would outshine all others because his wife was planning it more meticulously than ever. No one must even *think* of missing it. If anyone did, he would come in person to fetch them. Let them never say they had not been warned.

No one, as it happened, was thinking of missing the fete. Everyone looked forward to it as the high point of their summer, perhaps of the whole year, and smiled at the earl's needless threat and at his beaming pride in his wife's efforts.

CHAPTER TWO

O ne person who was waiting with more eagerness than usual for the Ravenswood fete was Gwyneth Rhys, daughter of Sir Ifor and Lady Rhys. A gentleman of Welsh birth and upbringing, Sir Ifor had inherited his title, land, and fortune from an uncle who had never married. At the time Sir Ifor had already owned land in Wales, and he had had a beloved younger brother with no land of his own and with a growing young family to feed. With the full knowledge and agreement of his wife, Sir Ifor had sold his land and home to his brother for five guineas and moved to England with her and Idris, his infant son. The following year Gwyneth had been born.

Sir Ifor missed Wales, for he had a large family of relatives there and a wide circle of friends and had lived a rich life in his home country. Wales returned the favor and missed him too, or at least the southwestern part of it, in which he had grown up, did. For as well as being a sociable, good-hearted gentleman, he was an organist of considerable talent and local renown. And he was a singer and a conductor of choirs. Music was in his soul, as was the case with many of his fellow Welshmen. And Welshwomen too, of course—that went without saying. He had brought his passion and his talents with him to England, however. Having discovered that there was no sizable pipe organ within an hour of his home in any direction, he had purchased one and had it installed in the village church, where he played it for Sunday services and upon numerous other occasions too.

He had inherited a church choir, all boys, and had trained them until they sounded like junior angels instead of a pack of disgruntled, growling dogs that would not have recognized a tune if one had tapped them on the shoulder. Soon after, he had added a few girls to their number, despite the misgivings of the elderly man who was vicar at the time. Sir Ifor had fixed him with a long stare, and the vicar had capitulated rather than find himself embroiled in an argument concerning the inferior status of women in the church. These volatile Welsh persons must be humored, he was rumored to have explained to a deputation of elders who had called upon him to question his decision. Sir Ifor had trained an all-women's choir too and a mixed choir, and occasionally an everyone-together choir. So far he had been unable to gather enough men for a choir of their own despite his rapturous descriptions of the male voice choirs in Wales.

Most of the residents of Boscombe and its surrounding areas considered Sir Ifor Rhys something of a local treasure. For everyone who did join his choirs—*even the boys*, for the love of God— actually enjoyed going to practice. Sir Ifor made them all laugh. More important, he made them want to sing. He convinced them that they *could* sing even though they suffered from that dreadful handicap of *being English*. And if they genuinely could not—there were, after all, a few people who were born with the affliction of tone deafness—there was nothing that could be done about it except to let them sing anyway.

It was not just Sir Ifor people valued, however. Lady Rhys—Bronwyn to her husband and close friends—had a lovely soprano voice, and Idris was a fine tenor. Gwyneth, after being dismissed for a few years by her fellow sopranos as one of those rare Welsh persons without a distinguished singing voice, had been discovered as she grew older to have a rich alto voice. But even apart from that, she was a fine harpist, though she was not heard nearly as often as many people would have liked, because the instrument was big and heavy. It could not simply be hauled about for all the impromptu concerts with which people entertained themselves at private gatherings.

Fortunately for everyone in the neighborhood, Sir Ifor had never expressed any intention of returning to his original home, which no longer belonged to him anyway. His English house had been named Cartref—the Welsh word for *home*, and that was exactly what it was to him and his Bronwyn. As for Wales, it was not *that* far away and could be visited at any time, despite the deplorable condition of the roads. And visit it he did. He spent a few weeks of every summer there with his family.

Gwyneth had turned eighteen just after Easter. She was no longer a girl but a woman, and her thoughts had shifted inevitably toward her future—toward romance and love and matrimony, that was. Not that she had not thought of those things before, of course. Like most of her female friends, she had dreamed of boys and happily-ever-after since she was twelve, maybe even younger. But there was a difference now. She was eighteen, and everyone would fully expect her to be seriously contemplating courtship and marriage. The young men she knew, and there were quite a few hereabouts, had begun to eye her with increased interest, just as she was eyeing them. Last summer, even though she had been only seventeen at the time, a few young neighbors and friends of her uncle and aunt and cousins in Wales had begun to look upon her with an interest they had not shown to any marked degree before. She had looked back with an answering awareness that they were no longer boys but young men. Attractive young men in some cases.

There was one problem, though. Or perhaps two.

One of those young men was Nicholas Ware, the Earl of Stratton's second son, who was just a year older than she. He was truly gorgeous to look upon, though she had fully noticed it only recently. Before then he had been merely her very best friend. He was good-natured and sociable and a huge favorite with all her friends, some of whom claimed to suffer heart palpitations if he should merely happen to glance their way. He was not a flirt, however, and was perhaps not even aware of the effect he was having upon the young female population of their neighborhood.

Nicholas had been Gwyneth's friend as far back as she could remember. A closer friend, in fact, than most of her female companions, who as children and growing girls had not been free to come visiting whenever they wished and, even when they did come, had been expected to remain in the drawing room with the adults or at least to stay somewhere within their sight while behaving with ladylike decorum.

Nicholas had come riding over to Cartref frequently, and it was for Gwyneth's company he came. They had spent hours and days of their childhood chasing each other and playing hide-and-seek among the trees and skipping rope and tumbling and climbing trees and chasing sheep—though that last was strictly forbidden and earned them a scolding if they were caught. They had talked and laughed endlessly and occasionally squabbled. She had ridden with him, at first on her pony while a groom hovered close by, and then on her horse, neatly seated on the sidesaddle she despised, or bareback and astride whenever she could avoid the scrutiny of that same groom.

As they grew older, Nicholas had still come when he was not

away at school. They had talked and talked, sitting up in a tree if it was a summer day, shut up in the parlor on colder days. She had told him about the freedom she always enjoyed when she was in Wales, running along the wide sandy beaches with her cousins and their friends, climbing the cliff faces, even swimming in the sea and diving beneath the foam of the waves. He complained to her of the tedium of school and the tyranny of the masters there and the bullying of the older boys, whom he delighted in defying. He even told her about the girls he and his friends would see occasionally despite the cloisterlike nature of the school, and of sneaking out occasionally to meet them—only to be disappointed by their giggling silliness.

Gwyneth's female friends were envious of her, for the gorgeous Nicholas Ware had eyes for no one but her. Yet to Gwyneth he felt a little like Idris did. Like a brother, that was, except more so. She tried sometimes to see him as her friends did and succeeded for a few moments. He was handsome and vibrant with life. Quite the stuff of romantic dreams, in fact. But then it was as though her eyes refocused and all she saw was Nick, her friend.

It was actually a little annoying.

He usually chose to sit beside her rather than anyone else at neighborhood parties and concerts, perhaps because conversation with each other never required any effort, or because they shared the same sense of humor. He always asked her first of anyone to dance with him at the assemblies—once she was deemed old enough to dance at them at all, that was. They could often amuse themselves for hours on a chilly or a wet day, singing duets while she played the spinet or the harp in the parlor. Occasionally her father came in to make a suggestion, the most common being that a duet was made to be sung *together*, in harmony with each other, not attacked as though they were in a competition to see who could finish first.

Sometimes she and Nicholas sang together at social gatherings during which all or most of the guests were expected to share their talents, however meager. And the suspicion gradually grew in Gwyneth's mind that perhaps the two of them were being looked upon as a couple, as potential marriage partners, even though Nicholas would be going away soon to begin his military career. The realization was a bit disturbing because the perception was not true. Moreover, it was actually damaging, for other potential suitors might be keeping their distance from her.

Specifically Devlin Ware, Viscount Mountford. Eldest son of the Earl of Stratton. Eldest legitimate son, anyway. Nicholas's brother. With whom she had been deeply, hopelessly, passionately in love all her life, or since she was eleven or twelve, anyway.

Unfortunately, he did not even know she existed.

He was four years older than she. That had seemed a very wide gap of time when she was a child. He had come to Cartref almost as often as Nicholas had, but he had come to spend time with Idris, his best friend and close to him in age. She had been about as visible to him in those days as a spider on the wall. Perhaps less so. But she had loved his visits anyway, except when he and Idris had gone off alone somewhere together. More often, though, she had been able to sit quietly in a corner, her head bent over some busy work, while they talked—about books and school and music and religion. Devlin had been a serious, earnest boy, quite unlike his younger brother, but she had loved to listen to him. He had had firm opinions and the knowledge to back them up. He had also, though, listened attentively to opposing ideas and sometimes acknowledged their merit. Not many people were like that. Most people, when they were apparently listening to an opposing argument, were really just waiting for the moment when they could jump back in to reassert *their* opinion. Very few people *listened*.

The age gap had seemed to narrow as she grew older, though she was still invisible to Devlin Ware. Not that she had done much to make herself seen, for she had started to feel uncharacteristically awkward and shy when he came. He was so serious-minded and intelligent and mature, and he had the title and would own the whole of Ravenswood one day. And in her eyes he was gorgeous, though in a quieter way than Nicholas or his father. Indeed, whenever other people talked about the Ware men, it was of those two they spoke with most admiration. Most people seemed not to have noticed Devlin's good looks, perhaps because he did not have the outgoing personality to go with them.

Gwyneth's stomach had started to tie itself into uncomfortable knots whenever he came to Cartref, and she had continued to hide in a dark corner or behind her mother lest he notice her and not like what he saw. Not that he would look. He never had. If anyone had asked him, he might well have said that there were just three members of the Rhys family—her father and her mother and Idris. Though that was surely an exaggeration.

As she grew up, she had wanted desperately for Devlin Ware to notice her, yet she did all in her power to see that it did not happen. Sometimes the hardest person in this world to understand is oneself, she had thought in exasperation. For it was most unlike her to hide, to cower, to be unsure of herself, to behave like a chastened mouse. *Most* unlike.

Finally, though, he *had* noticed her. It had happened last year when she had been behaving most like herself. Their paths had almost crossed while they were both out riding—separately. She had been about to turn up onto the line of hills that divided her father's land from his, and he had been on his way down. She had been riding alone—Nicholas had still been away at school. She had also been riding astride, as she had been allowed to do after she promised her mother and father one day when she was thirteen that she would never venture beyond their own property while so clad or so scandalously unaccompanied by a responsible male.

"The English are far more straitlaced than the Welsh, Gwyn," her father had said. "In some ways anyway. But since we are living here, you must try not to offend anyone unnecessarily and find yourself being called a hoyden."

"I despise that word, Ifor," his wife had said. "It is applied exclusively to girls. Have you noticed? I know a few wild boys, and people generally think none the worse of them—boys will be boys. I have never heard any of them called hoydens. But listen to your dad anyway, Gwyn. He gives good advice. Most of the time."

Gwyneth had been wearing breeches that day—also allowed on their own land, though her mother was beginning to make rumbling sounds of disapproval—and she had been hatless. Her hair had been streaming loose behind her in a tangled mass. She had not bothered to braid it or even tie it back before she left home. The whole episode had been unfortunate. She had told herself it was quite safe and unexceptionable to ride up over the hills, which were sort of her father's even if they were sort of the Earl of Stratton's too. She was not sure anyone had ever actually surveyed the hills to discover where the boundary line lay. Right down the center of the track? It seemed unlikely.

He had drawn rein when he was still some distance from her—Devlin, Viscount Mountford, that was—while she had felt every inch of herself blush, a reaction she had disguised by throwing back her head and staring defiantly at him since there had been nowhere she could literally hide. His eyes had swept over her from tousled head to booted feet in the stirrups, and he had nodded curtly and unsmilingly.

"Gwyneth," he had said by way of greeting—he had not even

paid her the courtesy of addressing her as *Miss Rhys*, even though she had been seventeen at the time. "I believe I will pretend this has not happened."

And he had turned his horse's head and ridden away back toward Ravenswood, leaving her to her own thoughts. *Well, at least he saw me today, no matter what he pretends to the contrary. And at least he does know I exist. He even knows my name.*

They had not been particularly consoling thoughts. He had not looked disgusted or angry or startled or . . . *anything*. He had not questioned or scolded or said or done something to give her an excuse to flare up at him. She flared anyway. What business of Devlin Ware, Viscount Mountford's, was it what she did or how she looked on her father's own land?

I believe I will pretend this has not happened.

How dared he! And what a very *stuffy* thing to say.

He was not in any way like his father or his brother. He was lean and dark haired and dour of countenance. Though *dour* was an unfair word to use. He did not glower or frown or display open ill humor. He was *serious* of countenance, then. And good-looking, even if no one else had noticed. He had very regular, finely chiseled features and blue, blue eyes. He did not make anything much of those eyes, it was true. He was not a man who smiled often, though he was *not* dour. His eyes were gorgeous. *He* was gorgeous.

He was a conscientious worker. He had apparently excelled at school—Idris had attended the same one, though he had been a class ahead of Devlin. He had studied hard at Oxford too, while Idris had apparently played hard, with predictable results academically. Her brother had scraped through his final exams, while Viscount Mountford had flown through his. Now he worked on the estate, alongside his elder half brother, who was their father's steward. Most young men of his social rank—or so she had overheard her father remark to her mother—were busy sowing wild oats at this stage of their lives. Though Idris was not. He was as devoted to their farm as Devlin was to his father's land. It was no wonder they were friends.

Gwyneth was not sure why she loved Devlin so passionately. Some people might call him dull, though admittedly she had not heard anyone go that far. But he was indeed very different from Nicholas and his father and even young Owen. Those three had a lively charm and appeal that appeared to be quite lacking in him.

It did not matter to Gwyneth. She loved Nicholas. But she was *in love with* Devlin Ware.

She had been for a long time. It was an infatuation she really must shake off now that she was grown-up, however, for it was time to experience attraction and flirtation and courtship and marriage with someone who was also attracted to her. She knew a few men who were—or would be if they knew she and Nicholas were not a couple.

What better place to turn her attention toward her future life than the Ravenswood fete, which everyone from miles around would attend, including every young, single male? She would even have a new dress for the occasion. Her mother had been urging her to have Mrs. Proctor, the village dressmaker, make one for her, and she had finally agreed. Something . . . *pink*, she had decided, though it was a color she usually avoided as being too daintily feminine for her vivid dark coloring. There was no chance of attracting Devlin's notice when she had not done so all her life. And her friendship with Nicholas was leading nowhere except to more of the same— which was very pleasant, but a woman needed more than friendship from a man after her eighteenth birthday. She needed romance and love and a husband and a home of her own and happily-ever-after.

She would look around with serious intent at the fete. Perhaps,

if the opportunity presented itself, she would do a bit of flirting and
see if she could feel a spark of romantic interest in someone who
was not Devlin Ware.

Who, after all, would *want* to be in love with someone like
him? Or married to him? Where would be the sunshine and the
laughter? The *passion*? Such thoughts were pointless, of course, for
she would want to be married to him. But it was time to be realistic.
Time to step out into the world and cast old dreams aside.

Gwyneth sighed and went in search of her mother.

B en Ellis had gone off to the island in the lake with one of the
gardeners to put a fresh coat of paint on the pavilion. He had
taken Owen with him but had left him on the bank of the lake
with another of the gardeners, who had been mending a slow leak
in one of the boats, a task that had caught the boy's interest. Now
Owen was helping paint the boat after having been given a work-
man's smock to wear, much to his disgust, and strict instructions at
least to try to get more paint on the boat than on his person.

Philippa was in the schoolroom with Miss Field, her governess
and Stephanie's, making ribbon rosettes to be presented to the winners and runners-up of the various contests at the fete.

Nicholas was looking over the equipment that would be needed
for the archery contest, to make sure nothing was missing and
nothing had deteriorated since last year. A few of the contestants—
Matthew Taylor, the carpenter, for example—would bring their
own bows and arrows, but most would not.

The Countess of Stratton was occupied with her endless lists,
convinced, as she usually was as the fete drew closer, that she had
surely forgotten something crucial, yet knowing with the rational
part of her mind that she had not. Her housekeeper would have

reminded her if she had, or her cook. Or Ben or Devlin, her right-hand men.

The earl was in the village somewhere, socializing, keeping out of everyone's way, though perhaps not out of the way of those villagers who had work to do. He was always welcomed anyway. It was hard to resist his hearty good nature.

Devlin was in the carriage house in the north wing of the hall, seeing to an overhaul of the maypole with one of the undergrooms. The pole itself was showing signs of rust and needed to be scraped and painted if it was not to present a sad spectacle on the big day. The ribbons, though they had been carefully stored in a long wooden chest, had nevertheless become tangled and twisted. A few of them were fraying at the edges and needed to be replaced. Others, though still intact, had faded after a few years of use and also needed replacing. The groom set about restoring the pole. Stephanie, who had escaped from the schoolroom to help her brother, patiently untangled the ribbons and straightened them, spreading them out along the floor beside the big traveling carriage, which was used once a year to convey her papa to London and once a year to bring him home and not very much in between. She smoothed the ribbons with plump fingers to see if they would need ironing. A fat braid of fair hair swung forward over each of her shoulders.

"I love the maypole dancing, Dev," she said. "It is my very favorite."

"Perhaps one day you will lead the dancers," he said, smiling at the back of her head.

"*Very* likely." She made a derisive puffing sound with her lips and continued with her task. "You have to be dainty and graceful and light on your feet. And *thin*. And *pretty* helps too."

None of which were possible for her, her tone implied. But there was no reason for it not to happen. She was neither physically lazy nor gluttonous, both of which manageable conditions were supposed to be main contributing factors to excess weight. The loss of her fat was not happening yet, however, and Devlin knew her appearance distressed his sister. He sometimes assured her he loved her just as she was—as he *did*—but she usually responded with that identical sound she had just made. She was his favorite sibling, though he loved them all. He loved Stephanie fiercely and dearly. Sometimes his heart ached for her.

"We will let them hang so they will not need an iron," he said of the ribbons, "and replace the ones that are damaged or old. I'll go into the village afterward to purchase new ones. Do you want to come with me?"

"In your curricle?" She jumped to her feet and turned a beaming face his way before smiling outright—her one claim to real beauty. "I do. And I get to choose the colors. You would probably pick black or gray. Or brown."

"I was planning to go on foot since the shop is no farther than a hop, skip, and jump from here," he said, and watched her smile fade. "But I suppose we can go by the scenic way, in which case a vehicle will definitely be necessary. The curricle it is, then, Steph, provided Mama does not have a fit of the vapors and forbid it. And you may choose the ribbons." He laughed as he tried to picture the faces of the villagers—not to mention his mother—if they arrived for the fete to discover black, gray, and brown ribbons fluttering from the maypole.

"Mama does not have vapors, Dev," she said. "She is not so silly. And she knows you always drive carefully when you have me for a passenger. I wish you would spring the horses sometimes, though. Nick might if I asked, but I know you would not."

"An old stick-in-the-mud, am I?" he asked her.

"You have a strong sense of responsibility," she said, stepping toward him and setting her arms about his waist to hug him, her cheek pressed against his chest. "I sometimes *wish* you would say yes, but I am always *glad* when you say no. I can trust you."

He kissed the top of her head. "Let's get these ribbons hanging and count how many new ones we will need."

A strong sense of responsibility. His father had put it a different way last year when Devlin, twenty-one years old and newly down from Oxford with a first-class degree, which he had earned with hard work and years of conscientious studying, had been spending a few months in London to kick up his heels and begin enjoying freedom and adulthood. It was something to which he had looked forward with great eagerness. He would have his father all to himself. Just the two of them. Two men together. His father, whom he had idolized his whole life and tried without much success to emulate, had been delighted to have his company and had encouraged him to sow some wild oats before the time came for him to settle down and marry and set up his nursery.

"And do not let anyone persuade you to do that too early in your life as I did, Dev," he had added. "Thirty is soon enough."

Devlin had been uncomfortably aware that both he and Nicholas had been born before their father turned thirty. Did he regret tying himself down with them so soon in life, then?

The earl had introduced his son to his clubs and taken him to Tattersalls and Jackson's boxing saloon and a fencing club. He had taken him to a few *ton* balls and private parties and select gambling houses. He had taken him to Vauxhall Gardens and the theater. After the performance at the theater, which Devlin had watched with avid interest, the earl had taken his son to the greenroom to meet and mingle with the performers.

Devlin had refused his father's offer to engage the services of one particularly alluring dancer to go to supper with him and—

presumably—to bed with him afterward. On another occasion he had refused to be introduced to the female proprietor of an exclusive house that catered to the needs of gentlemen who could afford the superior services of the young ladies who lived there.

His father had clapped him on the shoulder and squeezed while he laughed heartily and regarded his son with an indulgent smile. "You are in danger of becoming a dull dog, Dev," he had said genially.

Devlin had always longed to be like his father—open and amiable in manner, forever smiling and laughing. Loved by all, adored by his wife and children. Adoring them in return. Alas, it had always been impossible. An easy sociability did not come naturally to Devlin. His love for his family and friends and neighbors ran deep, but so did an inner reserve of manner he had never been able to shake off. And a firm sense of right and wrong and a belief in doing his duty, whether it was studying his hardest at school because his masters asked it of him and his father was paying the bills, or fixing up the maypole each summer because his mother trusted him to do it and it was important that it look fresh and new for their guests. One could not completely change the person one was born to be, it seemed.

A dull dog.

He should have laughed off the words and forgotten them. For his father had not meant any insult. The words had been spoken with humor and affection. Devlin did not doubt his father loved him as much as he loved Nicholas, his second son, who far more nearly resembled him.

He had been unable to forget, however. For those words had been spoken at just the time when a horrible, stomach-churning suspicion had been creeping up on Devlin. His father was meticulous about performing his obligation each spring and taking his place in the House of Lords even though it meant leaving his fam-

ily and going to London alone. He hated to leave, he protested each
year as he hugged them all and even shed a tear or two, and assured
them that the coming months would be dreary and endless until he
could return for the summer.

Devlin had never doubted his sincerity. But, when he was in
London himself, he discovered very quickly that his father did not
pine for his home and family in the country while spending all his
waking hours in London on House business or moping alone at his
town house. Rather, he enjoyed an active, boisterous social life. He
was something of a favorite with the *ton* and was invited everywhere.

He also seemed to be very well known in the greenroom of a
certain theater, especially by the actresses and female dancers.

He seemed also to be well acquainted with the proprietor of an
elegant house that was too exclusive to be known as a brothel.

And he had encouraged his son and heir to make free with the
services offered by both. *Sexual* services.

Devlin had not liked that side of his father—which was never
in evidence when he was at Ravenswood. He tried very hard not to
think about it, perhaps because he was afraid of where his thoughts
might lead him. His father after all had had at least one premarital
liaison when he was a young man. There was Ben as evidence.

No, Devlin had not wanted to think about it at the time. He
had chosen not to think about it since. Which was a bit unlike him.
Normally he would talk with his father about anything that bothered him in any way.

Perhaps, he had concluded, he really was just a dull dog.

Or, to use Stephanie's kinder description, a man with a sense of
responsibility.

"Come on," he said, grasping one of his sister's braids and tug-
ging gently on it. "Let's get ready and go purchase those ribbons."

CHAPTER THREE

M iss Jane Miller, the younger of the two sisters who ran the
general shop on the village green, helped Stephanie choose
ribbons. They had just had in a new supply, she explained, in all
colors of the rainbow and more.

"Choosing is not easy when there are so many lovely colors, is
it?" she said when she saw her customer dithering. "But look at this
orange one, Lady Stephanie. Is it not as vibrant as the loveliest sun-
set you have ever seen?"

"Oh yes, it *is*," Stephanie agreed. "I must have one of those.
And *that* one too. It is just the color of daffodils, my very favorite
flower. Lady Rhys told me it is the flower of Wales."

Devlin stood back, since his opinion as a mere male had not
been solicited. He nodded a greeting to the vicar's housekeeper and
held the door open for her as she left the shop, a laden basket over
one arm. He kept it open for Sally Holland, the blacksmith's daughter, as she entered and for Lady Rhys and Gwyneth, who came in
almost right behind her. Sally would have stood aside to allow them

to be served first, but Lady Rhys insisted, after thanking her, that it was only fair that they await their turn. Miss Miller, meanwhile—the elder sister, Caroline, that was—promised to serve Sally as quickly as she possibly could but also pointed out to her more illustrious customer that since Jane was already wrapping Lady Stephanie's ribbons, she might be free even sooner to offer her services.

"We are in no hurry at all, Miss Miller," Lady Rhys assured her. "And here is Lord Mountford waiting too, like patience on a monument. How do you do, Devlin? Is Stephanie purchasing ribbons? They must be newly arrived. There was not much of a selection when I looked a fortnight ago."

"Oh, Lady Rhys," Stephanie said, turning her head and beaming. "One of them is *just* the color of daffodils. Come and see. It is for the maypole, and Dev is letting me choose because sometimes I think he must be color blind."

Lady Rhys stepped up to the counter and Miss Jane opened the wrapping paper so she could see the ribbons Stephanie had chosen.

"Men often have execrable taste," Lady Rhys said. "They would probably choose gray or brown if left to themselves."

"That is *just* what I said." Stephanie giggled happily.

Devlin meanwhile was left standing beside Gwyneth. He nodded to her. "Good morning, Gwyneth. Or is it afternoon? I have lost track of time."

"So have I," she told him. "We have just come from Mrs. Proctor's. Mam and I were being measured for new dresses for the fete."

"Ah. For the daytime or the evening?" he asked. "Or maybe both?"

"I already have a gown for the evening," she said. "I have not worn it yet, though I have had it for a while. It was intended for the assembly after Easter, but we could not go. We all had colds."

"I remember," he said. "I was sorry. I missed you."

"I daresay it was Idris you missed, not I," she said.

It was a strange thing to say and not too gracious. "But I could not have danced with Idris," he said. "It would have looked odd. People would have talked."

Briefly and unexpectedly, she laughed. Gwyneth, he had always been aware, did not like him.

"Perhaps you will reserve the opening set of the ball for me," he said, and then regretted speaking so impulsively. "Or maybe you have already promised it to Nick, or intend to. How about the second set, then?"

It would have been far better to have kept his mouth shut. He could almost see her brain churning to come up with some reasonable excuse. He had never danced with Gwyneth. He had never asked, of course. *She did not like him.*

"I have not reserved any set for *anyone*," she told him. "Papa always says it ought not to be allowed, especially in a neighborhood where everyone knows everyone else. He says it is humiliating for a man to ask a lady for a dance only to be told someone else reserved it weeks ago. It makes him look and feel stupid, he says. *Twp* is the word he used. It is Welsh."

"Yes," he said. "Idris has called me *twp* a time or two. I shall wait until the evening of the fete, then, to ask you for a dance." That would give her plenty of time to think up another excuse.

She looked as though she was about to say something else, but Stephanie whirled away from the counter at that moment, her package clutched to her bosom, and beamed at Gwyneth.

"I am going to be allowed to watch the dancing until ten o'clock," she said, "even though I am not quite ten. But, as I explained to Mama, I *am* in my tenth year. Pippa had to wait until after her birthday. She is allowed to dance this year because she is fifteen. But she is terrified no one will ask her."

"I will ask her," Devlin said.

She made that sound with her lips. "You do not count, Dev," she told him. "You are her *brother.*"

"Ah," he said. "Did I give you enough money?"

"You did," she told him. "I even have one shilling and seven-pence ha'penny change to give back to you."

"Admirable," he said. "Good day to you, Gwyneth."

"Lady Rhys is going to the church because Sir Ifor is practicing the organ there," Stephanie said. "She just told me it could be a long wait."

"Ifor loses track of time when he is playing," Lady Rhys explained, turning from the counter for a moment. "Though I do not suppose that is news to anyone."

"I could listen to him forever," Miss Jane said with a sigh. "And even that would not be quite long enough."

"You said you would take me to the inn for lemonade in the coffee room before we go home, Dev," Stephanie reminded him. "May Gwyneth come too? *Will* you come, Gwyneth? *May* she, Lady Rhys?"

"Perhaps," Devlin said, "Lady Rhys would like to come too for some coffee."

"No, no," she said. "I am very ready to sit down in the quiet for a while and listen to the organ. But you go, Gwyn, by all means. We will know where to find each other."

"Then thank you," Gwyneth said, smiling at Stephanie. "That will be pleasant."

"I *would* show you the ribbons I chose," Stephanie said as they left the shop together. "But Miss Jane wrapped them up so nicely and tied them so neatly with string that I would make a mess if I tried to open the package."

"I will see them when they are hanging from the maypole," Gwyneth said. "Then I will let you know what I think."

She was looking pretty in a blue and white vertically striped dress with a blue spencer and matching bonnet. Her dark hair was confined in a tight knot on her neck. She always did look smart when in public, Devlin conceded as he stowed the package of ribbons behind the seat of his curricle and followed her and Stephanie, who were walking arm in arm toward the village inn on an adjacent side of the green. She very often looked quite different at home or on her father's land. He had once thought of her as a wild child. She had often gone barefoot outdoors during three seasons of the year, her long hair loose and disheveled down her back. She had often worn old, loose-fitting dresses, perhaps because she so frequently got her clothes dirty or even tore them. Devlin doubted there was a tree on her father's land she had not climbed or a fence she had not scrambled over even if there was a perfectly serviceable gate close by. Gates for Gwyneth had been made to swing on.

Devlin remembered one day in particular when a cat had been stuck at the top of a tall tree, mewing piteously. Lady Rhys had been anxiously muttering about gardeners and tall ladders and Idris had been callously predicting that the silly animal would find its way down eventually, as cats always did, and Devlin had wondered if he ought to volunteer to rescue it. Meanwhile, Gwyneth had simply climbed up and fetched it herself. *And* had her bare arms and knees badly scratched for her pains.

Ah, how he had loved her in those days. Though *love* was not the right word, he supposed, for he had been only a boy himself and there had been no sexual component to his feelings for her. He had envied Nick, who had run off to Cartref whenever he could and frolicked and laughed with her and encouraged all her excesses. Or perhaps she encouraged his. If he had been her friend, Devlin thought, he probably would have advised caution on a number of occasions for fear she would get hurt. And she surely would have laughed at him and done what she wanted anyway. Indeed, he would probably have goaded her unwittingly into additional wildness.

He could not have been Gwyneth's friend even if he had tried. Not as Nick was. He had just *wished* he could be.

His father was standing outside the inn, a tankard of ale in one hand, talking with three other men, one of whom was the vicar, and with one woman. She was Mrs. Shaw, the new resident of the village. She was apparently taking her tiny dog for a walk on a leash.

Stephanie was hugging their father while he held his tankard out at arm's length and patted her back with his free hand and beamed from her to Gwyneth to Devlin.

"I came with Dev to choose new ribbons for the maypole," Stephanie told him. "I got to pick the colors. Just wait till you see them. And now Dev is taking me for lemonade in the coffee room and Gwyneth has come with us because her papa is playing the organ in the church and Lady Rhys is going to sit and listen, but he is likely to play for a long time because he forgets about the time until he is reminded. But Lady Rhys will not remind him for a while yet. Do you want to come in with us, Papa?"

"Go on in and have a sit down," their father said, smiling genially. "I'll finish my ale and my conversation out here and see you at home later. I am delighted you are helping your mother with the fete. It will be the best one ever and a fitting testament to all her hard work. Am I the most fortunate husband in the world, or what? Though maybe your father would have something to say about that, Gwyneth."

The coffee room was empty and quiet and cool. After Stephanie had chosen a table by the window Devlin ordered drinks for them all: lemonade for his sister and Gwyneth, coffee for himself.

"If I were grown-up and really, really pretty," Stephanie said as the landlord withdrew to fetch their drinks, "and if my husband had just been killed in some war in India, I do not believe I would go to live somewhere in the depths of the country where I did not know a soul and no one knew me. Would *you*, Gwyneth? Would you, Dev?"

He had wondered about that himself. Mrs. Shaw was quite young, twenty-five or -six at the most. She was also extremely lovely. She dressed fashionably, and was very . . . He did not know quite what word his mind was searching for. *Provocative*, perhaps? But that was a bit harsh. She lived with an older woman, who was not, apparently, her mother or any relative. Devlin had never seen her, but he had heard her described as sharp-nosed and sour-looking and always dressed in black. Mrs. Shaw did not wear black—or even the gray or lavender of half mourning.

"I suppose she has her reasons," he said. "And they are her business, not ours."

"But I would like to *know*," his sister said with a sigh. "No one tells you anything when you are nine."

"Perhaps," Gwyneth said, "she is so distraught over her husband's death that she does not care *where* she lives, provided it is somewhere quiet."

"But then she would not care how she looks either, would she?" Stephanie said with irrefutable logic. "She clearly *does* care. I would not wear clothes like the ones she is wearing today just to take my dog for a walk. In the country. It would be silly. Did you notice her parasol, Gwyneth? It was all lace and show. It would not shield a person from a single ray of sunshine. I bet those are the sort of clothes ladies wear when they go walking in Hyde Park in London. Or on Bond Street. Or in the Pump Room in Bath. When they want to attract attention from men."

"I hate to dampen your need to know, Steph," Devlin said as their drinks were set before them. "But really, Mrs. Shaw's motivations are none of our business, are they?"

"I think Hyde Park is one place in London I would like to see," Gwyneth said. "And Vauxhall Gardens. By night, of course. It is said to be a magical place in the moonlight and lamplight. What would *you* like to see, Stephanie?"

Mrs. Shaw made Devlin feel a bit uneasy. And she did indeed remind him of London, which had not left a favorable impression upon him last year, when he had expected to enjoy himself but did not really do so. *Because he was a dull dog,* of course.

"St. Paul's Cathedral," Stephanie said. "And Carlton House. And all the galleries and museums. I wonder if Mrs. Shaw went to India with her husband. If she did, she surely would have needed more substantial parasols than that silly one she is carrying this morning. I think it would be awfully exciting and wondrously romantic to follow the drum with the man you loved. Don't you, Gwyneth?"

Gwyneth flushed a little and Devlin waited for her answer. He often wondered about her and Nick, though he had never talked to his brother about her. *Were* they sweethearts now that they had grown up? Surely they must be. Did they have an understanding? Was there likely to be a formal betrothal before Nick left in September to join his regiment? Was there any question at all of her following him? But he was only nineteen.

"I think it would be uncomfortable, moving from billet to billet," Gwyneth said. "Never having a settled home. It *sounds* romantic, Stephanie. I grant you that. But I doubt it is in reality. It also would be very stressful, though no more so, perhaps, than remaining at home and awaiting news. Military men *fight*. They get wounded and maimed. They get killed. Their wives surely live in a state of constant fear and anxiety. That poor lady might have lived through hell. We ought not to begrudge her that silly parasol now."

Stephanie was gazing at her, her half-consumed drink forgotten. "She does not *look* as if she has lived through hell," she said.

"People do not always show on the outside what they feel on the inside, though," Gwyneth said.

Ah. Devlin almost sighed aloud. No, indeed they did not.

"Is falling in love too risky a thing to do, then?" Stephanie asked. It was seemingly a rhetorical question. She did not wait for either of them to answer. "If I were in love, and if the man I loved returned my feelings, I would go to the ends of the earth with him and face dragons and volcanoes and invading armies with him. If anyone tried to stop me, I would elope with him and marry him and live happily ever after."

"Splendid!" Gwyneth laughed.

What the devil sort of fairy tales had Stephanie been reading? Devlin wondered.

"Don't elope, Steph," he said, smiling at her and patting her hand. "I want to be at your wedding. Proud brother and all that."

"You will wait forever, then." She sighed and lost her look of rapt ecstasy. "No one will ever want to marry me. Unless it is because I am Lady Stephanie Ware, daughter of the Earl of Stratton, and rich. No one will ever fall in love with me. I am sorry about that, Dev, for you are the eldest and will therefore have to look after me all through my spinsterhood."

"I will gladly look after you for an eternity if needs be," he told her.

"I think you may be pleasantly surprised, Stephanie," Gwyneth told her. "I think it altogether possible that the handsomest man in the world—and the most dashing and discerning—will fall very deeply in love with you and sweep you off your feet."

Stephanie made that puffing sound with her lips, but then she chuckled. "And the man in the moon may fall off it," she said, "and crash in the middle of the Atlantic Ocean."

"And on that note we had better get Gwyneth to the church before Sir Ifor and Lady Rhys grow tired of waiting for her and she has to walk home," Devlin said as he stood up.

"We would take her in the curricle, silly," Stephanie said. But she drained her glass and jumped to her feet.

The three men with whom the earl had been talking were still outside the inn when they left. Mrs. Shaw had gone on her way, though. So had their father, Devlin noticed.

Four children were out on the village green, to one side of the duck pond, throwing a ball from hand to hand. One of them waved to Stephanie, and she waved back and darted across the grass toward them, her braids bobbing against her shoulders.

"I'll see you by the curricle, Dev," she called over her shoulder.

He offered his arm to Gwyneth.

"You really do not need to escort me to the church, Lord Mountford," she said.

"I am to be abandoned by both my female companions, then, am I?" he asked her. "In full view of half the village? My reputation will be in tatters."

She smiled and took his arm after all. "I do love Stephanie," she told him.

"So do I," he said. "I just wish she loved herself a little more. But she looks in a mirror and, instead of seeing herself, she sees a fat child. *Are* you going to fear for Nick and worry about him after he joins his regiment?" he asked before he realized the question would leave his lips.

"Of course," she said. "The situation with Napoleon Bonaparte is getting nastier by the day. There are bound to be open hostilities soon, and the silly boy—*man*—is so eager to be a part of it all that sometimes I could shake him."

"He does know, though," Devlin said, "that war is serious business."

"Yes," she said. "He does. Oh, of course he does. I do him an injustice when I call his enthusiasms silly. Sometimes, though, I wish it was women who ruled the world. We would do so much better than men."

"Only, perhaps, because women do not have power," he said. "Perhaps if they did, they would soon begin to wield it as men do."

"Oh dear," she said. "Power really does corrupt, then?"

"I think perhaps it does," he said. "Not many people can hold firm to the noble ideal that power ought to be used in the service of those who do not have it."

This, he thought, was the longest conversation he had ever had with Gwyneth Rhys. And he was sounding as though someone ought to pick him up and shake the dust off him. Was it any wonder she had never liked him?

They had arrived outside the church. The doors stood open, and organ music spilled out.

"I think," she said, and he felt a bit breathless because she was smiling and looking directly at him, "all men should learn to play the organ or the cello or harp and pour all the passion of their soul into music. Or some other form of art. The world would surely be a better place. But since we do not live in a perfect world and I daresay my mother is feeling very hungry after missing luncheon, I had better go in there and suggest we all go home. Thank you for the lemonade, Devlin, and for your escort here to the church."

He had always noticed the slight lilt of a Welsh accent in her voice, though it was far less pronounced than it was with her mother and father, who often spoke Welsh to each other. He had not fully realized until today, though, how much it was part of her attraction. She had a low-pitched speaking voice to match her contralto singing voice. She had just called him *Devlin*.

He watched her disappear inside the church before he turned to look for Stephanie.

He drove her home by her favorite route and by far the longest one, over the crest of the hills between their land and Sir Ifor's. He flatly refused to spring the horses, but she exclaimed enthusiastically anyway over the steep drop on both sides of the track in places while she clung to the armrest of her seat on the one side and his coat sleeve on the other. Much good that would do her if he pitched them over.

Gwyneth had never totally abandoned her wild nature when she was at home, though it had been less in evidence as she grew older. Or so it had seemed to Devlin, who had viewed it from afar during his visits to Idris. She had continued to go barefoot outdoors, to leave her hair unbound, to run free. He had seen her sometimes running at play with the dogs or sitting on a stile reading. Once she had been up in the not-so-low branches of a tree with her book, a cat perched on a branch beside her and within reach of her caressing hand. She moved, it had always seemed to him, with a natural grace rather than with the trained deportment of a lady. But only at Cartref. Elsewhere she behaved with accepted propriety—as she had this morning.

It had always seemed to Devlin that she was bursting with passion—a product of her Welsh heritage, perhaps.

He had looked upon her for years now with a young man's yearning for what was unattainable. For it had always been clear to him that she was as different from him as night was from day. Yet he longed for her, for some share in that passion. He dreamed sometimes, with embarrassing foolishness, of running through a meadow with her, knee-deep in wildflowers, hand in hand, laughing. She played the harp, the instrument that to him looked most impossible to play, though it could produce music more haunting even than the organ. She played it well. She looked one with her harp when she was playing it. The instrument of Wales.

She did not like him. It was the one constant in his relationship with her—or, rather, in the total absence of a relationship. Or perhaps what she felt was not as active as dislike. Perhaps it was worse— a total indifference toward someone who was not of any interest whatsoever to her. Because he was dull and never wild. Or fun. Or spontaneous. He was the polar opposite of Nicholas, with whom she had had a close friendship all their lives and perhaps more than that now they were young adults. She had admitted that she would worry about him when he joined his regiment in the autumn.

Devlin had tried not to love Gwyneth. Loving her led only to pointless heartache, after all. For he would not cut in on a brother's preserve even if he could. Some things were simply not done. Besides, he loved his brother. And besides again, *she did not like him.*

He had tried not to love Gwyneth Rhys and had failed. He was hopelessly in love with her.

That truth had landed upon him heavily last year when he had come upon her at the foot of these very hills while they were both out riding alone. He had known before then—he had seen it with his own eyes—that she occasionally wore breeches, but he had never seen her close while she was wearing them. She had been wearing a loose white shirt with them, tucked in at the waist, and its very looseness had somehow drawn attention to her shapely bosom. Her legs had looked long and curvaceous through the tight-fitting breeches. Her hair, dark and glossy and untidy, had been flowing behind her, framing her oval Madonna's face. Her large blue eyes, a few shades darker than his own, had widened at the sight of him.

He had drawn rein, shocked to the core of his being. His body had reacted with sheer lust even while his mind had fought for control. His mind had won, of course—it always did. Ever the dull dog. He had looked her over slowly while steadying his breathing, had gazed into her eyes, keeping all expression from his own, and told her it would be better if he pretended this encounter had never happened. Or something to that effect.

That was what he had said and done instead of smiling and making some jesting remark, such as asking her if she was aware that she had lost her hat and her hairpins somewhere along the way. That might have drawn an answering smile from her to replace the cool, defiant look she was leveling upon him. Thinly disguised contempt.

He might have followed up that jest with a suggestion that he turn and ride back over the hills with her to admire the views. It had been a particularly clear day, he recalled. They might have spent a pleasant half hour or so together. Perhaps . . . But he had reacted predictably instead and she must have ridden onward, laughing at him. Or merely confirmed in her dislike of him. Certainly relieved to be away from him.

He had ridden off home. Hopelessly in love. Literally that, in fact—without hope. How could someone like him ever attract someone like Gwyneth Rhys, even if he *did* have his viscount's title and was heir to an earldom and property and fortune? Especially when there was his brother, who was everything he was not and with whom she was probably already in love.

"What about you, Dev?" Stephanie asked, breaking a long silence as they descended to flat land out behind the hall and there was no longer any danger to hold her attention. "Are you going to fall in love and get married and live happily ever after?" Her mind appeared to have reverted to their conversation at the inn.

"When there is someone for me to fall in love with, absolutely," he said, turning his head to smile fondly at her. "I know that to you twenty-two must seem ancient, Steph, but really I am *only* twenty-two. Give me time. And opportunity. One day she will appear— my forever-after dream woman. I will fall head over heels in love with her and she with me and we will marry—*not* by elopement but after all the usual formalities so the family will be able to celebrate with me. I will ask her to let you be a bridesmaid, and she will say yes because she will be in love with me and will therefore love you too. And we will live happily ever after."

His sister sighed. "Pippa too?" she asked him.

"Of course," he said. "I will ask my lady love to have both my sisters as bridesmaids."

"I had better hope, then, that she does not have eight sisters of her own," Stephanie said, and giggled gleefully as she patted his arm and gazed up into his face. "I would feel like part of a *procession*. Will you still love me after you find her?"

"Steph." He turned his head to look fully at her. "There is nothing on this earth that could stop me from loving you. Or in heaven or hell either, if you want all the alternatives covered."

"Ah." She sighed.

CHAPTER FOUR

The village of Boscombe more or less emptied out on the day of the fete as everyone crossed the bridge over the river and walked or rode in their gigs up the slight incline leading to the house.

People of all ages came, dressed in their best daytime finery, and people from all walks of life. The Reverend Paul Danver came from the vicarage on the green next to the church with Mrs. Danver and their three children, ranging in age from nine to fourteen. The Misses Miller closed their shop for one of the few times in the year—in addition to Sundays, of course—and came. As the elder of the two remarked to a group of neighbors while they waited on the lawn for the vicar's prayer to open the day's festivities, there was no point in keeping the shop open when there was no one to come shopping.

George Isherwood, the physician, came with Alan Roberts, the schoolteacher. Mrs. Proctor, the dressmaker, came with Audrey, her daughter. The day of the fete was always something of a triumph for the former, as a number of the women wore dresses she had

designed and sewn herself, with some help from Audrey. Oscar and
Amy Holland, the blacksmith and his wife, and their son, Cameron, and daughter, Sally, came as well as Mrs. Holland's mother.
Matthew Taylor, the carpenter, who had his shop above the smithy
on the village green, came with them.

And then there was Mrs. Barnes, once nanny to two generations of the Ware children at the hall, who came with Alice, her
great-niece. And Colonel Wexford with Miss Prudence Wexford,
his sister, and Ariel, his twelve-year-old daughter. And Mrs. Shaw,
the new resident, came alone, her companion being one of the few
villagers—perhaps even the only one—who stayed at home. There
were numerous others. The farm laborers all came from their cottages on the west side of Boscombe—it was almost like a village
within a village, the cottages almost identical to one another but
very picturesque nonetheless with their whitewashed walls and
thatched roofs and doors of different colors, which helped distinguish them from one another.

Families came from miles around, some of them modest landowners like David Cox and his wife, who supplied the village shop
with milk and eggs and vegetables in season. Others were tenants
of the Earl of Stratton. A few were landowners of some substance
and social prominence. The Rhyses were of this number, as was
Charles Rutledge, Baron Hardington, with his wife and children,
the eldest of whom was twenty-four, the youngest fourteen.

Members of the extended Ware family came if they lived close
enough, as many of them did. Some still bore that name. For others
it had changed upon the marriage of a Ware daughter. Some members of the family had come even if they lived at a considerable
distance, arriving the day before the fete and staying so they could
dress in the comfort of a Ravenswood guest chamber and consume
breakfast at their leisure. They would stay for a night after the fete

too. These house guests included Richard and Ellen Greenfield, parents of the Countess of Stratton, and their son George, the countess's younger brother, a childless widower.

On the earl's side the house guests included his mother, the dowager countess, and Margaret Beecham, her unmarried sister, with whom she now lived in what had been their childhood home. There were also his uncle and aunt Edward and Beatrice Ware, and his widowed aunt Enid Lamb, with Malcolm, her eldest son, and his wife, Jane, and two of their children. The earl's younger brother, Charles Ware, with his wife, Marian, and their three children had come to stay too, whereas the earl's elder sister, Eloise Atkins, arrived on the day of the fete with her husband, Vincent, and both their children, the younger of whom—Kitty—was with her new husband, Peregrine Charlton, this year and was already displaying to the observant eye evidence that she was in expectation of an interesting event.

By the middle of the morning all these family members were out on the wide, flat lawn before the house with neighbors and friends and villagers. It was crowded and buzzing with the noise of jovial greetings. The weather was, of course—had anyone really doubted it?—perfect for the occasion. The sky was clear, the air warm, the breeze slight. The only visible evidence of the breeze, in fact, was the fluttering of the brightly colored ribbons on the maypole on the west side of the lawn.

The Wares of Ravenswood itself were all outside too, greeting their guests with warm smiles and hearty handshakes and a few personal words for everyone, even those who labored on their farms every day except Saturday afternoons and Sundays and holidays— of which today was one. Those servants who were required to work were to be rewarded with a whole day off, for which they would be paid, on a day of their choice in August.

At last the vicar, in response to a gesture and a smile from the countess, took his place on the cobbled terrace at the foot of the wide marble steps, flanked by the Earl and Countess of Stratton and Viscount Mountford on one side and their other children on the other. Mr. Roberts, the schoolmaster, was helping Sir Ifor Rhys marshal into lines the members of the youth choir—which would include Owen and Stephanie after the prayer and opening remarks were finished—ready to take their places on the terrace to sing the songs they had practiced with great diligence for the past couple of months. The maypole dancers—the ladies in pastel-shaded dresses with floral wreaths on their heads, the men dressed in dark breeches and waistcoats with shirts to match their partners' dresses in color—were standing close to the maypole with the two fiddlers who would play for them.

An expectant hush fell upon the gathered guests as they turned their attention toward the terrace. The vicar raised both arms and invited everyone to bow their heads.

G wyneth stood on the lawn with everyone else, Idris on one side of her, her mother and father on the other. She was feeling unabashedly pretty in her new pink muslin dress. The bright shade had been the right choice, unusual though it was for her. She was not wearing a bonnet. Rather, she had had her maid gather her hair in a knot high on her head, with a cascade of curls and tendrils falling from it. They were all lightly threaded with small artificial flowers and leaves so that she looked, according to her father, like a spring garden.

She was smiling as she bowed her head for the opening prayer. She had been smiling all morning. And feeling glad about the pink dress and the fact that she looked like spring. For she had been fighting a bit of depression during the past week. It was quite illogical, but emotions did not always obey the rules of logic. They were not nearly as tidy as that.

Something had happened. It had all started a little over a week ago at the party Lord and Lady Hardington had held for the twenty-first birthday of James, their second son. It had not been a particularly grand affair because it was too close to the Ravenswood fete, Lady Hardington had explained. James himself had added in an aside to some of his younger listeners that the real reason was that he had threatened mutiny if they had insisted upon charades or blindman's buff or other such silly games. He had threatened to run away from home and never return if they suggested dancing.

There had been a lavish meal for the thirty guests, however, followed by cards in the drawing room and the inevitable impromptu concert before a light supper. Equally inevitably, Gwyneth and Nicholas Ware had been called upon to entertain the company with a vocal duet, for which Gwyneth provided the accompaniment on the pianoforte. They had both laughed as they took their bows afterward, for they had bungled their parts at one point and been forced to pause briefly to reestablish the harmony. Their audience had applauded them anyway, even Gwyneth's father, who had shaken his head as he smiled.

"They make a handsome couple," Colonel Wexford had observed. "Their voices are not bad either, especially when they keep in time with each other."

There had been general laughter.

"You are looking to add some good Welsh blood to your family line one of these days, are you, Stratton?" Lord Hardington had said.

"You need to be*ware*, Miss Rhys," the colonel had said, putting particular emphasis upon the second syllable.

More laughter.

"You are embarrassing poor Gwyneth, Andrew," the colonel's sister had told him, patting his hand. "And Nicholas too, I daresay."

That had been the end of the teasing, which had been perfectly good-natured. Someone else had taken their place at the pianoforte and the concert had continued. But there had been consequences. Two days later Nicholas had ridden over from Ravenswood to bring a couple of recipes Lady Stratton had promised Gwyneth's mother. He had sat for a while conversing with both her parents before turning to Gwyneth and inviting her to take the air with him since the rain of the previous day had stopped overnight and the ground had almost dried.

"We are going riding?" she had asked hopefully. The rain had actually lasted on and off for three days, and she was beginning to feel cooped up and in dire need of air and exercise. Her only real outing in that time had been to the birthday party, but that hardly counted as exercise.

"I had a short walk in mind," he had said, and he was frowning, she had seen when she looked closely at him. It was not an expression one saw often upon Nicholas's face.

Gwyneth had gone to fetch a shawl, and they had walked along the graveled paths, in the direction of the stile and the meadow beyond it.

"What is wrong?" she had asked him when they were far enough from the house not to be overheard through any open window.

"Wrong? Nothing," he had said. But he had not turned his head to look at her. His hands were clasped behind his back, and he was still frowning.

She had drawn breath to insist that *something* was the matter, but she had held her peace. If anything was bothering him—and *something* was—and he wanted to share it, he would get to it in his own time. Which was exactly what did happen.

"Gwyneth," he had said after a while, though he had not immediately continued. "Do you consider that we have a *courtship* going on?"

"No," she had replied forthrightly. "I would call it a friendship, Nick. Unfortunately it is harder than it used to be when you were ten and I was nine or when you were fifteen and I was fourteen to be simply friends—in other people's eyes anyway. Are you thinking of those rather tasteless remarks Colonel Wexford and Lord Hardington made at James's birthday party? They *were* embarrassing. I was very glad when Miss Wexford intervened and put a stop to it."

"So was I," he had said. "But it is not the first time such remarks have been made, is it?"

"No," she had said. He was frowning at the grass ahead of him.

"Look here, Gwyn," he had said at last, his voice abrupt. "I like you. I mean, I really do. I am very fond of you. But—well, good Lord, I am only nineteen. You are only eighteen. I am not in the market for a bride and probably will not be for at least another ten years. I do not want to be trapped into anything, especially now, when I am about to embark upon a new life and am looking forward to all sorts of adventures. It is an enormous relief to know you feel the same way. You *do* feel as I do, do you not? You are not just saying what you think I want to hear?"

"I am not, Nick," she had assured him. "I like you exceedingly well. I suppose I even love you. But not in *that* way."

He had looked at her at last, his cheeks a bit flushed. "The thing is, Gwyn," he had said, "that we should maybe stay away from each other between now and September. When we are in company with other people, anyway. At the Ravenswood fete in particular. If we spend most of the day in each other's company, as we usually do, and dance a few times with each other at the ball, there are sure to be cousins and aunts and uncles and neighbors galore who will notice and make something of it and remark on it, and before we know it we will find that we have an *understanding* and you will not be free to look for a husband after I have left and I will be plagued by guilt. Maybe it would just be best to stay away from each other."

"But will people then believe we have quarreled?" she had asked him. "And make something of *that*?"

"Well, I suppose we can occasionally exchange a few words and a laugh with each other before drifting apart again," he had said. "Dash it all, Gwyn, I wish people would mind their own business and let friends be friends without getting all silly about it and hinting at some grand romance when there is none. I do think we had better keep away from each other most of the time, though. What do you think?"

"It sounds like a very sensible idea," she had assured him, smiling at him and then laughing. "There is no need to look so tragic, Nick. There is not going to be one broken heart between the two of us, is there?"

He had laughed with her then and looked hugely relieved. "You are a jolly good fellow, Gwyn," he had said. "I have scarcely slept for the last two nights. I have tossed and turned instead and wondered if you would be hurt if I told you I do not want to marry you. The last thing in the world I want to do is to hurt you. I *like* you. I mean, I am not just saying it. I *do*."

"I know, Nick." She had laughed again. "And I feel just as you do. It would seem a bit like marrying my brother. Not at all the thing, in fact. I am glad you came and cleared the air. Now we can enjoy a simple friendship—but from a distance. And not at all during the fete."

He had taken his leave soon after, a spring in his step.

And the thing was, Gwyneth had thought as she had gazed after him, he was right, and she had been fully aware of it—and

concerned about it—before he came and made his painful explanation. She was dearly fond of him, but she could never *love* him. Not
in *that* way. It really was a relief to discover that he had no romantic
feelings toward her either. Now she was free to enjoy the fete as she
had wanted to enjoy it—looking about at all the other young men,
seeing if any were interested in her and if she was interested in
them. Perhaps even . . . No, *not* perhaps him. Devlin Ware hardly
knew she existed. She would be free to find someone new, even if
only for a little light flirtation.

But, oh dear, it did feel a bit upsetting that she and Nicholas
could no longer enjoy even a friendship. And it was all because they
were a boy and a girl suddenly grown into a young man and woman
and it was no longer quite the thing unless they were in a courtship.
Life was going to feel a tad flat for a while. A rehearsal for September, perhaps, when he would be going away to join his regiment and
would perhaps never come back. But a lurching of her stomach had
made her wish she had not thought beyond his actual leaving.
Never was a pretty brutal word.

So here she was at the fete, feeling festive and pretty—even if it
was a bit conceited of her to think so—and looking forward to all
the activities and possibilities of the day ahead. And a little dragged
down by depression. She had not set eyes upon Nicholas all week,
and this morning, while every member of the Ware family had
greeted her by name and spoken a few words to her—even *Devlin*,
who had commented upon how fortunate they were that the
weather was so lovely—Nicholas had included her in the general
remarks he had made to her parents and Idris but had scarcely
glanced at her and had not even spoken her name. He was finding
this hard, she thought, but . . . Oh, Nicholas! Everyone *would* be
thinking they had quarreled. And she really was missing him.

Being eighteen was not all sunshine and light, as she had expected it to be. But at least she was free to look about her today and *enjoy* herself.

The vicar began his prayer.

After the opening prayer and some brief words of welcome from the earl, the children's choir sang. They were unaccompanied but took their opening note for each song unerringly from Sir Ifor and remained miraculously on key and even in harmony with one another when they launched into two-part singing. The sopranos from the church choir soared, most of the others took the lower notes, which often comprised the main melody, and those few who were truly tone deaf at least managed to keep the correct rhythm as they growled a bass foundation to the whole. They all took their bow—which they had practiced to be done in unison— when they were finished, some of the boys giggling self-consciously and crossing their eyes, Owen among them, most of the girls, including Stephanie, puffing out their chests and beaming with pride.

Then it was the turn of the maypole dancers, who performed for almost half an hour while guests gathered in a wide ring about them and marveled at the colorful visual spectacle that whirled and dipped before their eyes as dancers performed the intricate steps with lithe grace and circled the maypole, weaving in and out and past one another, first plaiting their ribbons into what looked like a hopeless entanglement, and then magically unweaving them as they moved until they were all single ribbons again, each held by one dancer.

"I wish they could dance all day long," someone complained when they finally came to the end of their repertoire and acknowledged the enthusiastic applause, the women by curtsying low, their skirts spread about them on the grass, the men by bowing and grinning.

"But then we would miss our luncheon, Mavis," someone else said.

And everyone turned from the maypole to see that while they had been watching the dancing, long tables had been set up along the terrace and covered with crisp white cloths and laden from end to end with a large variety of foods and beverages. They lined up to serve themselves, having suddenly discovered voracious appetites.

Devlin was prepared to be busy all day long. His mother had organized everything down to the finest detail, of course, but one never knew when some unexpected crisis might arise. Besides, it was always good for the guests to see the family taking a constant interest in their well-being and in them. Being good hosts, no matter what social event had brought guests to Ravenswood, was something that was bred into the Wares at a young age.

Owen and Stephanie were directing the more elderly of the guests, including their grandfather and both grandmothers, to chairs that had been set up in groupings out on the lawn. Philippa and Nicholas were filling plates for them. Devlin helped some families find space on the blankets that had been spread on the grass. He held babies and small infants while their parents heaped plates with food. His mother was carrying drinks to various people while his father circulated among the groups, having a word with each. His laughter carried across the lawn along with theirs.

Ben was in the carriage house, gathering everything that was going to be needed for the children's races as soon as luncheon was over. He would be back before they started to help clear away any dishes or debris the guests had left behind on the grass and to help fold blankets and move chairs off to the sides.

It was the one day out of the year when the Wares worked alongside their servants, with very little thought for their own amusement or hunger pangs. It was how they drew enjoyment from the day.

After he had helped his brother clear the lawn for the races,

Devlin went down to the lake to check that the vendors' booths and other attractions were ready to go. He made sure all the boats and the requisite number of oars had been brought out of the boathouse and lined up on the bank. Then he strode off to the poplar walk some distance away, where the archery contest was to take place. But Nicholas had already made sure the area was properly roped off. He would be there later, he promised Devlin, before the contests began, to warn parents to keep an eye on their children. Devlin checked on the stable yard behind the hall, where the log-splitting contest was to take place later. But everything was under control— Ben was back there with Owen and a couple of Owen's friends, all of whom seemed to find it necessary to talk at once and at great volume.

He could relax now, Devlin told himself, and enjoy the afternoon with everyone else. Relax and let his mind wander. It had been wandering all day actually—to Gwyneth Rhys, just as it had all of yesterday and last night. The fete was always an exciting time. The arrival of family members as house guests the day before the great event only added to the anticipation. But this year Devlin felt more than usually restless. He had tossed and turned in his bed far more than he had slept on it last night. Because of Gwyneth. Because perhaps, maybe—though probably not, but just possibly—he might have a chance with her.

She looked vividly lovely today in a bright pink dress and with her dark hair styled in myriad curls and ringlets and threaded with tiny flowers. And she glowed, a smile curving her lips whenever he caught sight of her, as though she was bubbling over with happiness. As why should she not be on the day of the Ravenswood fete? But he had half feared she would be looking wan and dejected.

He had found out just yesterday from Nick what had happened a few days ago. His brother had ridden into the stable yard and dismounted while Devlin and Ben were examining the hoof of one of the carriage horses to see if the shoe needed to be replaced. Their father had mentioned that he fancied the horse was favoring that leg.

"I've done it at last," Nicholas had announced. "I did it almost a week ago, in fact."

"Congratulations," Devlin had said. "I can't see anything wrong with this shoe. Can you, Ben? And what is it you have done at last, Nick?"

"Had a talk with Gwyn," Nicholas had said, frowning and nodding when a groom offered to take his horse and brush it down for him.

"That sounds ominous," Ben had said. "No, I can't, Dev. There is no stone or anything lodged under it either. A quarrel, do you mean, Nick?"

"There was no quarrel," Nick had said. "She was very decent about it. And it turned out she felt just as I did. All this nonsense people have begun to spout about the two of us is nothing but—well, nonsense. I am nineteen, for the love of God. And Gwyn is only eighteen. That is hardly on the shelf, is it? I am fond of her, and if I were ten years older, maybe . . . But no, not even then. It must be because we have more or less grown up together. I cannot think of her in that way, and she says the same of me. It was a huge relief finally to talk about it."

"You were beginning to fear a leg shackle?" their half brother had asked, setting the horse's hoof back on the ground and straightening up. "At your age?"

"It has been enough to bring me out in a cold sweat, if you want the truth of it," Nicholas had said. "Though that sounds a bit disrespectful to Gwyn. I *like* her, dash it all."

"I daresay she grows a bit clammy too at the thought of being forced to follow you into mud and mayhem," Ben had said.

"So you have put an end to it." Devlin had straightened up too and wiped his hands on an old rag.

"We have agreed to more or less stay away from each other until I go away in September," Nicholas had told them. "I don't like it, but . . . Well, people can be very stupid."

So she was free. It was the thought that had hammered at Devlin's brain for the rest of the day, busy as he had been with the arrival of grandparents and aunts and uncles and cousins and everyone wanting to talk at once.

She was free. It was the thought that had set him tossing and turning all night.

He need no longer keep his distance from her out of deference to his brother. Not that she would ever have him, of course. And to his shame, he would not even know how to go about wooing her. But . . . Well, suddenly there was a glimmering of hope.

And she appeared to be very happy about her freedom, if her appearance today was anything to judge by. It might not be, of course. Her smiles and sparkling eyes, her pink dress, the flowers in her hair might all be a mask to disguise heartache. She had always seemed exceedingly fond of Nick, and that had never surprised Devlin. His younger brother had all the magnetic charm, not to mention good looks, that Devlin lacked. And ease of manner. And confidence in himself.

But she was free.

He had made the devil of a poor start with her this morning, however. He had gone to greet all the Rhyses after their arrival, as he had done with everyone else too, of course. He had exchanged a word with each of them. But what had he said to Gwyneth? He could not remember his exact words, but it had been something to do with the fine weather. *The weather.* To the woman he wished to impress. To the woman he wished to woo and marry. He had led the charge with remarks about *the weather.*

But she was free.

CHAPTER FIVE

G wyneth was with someone different every time Devlin glimpsed her after that, even once, briefly, with Nicholas, who was smiling and shaking her hand and then striding away in one direction while she moved off in another. She watched the maypole dancing with Audrey Proctor and Leonard Atkins, one of the Ware cousins. She ate luncheon with Wendell Lamb, another cousin, and James and Barbara Rutledge. Afterward she was down by the lake with Idris and two of the maypole dancers. Devlin could not recall the woman's name, but the man was Sidney Johnson, a prosperous landowner from five or six miles away, though he was still only in his early twenties. His father had died suddenly a year or two ago.

Whenever he saw her, she was sparkling and clearly enjoying every moment.

The maypole was still up, Devlin saw when he returned to the front of the house from the stable yard. The dancers had consented to give lessons to anyone who wished to experience the fun for themselves, and they were already starting. He strolled closer.

There were predictably more females than males interested in the dancing. Both his sisters were there. And Gwyneth Rhys. Two of the regular male dancers had made the numbers equal by joining the learners. Stephanie was clutching the bright orange ribbon as though her life depended upon not letting go. Her eyes were so focused upon the instructor that she did not even notice her brother. Pippa was bright-eyed and flushed. She was partnered with one of the dancers, a ginger-haired young man with freckles and a crooked smile. Mrs. Shaw was there too.

One of the fiddlers began to play, and, following the instructions one of the dancers called, the students circled the maypole, their ribbons weaving in and out and remaining miraculously unsnarled for a whole minute before one of their number—Pippa—ducked under her partner's arm at the same moment he tried to duck under hers and they bumped heads and everyone got tangled up and stopped with a burst of laughter and agonized giggles from Philippa, who apologized profusely.

The earl, laughing heartily, moved up beside Devlin.

"Pippa has inherited *something* from me, at least," he said. "I tried that a few times when I was a lad. I could get the steps right if I forgot the ribbon in my hand, and I could get the ribbon to work right if I ignored my feet. I could not do both at once, though. It was a bit like trying to play the pianoforte with both hands. It looks easy when you watch the experts."

"Most skills look easy if the performer has practiced long enough," Devlin said. "Sir Ifor on the organ, as a case in point."

"Oh, well done," his father called a minute or so later, after the dancers had performed a whole series of steps without mishap. "Very well done indeed." He applauded with enthusiasm.

Mrs. Shaw turned her face toward him and smiled with a lifting of the corners of her lips and a lowering of her eyelashes.

Good Lord, Devlin thought. Really. *Good Lord.*

"Did you *see* me, Papa?" Stephanie shrieked. "Did you *see* me, Dev?"

"I did indeed," Devlin said, his heart melting as it usually did when he looked into his sister's round, shiny-cheeked face. Her hair was in its usual braids.

"Splendid, splendid," his father called back. "All of you."

Gwyneth glanced their way too, but with an open, happy smile, not that . . . seductive? Was that the right word? Not that expression Mrs. Shaw had had on her face a moment ago when she looked at his father, anyway.

"Look!" one of the women dancers called from the cluster surrounding the instructor. "A spare young male, just standing there doing nothing. Lord Mountford, do please come and take Sidney's place at the maypole."

"That is not necessarily a good idea," Devlin said, grimacing and then laughing as his father slapped a hand on his shoulder and propelled him forward. "You may be sorry."

"I am an expert at untangling ribbons, Dev, if you should need me," Stephanie said. "Come and join us."

Sidney was the one partnering Gwyneth.

"Here," he said, grinning and extending an emerald green ribbon—one of the new ones—toward Devlin. "Take it. The worst that can happen is that you will wreck the whole dance and ruin everyone's day."

That amused everyone.

Devlin took the ribbon and glanced ruefully at Gwyneth. The sparkle in her had made a rapid disappearance, and he was unwillingly reminded of how she had been as a girl when forced to be in a room with him. She had always hidden in a corner or behind her mother and turned mute and become a totally different person from the wild, free, laughing girl he glimpsed from afar. She could not have made her dislike of him more obvious. He had found it a bit hurtful. Why exactly did she dislike him? What had he *done*?

"It is not as easy as it looks," she warned him now.

"It does not even look easy," he said, and her eyes lit with laughter.

He stayed for a quarter of an hour or so, until another group of would-be dancers had gathered. And actually it *was* as easy as it looked—which meant it was not very easy at all, but not impossible either, provided everyone listened carefully and followed the very clear instructions that were given before they danced and again *while* they danced. Devlin felt a bit as though he had two wooden legs at first, but he took his ribbon where he was supposed to take it and did not bang heads or collide with anyone else. He was not responsible for ruining anyone's day.

It was hard not to be distracted, though, for Gwyneth soon recovered her spirits, and smiled and even laughed as they danced. She looked directly at him a few times, and her smile did not dim. If anything, it grew brighter. Her cheeks were flushed, her eyes sparkling.

"You see what happens when people cooperate as a group instead of asserting their individuality?" he said to her as they relinquished their ribbons to the next comers. "Everything proceeds smoothly and everyone is happy." He was smiling, he realized—which was just as well. Perhaps the smile would blow the dust from his words.

"I do believe you have just devised a solution to the world's problems, Lord Mountford," she said, and she laughed and then kept on smiling the sunny Gwyneth smile he had seen a hundred times or more at Cartref, but never before directed at him.

It was by far the happiest moment of his day so far.

Mrs. Shaw was standing talking with his father. Pippa was being borne away by James Rutledge on one side of her and Cousin Clarence Ware on the other. She had a hand through an arm of each and was tripping along between them. Stephanie was making her way along the terrace with Douglas Danver and Ariel Wexford.

"I am going to check on the fortune-teller and the portrait painter in the courtyard," Devlin said to Gwyneth, and he kept speaking before he lost his courage. "Would you like to come with me?"

She hesitated for a moment and he was quite sure she was about to make some excuse. She did not, though. "I intend to have my fortune told today," she said. "I have not had the mettle any other year. I want to discover that I am about to meet someone tall, dark, and handsome."

"Well," he said. "I am tall and dark. Tallish, anyway. Will two of the three suffice? Or maybe one and a half of the three?"

"Oh, and you are handsome too," she said, and laughed again— and was all rosy pink beauty from her exertions about the maypole.

"Sometimes," he said, "fishing for compliments meets with quite spectacular success."

And were they actually . . . *flirting*?

She laughed once more and took his offered arm.

Had he been *flirting* with her? *Devlin Ware?* And had she been flirting right back? But here she was, Gwyneth discovered, actually walking with him, her arm drawn through his as they crossed the lawn toward one of the archways and the courtyard beyond. He might not be quite as tall as Nicholas or as dazzlingly handsome or as openly genial, but she actually found him more attractive. She always had.

The children's races had already begun, and he changed their course slightly so they could watch one or two of them. He congratulated the winner of a little girls' race and commended the rest for running so hard. He did the same after the little boys' race, and he would have turned away then. But the child who had come in eighth out of a field of ten—he was Eddie, Gwyneth saw, son of one of her father's grooms—burst into sudden tears and would not be consoled either by his mother's hugs and soothing murmurs or by his father's hearty reminder that big boys do not cry.

"But he is *not* a big boy," Gwyneth murmured. He was four.

"There is no point in coming in first in a race if there is no one coming up behind in second or eighth place," Devlin said, raising his voice to address himself to the child. "You have performed an important role, lad. That race needed every one of you."

Eddie looked up at him, sniffing and frowning. Unconvinced.

"Do you have any brothers and sisters?" Devlin asked.

"My sister. She is nearly three," the boy said. "And the baby."

His father was holding the baby.

"So you are the eldest," Devlin said. "There would be no point in calling yourself the eldest, though, would there, if there were no younger ones to make you feel older?"

The little boy thought about it. "But it would still be more fun to win," he said.

"My lord," his mother murmured to him.

"My lord," the child added.

"Alas, winning *is* more fun," Devlin said. "Keep trying. What are you really good at?"

Eddie thought. "I always find more eggs than Papa does," he said.

"Admirable," Devlin told him. "I love eggs, but I can never find any."

The child's tears appeared to have been forgotten by the time Devlin and Gwyneth turned away.

"Adults often assume that children's games and contests are sheer fun," he said. "We have short memories. They are anything but fun to the losers, and there are always far more of them than there are winners. I suppose they offer lessons in life, but why should children have to learn so early about failure?"

"But Eddie is good at finding eggs," she said. "I hope his parents praise him for that. I am glad you reminded him that there will always be something at which he can excel."

There was kindness in him, Gwyneth thought, even to the young child of a laboring man.

In one corner of the terrace, tucked in between the main block and the protruding section of one of the wings, a young man and woman had several pots of brightly colored paints opened up on a table between them. Both were wearing large aprons to protect their clothes as they transformed the faces of children into those of cats or clowns or princesses or ferocious warriors. Gwyneth had never seen anything like it before, but it had attracted a queue of eager children—some of them with more dubious-looking parents in tow. For the children were all wearing their best clothes.

"They assured my mother," Devlin explained, "that the paint dries almost instantly, that is does not smudge or come off on fingers, and that it washes off both skin and clothing without leaving any stain. My father has promised to have them locked up in a dungeon under the hall if it should turn out they have misled us."

"I would have *loved* that when I was a child," Gwyneth said. "I would have been Cleopatra."

"A lion for me," he said. "Oh, goodness."

Stephanie had appeared before them, her eyelids bright blue and glittering, her cheeks a shocking pink, her lips a bright and clashing red. She was beaming.

"Look at me, Dev," she said. "Look at me, Gwyneth."

"But who is this princess?" he asked. "Who let her in? No one invited her. No one would dare. She is far too beautiful. She will cast all the other ladies in the shade and have them all in tears."

"I do believe she is Princess Stephanie," Gwyneth said. "There is nothing to worry about, though, for everyone loves her to distraction because of her kindness and her sunny nature. The ladies do not resent her for being so much lovelier than they. They are too dearly fond of her. All the men admire her from afar, for she is *Princess* Stephanie."

Stephanie giggled and darted off to show herself to her father, who was watching the races with Colonel Wexford and Mrs. Shaw.

"Shall we find the fortune-teller?" Devlin suggested, and he took Gwyneth under the nearer archway and through the tunnel into the brightness of the courtyard at the center of the hall.

The scent of roses came to meet them. The courtyard had always been Gwyneth's favorite part of Ravenswood Hall, but she had never been able to decide whether she loved the cloistered walks about its perimeter best or the rose arbor and the fountain at its center. But why should a decision be necessary? Both were lovely, and they complemented each other, the one perfect for gentle exercise in the shade, the other ideal for quiet repose beneath the open sky.

The fortune-teller's tent had been set up in a far corner, just outside the cloister. The portrait painter—or, rather, the portrait *sketcher*, since he always used charcoal rather than paint at the annual fete—had set up his table and chairs and easel in the diagonally opposite corner. He was at work now on Doris Cox's portrait, while a small cluster of people, including her husband, watched over his shoulders.

As Gwyneth crossed the courtyard with Devlin, she felt very consciously happy. Quite bubbling over with happiness, in fact.

Soon, of course, he would move off to other duties, and it was possible she would come nowhere close to him for the rest of the day. Or for the rest of her life. But why depress herself with such thoughts? At this moment she was at his side, her arm through his, and she was going to enjoy it to the full.

Someone was coming out of the tent as they approached, and as good luck would have it, there was no one else waiting to go in. Gwyneth had been this close last year and the year before, but both times she had turned away at the last moment. She had been afraid of being told unwelcome news of her future, though it was an absurd fear when the fortune-teller was an entertainer rather than a genuine seer and always knew the sorts of things people wanted to hear.

"Perhaps," Gwyneth said, "it is best not to know what the future holds."

"Even if it offers a tall, dark, handsome stranger?" he asked.

Oh, even then, she thought, for she did not want to meet a *stranger.*

"Only if she can promise faithfully and not raise my hopes in vain," she said, and ducked under the flap of the tent before she could make an idiot of herself and lose her courage again.

The tent was dark blue and cut out most of the daylight inside. Gwyneth found herself standing in the blue glow of a lamp and confronting a crystal ball on a table covered with a dark cloth. A woman sat behind the table, dressed in a dark robe and hood with fair hair left loose and arranged in billowing waves over her shoulders.

She motioned Gwyneth to a chair on the near side of the table.

"Well?" Devlin asked when she came back outside a few minutes later and blinked in the sunlight.

"It was as I hoped," she said. "A tall, dark, handsome man and a love that will blossom very soon. But alas. He will leave me a short while later and go far, far away."

"Dastardly cur," he said.

"And not return for a long, long time," she added.

"Ah," he said, grinning at her. "There is to be a happily ever after, then, is there, even if you do have to wait a long time for it? Perhaps to her a week is a long time, and two weeks a long, long time."

"And perhaps it is a year and a decade." She sighed theatrically and laughed. But she was wishing she had not gone in there. For the handsome man with whom she was to experience love could not be Devlin, could he? Devlin would never go away from here. Duty would bind him to Ravenswood for the rest of his life.

"Your turn," she said.

"Mine?" He set a finger to his chest and raised his eyebrows.

"I do not see anyone else close by," she said. "Go in and find out about the dazzlingly beautiful woman who is about to step into your life and ensnare your heart."

"Hmm," he said. "That sounds like a wild story to me."

But he went into the tent while Gwyneth tried to shake off a foolish feeling of unease. She was not going to do *that* ever again. She did not want anyone predicting her future, even just an entertainer in a dark cloak and hood, bent over her crystal ball.

"Well?" she asked him when he reappeared.

"No mention of a dazzling beauty or an ensnared heart, alas," he said. "It seems I am a man of firm principle and am about to be faced with an impossible choice between a destructive truth and a corrosive lie. Whatever *that* is supposed to mean. Oh, and the choice I make will change my life and the lives of all around me forever."

"Oh gracious. For the better?" she asked him.

"She did not say," he said. "I think I ought to go back in there and demand some information about dazzling beauties. She is new here this year. The usual fortune-teller was indisposed. I would prefer the old one. This one sounds too much as though she might know what she is talking about. And who wants the truth at a summer fete?"

They both laughed.

"I had better go down to the lake and see if the needlework contests are being judged yet," he said. "My mother always likes it when one or more of us join her there for it. Do you want to come too?"

She did. Oh, she very much did. But she did not want him to feel he was stuck with her. And she had promised herself that she would spend the day meeting and mingling with as many single, eligible young men as possible.

"I am going to watch the archery contests," she said. "They will surely be beginning soon. I want to see if anyone can beat Matthew Taylor this year, though I doubt anyone can come close."

The village carpenter had not been beaten in the annual contest for men since he first entered more than ten years ago, when Gwyneth was just a little girl. He was a bit of a legend in the neighborhood. Some other men admitted that they entered merely in the hope of coming in second.

"I will see you later, then," Devlin said. "Enjoy yourself."

He would mingle with everyone throughout the rest of the day and the evening, Gwyneth thought as she made her way to the poplar walk and the archery contests. It was his duty, as it was for the earl and countess and Nicholas and Ben and Philippa and even the younger children. She must not refine too much upon the fact that Devlin had spent all of half an hour with her after being drawn into the dancing lesson at the maypole. Now he was on his way to watch the judging of the ladies' needlework contests, in which he could not possibly have any real interest. He was going because his mother would be pleased. And probably all the women who had entered their embroidery or lace or tatting in the various contests would be pleased too.

She had always known that Devlin was a man to whom duty was paramount. He performed it quietly and earnestly, but there was definitely kindness too in his dealings with others. At the children's races he had stopped Eddie's tears by having him remember that he was the best in his family at finding eggs. He was on his way to look at women's needlework. Nicholas, she saw as soon as she turned onto the poplar alley, had come to watch the archers. So had the earl.

Drat that fortune-teller, who had indeed promised her love with a tall, dark, handsome man but had ruined the effect by adding those dramatic details about his leaving her for long years before she saw him again. She was sure the woman had meant years rather than days or weeks even though her words had been unspecific. It was not at all what one expected at the summer fete. And what she had predicted for Devlin was plain horrible. If it was true, then he was in for a lot of anguish. He was to be faced with one of those wrong-if-you-do, wrong-if-you-don't sort of situations. Really, someone ought to have told that woman before she came here that no one expected or wanted her to be clever and mysterious and to frighten people half to death. People wanted her to make them smile and feel good about the future she predicted even if they did not believe for a moment that her rosy predictions would really come true.

Thomas Rutledge, Baron Hardington's son, was coming to join her. "You are looking awfully pretty today, Gwyneth," he said. "Pretty in pink. Can anyone beat Taylor, do you think?"

"I doubt it," she said.

He was tall and darkish and really quite nice looking. Thomas, that was. And only six years or so older than she was. Was he plan-

ning to go away somewhere anytime soon? For long years before
returning?

"Have you quarreled with Nick Ware?" he asked.

"Quarreled?" she said. It was not the first time today she had
been asked that. "No, of course not. But we are just friends, you
know, Thomas. We have been friends since childhood."

"Well, that is the best news I have heard today," he said, grinning at her. "Do you mind if I stand with you to watch?"

Everyone appeared to be enjoying themselves, Devlin thought
as he looked around while making his slow way down toward
the lake. Even his grandmothers, who were sitting on the lawn in
the shade of an elm tree, chatting with each other while his grandfather nodded asleep in his chair. Devlin stopped to see if there was
anything he could fetch them, and his grandfather jumped awake
to remind him that they had just had their luncheon and could not
possibly need anything else yet.

He stopped to talk with a group of the Ravenswood farm laborers who were standing below the hill on which the pavilion had
been built. Their children were dashing up to the pavilion and rolling, shrieking, down the grassy slope, best clothes notwithstanding.

Was this really the best fete ever? Devlin wondered. Or did it
just seem so to him because he had spent at least half an hour of it
in company with Gwyneth? He resumed his walk to the lake, only
to recoil in mock terror when three figures with the faces of mon-
sters and the bodies of young boys jumped from the branches of a
tree—one of them was Owen—and roared ferociously at him before roaring with laughter in most unmonsterlike fashion at his
reaction.

He was not really sorry Gwyneth had decided against accompanying him to the lake—or so he told himself. It was his duty to mingle with everyone, after all, to make every guest feel welcome, to make sure all were enjoying themselves.

The judging of the needlework would not begin for another half hour, he discovered when he reached the lake. He filled in the time by rowing his great-aunts Enid and Beatrice on the lake. He listened appreciatively to their chatter as they reminisced about fetes long past—in the village rather than at Ravenswood—and beaux their very young selves had sighed over before they settled for their respective husbands.

"Settled?" he asked, waggling his eyebrows at them.

They looked at him, looked at each other, and laughed gleefully like girls.

A short while later he stood beside his mother, watching the judging of the lace.

"There are such skilled people living in our neighborhood, Devlin," she said. "Both men and women. Have you seen the woodcarving items in the contest over there?" She pointed beyond the row of vendors' booths.

"I took a quick look earlier, but they had not all been set out," he said.

"They will be judged next," she told him. "Come with me, if you will. I have not seen your father."

"I daresay he is watching the archery," he said. "I am very glad it is not a family duty actually to judge any of these contests. How would one decide? All this lace is perfect. At least to my man's eyes it is."

"It is to mine too," she assured him.

They strolled along the line of stalls later, on their way to the wood-carving table, and he bought his mother a large false-pearl brooch, which was anything but perfect. It was eye-catching, however, and they both laughed over it. The vendors seemed to be doing a roaring business.

His mother, Devlin thought suddenly, was beautiful. He had always known that, of course, for surely every mother was beautiful to her children. What he had noticed today, however, as though for the first time, was that she was also young. One tended to see one's mother as old. At least as a child one did. But his mother was only forty now—they had held a special birthday celebration for her a few months ago, while his father was still in London. Today she looked younger even than that. It was surprising to discover that one's mother was still lovely and young and possibly desirable to any number of men. She was the perfect complement to his father. They were a dazzlingly good-looking couple.

"I believe Stephanie must have squandered all the spending money your papa gave her at this very stall," his mother said. "Have you seen her?"

"Decked out in cheap, garish finery, is she?" he asked. "To go with her princess's face?"

"One winces at the sight," she said. "Has she learned nothing from me or Miss Field about good taste?"

They both laughed as she fingered the brooch he had pinned just below her shoulder.

"Pippa left the maypole earlier on, looking very pleased with herself," he said. "She had two strings to her bow."

"Ah." His mother sighed. "I *wish* my children did not have to grow up. But two of you have already done so, not to mention Ben, and Pippa is not far behind. You were *such* an earnest little boy, Devlin. All big blue eyes and eagerness to please. And Nicholas was a bright-eyed mischief maker with hair that would never lie flat and teeth that were too big for his face until he grew into them a year or two ago. Owen is going to have a great growth spurt any day now and tower over me. And my baby is almost ten years old."

"But think of all the freedom you will have when we are all grown and settled," he said. "You will be able to go to London with Papa every spring and dance each night away."

"Mmm," was all she said by way of reply. "Ah, here we are. Just *look* at all these wonderful carvings, Devlin."

It had never seemed particularly odd to Devlin that his parents lived apart for the spring months every year while Parliament was in session. It was necessary, after all. His father had the duty of his aristocratic rank to serve his country. His mother had a duty to her family. The fact that duty took one of them to London and kept the other at home in the country was all just a part of the reality in which Devlin had grown up. Why would he ever have questioned it? It was only last year when he had gone to London himself after coming down from Oxford instead of coming straight home that he had realized most ladies of the *ton* went to London with their husbands each spring. More often than not their children went with them.

But the judging had begun, and there were the hands of the winners and other entrants to shake and congratulatory comments to be made. Afterward he made his way back up toward the house and the log-splitting contest in the stable yard. He supposed he had missed the archery contests. It was a pity, but he could not be everywhere at once.

Just as his parents could not be everywhere at once or together all the time. There was nothing strange about it. Just as there was nothing strange about their living apart during the spring months. He definitely did not want to start thinking about it with unease today of all days.

CHAPTER SIX

D evlin had indeed missed the archery contests, though he
soon heard that Matthew Taylor had won the men's again.

"By *a mile*, Dev," his brother Owen told him in a voice that
might have been heard all the way at the front of the house. "You
should have seen. He carries his sheaf of arrows on his back, like the
archers in olden times, and he pulls them out and shoots them one
after the other so fast that everyone thinks there is just one arrow
quivering in the bull's-eye when really there are five."

"It's true, Devlin," their cousin Clarence assured him at a volume to match Owen's. "I am going to get Papa to buy me a bow for
my birthday, and I am going to shoot with it every day until I am
as good as Mr. Taylor."

"Well, you can't be better, can you Clar?" Owen said. "There
isn't anything closer than the bull's-eye. I tried it myself last year,
but I gave it up after Papa told me I would never be able to hit the
long side of the barn from six feet away. That was not a very encouraging thing coming from my own father, was it?"

"The thing was, though," Devlin said, setting a hand on his brother's shoulder and squeezing, "no one would come within a quarter of a mile of the barn while you were practicing, and the milk cows inside were lowing piteously as a result."

Clarence cackled.

"Oh, you made that up, Dev," his brother said indignantly. "For shame. He is fibbing, Clar."

"Not very much," Devlin said. "On the other hand, Owen, you only have to cast a line into the river to come up no more than five minutes later with a fish at least three feet long. Sometimes I wonder if you even stop to bait the line. I can fish patiently all day long and go home empty-handed at the end of it."

"That's a bit of a whopper too," his brother said. "You need to watch that, Dev."

The three of them were in the stable yard, waiting for the log-splitting contest to begin. Idris Rhys had come to join them. So had Ben. It was always the most popular of the contests, together with the archery. The yard was soon crowded with men, women, and children. There were four contestants, brawny men with huge chests and bulging muscles in their upper arms and calves. They were all stripped down to shirts, breeches, and boots. The rules forbade the removal of shirts if there were ladies present—as there always were—but rules were made to be bent. The men's shirts were open at the neck and almost all the way to the waistbands of their breeches. The sleeves were rolled up as far above their elbows as the girth of their arms would allow.

Cameron Holland, the blacksmith's son, had been placed in the first pairing. The winner of each would go another round later to determine the overall winner.

Devlin had seen Gwyneth as soon as he arrived. She was amid a group of young people, both male and female, and still appeared to be enjoying herself. She moved away just before the contest started, however, and came to join her brother. Owen and Clarence darted away to join a crowd of other boys.

"Are you cheering for Cameron?" Gwyneth asked Idris.

"Of course," he said. "I always cheer for friends. And winners."

"Just look at those logs," she said, squeezing in between her brother and Devlin. "They look impossible to chop through."

"Not for Cam," Devlin said. "He is as strong as an ox. So are the other three, by the look of them. I would not like to bet on a winner."

He wondered if she had left her group and crossed the stable yard to join her brother—or him. She was certainly not avoiding him. She might have chosen to stand on Idris's other side but had not. He felt suddenly happy again. Nicholas was with a group of young men some distance away. He seemed to be enjoying himself too. He did not look heartsick.

The earl gave the signal to start when the first two contestants were ready, standing before their respective logs, feet apart, axes in hand. "Away you go, men," he said, and shot a pistol into the air.

A cheer greeted the sound and was succeeded by prolonged shouting and cheering and yelled encouragement as the two men attacked the logs with their axes. Cameron's split apart a mere second before his rival's. There was a renewed roar from his supporters and groans from his rival's. Gwyneth, beside Devlin, was actually jumping up and down with unladylike excitement and clapping. She glanced sideways at Devlin, her cheeks flushed again, her eyes sparkling. His father, on the far side of the area roped off for the contestants, was laughing too and cheering, one hand resting lightly upon the shoulder of Mrs. Shaw.

Devlin was annoyed at the twinge of renewed uneasiness he felt. His father was never a man to keep himself apart from others.

He had always been a hand shaker, often a hand *wringer*. He was a hugger, a cheek kisser, a shoulder squeezer. It was part of his appeal, perhaps, that he was never the distant aristocrat, holding himself physically aloof from all who were inferior to him in rank. Instead he was the friend and supporter of all. Devlin had never heard even a whisper of a complaint that his father's touches were unwelcome or inappropriate. He looked around for his mother, but she had not come for the log splitting. And by the time Devlin looked back, a mere few seconds later, Mrs. Shaw was standing alone in the same place, and his father, beaming happily, was shaking the hand of Oscar Holland, the blacksmith, no doubt congratulating him on his son's qualifying for the final round.

The second pair were less evenly matched than the first. One of them, an enormous giant from a neighboring village, cut through his log as though it had no harder a consistency than butter, while the other man labored mightily over his, though, to his credit, he did not give up until he had chopped through it.

"Not fair," he said, panting and grinning as he shook the hand of the giant. "Yours was made of soft wood while mine was made of iron."

"Well, man," the giant said, grinning back. "You have to know who to bribe."

The final bout was scheduled for an hour hence.

"Is it disloyal to confess that I do not hold out much hope for Cam?" Idris asked of no one in particular. "I am quite prepared to eat humble pie if he *does* win, but who the devil *is* that brute? I have never set eyes on him before. He has no neck. Did any of you notice? It is all shoulder muscle with a little bullet head on top."

"I would not let him hear you talk about him that way if I were you, Idris," Ben said. "I think it would be unwise to pick a quarrel with that particular man."

"Perhaps he is a gentle giant," Gwyneth said. "Someone over there told me he is a blacksmith, new to this part of the country."

"I am off to find a tree to sit under for the next hour," Idris said. "With a glass of ale. Did you put in a special order for this heat today, Dev?"

"Ben is in charge of organizing the weather," Devlin said. "Blame him if you do not like it. A cool drink does sound like a good idea, though. I'll come with you. Gwyneth, come for some lemonade?"

He did not expect her to agree. But a man could hope.

"Yes, please. That would be very welcome," she said, and when he offered his arm she slid her hand through it, as she had earlier, and he thought he must be the most fortunate man alive. Almost every single man between the ages of eighteen and thirty had been seeking her out today—except Nick—and she had spent some time with a number of them, though never with one exclusively for very long. Now here she was with him for a second time—and with her brother too, of course. Even through the sleeves of his coat and shirt he could feel the warmth and softness of her hand. He could smell her perfume, or the soap she used. It was a faint scent but very enticing. He had noticed it earlier too.

"Are you coming, Ben?" he asked.

"I'll stay and make sure everything is properly set up for the final," his brother said.

Light refreshments had been set out on the terrace—plates of fruit and sweet biscuits, pitchers of lemonade and ale, and an urn of tea, which many people favored despite the fact that it was a hot drink on a hot day. Devlin poured glasses of ale for Idris and himself, lemonade for Gwyneth.

"I see Mam and Dad are talking to Alice Barnes," Idris said. "Under a tree, wise parents. I am going to join them." Alice was Nanny Barnes's great-niece and was a rather pretty young woman.

"The courtyard will probably be cooler," Devlin said to Gwyneth. "Do you want to go and see?"

"Only if you can promise coolness," she said, and walked beside him under one of the arches.

There was still a buzz of activity about the sketch artist. A couple of people waited outside the fortune-teller's tent.

"She is not as popular as the usual fortune-teller," Gwyneth said, nodding in that direction. "I overheard someone saying she had come out of the tent in tears because she had been told that her betrothed was going to cancel their engagement the day before their wedding. But she was not to despair, for she would meet someone else very soon after. What sort of a thing is that to tell a woman at a summer fete?"

"My poor mother," Devlin said. "If she hears any of these stories, she will consider the whole fete a miserable failure and will take all the blame upon herself."

"Oh dear," she said. "Then we must hope no one *does* complain. I certainly will not. I love the countess. She is one of the kindest ladies I know."

Fortunately there was no one in the rose arbor at the center of the courtyard. It had always been one of Devlin's favorite spots. The roses grew in great profusion in beds about the stone fountain and over the trellises that had been constructed around it to give a sense of seclusion to anyone sitting on one of the wrought iron seats within. And it did indeed seem a bit cooler there after they sat down side by side on one of the seats, though perhaps it was merely the sound of gushing water that gave that impression. The midsummer scent of the roses was heady and might have seemed a bit oppressive without the sight and sound of the water. Devlin handed Gwyneth her lemonade.

"Thank you," she said.

"Are you enjoying the day?" he asked her.

"Oh, very much indeed," she said, her face a warm glow. "The Ravenswood fete always makes every other day of the year seem pale in comparison. But this year it seems more than usually festive and joyful."

"Does it?" She was smiling, but she was gazing at the fountain rather than at him. "You are not missing Nick?" As far back as he could remember the two of them had spent the fete days together and with other young persons of their acquaintance. They had always seemed to be exuberant and dashing about at a run rather than a walk. He had always felt old and dull in comparison. Though it had never occurred to him to be jealous. Only envious.

She turned her face toward him then. "He has told you what we have agreed to?" she asked. "We are just friends. Oh, I know people say that all the time when really they mean there is more. That is not true of Nicholas and me, though. I love him dearly, and I believe he loves me. But not in a romantic way. If we were of the same gender, I daresay we would be bosom friends for the rest of our lives. But we are not, and unfortunately some adults have a way of teasing young men and women who enjoy each other's company, as though embarrassing them is amusing and cannot possibly upset them or damage their relationship. It does hurt to be told, albeit with an indulgent smile, that I am angling after the son of an earl. It hurts Nicholas to be told that he is trying to introduce some Welsh blood into his line. We have agreed not to spend as much time as usual together before he goes away in September. Or *any* time together, as it has turned out."

"I am sorry that had to happen," he said. "I know Nick is sorry about it too."

"In a way, though," she said, looking back at the fountain, "it is not such a bad thing. Nicholas is free to mingle with his friends today—his male friends, that is. It will probably be the last fete for him for a long time. And I am free to spend the day with anyone I want. I am eighteen. And I must confess that I enjoy being free to admire and be admired. I enjoy a little light flirtation."

"But no more than that?" he asked.

"Not until he is the right man," she said.

The sounds of voices seemed far distant, though that was a bit of an illusion. The water in the fountain muted them. So did the trellises and the droning of bees among the roses. Neither of them spoke for a minute or two.

"Will you dance the opening set with me this evening?" he asked then. "Or is it still too early to ask?"

"I will," she said, and she looked around for somewhere to set her empty glass.

He took it from her hand. "Thank you," he said as he set it with his own on the small round table beside him.

They sat together in silence again, their shoulders not quite touching, until it was time to go back for the final bout of the log-splitting contest. It was a strangely companionable silence, during which he did not feel any of the usual social compulsion to find some topic upon which to converse.

Sometimes silence was perfect in itself.

And the day was almost at an end, though there was still the evening to look forward to, and more than ever now she had promised to dance with him.

H ere they come. My two ladies," Sir Ifor Rhys said a few hours later, rubbing his hands together and beaming at his wife and daughter in their evening finery. "I think after all I had better keep you both at home tonight. All the men will have eyes for no one else, and the women will be jealous."

"Well, I will have eyes for someone else," Idris protested, always more prosaic than his father. "Fine as they both look, Dad, I do not intend to spend my evening watching over Gwyn and Mam to make sure other men do not ogle them."

"Enough of all the silliness," Lady Rhys said, nevertheless looking pleased at the compliments. "It is time we were on our way."

The daytime activities of the Ravenswood fete had ended with a lavish outdoor picnic before everyone dispersed either to their own homes or to their assigned guest rooms to get ready for the evening. It was amazing any of them had any energy left for the ball, Gwyneth thought, but they always did. It was such a very special day. There was nothing else quite like it in the whole year. Just as one's appetite always seemed to expand at Christmastime, so did one's energy on the day of the summer fete.

She was wearing her new evening dress, a white lace tunic over a silken gown of pale yellow, with tiny yellow rosebuds embroidered about the hem and the edges of the short, puffed sleeves. The gown was high-waisted and low at the bosom—though not *too* low. With it she wore elbow-length gloves of white kid and dancing slippers and a narrow shawl. She wore also the pearl necklace her parents had given her for her eighteenth birthday, and the matching pearl earrings from Idris. Her hair was styled a little more simply than it had been during the day. It was smoother over her head, with only a few fine tendrils waving down from the knot high on the back of her head to trail along her neck and over her ears.

It had felt very good as she twirled before the mirror in her room earlier to know she was going to the ball this year as a woman rather than a girl. It was amazing what a difference turning eighteen made to one's expectations.

And, she had thought with one extra twirl, she was going to dance the opening set tonight with Devlin Ware. It would be the crowning moment of what had already been a happy day.

Despite what her mother had said just now, she was not yet moving toward the door and the carriage awaiting them outside. Instead, she was looking at Gwyneth, her head tipped to one side.

"Your first real ball since you turned eighteen, *cariad*," she said, using her favorite Welsh endearment—*cariad* literally meant *love*. "Has your heart been sore today, Gwyn? I did not expect young Nicholas to ignore you quite so completely, though we do know that the Wares go out of their way to mingle with all their guests, no matter who they are. And very proper and admirable it is too."

Gwyneth had told them she and Nicholas had been embarrassed by the teasing at James Rutledge's birthday party and had decided to spend less time in each other's company.

"Nick did not ignore me, Mam, or I him," Gwyneth said. "We spoke a few times. I was with other people all day, though, and busy trying to see everything at once and not miss a thing. I even rowed one of the boats for a while when I went out on the lake with Leonard Atkins."

"Was that the boat that went around and around in circles for all of two minutes until I got dizzy and stopped looking?" Idris asked.

"She did not sink the boat, though, did she?" her father said, setting one arm about her shoulders and hugging her to his side for a moment. "Well, Gwyn, young Nick Ware's loss is our gain. Much as he would be a grand match for you, he *will* be on his way to join his regiment in the next couple of months, and your mam and I have not been terribly excited at the possibility that you might decide to follow the drum and go off to war with him. That is no life for a woman, even a woman in love with a handsome boy like

Nicholas. There are some fine, upstanding Welsh lads just waiting to see you again next month when we go to visit the relatives."

"I will look them over, Dad, and see if I fancy any of them," she said, smiling, and kissed his cheek.

"And there are some fine, upstanding Welsh lasses waiting just as eagerly for Idris," he added.

Idris waggled his eyebrows and grinned at his father.

"We have to go," Lady Rhys said firmly. "The trouble with you, Ifor, is that you never know when to stop talking. I am glad to hear you are not nursing a broken heart, though, Gwyn. Though I do not suppose you would tell your mam even if you were."

She was not, Gwyneth thought as the carriage made its way back to Ravenswood, though a few times during the day she had missed Nicholas and felt a pang of regret at the absence of his easy, cheerful company. But once he had left Ravenswood in September to begin the military career he had dreamed of all through his boyhood, their friendship would inevitably have waned anyway. Although she was herself a conscientious letter writer, she doubted Nicholas was. And now it seemed unlikely that she would write to him at all. But how painful it was going to be, waiting for news of him from Ravenswood. He might be involved in any number of battles she would not even know about until weeks or months afterward. She would not know if he was hurt or . . . Well.

But truth to tell, it was not upon Nicholas that her thoughts dwelled as she looked ahead to tonight's ball. Specifically to the opening set. Would he remember? Well, of course he would. Duty had always come first with Devlin. He would always keep his word. She thought of him dancing about the maypole earlier, solemnly concentrating on his steps and the ribbon in his hand. She thought of him watching the youngest children's races and trying to console little Eddie after he lost his race. She thought of him smiling at Stephanie with her garishly painted face and calling her a beautiful princess. She thought of him in the stable yard, cheering on Cameron Holland in the final of a log-splitting contest, which he lost, and then stepping forward to shake the winner by the hand, sweaty and dirty though the man had been.

She thought—and her thoughts paused—of the half hour or so before that final bout when she had sat by his side in the rose arbor in the courtyard, neither of them speaking a word. Had it really been the happiest half hour of the day? Of her *life*? Why on earth would it have been, though? *They had not spoken.*

Because she loved him?

She had been infatuated with Devlin Ware for years. While girls of her acquaintance had gazed upon Nicholas and sighed over him and believed *she* was the lucky one who would end up with him, Gwyneth had been falling in love with his less obviously handsome, less openly charming elder brother. Much as she was fond of Nick, she was drawn by the unknown complexities of Devlin's character. She was sure they were there. It was so easy to judge people by looks and easily observable qualities. But no one could be fully known from those things alone. And some people were worth knowing to the depths of their being. To the innermost reaches of their soul. It was particularly true of the people one loved and believed one would love even more deeply when one knew all there was to know.

Gwyneth wanted . . . Oh, she dearly wanted to know Devlin Ware, Viscount Mountford. She wanted to *know* him.

But she must not refine too much upon the fact that he had spent time with her today, most notably that extraordinary half hour in the arbor. It had been his duty to spend time with his family's guests. No doubt other women could make the same claim. But . . . *No one else was going to dance the opening set with him this evening.*

She must take care, though, not to set herself up for heartache. Unwillingly she thought of what the fortune-teller had told her. She had been curiously disturbed by it. But no doubt the woman had heard of her supposed courtship with Nicholas. It was *he* who was going away soon, not to return, perhaps, for years.

"Here we are," her father said unnecessarily as the carriage drew to a halt outside Ravenswood Hall.

Her first real ball since she turned eighteen. She was going to enjoy every moment of it, no matter what. She was *only* eighteen, and she was not going to allow anything or anyone to break her heart or even bruise it. The whole of her adult life stretched ahead of her, and she was eager to begin living it. She was hopeful that she would not have to sit out a single set tonight. She would think about sore feet when tomorrow came.

Ah, and there was the opening set with Devlin to be enjoyed.

CHAPTER SEVEN

Devlin went to the ballroom early to make sure everything was in place and nothing had been forgotten, though he knew very well there was no chance of that with his mother in charge. Really he was just restless and eager for the evening festivities to begin. That was unusual for him. Dancing was not generally his favorite activity, though he always participated when it was required of him, of course.

Tonight he was going to dance the opening set with Gwyneth Rhys.

The ballroom looked like an extension of the garden. The French windows along the west wall were all thrown open to admit the cooling air of early evening, and the room itself was decked out with banks of fern and flowers in varying shades of pink, purple, and magenta. Violins and cellos and a flute were laid across chairs on the orchestra dais or propped against them, awaiting the arrival of the musicians. The grand pianoforte had been polished to resemble a mirror. So had the wooden floor. The two large crystal candelabra had been raised to their places just below the ceiling, all their candles alight even though it was not dark outside yet.

Dances in the country, even this grand annual ball, started at what in London would be considered an indecently early hour and were over by midnight. Many of those in attendance would have to be up in the morning to perform the usual early chores—feeding the livestock, milking the cows, nursing the babies, for example. None of those necessities would stop just because it was Sunday. And the vicar, kindly and mild-mannered though he was, would not be happy if he found himself delivering his morning sermon to an empty church.

Devlin crossed the room and stood in one of the open doorways. The ballroom was on the ground floor of the west wing and opened onto a broad, flat terrace—an extra dancing area on warm nights. Colored lanterns had been strung about the perimeter, though they had not yet been lit. They would be soon. The sun was getting close to the horizon and the light was turning dusky. It would not be a dark night even when the sun was down, though, Devlin suspected. The sky was clear, and he had noticed last night that the moon was close to the full. There would be lanterns in the trees on the south lawn too and in the courtyard.

A row of velvet-upholstered chairs had been set up about the edges of the ballroom, he saw when he looked back into the room. Just a single row. The room was really not large enough for a second. Besides, only elderly people ever wanted to sit through a ball here, and not even all of them much of the time. People wanted to dance at the Ravenswood ball, or at least walk about and mingle with their fellow guests. Even children who had passed their infancy were allowed to come, though only until ten o'clock. They were almost always well behaved for fear they might be banished early to the nursery. Devlin thought about the balls he had attended in London last year with his father. They had been far more formal and elaborate affairs than this would be, but none of them had been even half as lively and enjoyable as these balls invariably were.

He felt a sudden rush of almost painful love for Ravenswood, for his parents and siblings, for the extended family, for friends and neighbors from miles around. For the traditions that linked the generations down the years. He felt a welling of gratitude that he was heir to it all, that he would always belong here. He would marry and raise his own family here to perpetuate the same traditions, and one day it would all be his. Though he was in no hurry whatsoever for that day to come.

Tonight he would dance with Gwyneth.

He would dance each set following the first with a different partner, of course, as was expected of him as a Ware of Ravenswood. But during that first half hour he knew he would will time to stand still, which it was never obliging enough to do when a man was particularly enjoying himself. Today had been one of the happiest of his life, however, and he would surely always remember it even without the added memory of tonight. In the rose arbor this afternoon, though he and Gwyneth had said very little to each other, he had allowed himself to fall all the way in love with her. And to allow himself to hope, surely without utterly deluding himself, that perhaps she returned his feelings or might return them sometime soon.

His thoughts were interrupted when his father came striding into the ballroom and crossed the floor to join his son. The earl was looking very elegant in black evening coat and breeches, the newest fashion in London, with a waistcoat of silver brocade. His stockings and linen were very white in contrast, his shirt points high and crisply starched. He beamed at Devlin before looking around the room.

"Your mother is a genius," he said. "Everything today has proceeded without a flaw, and all because she has worked tirelessly for a month or more to bring it about. She organizes her army of helpers, and they do just what she tells them to do—without fuss and without argument."

That would include her telling his father to stay out of the way, Devlin thought with inner amusement. And just like the rest of them, his father had done exactly as he was told.

"I could not have done better for myself if I had tried, could I?" his father continued. "She is the perfect wife, the perfect countess. And she has given me handsome sons and daughters. Even Steph may grow up to be a pretty girl once she loses that baby fat."

"She is beautiful even with it," Devlin said.

"Oh, absolutely. Yes." His father laughed. "This will not be quite the elegant ball one grows accustomed to in London, will it? Nor will the company be as illustrious or the fashions as dazzling. But it will do very nicely indeed for a country party. It will make everyone happy. And that is our duty, Dev, mine and yours after me. To keep everyone happy—our wives, our children, our neighbors from far and near, and those men and women who work for us. We must always remember to put other people before ourselves. That is what your grandfather taught me, God rest his soul, and it is what I have tried to teach you. Not that we need to deny ourselves entirely, of course, for a man is entitled to some private pleasures of his own. But always remember to put other people first and you cannot go far wrong in life. Your mother—and your wife when you get one— must always be honored above all others. Kept content and happy."

Devlin smiled at him. It was moments like this one that he treasured above all others—father and son, earl and heir, alone together and talking of duty and responsibility, but in terms of service and love. Putting others first. Making other people happy. Yet entitled to some personal pleasure too—but then did not personal pleasure derive from giving it to others? By tradition the earl would lead his countess into the opening set tonight, and as always they would smile warmly at each other and about them at their family and guests of all degrees. They would radiate welcome and happiness.

It was what an Earl of Stratton and his countess must always do—did in the past and in the present, and must on into the future. It was tradition.

"I will always do my best to live up to your expectations of me, Papa," Devlin said. "Just as you have lived up to Grandpapa's."

His father squeezed his shoulder with a heavily beringed hand and laughed again. "Always so earnest, Dev," he said. "You need to learn to laugh more. And to enjoy yourself more."

He *did* laugh, Devlin thought. And enjoy his life. And show warmth and interest and fellow feeling to those around him. At least he tried. He lacked the outgoing nature and bonhomie of his father, it was true. Nick had it. He did not. But he could not help that. The magnetism that came naturally to them was a God-given gift and impossible to learn or even to imitate.

"Enjoy yourself tonight." His father gave him a final pat on the shoulder. "Here comes your mother with Pippa and Steph." He beamed his pleasure across the room and raised his voice as he strode toward them. "My love, as always you look quite exquisite." He extended one hand and bowed over the countess's when she placed it in his. He raised it to his lips as she smiled warmly back at him.

Philippa, flushed and pretty in pale blue, gathered the sides of her gown in her hands and twirled for Devlin's benefit.

"Lovely," he said. "You look quite the woman already, Pippa. Are you sure you are only fifteen?"

Stephanie's face had been scrubbed clean. It shone.

"I met a princess on the terrace this afternoon," Devlin said, wagging a finger at her and frowning in thought. "She looked remarkably like you, Steph. She was breathtakingly beautiful. Someone has coiled your braids around the back of your head. You look very grown-up. Turn and let me see."

She turned. "Breathtakingly beautiful," she muttered scornfully under her breath—and then giggled with glee.

"The loveliest hair of anyone in my whole family," their father said, beaming at her when she turned again. "Your crowning glory, Steph. Promise me that you will never have it cut."

"Caleb," the countess protested. "Long hair must always be trimmed once in a while to keep it healthy."

"I promise, Papa," Stephanie said, and stepped forward to hug her father about the waist.

T here was never a receiving line at the Ravenswood balls. What would be the point when all the guests had been at the fete all day, and the host family had mingled freely with them there? Nevertheless, the earl and countess and their older children stood close to the ballroom doors as everyone entered, welcoming them, shaking hands, and finding chairs for those who required them. Very soon the room was crowded and loud with conversation and laughter and the sounds of the musicians tuning their instruments.

Gwyneth gazed about the ballroom, eager to see how it was decorated this year. It was always a bit different. The countess, she suspected, worked hard to make sure the whole day did not grow stale with too much of a sameness from year to year. It must not be easy to achieve some variety.

There was not too long a delay before the earl mounted the steps to the orchestra dais, the countess on his arm. Something approximating silence fell even before he raised both arms to draw everyone's attention. He beamed about at them all.

"Now this," he said, "is what among the *ton* in London would be known as a sad squeeze. The ball would be deemed an instant success."

He waited for the inevitable laughter to subside before continuing with a few words of welcome and the hope that they would all enjoy the ball more than they had ever enjoyed any other. He reminded them that there were beverages and light refreshments available in the dining room just through the open doors at the other end of the room.

"But remember too," he added, "that there will be supper at half past ten, and my wife informs me that a banquet is even now being prepared. Leave room for it or she will be terribly hurt. Maybe even wrathful."

He smiled warmly at the countess, who was shaking her head. Everyone laughed again.

"Gentlemen," the earl said. "Lead your partners into the opening set, if you please. My most humble apologies to you all, however—the loveliest lady at the ball, the Countess of Stratton, is already spoken for."

There was yet more laughter, a few boos, and one ear-piercing whistle as he gave his hand to the countess and led her down the steps and along the room to place her at the head of the line of ladies that was already forming. He took his own place in the line of men opposite her, a space of a few feet between the lines.

But Gwyneth scarcely noticed. For Devlin, elegantly dressed in a dark blue tailed evening coat with gray knee breeches and white waistcoat, stockings, shirt, and neckcloth, was standing before her and extending a hand for hers.

"Gwyneth?" he said. "My dance, I believe?"

He was not smiling. Not openly, at least. But there was a glow in his eyes and behind his face that suggested he was smiling inside. Not just a social smile, but something for her alone. Or so she fancied. Ah, she had so looked forward to this moment, and now it was here. She set her hand on his, palm to palm, and he closed his fingers about it and led her to the head of a new set, the original one having already stretched the full length of the ballroom. She stood next to Susan Ware, Devlin's cousin, in the line of ladies while he took his place opposite her next to Dr. Isherwood in the line of men. He continued to look at her across the space between them with that same expression. Almost, she thought, as if he wanted to devour her. It was a look that sent shivers of pleasure through her body. She smiled with all the sparkle that was inside her, and his eyes crinkled at the corners.

Soon there were four long parallel lines of dancers, two of women, two of men. A few adults, mostly elderly people, and a crowd of children stood or sat off to the sides, watching. Gwyneth remembered those days of childhood and the longing to be grown-up and able to participate.

The orchestra struck a chord and the dancing began.

The pounding of several dozen feet on the wooden floor set a rhythm with the music of violins and cello and flute and pianoforte while partners joined hands and promenaded to their left and then to their right, both pairs of lines moving in unison with each other. With their immediate neighbors they formed arches of hands like mini maypoles as they paced in a full circle, changed hands, and paced back again. At the end of each pattern of steps the couple at the head of the line joined hands crosswise, and twirled down be-

tween the lines to take their places at the foot before the whole
thing began again.

Devlin smiled fully at Gwyneth as they twirled, the first couple
in their line to do so, and she laughed while everyone else in the
lines clapped in time to the music. The earl was laughing in his own
set as he twirled the countess. And ah, she had never, *ever* been happier, Gwyneth thought. Not even this afternoon in the rose arbor.
As happy, maybe, but not more so. How absolutely . . . exhilarating
it was to be eighteen years old and in love and full of hope that
perhaps she was loved in return.

But inevitably the music came to an end, and there was only a
leftover ball to enjoy for the rest of the evening. She tried not to feel
sad about it. How ungrateful that would be.

"Thank you, Gwyneth," Devlin said as he offered his arm and
led her in the direction of her parents, who had danced the set together. "Have you promised every other dance?"

"Only the next and the one after it," she told him.

"Are you willing to keep the set after supper for me?" he asked.

She looked at him in surprise. The Wares never danced more
than one set with the same partner, either at this annual ball or at
the Christmas ball or at any of the assemblies. It was a point of
strict etiquette with them.

"Yes," she said.

"It will be dark by then and the air ought to be cooler," he said.
"Perhaps we can step outside."

Step outside? To dance on the terrace? To take a stroll beyond it?
He did not elaborate.

"I would enjoy that," she said. She had not noticed until this
moment how breathless the dancing had made her.

"As would I," he said.

Nicholas was with her parents, all warm charm and cheerful

smiles. He was looking impossibly handsome in ice blue and silver and white. He had danced the opening set with Sally Holland.

"You are particularly lovely tonight, Gwyn," he said, looking her over appreciatively.

"So are you," she told him.

"Lovely?" He winced theatrically. "Not *handsome*? Or *manly*?"

"Just be thankful you did not use the word *pretty*, Nick," she said, and they both laughed.

"Enjoy the evening," he said as he and Devlin moved away to claim their next partners.

He had not asked her to reserve a set for him. She was both sorry and glad. Sorry because he was an accomplished dancer and an amusing partner, and he was her friend and she really was missing him and would miss him more after September. Glad because she could not bear to have anyone look knowingly at them tonight and make any of those pointed and teasing remarks that were always so embarrassing.

Her mother was looking rather intently at her. "That was quite an honor," she said, "being singled out by *Devlin* for the first set. It is a pity he is not as lively as Nicholas or quite as good-looking. He *is* a very steady and worthy young man, however."

"And the eldest son of an earl, Bronwyn," her father said, his eyes twinkling. "Never forget that."

"Oh. That was not my point at all, Ifor, as you very well know," she said, clucking her tongue. "One thing you would never be able to accuse me of is playing the part of conniving matchmaker. I want both Idris and Gwyneth to marry for love, as you and I did. When they are ready. I am in no hurry to lose either of them just yet."

Gwyneth turned with a smile to greet her next partner, Sidney Johnson, the handsome gentleman farmer and maypole dancer.

D evlin danced every set before supper with a different partner. He found time between sets to bring drinks to several of the older people, including one of his grandmothers. He spoke with as many guests as he could. He took a plate of sweetmeats out to a cluster of children who had gathered in one corner of the terrace.

He neither sat down nor ate during supper, but moved about the room, making sure everyone had what food they wanted and as much as they wanted. He occasionally signaled a footman to refill a cup with tea or a glass with lemonade or some stronger beverage. He talked with everyone, asked if they were enjoying themselves. Ben and Nicholas and his parents were doing the same thing, of course, his father with a glass in his hand. Pippa was seated with Gwyneth in the midst of a group of other young people, all of them talking animatedly and doing a great deal of laughing. It was the one group Devlin did not approach. His sister was doing duty for the family there, he told himself.

Eventually guests began to wander back into the ballroom to await the resumption of the dancing, and the young people in that group began to disperse. Devlin strolled closer, asked his sister if she had sore feet yet, chuckled when she told him she was having the best time *ever* and did not care if she woke up tomorrow with blisters on all ten toes, and finally turned to Gwyneth.

"My dance, I believe?" he said.

"It is." She looked at him with a face sparkling with exuberance, and he was reminded of how he had seen her from afar at Cartref as a girl. A free, happy spirit with boundless energy. She slipped a hand through his arm, and he led her into the ballroom and over to the French windows.

Darkness had fallen a while ago, but as he had guessed, the

outdoors was bright with moon- and starlight. Even beyond the terrace illuminated with colored lanterns it was possible to see the various features of the park—the temple pavilion on the hill nearby, the rise and fall of the land beyond, the clearly defined paths, the lake in the near distance with a silver band of moonlight across the water.

There were four people out on the terrace, in conversation with one another while they waited to dance. There were no children now. They had been sent up to the nursery before supper, grumbling and dragging their feet but reconciled to the inevitable by the promise of their own feast awaiting them there.

"Shall we take a stroll?" Devlin suggested. "Or would you rather dance?"

"I would love a stroll," she said.

They were not the only ones. The four people on the terrace had decided to walk toward the front of the house, where there would be more lanterns to light the lawn and a few chairs to sit upon while they enjoyed the cool air and the moonlight. They would hear the orchestra playing even if they did not return to dance.

Devlin did not follow them. He led Gwyneth across the terrace, down the slight grassy slope beyond it, along a flat stretch of lawn, and up the rise to the pavilion.

"Do you sometimes wish," she asked him when they were standing at the top, looking out at the view, "that your vocabulary would expand on certain occasions?"

"Sometimes," he agreed, "no words seem adequate to express deep feeling. Yet if we were to invent new words, the feeling would simply burst beyond them too."

"It would." She laughed softly. *"Lovely, beautiful, breathtaking.* What we are looking at is all those things, but so much more. It is . . ."

"Magnificent?" he suggested. "Majestic? *Nice?*"

They both laughed.

"Very nice," she said.

"But sometimes," he said, "words are just not necessary."

"As they were not this afternoon," she said.

He turned his head to look at her. "I was afraid that perhaps you thought me a dull fellow indeed for not introducing some topic to converse upon," he said.

"You must have known I thought no such thing," she protested, looking back at him. "It was perfect. It was a silence we *shared*."

"I thought so at the time," he told her. "But afterward I feared I had deluded myself and kept you from enjoying more of the fete in the company of someone more lively."

She turned her whole body toward him then, her free hand coming to rest on top of the other on his arm. "You are very differ-ent from the rest of your family, Devlin," she said. "I sometimes used to think that perhaps you were a bit arrogant—because you are the heir to all this and already have the courtesy title, because you are so handsome, and—"

"Me? Handsome?" And *arrogant*? He felt distinctly uncomfort-able. He ought not to have brought her—

"—and because you told me last year," she continued, "without a glimmer of a smile, that you would forget you had encountered me in breeches, riding astride my horse, my hair loose down my back. I do not believe it has ever been arrogance with you, though. I think you are just very unsure of yourself and your own worth."

"I beg your pardon for the way I behaved on that occasion," he said. "It is just that I—"

"I suppose," she said, "it must be difficult having a brother like Nicholas and a father like the Earl of Stratton—bright, shining stars who draw attention wherever they go. But Devlin, you do not need to compete with them."

"I—" he said, and wished like the devil he had not brought her out here but had been content simply to dance with her again. He felt gauche and dull and a bit miserable.

"You are unique and wonderful just as you are," she said. "To me you are far more attractive than they are, fond as I am of them."

He frowned, astonished, as he gazed into her face.

"You have *always* been more wonderful in my eyes," she said. "But you never knew I existed until we met at the foot of that hill last year and you were disgusted with me. And today . . . Oh, goodness, my tongue is running away with me. I am very thankful we are out here in near darkness, because my cheeks are burning and doubtless they are flame red. I will have nightmares about speaking out this way."

"Never knew you existed?" he said, and his frown deepened. "I went to Cartref often because Idris is my friend and your parents always made me welcome. But I went just as much to see you. You always hid from me indoors, as though you were shy or just did not like me. I believed it to be the latter, because when you were outdoors, as you very often were, and did not see me, you ran free and wild, more often than not with Nick. You played barefoot in your old dresses, your hair always loose about your face and shoulders. Even when Nick was not there, you ran and played and shouted and laughed with the dogs, and climbed trees and sat up in the branches, reading, as though it had never occurred to you that you might fall. I often longed to run free with you, but I was so much older and would have looked ridiculous. Besides, you did not like me. When I saw you last year, I was *not* disgusted. I thought you were lovely beyond words. But you seemed horrified to see me. I have always been so envious of Nick that . . . Well."

"He was never more to me than a friend and a playmate," she said. "And if I hid from you and was mute, it really *was* shyness. Only with you. Never with anyone else. For I always so desperately wanted you to *like* me."

"I did," he said. "Always."

They gazed at each other, their faces no more than a few inches apart. And Devlin reminded himself that she was only eighteen, that he was only twenty-two, that his father had advised him not to marry too soon in life but to enjoy himself first—as he wished he had done. His father had married his mother when he was twenty-six and she not quite eighteen.

Their marriage, though, had always been a happy one. And why wait when the love of your heart has just admitted that *you* are the love of hers?

He glanced back at the pavilion. There were seats inside, beyond the pillars, and some hope of privacy. In there they would at least not be visible from the terrace outside the ballroom, as they must be now. But it might occur to other people to come up here. The cool air and the moonlight were very inviting, after all, in contrast with the heat and noise and crowds in the ballroom.

The hill was bare of any trees on three sides—deliberately so. The pavilion had been built on its crest so that anyone sitting within could enjoy an unimpeded view over the park and the river and village to the countryside beyond. The fourth side was wooded all the way to the foot of the hill.

"Come." He released Gwyneth's arm and took her hand in his. He laced their fingers and led her around the outside of the pavilion and down the wooded slope. The trees were not densely packed. There was darkness among them, but not pitch blackness. He stopped when they were partway down and turned with her, setting her back against the sturdy trunk of a tree.

A narrow band of moonlight slanted across the lower part of her face and the upper part of her body. She looked lovely and delicate in her silk and lace gown of palest yellow. Her pearls gleamed in the dim light. Her lips were slightly parted, revealing her perfect white teeth. He set his hands on either side of her waist and instantly felt the soft warmth and the shapeliness of her. Her own hands came to rest on his shoulders.

He wished he had some experience to bring to the moment. Though perhaps it was as well he did not. He suspected this would be her first kiss—as it would be his. Perhaps it was fitting that they find out together what it would be like. He was not going to feel embarrassed by any gaucherie on his part. *You have always been more wonderful in my eyes,* she had told him a few minutes ago.

"Gwyneth," he murmured.

"Devlin." Her lips curved into a smile. "Kiss me."

And he did.

CHAPTER EIGHT

He kissed her. With warm, closed lips pressed lightly to hers. And Gwyneth thought the world might well have stopped. He was *Devlin*. Devlin Ware.

He drew back his head, but his hands, warm and firm, were still on either side of her waist. Distinctively a man's hands. Her own were gripping his shoulders as though her life depended upon not letting go. It was not quite dark down here, despite the trees. Moonlight shafted through the spaces between them and filtered between branches overhead. But she could not see his face, inches from her own. Not clearly, anyway. She knew, though, that his eyes were gazing very directly into hers, and she could imagine the blueness of those eyes. She was aware of music coming from the ballroom, but it seemed very distant. Strangely, it accentuated the quietness around them.

"I love you," he said softly, and Gwyneth thought her heart would surely burst, so filled it was with joy.

"I love you too," she said. "I have always loved you."

One of his arms wrapped about her waist to draw her closer while the other came about her shoulders. She slid one hand down over his chest and put her arm about his waist. She wrapped the other about his neck. And he was all solid, warm male. He was Devlin. She could feel his hard-muscled thighs pressed to her own as he kissed her again, his lips slightly parted this time. The heat and the shock of it made her knees feel weak. There was a curious, dull throbbing between her thighs and up inside her. His hand was moving down from her waist to press her firmly against him, and she was not so ignorant that she did not know what she felt there. Her lips parted against the pressure of his and she kissed him back with all the hot ardor of her youth and her love for him.

At last, she thought. *At last.*

"Gwyneth," he murmured against her lips after what might have been moments or minutes or hours—she was not keeping count. "What a perfect day this has turned out to be. My love." He spoke the words with some wonder, as though he were testing them, and she laughed softly at the simplicity and extravagance of them. "You are so beautiful."

She almost replied by telling him that so was he, but it would be too reminiscent of what she had said as a joke to Nicholas earlier. It would not be a joke if she told Devlin he was beautiful, but he might think it was. He might be hurt. Oh, she did not know him well at all yet, she realized. There was so much to learn about him, so much to know. But the thought exhilarated her, for there would be time for the learning and knowing. A lifetime. She felt no doubt that they would have that together. This was not dalliance, the fleeting passion of a moment.

His forehead touched hers as he fondled her breasts with light fingertips through the lace and silk of her gown. She ran her fingers through his hair—short, thick, smooth, warm.

"May I call on your father tomorrow?" he asked her. "Or am I being ridiculously hasty? There has been one day of courtship. One perfect day. Ought I to wait longer? But it is not as though I have not known you and loved you forever—as you say you have loved me. *May* I call?"

"Yes," she said, and laughed softly. "Oh, yes, Devlin. It has been far longer than one day. It has been forever."

"I will prepare a pretty speech to make you on bended knee after he has given his consent," he said. "*If* he gives his consent. Will he?" He laughed then too, and she loved the happy sound of it.

Ah, she would make him laugh all the time from this day forward. She would make him *happy*. Because she herself would be happy.

He kissed her lingeringly again before sighing. "We must be going back soon," he said. "I am obliged to show myself in the ballroom and dance with other partners."

"And I have promised the next set to Mr. Greenfield," she said. "Your uncle."

Devlin kissed her once more, his hands cupping her shoulders. But he lifted his head sharply after a few moments and held it in a listening attitude. "Dash it," he muttered. "There are some people coming. Up to the pavilion, I suppose."

Gwyneth could hear them too—low female laughter and the soft murmur of a man's voice. It was hardly surprising. The ball was in its final hour and the night was cool and lovely. The temple pavilion was picturesque and private and not very far from the ballroom. It was the perfect setting for a little moonlit romance.

"We had better creep away like thieves in the night," Devlin whispered in her ear, laughter in his voice. "So that they will not embarrass us and we will not embarrass them. We will go down through the trees to the bottom of the hill and around the side and back up to the house. They will probably be too busy to notice us anyway."

He moved back from her and took her hand in his. But before they could begin the descent the woman spoke from the pavilion above them. She did not speak loudly enough for her words to be distinguished, but there was something familiar about her voice.

If only, Gwyneth thought much, much later—too late, far too late. *If only* she had said nothing at that moment, the world might have continued on its course and . . . Ah, but she did say something, albeit very softly. And so the world changed course and everything changed with it.

Everything.

"That is Mrs. Shaw," she murmured.

The new resident of Boscombe. The widow who had lost her husband in the Indian wars, poor lady, and come to live here, though she knew no one and no one knew her. That fact had puzzled everyone, for she was young and beautiful and always dressed fashionably, her year of mourning presumably at an end, and one would have expected her to have chosen a more sizable town or a spa such as Bath. Did she have no family to go to? Did her late husband have none? So far she had not seemed particularly interested in making friends here, though admittedly she had not been here longer than a few weeks. She had been at the fete today, however, and had appeared to be enjoying herself whenever Gwyneth set eyes upon her. She had joined in the maypole dancing lesson. And she had come back for the ball tonight.

Devlin had gone very still, his hand tight about hers.

The man laughed. And there was no mistaking that laugh. There was only one like it, and it was very well known. He took laughter and good cheer with him wherever he went. The Earl of Stratton. Devlin's father.

He had brought Mrs. Shaw here to show her the temple and the view from it at night. The moonlight was probably still shining in a band across the waters of the lake.

Gwyneth's hand was beginning to hurt.

"We really must be careful, Cal," Mrs. Shaw said, her voice quite distinct now. "We mustn't stay up here long. You can come to me later tonight. It will be safer."

"Half the family is staying at the hall, alas," the earl said—there was no mistaking the fact now that it was he. "It will be impossible for me to slip away, Liza. And I cannot miss church in the morning."

She laughed, a throaty, seductive sound. "I suppose I had better not miss it either," she said. "Village life is very quaint."

"I told you it would amuse you," he said. "A quick ten minutes here, then. No one will come. And if anyone does, I am playing friendly neighbor and genial host, showing you the moonlight on the lake."

They were not speaking loudly, but their voices were disastrously clear. As was their intent—and their familiarity with each other.

Oh dear God.

"Come on," she whispered to Devlin. "We must get back before this set ends."

But his hand was like a steel band about hers, and though she was not touching any other part of him, she could sense the rigidness of his body.

He moved then. But not downward with careful stealth, as he had intended. Rather, he strode upward, drawing her along with him. Perhaps he had forgotten she was even there.

"Devlin," she whispered, desperate to stop him.

He ignored her. It was too late anyway. They were at the top of the rise and moving between two of the pillars of the temple.

Gwyneth was aware briefly of the two figures sprawled on one of the love seats, clasped in each other's arms, of the fact that at least one of Mrs. Shaw's silk-stockinged legs was exposed to the knee. Then Devlin spoke, and the two of them jumped to their feet, and the earl stepped in front of Mrs. Shaw, shielding her while she shook out her skirts.

"Get her out of here," Devlin said, his voice tight with fury. "Get her away from here. Right away. Now."

"Dev." His father's voice sounded quite as it normally did, except perhaps for a little breathlessness. "Taking the air too, are you? With Gwyneth, I see. A beautiful evening, is it not? A fitting end to what has been a perfect day. Don't jump to conclusions now. I have been showing Mrs. Shaw the lake with the moonlight on it. I suppose, though, we ought not to linger here, welcome as the cool air is. We should all be making our way back to the ball."

"Get her away from here," Devlin said. "Away from Ravenswood. Away from Boscombe. Get her back to whatever love nest you usually keep her in."

"You are being overhasty and a bit offensive, Dev," his father told him.

"Yes," Devlin said. "A dull dog. Get her away."

"Cal." Mrs. Shaw took a step forward and set a hand on the earl's arm. "I will walk home. It is not far, and it is not a dark night. I do apologize, Lord Mountford. Your father kindly offered to show me the lake from up here, and the promise of some fresh air tempted me and made me forget that our coming here together might be misconstrued."

"I have not misconstrued your use of the name *Cal*, ma'am," Devlin said, his voice cold with stiff contempt as he turned briefly toward her. "Or the proprietary hand you have placed on my father's arm. I have not misconstrued the compromising position in which I found you." His attention snapped back to his father. "Get her out of here."

"It is time you calmed down, Dev," his father said, "and remembered who you are and where you are. And whom you are with. I apologize for my son, Gwyneth. Sometimes he can be a bit hotheaded. Stay out here for a few minutes longer, the two of you, while I escort Mrs. Shaw back to the ballroom in time for us both to join our next partners. You and I can talk tomorrow, Dev, if you deem it necessary."

He drew Mrs. Shaw's arm beneath his and walked briskly away with her down the slope in the direction of the ballroom. The music was ending.

"It is time I *remembered who I am?*" Devlin said to his father's retreating back. His voice was raised now to be heard from a distance. "I am Devlin Ware, Viscount Mountford, heir to the earldom of Stratton. *Sir.* And *where I am* is Ravenswood Hall, ancestral seat of the Wares, home of my mother, the Countess of Stratton, and of my sisters and brothers. I am *with* Gwyneth Rhys, daughter of Sir Ifor and Lady Rhys, our neighbors. I will *not* have this home sullied with the presence of *your whore. Sir.*"

He was striding down the slope in pursuit of his father, Gwyneth's hand still clasped tightly in his.

"Devlin," she said, laying her free hand on his sleeve, desperate for him to halt and to be quiet. Though it was too late for that, of course.

There was a small group of dancers out on the terrace. They were no longer dancing, though. There was no music to dance to. And they had become aware of raised voices coming from the direction of the hill. A hush had fallen on them, and they had turned to find out what was happening. A few people inside the ballroom had moved closer to the doors too.

"Devlin," Gwyneth said again. "Don't make a scene. Talk to your father tomorrow."

She was aware of feeling slightly sick, as though she might disgrace herself any moment and vomit. She was aware that the opportunity to avoid a scene was narrowing but that Devlin appeared not to have seen the disaster that was looming. Or perhaps he was seeing a greater disaster and was unable to think rationally about the immediate crisis that was upon them.

The earl had reached the terrace. He spoke, and included everyone in his geniality, as he always did.

"The moonlight on the lake looks quite magnificent from the temple up there," he said. "It is well worth the walk and the bit of a climb. I thought Mrs. Shaw might appreciate it as a newcomer here, but alas we interrupted my son and Gwyneth Rhys up there admiring the view before us, and I do believe they did not appreciate our company. My son was quite upset by it, in fact."

There was laughter, as there so often was when the earl spoke. Laughter at least partly at her expense, Gwyneth thought. But maybe it was not too late . . . She turned to smile at Devlin and inform him that she must go in so that his uncle, her next partner, would be able to find her.

Please do not say anything else. Not here. Not now.

He did not even give her a chance to get a word out or to pull her hand free.

"That woman is not going inside the ballroom," he said in a disastrously loud and clear—and clearly furious—voice. "She is leaving here. Is it not enough that you keep her in London—I assume you *do* keep her in some cozy love nest there? Did you have to bring her to Boscombe too for your entertainment through the summer? And to Ravenswood itself today? Have you no sense of decency whatsoever? She is not going inside to be in a room with my mother and my sister. And my grandmothers. How *dare* you, sir? Get her away from here *now*."

"Dear God," Gwyneth murmured, and closed her eyes. But there was nothing God could do about the disaster that no longer loomed but was fully upon them. And closing her eyes would not make the whole scene disappear. She drew a shaky breath. And at last Devlin released his hold on her hand.

When she opened her eyes a mere second or two after closing them, it was to see that the attention of surely everyone inside the ballroom had been drawn to the scene out here on the terrace. The doorways were crowded with people, some of them demanding to know what was happening, others shushing them so they would miss nothing.

She had never seen the earl nonplussed. She had never seen him without his affable smile and genial manner. But in the light of the colored lanterns his face looked ghastly, and his smile looked painted on. It was a smile without any light behind it.

"I am afraid my son must have caught a touch of sun during the day," he said. "He has forgotten his manners. He will no doubt apologize tomorrow—to his mother for disrupting the ball over which she has worked so hard, to Mrs. Shaw for—"

"You will *not* mention my mother and *your whore* in the same breath," Devlin said through bared teeth as he took a menacing step toward his father. "How dare you! Get her out of here."

"Cal," Mrs. Shaw said, and laid a hand on his sleeve as she had done up at the temple.

"And *get your hand off my father*," Devlin said.

Gwyneth wondered if he even realized how many people were looking on and listening. But dear God, how were they all going to extricate themselves from this mess? Mr. Greenfield was squeezing his way past the dense crowd in the nearest doorway, she saw, and stepping out onto the terrace. For a foolish moment she thought he must be coming to claim his dance with her. But he was looking grim and tight-jawed.

"Dev," he said, putting one hand on his nephew's shoulder and speaking softly, though no doubt everyone could hear. "Leave this to me. Caleb, go in and get the next set of dances going. Mrs. Shaw, ma'am, allow me to walk you home. If any of your belongings are inside, I will see that they are brought to you later."

Even then Gwyneth entertained the hope that all would be well. Mrs. Shaw smiled graciously at Mr. Greenfield, murmured thanks, slid a hand through the arm he offered, and allowed herself to be marched off at a brisk pace toward the front of the house.

It was not a hope that lasted, however, for Mr. Greenfield senior, the countess's father, had followed his son onto the terrace. A dignified, silver-haired gentleman of trim build and proud bearing, he spoke first to his grandson.

"Go somewhere private, Devlin, to your room, perhaps, and compose yourself," he said quietly. "Come to the drawing room in half an hour. Caleb, this ball is over. Go inside and make the announcement. I will see you in the drawing room in half an hour."

"We must not ruin Clarissa's ball over a slight family quarrel," the earl said in an attempt to reassert his old jocularity of manner. "What has happened to the orchestra? I must go and have a word with them."

"The ball is at an end," Mr. Greenfield said. "It has been a very pleasant day and a lovely evening, but it is over. It is time for these good people to go home. Go and make the announcement, Caleb. It is what my daughter sent me to say."

Devlin went without another word and with only one hard look at his father. He did not enter the house through the ballroom doors but strode off toward the front. It seemed to Gwyneth that he had probably forgotten her very existence.

The earl swayed a bit on his feet and looked about in an obvious attempt to gather the shreds of his dignity about him. But Gwyneth did not find out if he succeeded or not. Her father suddenly appeared at her side.

"Here you are, Gwyn, *fach*," he said, taking her arm in a firm clasp. *Fach*—little one. It was a Welsh endearment he had not used with her for many years. "Come along. It is time to go home."

Her mother appeared at her other side and took her other arm. "I am so sorry you had to get caught up in that unpleasantness, cariad," she said. "I do not know *what* it was all about. I cannot believe that the earl would . . . And I am stunned that Devlin could so forget his manners as to cause a public scene like that. And you caught up in the middle of it. We will get you home and make a nice cup of tea, will we, and perhaps by tomorrow . . . Oh, but the poor, poor countess. She does not deserve any of this."

They made their way along the side of the house toward the north wing and the carriage house, where all the carriages had been taken and lined up in such a way that they did not block one another. Idris was there with a groom, hitching the horses to their carriage. He handed his mother inside, and then turned to pull Gwyneth into a hug.

"Your happiest day, I daresay, Gwyn," he said, his voice not quite steady. "And I know Dev well enough to have seen that it was his too. That damned scoundrel, Stratton! Good God, I could punch his nose out the back of his head."

"Language, Idris," their father said, but he said it halfheartedly, and Idris did not apologize. He helped Gwyneth into the carriage to sit beside her mother, who set an arm about her shoulders and cuddled her close, just as though she were a little girl again and suffering some earth-shattering disappointment, such as discovering when she went to the village shop with her penny that the sweets she had set her heart upon had sold out half an hour before.

They drove home in silence. Goodness only knew what the morrow would bring. But Gwyneth knew something with utter certainty. Tomorrow would not bring Devlin to talk with her father and then to deliver his carefully rehearsed speech to her from bended knee.

For the world had just ended.

And, God help her, she did not believe she was exaggerating.

CHAPTER NINE

D evlin had changed out of his evening finery. He was the only
one who had, though, he saw when he stepped into the
drawing room forty minutes after leaving the terrace. He had heard
voices below the window of his room and the sounds of horses and
carriages and, without looking out, assumed everyone had left. He
could hear no music.

He had not known what to expect. He had not even known
until the last moment that he would go down and find out. He had
done so only because he could not think of what else to do. Go to
bed? Sleep soundly and wake up tomorrow to discover that the last
hour or so had been a bizarre and horrible nightmare? His fury had
spent itself and left behind a dull, flat feeling and the conviction that
nothing would ever be the same again. He had come down in obedience to his grandfather's command. And that command was strange
in itself. His maternal grandfather was the mildest of men. More than
once Devlin had heard him say that he minded his own business
and expected other people to mind theirs, and they usually did.

But tonight Grandpapa *had* been minding his own business. His daughter, the Countess of Stratton, Devlin's mother, was his business. He had taken charge when it had become necessary for *someone* to do so.

Devlin had not known what to expect in the drawing room, but now he saw. The room seemed crowded, large as it was. His father was standing before the fireplace, facing it, gazing down at the unlit coals, his hands clasped at his back. His mother was seated, not in her usual chair by the fireplace, but some distance from it. She sat very straight, her back not touching that of the chair, her hands clasped in her lap. Her face was the color of alabaster but perfectly composed. Nicholas was standing beside her chair. Philippa, looking pale and mulish, as though she had recently been arguing with someone—perhaps someone had tried to send her to bed—was seated on a sofa near one of the windows, between her two grandmothers. Ben was behind and to one side of the sofa, standing in the shadow of the heavy curtains that covered the window. Devlin's grandfather was standing on the other side of the sofa.

There were other people in the room too, all family members. George Greenfield was there, back from escorting Mrs. Shaw home. Charles and Marion Ware, the earl's brother and sister-in-law, were there, as were his sister and brother-in-law, Eloise and Vincent Atkins. Edward Ware and Enid Lamb, the earl's uncle and aunt, brother and sister of his late father, were there too.

The drawing room door closed quietly behind Devlin. He did not move from where he was, just inside the room. Apparently he was the last to arrive. The grand entrant. The star of the show.

"We find ourselves in a situation," his grandfather said, breaking what had probably been a lengthy and uncomfortable silence while they awaited him.

It was such a massive understatement that Devlin might have laughed if he had remembered how.

If it was a conversational cue, it fell flat on its face.

"You have some explaining to do, Devlin," his grandfather said.

"*I* do?" No one was looking at him, Devlin noticed, except for his grandfather and his uncle George, who was frowning. "*I* have something to explain? My father has dishonored my mother by bringing his mistress not just to the village here, but right to Ravenswood itself, and *I* have something to explain? He had her up on the hill inside the pavilion, not a quarter of a mile from where my mother and my sister were dancing in the ballroom, and I have something to explain? I told him repeatedly to get her away from here. But perhaps I did her an injustice by calling her a whore and demanding her removal when he was at least equally guilty. Perhaps it was *his* removal from Ravenswood I should have demanded."

"Enough, Devlin," his uncle Charles said. "And watch your language, if you please, in the presence of ladies. It was you who caused the public scene from which it will be extremely difficult, even perhaps impossible, for the family to recover fully."

Devlin's eyebrows rose in disbelief as he looked from one person to another. With one or two exceptions—most notably his mother and his father—everyone was looking at him now. But no one was jumping to his defense. No one was pointing the finger of blame at his father.

"What is this?" he asked. "Am *I* the one on trial here?"

The dowager countess, his grandmother, his father's mother, answered him. "I never thought to hear any grandson of mine so disgrace me and his mother and his father. And his whole family."

What?

"Disgrace my *mother*?" he said. "It was in defense of her that I spoke out. It is my *father* who has disgraced and dishonored her and, in the process, his children. And you, Grandmama, and all his family and Mama's by association. Was I to turn my face away and pretend I had not noticed when I caught him in that pavilion in a thoroughly compromising position with that woman? Ought I to have pretended I did not *know* what he was doing, what he had done? Was I to smile and dance afterward as he brought her back to share a roof with Mama? And with Pippa? And with you and Grandmama Greenfield?"

"In a word, yes," she said, her voice flat and very distinct.

"I do not believe what I am hearing," he said, his eyes seeking out Nicholas and Philippa and Ben in the shadows. None of them were looking at him now. "Was I to condone *adultery*? By my father? Against my mother?"

His father turned at last to face him. Devlin hardly recognized him. Gone was all the good humor and geniality. His face looked pale and drawn, his eyes dull, his mouth a thin line. He looked every one of his forty-eight years.

"It is time, Devlin," he said, "that you grew up. There is a real world out there, my son, which I ought to have forced you to discover when I had the chance last year after you came down from Oxford, waving your diploma as though book learning alone had made a man of you. I was derelict in my duty then. Tonight you have exposed your mother to shame and pity and untold suffering. I do not know quite what I am to do with you."

Shame? His mother was to feel *shame?* Had the world turned upside down? Devlin gazed at his father in shock and disbelief. But there was more to come. His mother spoke for the first time.

"You must go from here, Devlin," she said.

He swung about to gaze at her. She had not moved except, perhaps, to lift her chin a little higher. She was not looking at him.

Or at anyone else, it seemed. And the revelation hit him like a giant fist to his stomach.

"You *knew*," he said.

She knew about his father's infidelities when he went to London each spring. Perhaps she had known too about Mrs. Shaw, if not before today then at some time during the day. Perhaps everyone had known. Perhaps the whole world did. Except him. For him there had been only unease and niggling suspicions, which he had determinedly ignored—and then the truth bursting upon him like an erupting volcano tonight. Was he a total idiot?

It is time, Devlin, that you grew up.

What, for the love of God, did growing up mean? Accepting corruption as a normal part of everyday life? Recognizing that morality meant nothing at all except as something to be preached from a pulpit or taught in a classroom?

"You must go away, Devlin," his mother said again.

And no one spoke up to protest how illogical it was that it was her son she chose to send away, not her husband, who had probably slept with countless other women during the years of their marriage, until now he had gone one step further and brought his latest mistress to the village beyond their gates and even right into their own home. He would have . . . *rutted* with that woman up in the pavilion if he had not been interrupted.

Devlin looked at his mother, who was not looking at him, and at his father, who was, before turning on his heel and leaving the room.

D evlin had no idea what time it was when the door of his bedchamber opened behind him. It was not morning yet, though. He was standing at his window, looking out onto blackness. Even the moon and the stars seemed to have run away to hide. There was no sign of dawn yet on the eastern horizon. His bags were ready—he had packed them himself without summoning his valet. He had been tempted to leave during the night, but there were people to whom he must say goodbye. The children. Owen and Stephanie. He could not leave without a word to them. He turned his head to look over his shoulder.

Ben and Nicholas and George, his uncle.

He turned back to the window without either greeting them or telling them to get out.

"The woman will be gone in the morning, Devlin," his uncle told him. "I have made the arrangements, and I will go to see her on her way. She does indeed have a place to go to in London."

"Perhaps she should move in here instead," Devlin said. "My room will be vacant. Perhaps my mother would welcome her here in a three-way relationship. One big, happy family."

"I can understand your bitterness," his uncle said.

"Can you?" Devlin turned to look at the three of them. "Even though I appear to have broken a cardinal rule of polite behavior never to notice or refer to or expose the underbelly of . . . Of what? Evil? Corruption? Never to disturb whatever-it-is and thus upset people."

His uncle sighed. "What has breaking that rule accomplished?" he asked, coming farther into the room and sitting, uninvited, on the end of the bed. "What has it accomplished for my sister, Devlin? And for my niece? And for those poor children who are fast asleep in their beds and do not know yet what will be facing them in the morning and the coming days?"

"Does the truth count for nothing, then?" Devlin asked. "She knew, did she not? My mother? She has probably known for years. I suppose everyone else has too. Except me, and even I have been suppressing vague suspicions for longer than a year lest they become less vague and force me to do something about them. We have all been living a cheerful, genial, laughter-filled lie. Because it is *not the thing* to tell truth and upset the status quo. It is not *genteel*. It is not *good manners*."

"Mama's life is going to be difficult, to say the least, from this day on, Dev," Nicholas said. "One wonders if it will ever be bearable again, in fact. Pippa is having a sleepless night and has apparently been vomiting. One can only imagine how it is all going to affect Steph and Owen."

Devlin glared at him. "Did *you* know?" he asked.

"No," Nicholas said. "I did not, though I cannot say I was surprised. I suppose I have been like a lot of other people, you included apparently, not *wanting* to know and so not asking questions I might otherwise have asked. Is it really credible, for example, that our father has spent a few months of every year of our lives alone in London, during the height of the Season, *without* mounting mistresses? Ever? I just wish he had kept them there and not brought one of them home here with him. For *that* I will find it difficult to forgive him. If I ever will."

"Yet you said nothing in the drawing room earlier," Devlin said.

"No," his brother admitted. "No, I did not, Dev. What was there to say?"

"That our father is nothing but a damned whore himself, perhaps?" Devlin suggested.

"Good God," his brother said, and stopped to swallow rather loudly. "I just think you may have destroyed more than you realize tonight, Dev. We cannot simply tear down the whole framework of our lives in the name of righteousness. Yet I believe that is what you have done. What will be left now—for Mama, for our sisters and Owen? For you?" He inhaled slowly and audibly. "For me?"

"*I* have destroyed an awful lot," Devlin said. He did not even bother to make it into a question. "Yes, it was all my fault. I understand, Nick. It was not our father's fault, but mine. He is only guilty of adultery and debauchery and blatant disrespect for his wife and family. I am guilty of something far worse—of telling the truth."

He *did* understand too. At long last. He had misunderstood his world all his life. He had assumed it was built upon truth and light and honesty and decency. But it was not. It was all about appearances, about respectability, about preserving a facade that was essentially empty. And by misunderstanding, he had torn down that flimsy illusion to discover there was nothing left. Only human suffering. In particular, his mother's. And he was the cause of that suffering. Not his charming, laughing, philandering father, whose infidelities she had somehow managed, preserving a life for herself despite them. Not his father, but *him*, Devlin, with his unconsidered righteousness.

And what had happened to Gwyneth? He had not even missed her until he had come up to his room here in obedience to his grandfather's command. How deeply had he embarrassed her?

He looked at his half brother, who had not said a word yet, either in the drawing room earlier or now. "And what about you, Ben?" he asked. "Do you have anything to add? Any further coals to heap on my head?"

Ben eyed his bags, packed and ready to go, and then looked at him. "When are we leaving?" he asked.

Devlin regarded him in silence for a moment.

"*What?*" he said then. "*We?*"

"I am going with you," his brother said.

"*Why?*" Devlin asked.

Ben half smiled, though there was no amusement in his expression. "I am the son of one of his whores, am I not?" he said. "The *only* mistress he ever had, of course. Because he loved her dearly and passionately. Or so he has told me more than once. He would have married her, but he was an earl's heir with obligations, and she was not an eligible bride. His heart broke when she died, and would never quite mend. Though he has me to remember her by. A favored son though he cannot in all good conscience have actual favorites among his children. It would seem, Dev, that I have been as naïve as you but with less excuse. I am older than you. I have always believed him because I have wanted to. But I have always known that I am nevertheless the bastard son of a whore. It is now obvious that my mother—my *mother*—was *just* one of countless numbers of whores our father has used. Does that answer your question?" His voice, trembling with bitterness, was almost unrecognizable. Tonight, Devlin realized, had shattered Ben's illusions as surely as it had shattered his own. Ben's mother had been dishonored tonight just as much as his own had.

Nicholas had turned his back on the room. He was weeping silently, Devlin realized with a terrible lurching of the heart.

What had he done?

S tephanie was an early riser. When Devlin tapped on the door of her bedchamber just before seven o'clock and opened it cautiously, he found her fully dressed and sitting on her bed, reading, her back propped against the pillows, one braid over each shoulder, her knees drawn up before her. Her eyes took in his travel garments and she snapped shut her book, smiled sunnily, and swung her legs over the side of the bed.

"Are you going riding?" she asked. "Let me come too. I can be ready in a minute."

"Owen is still sleeping," he said. "I need to talk to the two of you."

"He will grumble and complain and hide his head under his pillows if you try to wake him," she said. "Then he will be in a bad mood all morning. He is going to have to get up for church later, but not quite yet. Tell me and I'll tell him."

"Come with me to his room," he said.

She looked more closely at him. "What is wrong?" she asked. "You look as if you have not slept at all. You haven't, have you?"

"Come with me," he said instead of answering her question. And they went together into Owen's room. Ben was in there, standing with folded arms to one side of the door.

"You too, Ben?" Stephanie said in a whisper. "He is going to be awfully cross if we wake him. He was up half the night talking and laughing with Clarence. I heard them. I would have come and thrown pillows at them, but it would have been two against one. It would have been a massacre."

Young Cousin Clarence was still fast asleep in his own room next door. Ben had checked.

"Owen." Devlin touched his brother's shoulder and then shook it gently. "Wake up for a minute. I need to talk to you and Steph."

Owen tried to shake off his hand while growling a protest. "Wadduyouwant?" he asked crossly when the hand did not go away. "Lemmealone. Goway."

"Wake up," Devlin said, and his brother opened his eyes, looked from one to another of his visitors, and yawned hugely without covering his mouth. Then he looked more alert.

"Oh, I say. I suppose this is about the vase," he said. "It wasn't me who smashed it, Dev. But we were all in a group, and there was a bit of horseplay going on, and . . . Well, the vase got knocked over and smashed. I knew Mama would be dreadfully upset because it was worth a fortune and she liked it, but the middle of a ball didn't seem the right time to tell her. That's why I hid the pieces. I would have told this morning. And I'll take the blame. It was as much my fault as . . . Well, as *his*. I am not going to say his name. I promised I would not."

"It is not about the vase," Devlin said. "I have come to say goodbye. It is still very early, but I did not want to leave without telling the two of you."

"Oh, you are *going* somewhere," Stephanie cried. "Where? How long are you going to be gone? Can we go too?"

"I am not coming back, Steph," Devlin said. "I am leaving."

"*What?*" Owen was awake now and sitting up. His hair, flattened on one side, stood up in spikes on the other. "You cannot do that, Dev. You are the *heir*."

"There was a bit of an upset last night," Devlin said. "A bit of a quarrel. And I am going away."

"But—" Stephanie stared at him openmouthed for a moment. "But you *never* quarrel with anyone, Dev. Owen and I are the only ones who do. And sometimes Pippa. You cannot leave just because of a *quarrel*. What was it *about*?"

"I caused a bit of a scene at the ball," Devlin said. "No, it was more than *a bit*. I caused a big scene, which you will no doubt hear about in the coming days. I do not want to talk about it now. But Mama told me I must leave. So I am going. Now, in the next few minutes. I came to say goodbye first."

Owen was on his feet. "*Mama* told you to leave?" he said. "That is a bouncer, Dev. She would never say any such thing. Not in a million years. You cannot go. Papa needs you here. *Ben* needs you here. Tell him, Ben."

"I am going too," Ben said. "I am going with Dev."

"But you *can't*," Owen cried, a bit wild-eyed now. "You can't *both* go. Everyone knows the two of you run the whole estate. Everyone knows Papa could not manage on his own. What are we going to *do*? And Nick will be leaving in a couple of months."

"You will manage," Devlin said. "Papa will find a decent steward, and you and Steph and Pippa will love one another and mind Mama and Papa, and you will all manage. Oh, devil take it." He looked down suddenly and slapped one palm against the other a few times. He could not collapse now.

"No," Owen cried. "No, this is *not right*. Whatever you said or did, Dev, you need to apologize. You cannot just go. I'll hate you forever if you do. I'll never forgive you. And you too, Ben. I thought you were our *brother*. I thought you *cared*."

He dashed for the door, barefooted, creased nightshirt flapping about his legs, and yanked the door open. He dodged Ben's reaching hand and ran out before slamming the door behind him.

Stephanie looked as if she had been turned to stone. Until she inhaled audibly and looked first at Ben and then at Devlin.

"I don't want you to go," she said, and her eyes were suddenly huge in her face as they filled with tears. "I don't want Ben to go, and I don't want *you* to go. De-e-ev."

He gathered her into his arms and held her tightly. He kissed the straight part at the top of her head as she wailed and cried the great gulping sobs of a distraught child. He closed his eyes so that he would not see the expression on Ben's face.

"I don't want you to g-g-go," she said again when she finally could. "Don't go. Please don't go."

"I have to," he said. "I have to go. Steph, I love you. I will carry you here forever." He pressed a hand to his heart. "And Owen too. Tell him that."

She shook her head slowly. "I don't want you to go," she said, her eyes red, her cheeks blotched with color. "I want you to talk to

Mama. Whatever you did to make her so angry, she will have cooled down by now. And she cannot want you to go forever. She *cannot.* Go and tell her you are sorry. Go and tell her you do not want to go away, that you will make amends. Go and tell her we cannot do without you. That I cannot. De-e-ev. Don't go. Go talk to Mama."

"Come," he said. "I'll take you to Miss Field."

"No," she said. "I do not need my *governess.* You are not going to do it, are you? You are not going to talk to Mama. Just go, then."

He hesitated.

"Go," she said again. "Go, go, go."

He turned to the door.

"Ben," she wailed then. "Ben, I don't want you to go. Don't go."

Devlin left the room as his brother's arms were closing about her.

Oh, God, Devlin thought. Let this be over. Please let it be over. Let us be gone. But . . . His mother. *Would* she have changed her mind this morning? *Ought* he to talk to her directly? Apologize? Tell her he wanted to stay?

But *did* he? *Would* he if she offered a reprieve? Would he stay here in a house with his father? But ought he at least to say goodbye to her?

A few minutes later he was tapping at the door of her dressing room. It was opened partway a moment after that and his mother's longtime dresser peered out at him—minus her customary smile.

"Millicent," he said. "Ask my mother if I may take a few minutes of her time, will you?"

She shut the door without saying a word and left him standing outside, hoping his father would not come out of *his* room as he waited here. All of two minutes must have passed. They felt more like ten. Finally Millicent half opened the door again and fixed her gaze somewhere in the area of his chin.

"Her ladyship says no, Lord Mountford," she said, and closed the door quietly again before he could react.

Her ladyship says no.

His mother.

His mother had refused to see him.

Philippa was out behind the carriage house, pale almost to the point of greenness, with dark circles beneath her eyes; she was hugging her arms and hunching her shoulders because the early morning was chilly and she had not brought a shawl with her. She was standing beside Devlin's curricle, which was ready to go. A groom had just finished strapping his bags and Ben's to the rear of it. Ben was rubbing the back of her neck with one hand.

She looked at Devlin with haunted eyes.

"Go and talk to Mama," she said. "Please, Dev? She cannot possibly have meant what she said last night. And even if she did, she will have changed her mind this morning. This whole . . . *thing* will be patched up soon and forgotten about. It is what always happens. Go and talk to her. Grovel if you must. Just please do not go away."

"She will not see me," he told her.

She walked into his arms then and pressed her face to his shoulder while reaching out one arm to draw Ben too into her embrace.

CHAPTER TEN

S ometimes I find myself quite annoying," Lady Rhys said. "I have a very late night and think to myself that it does not matter. I will simply make up for it by sleeping on in the morning. But does it happen? It does not. I wake up at my usual time notwithstanding, and when I direct myself quite firmly to go back to sleep, myself does not listen."

"And it seems you have trained us all to be just like you, Mam," Idris said. "Here we all are to prove it."

All four of them were up and seated about the breakfast table at their usual hour, and Lady Rhys was talking for the sake of talking, in Gwyneth's opinion. With unnatural cheerfulness, just as though the world had not come to an end last night. Just as though she had not noticed that her daughter was toying with the food on her plate, moving it from place to place but not into her mouth.

"I needed to be up anyway," Sir Ifor said in an identical tone of voice. "I want to get to church early. I have no idea how many of the choir boys and girls will turn up today and which of them will bring their voices with them. There may not be enough of them to drown out my mistakes, and I chose some tricky pieces for this week."

Her father *never* made mistakes, Gwyneth thought. The more complex the piece of music, the more brilliant his playing became. She knew a few people who were willing to admit that they went to church for the sole purpose of listening to Sir Ifor Rhys play the organ.

"I'll go with you, Dad," Idris said. "We can take the gig. It's a nice enough morning. Mam and Gwyn can come later in the carriage."

All this hearty cheerfulness was going to make her scream in a minute, Gwyneth thought. It was time someone addressed the issue that was on all their minds and had probably kept them all awake half the night. More than half in her case. But before anyone could broach the topic, her mother and Idris both turned their heads sharply toward the window, and Gwyneth heard it too. Some sort of carriage. Pulled by more than one horse.

"There is someone coming here at this hour?" her mother said. "On a Sunday?"

Idris pushed back his chair, got to his feet, and went to the window. "It is Devlin," he said. "And Ben Ellis. In Dev's curricle."

Gwyneth felt a great surge of joy. *He had come.* But it lasted no longer than a moment, for everything was wrong with the picture that had rushed to her mind. It was very much too early. It was a Sunday morning before church. He had his half brother with him. And after last night it was impossible that he was coming courting. She was very glad she had not leapt up from her chair.

Idris went striding out of the room while Gwyneth's parents exchanged glances and Lady Rhys looked with some concern at her daughter.

"One of us must have left something at the hall last night," Sir Ifor said, "and they have come to return it." He set his napkin beside his plate and rubbed his hands together.

Idris returned within a minute or two with Devlin, who was looking pale and grim and tight-lipped—and was dressed for travel.

Sir Ifor and Lady Rhys both rose to greet their visitor. Gwyneth stayed where she was. She wished she could sink beneath the table, for this was the Devlin she had known all through her growing years. He did not even glance her way. And her instinct again, as it had been then, was to hide. Yesterday had been a dream more wonderful than anything she had ever imagined, but it had ended in a nightmare.

"Where is Ben?" her mother asked while her father shook Devlin's hand.

"He will not come in," Idris explained. "He is going to stay with the horses."

"Come and sit down, Devlin, *bach*," Sir Ifor said, using an unexpected Welsh endearment. "Have some breakfast with us. I daresay you have not had any yet. Idris will go back out and persuade Ben to join us. One of our grooms can watch the horses."

"I am not staying," Devlin said. "But thank you for the invitation, sir. Lady Rhys, I am sorry to interrupt your breakfast. I wished to apologize for involving your daughter in that rather . . . sordid scene last night. It was unforgivable of me. I did not intend to draw her into it, but that is no excuse. I—"

Gwyneth's mother held up a staying hand. "Say no more about it, Devlin," she said. "No one will think the worse of Gwyn for taking a stroll outside with you during the ball. A number of other people were doing the same thing. Ifor and I knew she had gone, and we did not worry in the least because we know you to be a steady, responsible young man. And never mind about that scene, nasty as it was while it was happening. I daresay it will all be forgotten within a few days as such things always are. Let me—"

"I came also to inform you that I am leaving," he said. "Ben is coming with me. We will not be back. At least I will not."

Gwyneth, gazing at him from her place at the table, felt as though someone had constructed a sort of tunnel between herself and him. Everything outside it receded into darkness. Everything within it was sharp and icy cold.

"Not be back, Dev? Have you taken leave of your senses?" Idris asked him. "You run Ravenswood and all the other properties too. You and Ben between you. You told me after you came down from Oxford last year that this is where your heart is and you would never willingly leave here again."

"I am leaving, Idris," Devlin said. "I will not be back."

Gwyneth fought to save herself from fainting. She had never fainted in her life. She had no patience with vaporish women.

"I was wondering," he was saying, "if I might have a word with Gwyneth before I go. Alone if it is possible. With your permission, ma'am. And with hers."

The tunnel had opened back up a bit through the sheer effort of her will and the slow, deep breaths she was taking. She was *not* going to faint.

"But of course," her mother said. "If it is all right with Gwyn."

"I am going to have a word with Ben," her father said. "Come with me, Bronwyn. You too, Idris."

Idris stood frowning intently at Devlin for a while before turning to follow his parents outside. Gwyneth got to her feet, and she and Devlin faced each other across the table.

"I have to go," he said. "It seems that what happened last night was my fault, and I am the one who must leave."

"It will all be forgotten in a while," she said, "and you will be able to return."

She did not for a moment believe what she was saying.

"No, Gwyneth," he said. "Even if I could come back, I would not. Everyone—my whole family—has lived with a lie for years and years. Perhaps all the years of my parents' marriage. My mother has lived with it. Perhaps especially her. Even I have had niggling suspicions for longer than a year but have suppressed them because I did not want to dig deeper and perhaps discover that they were well founded. I did not know for sure until last night, but I have not been entirely innocent. I do know now. And it seems I made my decision last night not to be a part of the happy illusion that everyone condones by refusing to acknowledge the truth. Even my mother's own family—her parents and her brother—have perpetuated it. All of them are doubtless frantically thinking at this very moment of ways to reconstruct the illusion so that *normal* life can resume. There has been nothing normal about our lives. I will no longer ignore the truth just because it is the convenient and polite thing to do. I will not live beneath a roof with that man again. I cannot."

That man. He was talking of his father, whom he had clearly always adored. Whom everyone had. Or did. Oh dear God.

"Where will you go?" she asked him. "What will you do?"

"To London first," he said. "I have money of my own. I am going to purchase a commission. In a foot regiment if they will have me. I daresay they will, though. The fight against Napoleon Bonaparte is heating up, and it is going to be a long and brutal one, I suspect."

Gwyneth swallowed and gripped the edge of the table. Not *Devlin.* No one could be less suited . . . She tried to speak, but no words came out. She did not even know what she wanted to say. Her mind was refusing to function properly. He was leaving. Leaving Ravenswood. Leaving her. Forever. He was going to be an officer in a foot regiment. He would almost surely be killed and she would never see him again after this moment.

She would never see him again even if he lived. He was leaving.

"I am sorry, Gwyneth," he said. "I am *so* sorry."

She nodded and looked down at her hands. How absurd, really. This time yesterday he was just a dream from the days of her youth. This time yesterday a scene like this was unthinkable. If all had stayed as it was this time yesterday he would not even have been on that hill to overhear his father and Mrs. Shaw in the pavilion. *None* of last night would have happened. None of this would be happening now.

And suddenly he was behind her and his hands were gripping her shoulders and she was turning and burying her face against him.

"I am so sorry," he said again, his voice low and unsteady against her ear. "Forgive me for saying this, for I have no right and you must forget me immediately. Today. But I do love you, Gwyneth. With all my heart. I will always love you."

"If you loved me," she heard herself say, pressing her hands against his chest so that he would move back from her, "you would not have made that public scene last night, Devlin. I begged you not to, but you did anyway."

The words, bitterly spoken, seemed not to be coming from her. They were not what she was *thinking*. She was not thinking at all, in fact. She was all pure, raw agony.

"Yes," he said, gazing at her. "You did, Gwyneth. And I did. Accept my apologies, please."

"And if you loved me," she said, "you would not be leaving me in this cowardly manner. You would be staying here and fighting for me. You would be persuading Dad to let you marry me, and you would be taking me off to Wales or somewhere to set up a new life with me instead of with your stupid foot regiment. You know *nothing* about love. You have never loved me. You scarcely knew of my existence until suddenly yesterday you thought you fancied me and got stirred up by a bit of moonlight and music. And *lust*. And you called it love. You do not know the meaning of the word. A man does not leave the woman he loves."

He gazed at her with that closed-off Devlin look of his—the one he had used on her a year ago when she had met him at the bottom of the hill while they were both out riding. "I am so sorry," he said. "I cannot offer you so little. It would be the ultimate act of selfishness."

"One's heart is such a little thing, is it?" she asked scornfully. "There is no warmth in you, Devlin. No *give*. You are all inflexible righteousness. I have never loved you either. How could I have? The man with whom I have been infatuated does not even exist. I saw you, and I made you into the image of my dream man. You are not the only one who learned truth last evening. I learned it too. I saw that I have loved an illusion. I do not even *like* the real Devlin Ware. I am glad you are going away and never coming back."

"Gwyneth," he said, and reached out a hand for her.

She batted it away. "Go on," she said. "Go. I have to get ready for church. *Go.*"

And he dropped his hand to his side, made her a formal bow, and strode from the room without another word.

By the time the sound of horses' hooves and carriage wheels came from outside, Gwyneth was on her knees on the floor, her head bowed forward, the heels of her hands pressed to her eyes.

And now, she thought as the sound of the receding curricle grew faint and then disappeared altogether, it was too late to call him back. To tell him she had not meant a word of what had just come pouring out of her. To tell him, as he had told her, that she loved him with all her heart and always would.

Though she would never see him again.

I t must have been close to noon when they made their first stop to change the horses and have something to eat, though Devlin ate less than half of his meat pasty and noticed that Ben ate very little more of his own. They had been back on the road for half an hour or so, Ben at the ribbons now, before Devlin spoke—the first to break the silence between them since they had left Cartref.

"So, what are you going to do, Ben?" he asked. "After we have reached London, that is."

"Hang about there for a few days at least," Ben said. "Then go with you."

Devlin turned his head sharply and looked at him. "I'll probably get sent out to the Peninsula sooner rather than later," he said. "You know I am planning to purchase a commission. In a foot regiment. Perhaps the Ninety-Fifth—the Rifles."

"I will go there with you," Ben said.

"As a fellow officer?" Devlin asked.

"Not as a military man at all," Ben said. "I have money. I suppose you are aware that our . . . father settled a tidy sum on me right after my mother died. It was in trust until I turned twenty-five, which I did earlier this year. It has grown into something of a fortune over the years. And then there has been my salary, which has been largely unspent. I will not spend any of what I have on a commission, though. I do not believe in killing people against whom I have no grudge. I could do it in self-defense perhaps if there was no alternative, or in defense of someone dear to me. But not just because I was ordered to do it in some senseless battle."

"Then why would you come with me?" Devlin asked.

His brother did not answer for a while. Finally he said, "Because I think you might need me, Dev. You are a bit of a dangerous innocent. You see everything in terms of good and evil. Right and wrong. Truth and lies. With nothing in between. Yet in this world we live in almost everyone fits somewhere between those extremes."

"We all have to compromise?" Devlin asked. "I suppose you agreed with everyone last night and saw me as the big villain, the one who would not condone the Big Lie. Why the devil did you come with me today, then?"

"I told you why," Ben said. "My mother may be dead, but she was and is and always will be *my mother*. And you were the only one of all of us who was right, Dev. That does not necessarily make what you did right. But you made me see the truth that I suppose I have always known and have pretended not to know—that my mother was no more to my father than a cheap whore. Or maybe not so cheap. I will never know, but I hope for her sake she demanded and got an exorbitant price. She meant so little to him that he went and married your mother even though there was me. And then he kept on whoring while keeping up that pretty image of devoted husband and father and friend and neighbor. The perfect aristocratic family in the perfect setting. Even I was somehow folded into the image without tarnishing it. You were the only one who ultimately could not be folded in. You need looking after, Dev. I don't know how you will manage otherwise."

"The army probably does not allow brothers to accompany its officers to war," Devlin said.

"Then I will go as your servant," Ben said, shrugging. "As your valet."

"I believe they are called batmen in the military," Devlin said. "You really want to go with me to play nursemaid and polish my boots and clean my weapons, do you?"

"I'll probably tell you to do them yourself and mine too while you are at it," Ben said. "But yes, I am going with you."

Another half hour or so passed before they spoke again.

"Ben," Devlin said. "I always knew your story. I knew that though you were older than me you could never inherit the title or Ravenswood. I knew you were sent to a different school from the one Nick and I attended and now Owen. And all because you are not a Ware, though your father is. But I can honestly say, for what it is worth, that I have never thought of you as somehow inferior to the rest of us. You have always been my brother, as important to me as the others. I swear this is true."

"Yes," Ben said after drawing the curricle farther to the side of the road as they passed a stagecoach coming in the opposite direction. "Yes, I know."

"You did not come with me *just* because you thought I would need you, did you?" Devlin asked him. "You came at least partly because what happened last night made you feel very alone. It made you feel you did not belong at Ravenswood after all. You need me as much as I need you."

"You talk too much," his brother said, which was a funny thing to say when they had been traveling side by side for hours in almost complete silence.

"Well, that makes two of us," Devlin said. "Not talking too much, I mean. All alone. Not belonging."

"The difference being that you are still the heir," Ben told him. "You cannot *not* belong, Dev. Sooner or later you will have to go back whether you want to or not."

"Would to God it were not so," Devlin said. "I envy you your freedom from all that nonsense, Ben. But you will never be entirely alone, you know. Not as long as I am alive."

PART TWO

❧

1814

SIX YEARS LATER

CHAPTER ELEVEN

L eaving home forever was not possible, of course, when one happened to be the heir to an earldom and everything that went with it. In the case of Devlin Ware, forever lasted for six years and one month. At the end of that time he was on his way back home. Or, more accurately, on his way back to Ravenswood, which was not quite the same thing. Not *nearly* the same thing, in fact. Ben Ellis was with him.

Devlin had indeed purchased a commission in the 95th Regiment of Foot (the Rifles). He had not purchased any of his later promotions. He had earned them on the battlefield. It had not been impossibly difficult. The mortality rate of British officers during the Peninsular War had been shockingly high, and vacancies had to be filled, if not by purchase, then by merit and seniority.

He had arrived on the Peninsula in time to be part of the brutal winter retreat of the British forces under the command of Sir John Moore from Spain to Corunna in Portugal. He had been there for the Battle of Corunna. After that he had fought in so many engagements, ranging from minor skirmishes to sieges to massive all-out battles, that they tended to blur together in his mind so that he could not always remember whether a particular incident had happened at the Battle of Talavera or at Bussaco or Almeida. Or perhaps Vitória or Roncesvalles. He had been there for all of them and more.

He did remember the Battle of Toulouse, however, fought in the South of France on April 10 of 1814, because it was the final battle of the war. Over several years, British regiments had gradually trudged and fought their way out of Portugal and across Spain and over the Pyrenees into France, where they fought again, and finally it was all over. Napoleon Bonaparte abdicated as emperor, Marshal Soult agreed to an armistice with the Duke of Wellington, and Bonaparte was sent into exile on the island of Elba. Captain Devlin Ware—the only name by which he would allow anyone to address him—had had enough. The war was all over for him too. He returned to England, sold his commission, dealt with other necessary business in London, and was now on his way to Ravenswood.

It was two years since he had been summoned to return there. But he had ignored the summons at the time and remained with his regiment to lead his men to the bitter end of the fighting.

Two years ago his father had dropped to the floor of the taproom at the village inn. He had been dead before he reached it.

Devlin Ware, seventh Earl of Stratton, peer of the realm, owner of Ravenswood Hall and a number of other properties and a vast fortune besides, had been summoned home by his father's solicitor, now his own. He had been summoned too by a brief, formal note from the countess, his mother. He neither answered nor responded to either one. Ben had done so, he suspected, but they had not talked about it. They did not talk of what had once been their home or about any of the other people who had lived there and presumably still did. He believed Ben had kept up some sort of correspondence with some of them, but Devlin never asked and Ben almost never volunteered information or comment. Devlin had not corresponded with any of them, even the total innocents. The children. He had always thought it would be best if they considered him dead. Sometimes he almost wished he were.

He had not been killed in six years of relentless, ferocious warfare, however. He had arrived back in England relatively intact. He had all his limbs and both eyes, and surprisingly few scars. The worst of those he did have was unfortunately visible. It slashed across his forehead and through his eyebrow, and across the top half of his cheek, but the saber that had done the damage had missed his eye by some miracle that defied understanding. It had also failed to separate the top half of his head from the rest of his body. If there were other, inner scars, he did not know of them or care about them. He was a battle-hardened warrior with a battle-hardened mind, and that suited him fine.

He had been known in his regiment as a hard and ruthless officer, demanding a great deal of his men, but never more than he demanded of himself. He had held them to a high standard of conduct and achievement, but he had had one quirk of nature that had prevented many of his men from outright hating him and had even inspired a few to devotion and the determination to protect him from hostile fire. A number of enemy skirmishers died from rifle fire as they tried to pick off Captain Ware, conspicuous with his red officer's sash and sword. Unlike almost every other officer of any rank, he gave second chances except when they were impossible to give, as in a deliberate murder, for example. If one of his men ran in panic from battle, his recapture meant instant execution—except with Captain Ware, who stood the offender up in shirt and breeches

and nothing else before a punishment parade of his peers, all standing rigidly to attention, and gave the man the choice between an
ignominious death by hanging and a position at the very center of
the front line in the next battle. All, without exception, had chosen
the front line, and some had died an honorable death there in the
next battle. A few had distinguished themselves with extraordinary
bravery. Captain Ware gave a second chance but never a third.
Most men did not need a third.

His own courage could never be called into question. He volunteered a number of times to lead a forlorn hope, an advance force
of elite volunteers who led the charge against a seemingly impreg-
nable position and were almost certain to die so that the regular
forces behind them could smash through to victory. On one of
those occasions he had been chosen and led his fellow volunteers to
what was a successful siege but at the terrible cost of the deaths of
nine out of every ten of them. Lieutenant Ware was careless of
death himself, but it did not find him on that day or any other. He
was awarded his captaincy as a result of that forlorn hope.

His courage, his toughness, his tenacity, his cold adherence to
duty made him feared, respected, and revered all at the same
time—and by the same men.

During those years he made up for the celibacy of his youth
and young manhood. He chose his women exclusively from among
the camp followers—washerwomen, cooks, wives, and widows—
though he never slept with any of the wives. There were widows
enough. Many of them had come to the Peninsula with their husbands as winners of one of the lotteries that decided which women
would be allowed to accompany their men and which would not.
Those husbands often died in battle, but their widows rarely returned home. How would they have got there? What would they
have done when they went back? They stayed and worked and re-

married and as like as not were widowed again. It was a constant cycle. There were always men only too willing and eager to take over from dead husbands and have a woman all their own. Most of the women were clean, honest, hardworking, foulmouthed, tough, cheerful, and lusty.

Devlin liked them as a group. He rarely slept with the same woman twice, but few if any of them resented that fact. The women did not expect that an officer would ever marry them, after all, but it was definitely something of a coup to have been seen disappearing inside an officer's billet during an evening. And if any of them were apprehensive about Captain Ware's reputation as a cold, hard commanding officer, they were soon able to pass on the reassuring information to other women that he was lovely in bed—always clean and freshly shaved, considerate, respectful, almost gentle. And that he took his time about the main business, Lord love him, and let them have a good time too. Also that he was very generous *after* bed, though, none of them being whores, there was never any demand or expectation of being paid. He gave gifts of money anyway, yet never made them feel like whores. Many of them would not have minded being invited back for more of the same, though they were far too sensible to expect it or to waste their energy sighing over him when there were plenty of other men to go with or even marry.

Ben remained with his brother throughout those years, except for the two-month period he spent with Nicholas, who was so severely wounded at the Battle of Talavera that it seemed certain he would lose a leg and very likely his life as well. Devlin spent a week with him too, but when duty called him back to his regiment, he went, leaving Ben behind. Ben in turn had proved himself to be a force to be reckoned with when he was confronted by surgeons— nothing but *sawbones* to his mind—who thought they were going to get away with sawing off his brother's leg when it was not *by God* necessary and they would do it at peril of their lives. Nick kept his leg and, ultimately, his life.

Devlin did not see much of his brother apart from that one-week stretch, when Nicholas was so crazed with fever and pain that it was doubtful he even knew that two of his brothers were hovering over him like fierce, cursing angels the whole time. He was a major in a prestigious cavalry regiment. He was always resplendent in scarlet coat with copious amounts of gold lace and facings. His fellow officers were almost all sons of aristocratic fathers. Devlin was one rank lower and attached to a regiment that had little prestige, except for the growing respect for the rifle as a superior weapon to the musket, which other foot regiments still used almost exclusively. He also looked less striking in his green uniform coat. His fellow officers were mostly sons of the gentry. Just as he liked it. He wished he were one of them. He wished he could exchange mothers with Ben. Or exchange ages with Nicholas.

Ben was not himself a military man, of course. He was not a servant either, despite his official designation as Devlin's batman. If he did all those things a real batman would have done, but without the salary—which he had flatly refused—and without being told, then he did them for something to do, he had explained once when his brother had protested. He nursed Devlin through his various injuries except on those occasions when Devlin told him, usually through gritted teeth, to *stop fussing, damn it, Ben—it's a mere scratch.* Occasionally, and probably against every military rule that had ever been written, Ben fought in defense of his brother when he had found himself close to the battlefront, and then in defense of his brother's men, and ultimately in defense of himself. He bore a charmed life, however. The closest he came to being wounded in all of the six years was a slight burn on the outside of one arm as a musket ball whistled by him, too close for comfort, when he was in his shirtsleeves. He grumbled about his damaged shirt and made no mention of the burn.

Like his brother, Ben chose from among the camp followers for his personal comfort. Unlike his brother, though, he picked one woman and kept her—and only her. She was large and strong and plain faced and had red hands and arms from the large washtubs at which she labored every day. She was also true to her man, and Ben was content with her. When she showed signs of getting big bellied and he confronted her on it and she admitted that yes, she was with child but he need not bother his head over it, he went and found the regimental chaplain and married her.

"I am not going to have Marjorie called whore on my account," he explained to Devlin, whom he had asked to be a witness at the wedding. "She is a good, decent woman, Dev, and she deserves better. And no son of mine is going to be called bastard."

They called their daughter Joy Ellis, and Devlin did not think there was any irony in the naming. He believed that Ben, in his own quiet way, loved his wife and was happy. He buried her and mourned her with stonelike demeanor when she died somewhere in the Pyrenees of a chill they could not stop to treat properly as they slogged and fought their way into France. She had looked after the infant with uncomplaining devotion, and after her death Ben tucked the child inside his almost-warm-enough greatcoat, next to the heat of his body, and she spread her hands against his neck, nestled her curly head beneath his chin, and nuzzled the collar of his coat, cooing contentedly. She was almost one year old, fully weaned, and not yet quite able to walk. Ben trudged onward without complaint, holding his Joy close to his heart and the rest of his gear and hers on his back.

Now they were in England and on their way to Ravenswood,

the three of them. Ben had not yet hired a nursemaid for his daughter, unwilling as he was to let her out of his sight. Devlin had had several appointments with his solicitor in London. After one of these, on the man's advice, he had visited a tailor to turn himself into a proper English gentleman and had purchased a carriage grand enough for the Earl of Stratton to ride in and four horses worthy of pulling it and him. Ben had also purchased new clothes for himself and his daughter. So here they were, having run dry of excuses for delaying in London, and traveling in far greater pomp and luxury than they had six years and one month ago when they had been going in the opposite direction.

Devlin had written a brief note to his mother, advising her of their impending arrival.

He had not written to anyone else and had not asked news of them either from his solicitor or from Ben. Philippa would be twenty-one now. He did not even know if she was married. Owen would be eighteen. Finished with school. Perhaps about to go up to Oxford? With a career in the church as his objective? It had seemed unlikely when the boy was twelve, but that was a long time ago. Stephanie would be fifteen. Almost grown-up. So many missing years. He ought perhaps to have maintained contact with them. But his very survival—or the survival of his sanity, anyway—had seemed to depend upon his cutting all ties, all news, all knowledge of what he had left behind. And all memories too.

It was impossible to stop oneself from thinking, of course. Thought happened whether one wanted it to or not. But he *had* stopped himself from thinking of what had once been home. He had done it with a ruthless effort of will, filling his mind with his new life. He had chosen a military career quite deliberately. There would be much upon which to focus his attention, he had thought. And he had been right. Fortunately he had always devoted himself to duty. He had not found it hard to transfer that training to his duties as an officer during wartime.

When the news of his father's death had been forced upon him, it had been like something coming from another lifetime. One in which he was no longer interested. He had treated it as mere information, to be dealt with later. Now *later* had come. Though he had still not dealt with that death emotionally. Just as he had not dealt with thousands of other deaths he had witnessed. He had killed emotion while he was driving his curricle away from Ravenswood and then Cartref all those years ago.

He had not thought of Cartref or any of the people living there since.

It was impossible to know what sort of welcome he would receive at Ravenswood. Or what he would have to offer in return. They were all strangers to him now, the people living there, as he would be to them. People he had once loved. But what was love? He no longer knew or wanted to know. He thought suddenly of Idris Rhys, his closest friend while they were both growing up and a little beyond their growing years too. If Idris had written to him after he left, it was Ben who would have opened the letter and perhaps replied to it. Though it was doubtful Idris *had* written. He had not been happy during their final encounter. And his very words came back, as though they had been spoken yesterday.

Dev, he had said just before Devlin climbed to the seat of his curricle beside Ben on that final morning, *you have broken her heart, and it will go hard with her. Don't do it, man. Find some other course of action. There is bound to be something. Dad will help you. I will help you. Just don't be an idiot. It always has to be all or nothing with you, though, doesn't it?*

Her.

You have broken her heart.

And just like that, his thoughts landed where they had always least wanted to go.

Upon Gwyneth Rhys.

She would be twenty-four now. Undoubtedly married. But not to someone local, he hoped. He would rather not see her again. Perhaps she had married someone from Wales, where she had gone each year with her parents and Idris to visit relatives. Or where they had used to go. Who knew what changes might have happened in the past six years?

. . . and it will go hard with her.

If she had allowed her heart to be broken after a one-day courtship and one inexpert kiss, then the more fool she. He did not think Gwyneth was a fool, though. She would have shaken him off, like dust from her bare feet, and run laughing into the wind, her dark hair streaming out behind her. Then she would have found someone else. Not Nick, though. His brother had left home soon after *he* had, and unlike Devlin, he had not sold out when the wars ended. He was probably in Paris with his regiment at this moment.

The carriage brought them inexorably closer to Ravenswood, and Devlin thought for the thousandth time that he really did not want to be doing this. But he no longer had any choice. The wars were done, he was no longer Captain Ware of the 95th, and duty was calling him in another direction. He was the Earl of Stratton.

He could not even think of Ravenswood as *his*. He could not imagine his mother as she might be now, forty-six years old and widowed. He could not picture his brother and sisters, the younger ones, who would all have grown up since he left. Even Stephanie would be on the brink of womanhood.

Had he changed the course of all their lives beyond recognition? Perhaps even beyond bearing? But how could he not have? On one perfect day at the end of July in 1808 they had all been at a

Ravenswood fete, living the grand illusion—one close, happy family in the midst of happy extended family members and neighbors. Not a cloud in their sky, either literally or figuratively. But before that day was over, the illusion had been shattered, possibly beyond repair. And the very next day the two oldest sons, one the heir to the earldom, the other the steady, competent steward of the estate, had been gone, never to return. Not for six long years anyway. How could everything *not* have changed drastically from that day on? Even before the death of the earl. And certainly after it.

And had he, Devlin, been solely responsible for it all? Or had that been on his father? Devlin still did not know the answer. Perhaps because in six years he had not asked. Nor had he seen the effects of what had happened on that fateful evening—or heard about them. By his own choice.

A man of extremes, Ben had once called him, with no tolerance for what went on in the middle, between the two extremes, where most people did their living. Was he still that man of extremes? He did not even know.

He glanced at the child asleep on Ben's lap beside him, her cheeks flushed, her mouth partly open, her cocked thumb fallen out of it. She was now almost a year and a half old. Ben had played with her with what seemed to Devlin like infinite patience after their stop for luncheon until she succumbed to the motion of the carriage. Ben loved that child with all the quiet passion of his steadfast heart. For a moment Devlin felt the soreness of unshed tears at the back of his throat because *he* had not loved for a long, long time. He had lusted and enjoyed, liked and respected, but he had not loved. He did not believe he ever could again. He had not died on the Peninsula, but something in him had.

Ben must have felt his brother's eyes on him. "I will not be staying for long, Dev," he said.

Ah. Devlin had wondered about that but had been a bit afraid to ask. It had become too ingrained in them that nothing concerning home be as much as mentioned between them. Almost as though their history as brothers had been erased and only the fact of it remained. *They were brothers.* Ben had tried a couple of times in the first year or so to mention a letter that had come from some member of the family, sometimes addressed to him, sometimes to Devlin, but when his brother had not asked for details, he had not volunteered any. Soon he had stopped even mentioning letters.

"Why?" Devlin asked. Why would Ben not be staying for long?

"Ravenswood is not really my home," Ben said. "It is where I grew up because my father took me there after my mother died. Now my father is dead too."

It was the first time that fact had been mentioned openly between them since the day Ben had forced those two letters upon him—the ones from the solicitor and the countess—looking as he did so as if he might have been weeping. Though even then they had not talked about the fact that their father was dead. Devlin had read both letters, folded them carefully, and handed them back. Ben had disappeared for a few weeks after that. Devlin suspected he had gone to see Nicholas. Perhaps they had grieved together. He had half expected that Ben would not return, but he did.

"But your brothers and sisters are not dead," Devlin said. "I am not, and Ravenswood is mine."

Perhaps that was the problem, of course. Ben was older than he, the eldest son of the late Earl of Stratton, but it was Devlin, his second son, who was now the earl and owner of Ravenswood in his place. He was the one who bore the name Ware. Just because he had been born within wedlock while his elder brother had not.

"I will not be staying for long," Ben said again. "I need to make a home for my daughter."

"Where?" Devlin asked.

It seemed Ben had been thinking about it. "I was wondering if you would sell Penallen to me," he said.

Penallen? It was one of the minor properties Devlin had inherited from his father. It was close to the sea and a picturesque fishing village, twenty miles or so from Ravenswood. They had gone there once when Devlin was a very young boy and Nicholas had been little more than a baby. He had a sudden vivid memory of the salt smell of the sea and of the fish Ben had brought back from a morning spent out on a boat with some of the fishermen. He had been almost bursting with pride as he displayed them for everyone's admiration. The family had not gone there again. The house, which Devlin could not remember at all, was not large enough for his father's tastes. Ben had been there a few times, though, in his capacity as their father's steward. It was not one of the entailed properties. It could be sold. For the first time Devlin wondered why his father had not left one of the unentailed properties to his eldest son.

"There will be no need to—" he began.

"Do *not* tell me," Ben said, cutting him off, "that you will give it to me. I will buy it. If you will sell. I can afford it."

Devlin wondered if his father's not leaving him one of the properties had hurt Ben, implying as it did that only the gentry were worthy of owning land. The legitimate sons of the gentry, that was.

"You do not know my price yet," Devlin said, flashing his brother a grin. "But don't leave too soon, Ben." *I am going to need you.* He almost said the words aloud, but it would be grossly unfair. His brother had stuck by him all this time, though it could not have been easy. Now he had a life to get on with. A life that centered about his daughter.

Joy had flung up one arm to touch Ben's face. He held her tiny wrist and kissed her hand, gently pulling back her fingers with his thumb, and she smiled without opening her eyes, smacked her lips a few times, and curled deeper into him.

And Devlin realized the fathomless depths of Ben's love for his child. He held the whole of his world in his arms. His own flesh and blood. His *family*. Whereas Devlin's family, large and extensive, was estranged from him. By his own doing? By theirs? A bit of both? His mother was the only one of them who had actually told him to leave. She was also the only one who had summoned him back home. Though, to be fair, he had not given any of the others an opportunity either to invite him to return or to tell him to go to the devil.

And he had ignored the only summons he had received— summons or invitation, depending upon one's perspective, he supposed. For two years.

"We are going to be there soon," Ben said, and Devlin glanced with a heavy heart at the increasingly familiar landmarks beyond the windows.

CHAPTER TWELVE

Gwyneth was out riding. She had been feeling restless and in need of air and exercise—and solitude. She was riding side-saddle, her riding habit both smart and fashionable. Her hair was dressed neatly beneath a matching riding hat. She had refused the company of a groom, having assured him that she did not intend leaving her father's land. She was up on the highest point of the hills on its western border, looking down upon the river and the village of Boscombe and miles of land beyond it. And, on this side of the river, Ravenswood's park and the hall itself in the middle distance.

She had drawn her horse to a halt. For a carriage drawn by four horses had just crossed the bridge from the village and was passing through the gates on its way to the hall. It was impossible from this far away to see if it was a carriage she would recognize. But no one coming from a mere few miles away to pay a visit would be using *four* horses. If, on the other hand, that vehicle had left London this morning, this was about the time it would be arriving.

Word had spread to every corner of the village and the surrounding countryside, as even lesser news and gossip invariably did, that the Earl of Stratton was coming home today. He had written to the countess, advising her to expect him. It was doubtful that the countess herself had spread the word except to inform her immediate family and the servants who would be involved in preparing for his arrival. But that had been more than enough. Many of the Ravenswood servants, though possibly warned of dire consequences if they gossiped, would not have been able to resist whispering the exciting news to a relative in the village or to one of the Misses Miller at the shop or to Mr. Holland at the smithy or to a fellow servant at another house. One would have a better chance of containing a wildfire in a hurricane than gossip in the English countryside.

He was coming home. Forever had not lasted forever after all.

The carriage was drawing to a halt on the terrace before the house, but it was impossible to see who would alight from it or even how many persons. There had been some discussion about whether Ben Ellis was likely to return with his brother, or even Major Nicholas Ware. Nobody knew, however. It was known only that the Earl of Stratton was coming.

Gwyneth, watching intently though she could see very little, told herself that she had arrived at this particular place at this particular time purely by chance. Why would it be otherwise? Once upon a time she had fixed both her twelve-year-old eyes and her girlhood dreams upon a seeming impossibility—a boy several years older than she, her brother's best friend, a boy with a title and the prospect of a far more illustrious one. A boy beyond her reach, *not* because of the titles, but because he was *older*, and his serious demeanor made him seem older still, and he did not know she existed. She had been quite lovesick over him for years, even while she had enjoyed a close friendship with his younger brother. And then for one day—just *one* out of all the days she had lived in her twenty-four years and a few months—that infatuation had blossomed into a glorious, unlikely romance, complete with a kiss on a darkened hillside and a mutual declaration of eternal love. And a proposal of marriage.

The very next day, he was gone.

Such a grand, sad tragedy. *One day.* A long time ago. There was no reason for the news of his impending return to have brought her up here on the chance that she would witness it. And what was she seeing anyway? A carriage and horses that *might* have brought him from London. So what? What did it have to do with her?

Perhaps Nicholas had come with him. She tried to pin her thoughts upon that possibility, for Nick had once been her dearest friend, and she had wept bitterly the day he left Ravenswood to join his regiment. She had died a number of little deaths over the following years as this corner of the world had received news of deadly battles fought and won or lost weeks, even months, before. Sometimes word of wounds Nicholas had sustained and somehow survived had seeped out of the hall by the usual means. It had been heartsickening to know that every bit of news was old by the time she heard it. To know that perhaps he had been wounded again. Or worse. He might be dead and no one here knew it yet.

There was never any news of *him*. Except that he became Earl of Stratton upon his father's death two years ago, so he must at least have been still alive then. Now he was coming home. He had survived the wars.

The carriage was moving off from the front of the hall and Gwyneth's horse snorted and pawed the ground, eager to be moving again. She held it still. Whoever had descended from the carriage had gone inside, and she was none the wiser.

She thought of him as the Earl of Stratton. Nick's elder brother, who had succeeded to the title two years ago. She did not think of him by any other name. A girlhood infatuation, a one-day flaring of exuberant, passionate romance when she was eighteen and on the cusp of womanhood—what, after all, had it left behind that was of any significance except a few memories she might draw out and dust off when she was old and gray and rocking in her chair before the fire and smile over a little sadly for the pain she had allowed herself to suffer just because she *was* young? At present the memories were safely packed away somewhere deep inside herself where they caused no pain at all.

She had moved on from that brief, seemingly unbearable agony, that girl who had been herself. She had gone to Wales with her family a couple of weeks after and been caught up within the warm affection of the larger family there with all their friends, who lived boisterous, passionate, laughter-filled and music-centered lives—or so it had always seemed to her, though doubtless they experienced their own upsets and tragedies and disappointments. They had been a balm to her shattered dreams that year, and she had almost got herself betrothed to a pleasant young man she had known most of her life.

Almost but not quite. She had found herself saying no to his stammered marriage proposal when she had fully expected to say yes. Then she had watched his expression change, *not* to one of anguish, but to one of . . . relief? It had suggested to her that he had offered out of pity more than romantic love. Her mother had had much the same look on her face when Gwyneth had told her. She had been wise to refuse, her mother had said, for accepting would not have been entirely fair to the young man.

She had not needed her mother to tell her that, though. She had liked him too well to use him to soothe a bruised, perhaps even broken, heart. The whole family had hugged and fussed over her far more often than usual that summer and dreamed up all sorts of treats for her amusement and otherwise showed her how much they loved her.

It had been soothing and devastating.

They had gone to London the following spring. Her father had leased a house in a fashionable part of Mayfair, and he and Gwyneth's mother had used connections she had not even realized they had to secure introductions to influential people. Gwyneth had even been taken to one of the queen's drawing rooms to make her curtsy to Her Majesty. After that she had been caught up in a dizzying round of social entertainments—balls and routs, theater performances and Venetian breakfasts, strolls and rides in Hyde Park and drives to Kew Gardens, dinners and one dazzling evening at Vauxhall Gardens, listening to music, dancing, and watching the fireworks. She and her mother had been sent vouchers to Almack's, a coveted mark of distinction indeed. She had received two very eligible marriage offers, one from a baron, and had given serious consideration to both before declining. Since then she had attended several house parties to which she had been invited by friends she had made in London. She had attended part of another Season two years ago with one of those friends and had received and rejected another marriage offer.

She was very much in danger, she had begun to think after that particular occasion, of ending up on the shelf, a spinster with nothing to do but care for her mother and father, if they should ever grow old enough and infirm enough to need her care. There was no sign of either affliction yet. Worse, she might end up alone in *her* old age and dependent upon Idris to give her a home with him. That would be a dreadful fate, for Idris, at the age of twenty-nine, was in a serious courtship of Eluned Howell, daughter of one of their father's closest friends in Wales. Gwyneth loved her dearly, but she did *not* fancy being an unmarried sister-in-law in her house-hold. No doubt Eluned would not fancy it either.

Gwyneth did not believe she was going to end up alone, how-ever. For Idris had stayed on in Wales after she and her parents came home from there a few weeks ago, and he had just let them know that he was coming in a few days' time and was bringing Aled Morgan with him. Gwyneth had met Aled last year when she was competing in the harp contest at one of the *eisteddfodau*, or arts festivals, for which Wales was famous. She had won the contest. Her father had undertaken the Herculean task of taking the youth choir there too, and Gwyneth had accompanied them with her harp. They had placed third, one position higher than they had two years before. Aled Morgan had not been an entrant in any competi-tion himself, but he was a well-known musician and conductor. He had conducted orchestras and choral works in London and Edin-burgh as well as in Bristol and Cardiff and Swansea. The prince regent had shaken his hand after one performance—though it was not Aled himself who had told Gwyneth that. He was not a boast-ful man.

He was a pleasant, mild-mannered man in his middle thirties, passionately involved with music. He had gone out of his way to commend Gwyneth on her harp playing. He had persuaded her to play just for him one evening—the large festival tent had been empty, but people milled outside and so made her being alone with him inside not quite improper. He had watched her intently while she played and afterward had kissed the back of her hand and told her he hoped they would be friends. She had seen him again this summer, and he had made it very clear that he wished to move their acquaintance to another level. Now he was coming to Cartref at her father's invitation, to see and listen to the organ at the church. He was also coming because of her, Gwyneth believed. She fully ex-

pected that he would propose marriage to her while he was here—
he had hinted as much when he took his leave of her the evening
before she came home with her mother and father.

And this was a proposal she would accept. It was high time she
was married. She was twenty-four. More important than any unease she felt over her advancing age, however, was the fact that she
was very fond of Aled. They had a great deal in common and never
lacked for topics to draw them into deep, animated conversation.
He would be a kind husband, she was sure, and an intelligent and
constantly interesting companion. He would treat her as an equal.
He professed to admire her as much as she admired him. He had a
wealth of friends in all parts of the country. She would have a stimulating and varied life with him. He was not a vastly wealthy man,
she believed, but he could undoubtedly offer her a comfortable and
secure life.

She was not going to wait any longer for love—romantic love,
that was. It was for the very young and was, moreover, extremely
precarious and ultimately painful. Poor young people, who had to
discover the truth of that for themselves! It was so much more sensible to marry for affection and shared interests. And really, affection was a form of love, but more stable and longer lasting than
romantic passion. She felt a warm affection for Aled.

She had been staring at Ravenswood for a long time, she realized. Long after there was anything to see. Her poor horse had even
given up dropping hints about moving on and was nibbling for-
lornly at the scrubby grass beside the track.

She turned toward home and the pleasant prospect of seeing
Aled again within the next day or two. It was just a pity that the
Earl of Stratton had chosen almost the same time to come back to
Ravenswood to offer an unwelcome distraction. But he had to come
sometime, she supposed, and now was probably as good a time as

any, now that the wars were over, the harvest was in, and the winter had not yet descended upon them.

It did not really matter to her anyway. While the neighborhood for miles around buzzed with the news that he was back, she would have something and someone else to hold her attention.

She *so* looked forward to Aled's coming here, to her own home and her own neighborhood this time. She wanted to be seen with him. He was a distinguished, good-looking man. She wanted her neighbors and friends to see that she had indeed and at long last moved on in life, that the return of the Earl of Stratton meant nothing whatsoever to her.

It would be lovely if she did not have to see him at all, though she supposed that was not a realistic wish. Well, then. When she *did* see him, she hoped she would have Aled by her side.

It had been one day. Just *one*. More than six years ago.

Their approach had been noted.

It had probably been watched for all day, in fact. The main street through the village and the village green had been unusually busy with people, all apparently just going innocently about their business, though all had stopped and fixed their gaze upon the carriage as it passed on its way toward the bridge. And now, at Ravenswood itself, the butler and a number of footmen and grooms, all smartly dressed as though for a special occasion, were out on the terrace, the butler waiting to open the carriage door and set down the steps lest the coachman Devlin had hired in London be incapable of doing so himself, the footmen ready to carry what they must be expecting to be a great mountain of baggage inside and up to their relevant chambers, the grooms to lead away the carriage and horses.

"And so it begins," Devlin murmured.

Ben was busy with Joy, who was making grumbling noises at having her sleep disturbed.

"Welcome home, my lord," the butler said, bowing importantly from the waist as Devlin descended the steps. "Welcome home, Mr. Ellis. And Miss Ellis."

Devlin had not been sure if anyone here knew of the existence of Ben's daughter. Apparently they did.

"Thank you, Richards," he said. Everything outdoors was immaculate. Even the sheep below the ha-ha had looked as though they might have been washed for the occasion, though it seemed unlikely. Poor sheep if they had been.

The butler preceded them up the steps to the open front doors and bowed them inside the great hall. Devlin saw immediately what he had feared he would see and had hoped he would not. The servants were all there, lined up on either side of the entrance, the women on one side, the men on the other, as though they were about to perform some stately dance. All of them were in their best uniforms, clean and freshly starched and ironed. But even as the women all curtsied at a signal from the housekeeper and the men all bowed, Devlin became aware that he was not to escape the full flowering of this homecoming farce. A group of people stood facing him beyond the servants, forming a still, silent tableau.

The family.

His mother stood between two young ladies on her left and a young man on her right. None of them were smiling, and none of them came rushing down between the lines to hug him and Ben and welcome them home. He understood the reason, of course. They had not congregated here to greet the son and brothers they had not seen for years. They had done it as a formal, almost ceremonial gesture to welcome the Earl of Stratton to his principal seat. As though the earl were some impersonal being. But really he had not expected any different, if he had expected anything at all. He might have hoped this first encounter would take place in some private apartment—the drawing room, perhaps—but instead it was to be in a public setting. And of course it would be reported far and wide long before this day was over.

Perhaps that was the whole point.

His return was a necessary evil as far as the family was concerned.

"Mrs. Padgett?" he said, acknowledging first the housekeeper and then each of the two lines of servants with an inclination of his head. He glanced at Ben, who was looking toward something at which Joy was pointing, and strode forward between the lines without waiting to see if his brother was coming too. But this, of course, was all about him, not Ben. He could hear his boot heels ringing on the marble tiles as he went, the only sound in the hall except the slightly softer thud of Ben's boots as he came along behind him.

Well, let them have their moment. He had inspected silent ranks of soldiers more times than he could count. This would not disconcert him.

His mother, he observed as he drew closer, had changed. Not so much in outer appearance—she was as elegant and poised as she had ever been. There still appeared to be no gray in her dark hair. She was perhaps a bit thinner. Her cheeks were more hollowed than he remembered, but her face was unlined and she was still beautiful. The change in her was something indefinable. There seemed to be a certain loss of charm and warmth, though it was surely not possible to form an accurate impression so soon, especially when she was looking at the son she had banished six years ago and refused to receive before he left. She just somehow did not seem like his mother. Perhaps he did not seem like her son. The light appeared to have gone out within her, whatever the devil that meant. But that was it, of course. That was what had changed.

They stood and looked at each other for several wordless moments after he halted a few feet away, neither of them flinching. Or smiling.

"Mother." He held out his hand and, when she set her own within it, he bowed over it and made the quick decision *not* to raise it to his lips. It was icy cold and lay limp in his clasp. He had never called her *Mother*. He had not planned to do so now. But how could he call her *Mama*? He could not. "I trust I find you well."

"Stratton," she said. "Thank you. You do. Welcome back to Ravenswood." She looked beyond his shoulder as her hand slid free of his. "Welcome home, Ben. And this is Joy?"

Stratton and *Ravenswood* to him. *Ben* and *home* to his brother. She had chosen her words with deliberate care, Devlin thought.

The child had burrowed her head as far inside Ben's coat as it would go.

"She can be a bit on the shy side," Ben said. "Thank you, Mother. It is good to be here." He had always called her *Mother* in order to distinguish her from his mama, whom he could barely remember, he had once told Devlin.

Devlin turned to the elder of his two sisters. Philippa. She was no longer the girl he remembered. She was a young woman, whose looks had lived up to all the promise of her youth. Honey blond hair, a delicate complexion, blue eyes with long lashes a shade or two darker than her hair, a slender build—even to a brother's eyes she was a rare beauty. But where were the sparkling eyes, the rose-petal cheeks, and the bright animation he remembered? Perhaps it was only this difficult moment that had banished them. The difficult moment or the whole fact of his return. She had not hated him when he left, but could he blame her if she did now? He had not done anything in all that time to retain her love or even discover if she lived or was dead—or married.

"Philippa." He extended a hand for hers, and she gave it to him after a small hesitation. It was limp and cold, like their mother's. There was no sign that she was married, he thought with a glance down at her left hand. Why was she not? How had her life changed after the age of fifteen? He had absolutely no idea.

"Stratton," she said. Her eyes did not quite meet his. "Hello, Ben. And Joy."

Stephanie had grown a great deal, as was to be expected between the ages of nine and fifteen. She was slightly taller than Pippa. But otherwise she still looked much the same, was just a larger version of herself. Her flaxen hair, in heavy plaits, was wound over the top of her head like a double halo. Her face was round and shiny. She had not lost any of her baby fat. Poor Steph. The only real difference, apart from height, was the paleness of her face and the dullness of her eyes.

"Steph," he said, and held out both hands, perhaps a little recklessly, as any rejection on her part would be avidly noted and reported upon by the silent lines behind him.

"Devlin." She set both hands in his and even wound her fingers about them. She raised her eyes to look into his face and roam over it. "You got wounded. No one told us." Her words and her expression accused.

"I lived," he said.

She nodded and removed her hands from his before turning to their brother. "I am glad you are home, Ben," she told him. "And I have been longing to meet Joy. Will she let me see her face? She has awfully pretty hair."

It was short and curly and unruly at the best of times. Now it looked rumpled. But she peeped—and smiled widely before ducking her head back under the safety of Ben's greatcoat.

"And she has a pretty face too," Stephanie said. "I am Aunt Stephanie, Joy. I have been waiting for you to come and play with me."

Devlin had turned to his youngest brother, grown surely to nearly twice the height he had been at the age of twelve. He was slender almost to the point of thinness. He was also a handsome lad with his shock of fair hair and his blue eyes, which gazed at his brother with an inscrutable look.

"Owen." Devlin extended his right hand and found that he was looking slightly up at his brother.

"Do all officers have that same look about them as you do?" Owen asked, shaking Devlin's hand with a firm clasp. "Hard, I mean. And scarred. I am glad you are home, Devlin, even though I do not know quite what it is going to mean. And you too, Ben. It will be good to have brothers around again. To outnumber our sisters." He actually grinned, the first of them to smile, and in his face Devlin saw the impish boy he had known—and also the alluring sort of family charm that had passed him by and was going to make Owen irresistible to women in a few years' time. Or perhaps already? He *was* eighteen, after all. A young man.

"You will wish to go to your rooms to freshen up before joining us for tea in the drawing room," their mother said. "Mrs. Padgett will direct you. Will you take the child to the nursery, Ben? One of the maids has been appointed as temporary nurse, unless you have brought your own."

"I have not, Mother," Ben said. "Not yet. But Joy will stay with me in my room, at least for a while. And she will come to tea with me if it is permitted."

"Of course," she said.

Devlin was about to say that they would not need Mrs. Padgett to show them to their rooms. But which *were* their rooms now? It was altogether possible—even probable—that his mother had moved out of the earl's suite above the drawing room and had it prepared for Devlin. Ben might have been moved from his old room to Devlin's since it was front-facing and a bit larger. Or perhaps his mother was now there.

Did it matter?

"Thank you," he said, and turned to find the housekeeper waiting to escort them upstairs. Like visitors in their own home. He felt more like a stranger than a visitor actually. An unwelcome stranger to all except perhaps Owen, who on the last Saturday of July six years ago had had three older brothers at home, just one the following day, and none a couple of months later. And no father either four years after that.

As he followed a silent Mrs. Padgett from the hall, a silent Ben at his heels, Devlin wished with all his being that he was back in France somewhere with his regiment. As Captain Ware, who had somehow been in control of his own world even while the larger world around him was in chaos. *The Earl of Stratton* did not sound like himself. Or feel like himself.

Ravenswood did not feel like his home.

CHAPTER THIRTEEN

I t was amazing, Devlin thought over the following few days, how he could spend time with people—his own family in this case— take his meals with them, occupy a drawing room with them during the evenings, converse with them enough that there were no awkward stretches of silence, and yet find that he did not feel he knew them any better than he had the day he returned.

Though he learned one startling piece of news. When he asked at tea on the first day about the extended family—his grandparents, aunts and uncles, and cousins—he was told that his paternal grandmother, the dowager countess, had died last year during the summer. She had been Ben's grandmother too, of course. Had he known of her passing? Devlin had not asked him.

After dinner on that same day he told them all that he would be spending much of his time during the coming days with his steward, familiarizing himself again with his properties, reminding himself of his duties, talking with his workers, making sure everything was functioning as it ought.

"But are you not going to be the steward here again, Ben?" Owen had asked. "I do know Mr. Mason has been feeling a bit anxious about it."

"His position is quite safe," Ben had told him, "provided Dev is satisfied with his work, of course. I'll be setting up home somewhere else in a short while. It is high time. I am thirty-one years old. And I have a daughter to raise."

"Oh, Ben," Philippa had cried. "Not too far away, I hope. Not when we finally have you home again."

"I am not sure yet," he had told her. "But you will be able to come and visit, you know. I daresay I will find a house somewhere that has at least one extra bedchamber."

Devlin had also told them that he would be establishing himself in the neighborhood in the coming weeks by calling upon his extended family and neighbors. Visiting, making polite conversation while sipping tea and nibbling on cake, was not something he had ever enjoyed. Now it was something he dreaded. Would he find doors slammed in his face? It seemed unlikely, though it was a possibility. Would he find rigidly polite, stony-faced hosts, rather like his mother? Would the Ware and Greenfield families turn their collective backs upon him? He had no idea what to expect. None of it mattered, however. He was the Earl of Stratton, he had chosen to return here to take charge of his inheritance, and he would not now cower on his own land, afraid to face the world beyond his gates.

It was important that everyone, including his mother and siblings, understand that from the start. He had not wanted what was now his life, but since he had no real choice in the matter despite ignoring it for the past two years, he would do what had to be done.

His mother had surprised him at that point by informing him

that she had arranged a tea in his honor to be held three days hence. Invitations had already been sent out and acceptances returned.

"Your family and neighbors will naturally wish to come and pay their respects to you, Stratton, now that you have finally returned home," she had explained. "I thought it as well to invite them to come all together rather than have a constant stream of callers for the next week or two. I guessed you would not wish for that."

"No," he had agreed. "I would not."

His mother had always enjoyed entertaining. She had been known for her openhanded hospitality. But that had been then, while this was now. She did not look delighted at the prospect of this welcoming party she had arranged for her own son. She would be doing it out of a sense of duty, of course. Always that word—*duty*. And it struck him as it never had before that there were strong similarities between his mother and him, even though there was now this cold, stiff near-estrangement separating them. She had not forgiven him for his public display of outrage on her behalf, and he . . . Well, he had not forgiven her either, had he?

This tea, he could confidently predict, would be a grand and formal affair to rival his homecoming reception earlier. And of course almost everyone who had been invited would come, out of sheer curiosity if for no other reason. He would certainly not expect any warmth of welcome from the occasion, though. But he had none to offer in return anyway.

Joy turned out to be a welcome distraction to them all during those early days, as very young children often are. She clung to Ben at tea on the first day and only occasionally peeped at her new relatives. Then Owen took a large white handkerchief from his pocket and, without saying anything, made out of it a bird with wings that fluttered. The bird chirruped cheerfully through lips Owen managed to keep motionless. Joy peeped and stared. Then Owen slowly pulled a long, thin white worm from the bird's beak until the whole thing collapsed in on itself. Joy chuckled and pointed and looked up at her father.

After that Stephanie crossed to the pianoforte and picked out a simple tune on the keyboard. When Joy peeped, she beckoned.

"Come and see," she said. "Come and play too."

At first Joy hid again. Then, when Stephanie resumed playing, she wriggled off Ben's lap and toddled over to take a closer look. Soon she was on Stephanie's lap and banging both palms down onto the keys and looking up over her shoulder for approval. Philippa went to dance beside the pianoforte and then coaxed Joy to dance with her while Stephanie played. Joy, holding her aunt's hands, bounced on the spot in time to the music and laughed while looking to make sure her father was still where she had left him and could see her.

During those days not a single mention was made of Devlin and Ben's father. Yet his presence seemed to loom over every moment the family spent in company with one another. There was something about the atmosphere that was heavy with unspoken sentiment and unresolved issues. Yet no one showed any willingness to address any of them. Least of all Devlin. His father was like a yawning black hole in his memory.

In many ways nothing had changed. They had never spoken truth to one another, this family, though Devlin had not realized it until six years ago. They had lived with illusion and considered themselves happy. They did not speak truth now either. Not that they spoke falsehood. They said nothing at all that had real meaning, that addressed the great awkwardness that lived in their midst, almost like another family member. For the moment he was content to leave it that way. He did not want to stir up anything, least of all emotion. There were other things upon which he could concentrate his attention.

He spent much of his first full day at home in consultation with John Mason, the steward his father had employed to replace Ben. He appeared to be a good man, about the same age as Ben, a bit dull and plodding, maybe, but he was not being judged on his personality. He kept clear, thorough records, and the estates had shown a decent profit for each of the past six years. Whether any of those profits had come at the expense of the workers remained to be seen, but the records did also show a slight increase in wages for three of the six years and evidence that repairs and general maintenance had been done on the laborers' cottages in the village.

Ben had declined Devlin's invitation to join them. He had insisted upon behaving like a guest, happy enough to be here, but not involved in any of the workings of the home where he had grown up.

Now, this morning, on their second full day at home, a beautiful, blue-skied early-autumn day, Ben had taken Joy out in the gig for a drive about the park. Stephanie, after appealing to Miss Field for time off from her lessons, had gone with them.

Devlin wandered outside for a while, noticing how a few of the leaves on the trees were beginning to change color and feeling unexpectedly cheered by the prospect of witnessing the whole glory of an English autumn this year—and winter after it. Winters on the Peninsula had been brutal. They had been responsible for the deaths of far too many of his men. He had not seen much of the park yet, but what he had seen was encouraging. There had been no neglect. Everything was looking pristine. Everything close to the house, of course, would have been spruced up for his homecoming. He would see the more distant parts of the park in the next few days, though probably not tomorrow. That was the day of the infernal tea.

He turned when he heard the front doors opening. Owen was

running lightly down the steps. It was still a bit of a shock to see him as a man. A very young man, it was true, but definitely no longer a boy.

"I am off to the village to pick up some silks for Mama's embroidery," he explained when he saw Devlin. "I'll call on Brad too while I am there. Mama is in no particular hurry for the silks."

"Brad?" Devlin raised his eyebrows.

"Bradley Danver," Owen said. "The vicar's son. We have always been friends. Remember? I lent him a book about a month ago. Have you noticed how people never return books unless you prod them? I am going to do a bit of prodding. I *like* that book."

"I'll come with you if I may," Devlin said on impulse. The thought of walking into the village for the first time was a bit daunting, but it had to be done. Now was as good a time as any.

"Brilliant," Owen said cheerfully, and they fell into step beside each other. Once they were clear of the house and alone, Owen turned to him. It was the first time Devlin had been alone with any of his siblings, besides Ben, of course. "Tell me what happened, Dev. I have been itching to ask, but violence and warfare are something one cannot talk about when there are women present. They might swoon or turn green or even puke. It must be dashed uncomfortable being a woman, I would say. It looks to me as though the top of your head came damnably close to being sliced right off."

"It was a glancing cut rather than a deliberate blow," Devlin told him. "If it had been deliberate, I would not be here talking with you now. There was enough blood to fill a lake even so, and I really did think I was done for. I thought I was blind too for a while, until I realized everything was red rather than black. Ben worked his magic on me after a surgeon had patched me up, and here I am, intact except for an ugly scar."

"I bet women don't see it as ugly," his brother said. "Women are funny that way. Though they would probably be prostrate on a couch with burned feathers being waved under their noses if they ever heard about that lake of blood. Better not tell 'em, Dev. Did you meet lots of them? Women, I mean. Ben obviously did."

Devlin paused for a moment, grateful for the ease of his brother's conversation. While his exuberance had been sometimes annoying when he was a boy, now it felt rather welcome. "Ben met *one* of them," he told his brother. "He made her his wife and had a child with her. He mourned her without fuss when she died, but he *did* mourn. Very deeply. He is a good man, Owen. A brother to be proud of."

"He always was," Owen said. "I always thought it a dashed shame he was a— Well, that his mother was never married to Papa. Though that would have relegated you to the position of spare rather than heir—would it not?—and *he* would have been the earl now rather than you. Tell me what it was like out there, Dev. Nick's letters have always been full of good cheer. One would swear he went there to enjoy some sort of Grand Tour. Ben's letters, on the other hand, were always so dry, one half expected the paper to crumble to dust in one's hand. And your letters were nonexistent."

"Did you resent that?" Devlin asked. He had not written because he could not risk cracking the emotionless shell he had built to hold himself together. He had not thought of how his silence might hurt his siblings, who had loved him and whom he had loved. He had *dared* not think of it.

His brother thought. "I don't know if *resented* is the right word," he said. "*Hated* would be better. I hated that you did not write. Not even to Steph, who worshipped the ground you trod upon. As though none of us existed. As though you did not care. Not even when . . . Well, not even then."

"Not even when our father died," Devlin said, somehow getting his mouth about the words. And Stephanie . . . *who worshipped the ground you trod upon.* The very idea of it cut into him like a whip.

"It was *awful*," Owen said. "He was in his cups. As usual. He fell and hit his head against the corner of the counter in the tap-room at the inn."

Good God! Devlin had always assumed it was a heart seizure. Had the letter from his father's solicitor not specified that was the cause of his death? Or had he worded the letter in such a way that Devlin would make that assumption? His father had been drunk? *As usual?*

"The head at school told me he had had a heart seizure," Owen said. "That is what everyone here believes too. Or pretends to believe. Everyone always *pretends.* Have you noticed that, Dev? Did they do that during the wars too? It is as if truth does not really matter, but only what you want to believe is the truth."

Oh yes, that Devlin noticed right enough. The noticing had ended life as he knew it six years ago. It seemed that at the age of twenty-two he had been more naïve than Owen was now at eighteen. "Perhaps," he said, "some people find it more comfortable to see their world the way they want it to be. Do you think?"

"Instead of the way it is," Owen said, shrugging. "Look, Dev, I don't know exactly what happened the night of that fete. You did not tell us before you left, and no one would tell us the next day or anytime after. But it must have been drastic for everything to change as it did. Not just every*thing*, but every*body*. I worked it out, of course. Twelve-year-olds are not stupid, and they have ears. I think I am almost certainly right. But I do not *know*, and it irks me now that I am grown-up. Anyway. You will tell me one of these days. And you will tell me what it was like out on the Peninsula. But here we are coming up on the shop. Now, what did I do with that piece of paper Mama gave me? She will roll her eyes if I go back with the wrong color silks and mutter darkly that she might have known to come herself. Ah, here it is."

They were indeed in the village by then, and a few heads had turned their way. One woman whom Devlin did not recognize, someone's servant by the look of her, curtsied hastily to him. The last thing he felt like doing was to go right into the Misses Millers' shop. He would have preferred a bit more time alone with his brother, getting to know him, sharing thoughts and even perhaps some memories. But Owen plunged on inside and Devlin followed.

He was greeted by the sisters and their two customers with surprised curtsies and obsequiousness—no, perhaps that was unfair. He was addressed at least four times as *Lord Stratton* and a few more times as *my lord*. He tried to recall if that was what everyone had always called his father and supposed it was. How else would they have addressed him?

He went as far as the rectory with his brother, and stood at the gate watching him dash inside to join his friend after the vicar and his wife both came to the door to invite him in—and to greet him as *Lord Stratton*.

"I will not come in, thank you," Devlin told them. "But I hope I will see you both at Ravenswood tomorrow afternoon?"

He would indeed, they assured him.

"Is that Sir Ifor Rhys playing the organ in the church?" he asked.

"It is," the vicar told him. "He has a famous conductor with him—Mr. Aled Morgan. He is a guest out at Cartref. The Prince of Wales shook his hand after an orchestral performance in London a year or two ago. They have been in the church for an hour or more."

"Perhaps I will step inside, then, and listen for a while," Devlin said. "I will try not to disturb them." The church would be somewhere to hide for a while since he did not fancy strolling about the green alone but did not want to go back home so soon either. More important, though, he had always loved the sound of the organ in this church. When Sir Ifor was playing it anyway. It was not just music that came from the instrument when he played. It was sheer emotion. Sheer beauty.

He opened the church door quietly and slipped through. He closed it softly behind him and was engulfed in familiarity. There was a certain quality to the light inside here as it filtered through the stained glass windows. Something suggestive of eternity. Something that induced serenity. There was a familiar chill too, which was not quite coldness. And there were the mingled smells of ancient stone and prayer books and candles and incense.

He had been given similar impressions by other churches, but there was something unique about this one. It spoke of home as Ravenswood no longer did. He felt a sharp stabbing of nostalgia— pain and regret and a wish that history could be changed. And a knowledge that it could not. Not if one was honest with oneself about what was real, that was, and what was merely wishful thinking—like his father having died of a heart seizure.

Somewhere—if he allowed it in—there was terrible pain in knowing that he had turned into a drunk.

The organ was playing something both intricate and majestic, though he did not recognize what it was. His eyes adjusted to the gloom, and he could see Sir Ifor seated on the organ bench while another man stood behind and to one side of him, bending forward, apparently totally absorbed in what he saw and heard.

Devlin went to sit at the end of the back pew, and for the first time since coming home, it seemed to him, he relaxed. Perhaps it was the first time since he returned to England. He closed his eyes briefly and gave himself to the comfort his senses brought him. But sight was one of those senses, and he loved the sight of the church interior on a sunny day. He opened his eyes again.

And found himself looking at a fourth occupant of the church. Someone he had not noticed when he came inside. She was sitting with her back to him, several pews ahead. She was still and quiet and gazing toward the organ.

Gwyneth.

Was she not married and gone from here, then? He wished like the devil that she had gone away. He felt rather as though he had been punched low in the abdomen.

It was impossible to know if she had heard him come in or, if she had heard someone, whether she knew it was him. Perhaps it could not be inferred from her utter stillness that she did. When one was immersed in the total enjoyment of something, one did not fidget.

Did one also look tense, though?

He could get up and leave as quietly as he had come. He *should* do it. He did not want any encounter with her. Dash it all, he did not. Yet he continued to sit and gaze at her. Numbness, he thought, sometimes felt a little too much like pain. Yet there had been just one day. *One.* Six years ago.

And then it was too late to take the initiative. She stood up abruptly, moved out from her pew, and came along the aisle toward the back. She stopped beside him. By that time he was on his feet too.

They gazed at each other in the semigloom. A shaft of colored light caught one side of her bonnet and left her face in the shade. But he could see her well enough. It was not a girl's face he looked into but a woman's. She had not changed a great deal, though. She was still dark haired and beautiful—with firm jaw and flashing eyes.

"I am going outside," she said just as the organ music was building to a grand crescendo. "I need some fresh air."

"I'll come too," he told her, and for a few moments she continued to gaze at him while he wondered if that was what she had intended.

The music came to a close.

"Dad." Gwyneth turned her head.

But the men were already talking to each other with passionate intensity.

"Dad." She raised her voice a bit.

They were too involved with what they were talking about to hear her. The man with Sir Ifor—Morgan, had the vicar said?—was leaning forward to play a chord on the lowest keyboard.

"They do not know anyone else even exists," Gwyneth said. "They probably will not come back to earth for another few hours."

She turned and led the way outside without looking to see if Devlin was following her.

CHAPTER FOURTEEN

G wyneth had been feeling irritated. Which was a bit of an understatement, for there was more than one cause of her bad mood.

For one, she had *not* been looking forward to tomorrow and the tea to which they had all been invited at Ravenswood Hall—even Aled. An invitation had been delivered for him just this morning to prove how quickly news traveled. Normally a social event might have been a welcome break from the monotony that often threatened life in the country, and these days events at the hall were rare. But the formal invitations that had been sent out had stated quite clearly that the tea was in honor of the return to Ravenswood of the Earl of Stratton. No mention of *Devlin* or *home* or the pleasure their company would give the countess. Even Gwyneth's mother had remarked that there was something a bit chilling about the card.

Who knew what was to be expected? Opinion had always been divided, quite sharply in some instances, on that scene Devlin had created before leaving home. Some people claimed to have suspected that Mrs. Shaw was the old earl's mistress and to have been uncomfortable and outraged on the countess's behalf and that of her children. Those people tended to defend what Devlin had done. Others pointed out that his ill-considered outspokenness had hurt his mother and his sisters and young brother as much as they had chastised his father, perhaps more. Those people were of the opinion that good manners were sometimes of greater importance than the truth. Now a sizable number of both groups, as well as those, like Gwyneth's parents, who refrained from giving any opinion or passing any judgment, were to gather at Ravenswood to face the very man who had hurt his family and divided the neighborhood.

Gwyneth did not want to be one of them. It was a farce, what the countess was doing. And how would *he* react? She did not want to know. She did not want to see him. Her connection to him was history, and she would have preferred to leave it that way. But . . . good manners dictated that she go. And since this morning she did not even have the excuse that she ought to remain at home to keep Aled company. He was delighted to have been invited.

"I will be pleased to be your escort, Gwyneth," he had said, even though Mam and Dad and Idris would be going too, and they had always been escort enough for her—if she needed an escort at all.

She had been feeling depressed about that, then, even before coming to the church this morning—Aled had persuaded her to come, against her better judgment. She had allowed herself to be flattered by his attentions. Foolish her! For one hour passed inside the church and then two, and a third was in progress. And she understood what of course she had already known—that for Aled music was his life and his soul. Everything else was secondary. She did not really doubt that he loved her, but she did not come even close to being the foremost love of his life.

She was going to have to decide if she could live with that reality. At *just* the time she was feeling all ruffled over Devlin's return and trying to persuade herself that she was not ruffled at all, that his coming home meant nothing whatsoever to her. She desperately needed the reassurance of Aled's preference for her, yet all he could think about was that wretched pipe organ. It had been her harp last evening, but that was small comfort today.

Today she was feeling both bored and annoyed. No one liked to feel neglected. And no one liked to feel petty and childish for feeling neglected.

But then . . .

Well, then the church door had opened quietly behind her. She had glanced back and then turned her head sharply forward again. And prayed desperately—she was in the right place for it—that he would close the door and go away. For a few minutes she had tried to convince herself that he had done just that. Tried but not succeeded. For there had been prickles down her spine, and if she did not soon do something decisive, she would surely scream.

So she had got up and turned. And without even looking at him, she had known he really was there and he really was Devlin.

Oh, he had changed, she thought less than a minute later, gazing at him as he gazed at her, only a couple of feet separating them. Not beyond recognition, but . . . fundamentally. He looked years older. There was a roughness about him, though his hair was neatly combed and he was clean shaven and well dressed. Perhaps it was because his face was swarthier or more weather bronzed than it had used to be, though it was not easy to see clearly in the dim light of the church. There was a hardness to the look of him. It was in the set of his jaw and mouth and in the direct, cold gaze of his eyes. Or perhaps it was the wicked scar that crossed his forehead and the upper part of one cheek and sliced through his eyebrow and made her knees feel weak. He looked dark and ruthless. Even cruel. For the first time it occurred to Gwyneth that his name suited him—Devlin. It was not far off *devil*, was it?

Was this what war did to a man? Was this what it had done to *him*? Or had something else done that and war had merely accentuated it?

She knew without any doubt that she wanted nothing—absolutely *nothing*—to do with this man. She had to make an effort not to take a step back from him. And yet . . .

And yet she had told him she was going outside for some air, and there had been an implied invitation in her words. After failing to attract her father's attention though she had called his name twice, she left the church, and he followed her.

Devlin Ware, Earl of Stratton. Not the boy and very young man with whom she had fancied herself in love. A stranger.

Perhaps this was a fortuitous meeting, she thought. It would get the first dreaded encounter behind her, and she would not have to hate quite as much the thought of tomorrow with the necessity of coming face-to-face with him before the interested gaze of a number of her neighbors. Tomorrow she would be able to concentrate upon introducing Aled to them all and basking in the pleasure of being in company with a distinguished man who was obviously courting her. He had talked of *escorting* her rather than just going along with her and her family.

She hesitated for a moment outside the church, but she did not want to stand here with him, eye to eye, visible to anyone who passed by—or peeped from windows. She set out along one side of the green.

"It is a lovely day," she said. "Sunny. Warm. No real wind."

"A quite perfect autumn day," he said, and his voice was surely deeper than it had used to be. A bit gravelly.

"I trust Lady Rhys is well?" he asked after a few moments, when her frantic mental search for something else to say about the weather had yielded nothing.

"Oh yes," she said. "She is perfectly well. Thank you."

"And how—"

"Idris—"

They spoke simultaneously, and stopped talking simultaneously.

"After you," he said.

"Idris came from Wales yesterday," she said. "He stayed two weeks longer than we did. He brought home news of his betrothal to Eluned Howell. She is the daughter of one of my father's close friends."

"You must all be happy about that," he said.

"Yes indeed," she assured him.

"And when is the wedding to be?" he asked.

"The date and the place have not been decided upon," she said. "But I expect it will be in Wales."

"Ah," he said.

He had not offered his arm when they left the church, for which fact she was very thankful. She would have had a hard time taking it. She felt an inward shiver at the mere thought of touching him, this man who was Devlin and yet somehow was not. This man with whom she was conducting a ridiculously stilted conversation.

She was half aware as they strolled along a second side of the green that they were attracting some attention. Or rather that *he* was. For everyone, of course, was avid for their first glimpse of him, the man who, rightly or wrongly, had wreaked such havoc with all their lives six years ago, when Ravenswood had abruptly stopped being the center of the universe to those who lived near it. When all the bright entertainments that had been the center of their social lives had ceased and the Countess of Stratton in particular had become a near recluse, all the sparkling warmth of her charm gone. When the three adult Ware brothers had left home, not to return. When the earl, it was rumored, had taken to drink and became a somewhat pathetic figure as he continued to behave in the village as though nothing had happened.

The conversation had lapsed, and Gwyneth wished with all her heart that she had remained in her pew at the church and pretended she had not known Devlin was sitting behind her. She could not remember feeling as uncomfortable—or as miserable—as she was feeling now.

They did not turn onto the third side of the green and so back in the direction of the church. Rather, he veered off, and Gwyneth followed him onto the bridge over the river. He stopped halfway across, and they stood side by side looking along the water. There was a hint of yellow in the trees. Soon the leaves would be multi-colored and there would be that desperate feeling of beauty that must be enjoyed to the full *now* before winter descended and stripped it all away.

"But spring always comes," she thought, and then felt very foolish because she had actually spoken the words aloud.

"Does it?" he said, and it seemed to her that there was a bitter sort of cynicism in the brief question.

He folded his arms along the top of the stone balustrade and leaned against them. "I thought you would be married by now, Gwyneth," he said.

"No," she said. "Not yet." Had he hoped she was married and gone from here? Did it matter to him either way? Did *she* matter? But how could she? There had been that one day. Sometimes she chastised herself for having made so much of it. *One day* out of all the days of her life.

He nodded.

"What happened?" she asked, desperate to change the subject, though then she wished she had not asked something so personal.

He turned his head her way, and she looked into the rough hardness of his scarred face. She tried not to remember what he had looked like on that one day when they had been in love with each other.

"Here?" he asked, indicating his scar by moving one finger diagonally in front of his face. "I did not step back from an enemy saber quite soon enough for it to miss me altogether. I do not look nearly as pretty as I did as a young man, do I?" His tone was mocking. His eyes searched her face. "You, on the other hand, are prettier than you were. Did you dance about the maypole at the fete this year?"

He did not know? "There was no fete," she said.

He raised his eyebrows. "Bad weather?" he asked.

"There has been no Ravenswood fete for six years," she told him.

He gazed at her, his look inscrutable. "And the Valentine's treasure hunt?" he asked. "The Christmas ball?"

She shook her head. "Only the children's party on Christmas Eve," she told him.

"And the village assemblies and the children's drama nights?" he asked, frowning.

"There have been dances in the assembly rooms above the inn," she said. "There will be one next week, in fact, to celebrate the harvest. The church has proved big enough for special school events."

He continued to gaze at her, nodding slowly. If it was possible, he looked harder than before, his eyes colder. He really had not known, she realized. The past six years were a blank to him as far as this part of the world was concerned. *Oh, Devlin. Why did you do that to yourself?*

"I do not suppose I have been very popular in these parts if I am blamed for all these changes," he said, a curious twist to his lips that was not quite a smile. "Or was it my father who was blamed?"

She stared at him mutely, but he held up a staying hand before she could frame an answer. "That was altogether an unfair question," he said. "I beg your pardon. Why are you not married, Gwyneth? I cannot believe no one has ever asked you."

She could feel her cheeks grow warm. For he ought to remember that one man at least had asked her. Six years ago, not even a mile from here. And she had said yes. But really, how dared he ask such a question? It was none of his business. She answered anyway.

"I have had a number of eligible offers," she told him. "None of them suited me."

"Waiting for love, are you?" he asked.

Oh, his eyes! And his lips, with that curious twist to them that was not a smile. Could this possibly be Devlin? This man with his ill-mannered, intrusive questions? Was he *trying* to hurt her? Or annoy her? Or . . . or *what*? But she was not going to quarrel with him. Or simply walk away back to the church.

"I am waiting for someone with whom I can be comfortable," she told him.

"It sounds dull," he said.

He was definitely trying to provoke her. But why? Because he now disliked her? But surely dislike would merely breed indifference. Because somewhere deep inside this strange, stony exterior, then, there was pain of some sort? It was impossible to know, and she did not *want* to know. Oh, she *wished* she had stayed in her pew.

"Comfort is never dull," she said. "It is—" But there was nowhere to go with that sentence.

"Comfortable?" he suggested.

"Yes," she said, and then she was horrified and definitely *not* comfortable when they both smiled at the same moment. A real smile on his part. Not just that twist of his lips.

Her stomach felt as though it had turned over. For during that moment he had looked just like . . . Devlin. Though Devlin had not often smiled—except on that last day, which she would really rather not remember.

"Are there any comfortable men on the horizon?" he asked her.

The mockery with which he had asked the last few questions had gone. "Yes," she said, though she was not sure that it was a comfortable life she could expect with Aled. Interesting, perhaps. Stimulating, almost surely. Anyway, he had not asked yet.

"He is a fortunate man," Devlin said, straightening up. "I had better walk you back to the church before Sir Ifor misses you and organizes a search party. Is that likely to happen? Or should we walk up to the hall so I can drive you home in the gig? I can stop in at the church on my way back to let him know where you are."

It was tempting. To go home, that was, to seek out solitude until she had found some composure. But she would have to walk all the way up to the hall with him and then ride beside him in a gig. And the chances were that her mother and Idris would see him and come out to speak to him and invite him inside. She was not prepared for any of that. This had been quite enough for one day.

"I will go back to the church," she said. "You do not need to escort me."

"But I will," he said. "It is what gentlemen do, I believe." They walked in silence for a short while before he spoke again. "The man in the church with your father is a fellow musician?"

"Aled Morgan," she said. "A Welshman, as his name would suggest. Yes, he is a musician of some renown. He sings and plays a number of instruments, but he is best known, even outside Wales, as a conductor. I believe he will soon be conducting orchestras in places like Vienna and Paris and Rome now that the wars are over."

He had his head turned toward her. "Ah," he said softly.

She thought of how a brief, chance moment could change the whole course of life for many people. If Devlin had suggested returning to the ballroom a minute sooner than he had that night, or if his father had brought Mrs. Shaw—if that had been her real name—up to the pavilion a minute later, would they be married now, she and Devlin? Perhaps with little ones? Would his father still be alive? Would all of life in this place have proceeded as it always had? Would there have been fetes and Christmas balls and . . . happiness?

But who could know? One could never predict the future, and the past could never be changed. The only influence one could ever have upon one's own life or the lives of other people was in the present, yet the present was such a fleeting thing, gone even as one thought of it. Then one was confronted with yet another present moment, and so on throughout a lifetime. Each moment unveiling choices and decisions, any of which might have long-lasting consequences. It was a dizzying, even frightening thought, for any hope one might have of permanence or stability was just an illusion.

The organ was still playing inside the church.

"I am going to stay out here for a few minutes longer," she said, turning to him. "I am going to wander about the churchyard. I always enjoy reading the gravestones and contemplating the long history of this place where I live and the ongoing connection of families through the generations. I find it soothing rather than morbid. Thank you for walking with me."

But something had happened to his eyes. They had turned opaque—if that was the right word—as though he had shut himself up inside himself so that the world would not see in. And she remembered with a great sinking feeling that his father was buried in the churchyard and in all probability Devlin had not seen his grave.

"It was my pleasure." He inclined his head to her and turned to stride away diagonally across the green, skirting the duck pond as he went. Striding, like a military man.

Gwyneth felt the soreness of tears prick the back of her throat.

Oh, she did not *want* this.

Whatever *this* might be.

H e ought not to have told Gwyneth she was prettier now than she had been, Devlin thought as he strode homeward up the drive. For one thing, it had sounded condescending. For another, it was not really true. She had been a pretty, vibrant girl. Now she was a woman, and some of the vibrancy had gone. Or perhaps it was just being with him that had dampened it temporarily. *Pretty* was not the best word to use of her now anyway. She was beautiful.

And presumably she was in some sort of a courtship with that musician with a Welsh name. Somebody Morgan. They almost certainly had a great deal in common and were therefore well suited. Did she still play her harp? Did she still sing?

His mind was abuzz with her, and he did not like it. He had liked being a military officer. It had enabled him to focus his mind entirely upon his duty and the task at hand. He would not say he had not thought at all during his years on the Peninsula. It was, after all, impossible *not* to think. But there had been enough to occupy his mind every day, so that his thoughts had rarely strayed. When they had, he had brought them firmly back to the present before they could take root in the past.

Now his thoughts were straying all over the place, and he did not know what to do to control them. For he must live here. It was his duty to do so, and ultimately duty had always been the guiding principle of his life. In being here and doing his duty as Earl of Stratton, however, he must also relate to his family and, to a lesser degree, to his neighbors. He had known that. He had even spoken about it on his first evening at home. The Rhyses were his neighbors. And so, God help him, was Gwyneth, for she was not yet married or even betrothed. She would surely have said if she had been. She had told him that Idris was engaged, after all.

Memories were asserting themselves after years of being suppressed. He was remembering things she had said to him the last time he had spoken with her—at Cartref the morning he left, when he had gone to say goodbye. And suddenly it was all as though it had happened yesterday.

He stopped to watch the sheep amble about the meadow below the ha-ha. One of them looked up and greeted him with a baa. Sheep always sounded comically human, he thought.

"And good day to you too," he said—and felt a sudden, unexpected gladness that he was in England, that he was home, that this land was his. His in trust, to nurture while he lived and to hand on to his children and his children's children, as it had been passed on to him.

His father's mortal remains were in that churchyard.

He walked on, thinking desperately about sheep. He had missed the shearing this year—and for the past six. He had always enjoyed the shearing.

If he loved her, Gwyneth had told him on that long-ago morning, he would not have made that public scene the night before. She had begged him not to, but he had done it anyway. Had she been right? If he had loved at all—his mother, his brothers and sisters, his friends and neighbors, *Gwyneth*—would he have kept quiet and confronted his father privately the next day? Had the choice been between love and truth? But were they not the same thing? Or, when he thought he had acted out of an adherence to the truth, did he really mean *righteousness*? *Righteousness*—the need to judge and condemn in the name of a perceived truth. He had chosen righteousness. But also truth. And surely love too. It was his fierce love for his mother and his sisters that had so incensed him and convinced him that he could not allow the terrible indiscretion to continue one moment longer.

He hated questions that had no clear answers. Had he done the right thing? The wrong thing? Did it really matter? He had done what he had done.

He could hear more of her words suddenly, just as if he were back in the dining room at Cartref that morning:

And if you loved me you would not be leaving me in this cowardly manner. You would be staying here and fighting for me. You would be persuading Dad to let you marry me, and you would be taking me off to Wales or somewhere to set up a new life with me instead of with your stupid foot regiment. You know nothing about love . . . A man does not leave the woman he loves . . . There is no warmth in you, Devlin. No give. You are all inflexible righteousness . . . I do not even like the real Devlin Ware. I am glad you are going away and never coming back.

Ah yes. She had used that ugly word—*righteousness*.

He had left her. He had not stayed and fought for her or for his ability to love at all, which had been slipping fast from his heart and was soon to be gone altogether. He thought of Ben and his Marjorie, such an unlikely couple but bound by a fidelity that was never demonstrative but was as steadfast as a rock. It would have lasted for a lifetime, Devlin was sure. It *had* lasted for Marjorie's. And now Ben had Joy. Devlin thought of the women with whom he had lain, of the enjoyment he had had with them, of the liking and respect he had felt for every one of them.

But never a spark of love.

Had he been punishing himself when he left Gwyneth behind? For the fact that he had hurt his family? For perhaps destroying it? All for the sake of a truth that the adults among them, *even his mother*, had already seemed to know?

Yet he still felt sick to his stomach at the thought that his father had brought his mistress right into the home of his wife and children. Had the terrible indiscretion of it, the *danger* of it, somehow titillated him? He had been going to fornicate with her in the pavilion, only a stone's throw from the ballroom, where his wife and his children were dancing. It was too bad that unbeknown to him *one* of his children had been closer than that, kissing his love down among the trees.

When he reached the house, Devlin was reluctant to go inside, where he might encounter his mother. He had still not been alone with her and did not want to be. They might find that they had to talk about more than just the weather and the health of every family member and acquaintance they could think of. Instead of proceeding up the steps, he went beneath one of the arches and through the tunnel to the courtyard and the rose arbor, though he realized the roses would no longer be blooming and that the fountain might have been turned off in preparation for the winter. The courtyard nevertheless would provide a quiet sanctuary for a while.

Too late he saw that there was already someone there—Philippa. She was alone and had nothing in her hands with which to occupy herself. They were holding the edges of her wool shawl. It was a lovely autumn day, but she should probably be wearing something warmer than that. The fountain was still turned on. She was gazing at it, but she turned her head to watch him coming. He could see that she was as sorry to see him as he was to see her. He could have turned and walked away. Perhaps he ought to have done so since it appeared she had come here for some solitude, just as he had. Instead he sat down on the love seat adjacent to hers.

He was home and he was master here and head of the family. This was not a fleeting visit. He was here to stay because it was his duty to do so. He could not avoid close encounters with his family forever. And did he really *want* to? He had given up everything six years ago for the sake of truth. He still believed in it as a fundamental value of life. Yet the opposite of truth was not *just* lies. It was also avoidance, the ignoring of what was uncomfortable. It was what he had done for his last year at home. It was what the adults of his family had done for years and years. Was he going to be content to perpetuate that? By simply saying nothing? By letting life just drift on, meandering about the silences?

Damn it all, why had he come back?

For a few moments he watched and listened to the fountain.

"I have been told," he said then, "that there has been no summer fete here for the last few years."

Pippa was looking at him, as she had done since his return, with an expression that was not openly hostile but was actually a bit worse. It was blank, lifeless. Or, if not quite that, then spiritless. "Not since I was fifteen," she said.

"Why is that?" he asked.

She shrugged. "It was a lot of work. Mama did not want to do it any longer."

With him and Ben and Nicholas all gone, that made sense. Organizing the fetes had involved an enormous amount of work for the whole family, not just their mother. The whole family except their father, who had always been useless. It was strange how the rest of them had skirted about that fact, perhaps convincing them-selves that his great geniality to all was his contribution to prepar-ing for the various social events at the hall. And perhaps it really had been a contribution of some value. There had always been an atmosphere of happy anticipation surrounding upcoming events at Ravenswood.

"What was the *real* reason?" he asked.

She looked away from him.

"I am sorry," he said. "That was probably an unfair question. Was it terrible, Pippa? After I left?"

She shrugged. "What do *you* think?"

"Was it my fault?" he asked. Another unfair question. And even he was unable to answer it.

She pondered how to answer before replying. "We danced about the maypole with that woman," she said. "Stephanie and I. Gwyn-eth Rhys too. Even you. I do not suppose she even was a widow. Or married. There was no husband who died tragically in the Indian wars. *Shaw* was probably not even her name. It would be too easy to put all the blame on her, though, as many people do. I suppose women like her are always seen as most to blame. But sometimes I think they do what they do because they have no choice. Because they do not wish to starve. How provoking of them!" She gave a hollow little laugh.

She had not answered his question, he noticed.

"Do you have any beaux?" he asked her. "I more than half ex-pected that you would be married by now."

She shrugged again, so unlike the old Pippa, who had glowed with youth and the eager expectation of courtship and a brilliant love match and a life vibrant with happiness as soon as she turned eighteen. "I am not interested," she said.

Chilling words. She was *twenty-one* years old.

"You are *Lady* Philippa Ware," he said, "daughter and sister of an earl. Have you never gone to London for a Season? You looked forward so much to doing that, I remember."

"I would not go when I was eighteen," she said. "I did not want to. Then, when I was nineteen, Papa died. We were not quite out of mourning for him last year until well after Easter. By then Grandmama Ware was very sick, and then she died. We were still in mourning for her in the spring this year." She told her story of crushed dreams and dashed hopes in a flat voice, as though really they were nothing at all. Her following words confirmed that impression. "It did not matter anyway. I did not want to go. No one teaches you that the future is not assured, do they? They teach you useless things like the plays of Shakespeare and the difference between *who* and *whom*. They teach you to add and multiply and divide. They teach you to find Italy and India and China on a map, and how to paint in watercolors and embroider your initials across the corner of a handkerchief without pulling the linen out of shape. You have to learn all the important things from life itself."

"You will go to London next year," he said. "I will take you myself." He was going to have to take his place in the House of Lords anyway.

She looked at him with weary scorn. "You cannot promise any such thing," she said. "You may be dead by then. I may be. Besides, I will be twenty-two next year. I will be *old*."

"You will be greatly sought after," he said. "There *is* happiness awaiting you, Pippa."

A fine one he was to promise her that. What the devil did he know about happiness or courtship or love? Only that all three could be crushed in a moment and ought never to be risked.

She was looking steadily at him, apparently unconvinced. Or—worse—uninterested.

"Devlin," she said, "are you really going to stay?"

"I am," he said. "It is my duty to take on the role of Stratton and see to it that Ravenswood thrives at least in material ways. I am not like our father and never can be. I cannot light up a room or a village street with my mere presence. But I will always do what I can see needs doing. Like seeing to it that you have your Season in London next year and your chance for happily ever after."

She was still gazing at him. "No one can ever be someone else," she said. "But even if you *could*, Devlin, or if you could at least be *like* Papa, I would not want you to do it. I loved him with all my heart, but he did not love us."

Her words chilled him again.

"He loved us in his own way, Pippa," he said, and thought with some surprise that it was probably true.

"It was not good enough for me," she said. "I think the only person he really loved was himself."

Strangely, Devlin was not sure about that either. He had determinedly not thought of his father all these years. But the man had beamed love to all around him. Maybe it was not a pure love, since he undoubtedly took a great deal of pleasure for himself at the expense of those nearest and dearest to him. But it was love he had given them nevertheless. They could not possibly have been so deceived by him if it had not been. Could they?

His father had been a . . . *complex* being, Devlin thought, and was contented to leave it at that. He did not want to analyze him. He did not want to think about him at all.

He did not ever want to step into the village churchyard.

"Pippa," he said. "I ought to *ask* you rather than *tell* you, ought I not? You are an adult. What have the past six years been like for you? What may I do for you? How can we mend what is broken? Is it even possible?"

She looked at him for a long moment. "You were not to blame," she told him. "Even though the consequences were terrible, I was never really sorry that you did what you did. I was actually proud of you. For if you had waited and talked privately with Papa and even perhaps with Mama and the grandparents, everything would have been hushed up when it needed to be shouted from the rooftops." She paused then. "There is one thing I *do* blame you for, though. Papa died more than two years ago. We waited and waited for you to come home, but you did not come. Steph worshipped you, Dev. She took to hanging about down by the river, and though she said nothing, I know she was watching for you. For *two years.* And Owen has needed you terribly. He had three older brothers and then none. And not even letters from you. Nothing. Just silence. Because you could not bear to think of us, I suppose. And now you have come back all turned to stone. Or so it seems. And talking about how you are going to take charge."

He gazed mutely at her. What the devil was there to say? He closed his eyes and hung his head.

"You are not the only one who has suffered," she said, getting to her feet. "It is chilly out here. I am going inside."

He let her go and stayed where he was. And realized something with a sinking heart. For six years he had shut himself up inside himself in an act of self-defense that was incredibly selfish. And now he had come home to do his duty. But cold duty was definitely not going to be enough. He was indeed going to have to mend what was broken in this family. Yet he was surely the least suitably equipped man on earth to do so.

Then he frowned as he heard the echo of something Pippa had said when she was talking about going—or rather about *not* going— to London for a come-out Season. *I would not go when I was eighteen,* she had said. *I did not want to.*

Why?

Their father had still been alive. Things had changed here at Ravenswood for the worse, but would not that very fact have made her all the more eager to escape to the pleasures awaiting her in London? Would she not have dreamed all the more of meeting someone and falling in love and marrying and all the rest of it? She had been *eighteen*, for the love of God.

What the devil had happened?

CHAPTER FIFTEEN

Those days when there had been frequent social gatherings of any considerable size at Ravenswood Hall were long in the past and almost forgotten about by some. They were sadly missed by others. Now, however, all the families with some claim to gentility in the village and beyond had been invited to a formal tea, and their numbers were expected to be so large that it was to take place not in the more intimate setting of the family drawing room or dining room, but in the largest of the reception rooms in the west wing, a room exceeded in size only by the ballroom and the gallery.

The occasion had been billed as a welcome-home reception for the Earl of Stratton. And everyone, it seemed, wanted to attend, whether they felt kindly toward the earl or not. They wanted to see what changes a six-year absence had wrought in his appearance and to hear him speak if he should deign to do more than bow politely to them. They wanted to be able to discuss him afterward with one another and pass on their observations to anyone who had had the misfortune to miss the occasion. That number was not likely to be large, however. It was being said that not a single invitation had been rejected.

Gwyneth's feeling of relief over having already seen Devlin and spoken with him had dissipated overnight. For it was not enough to have come face-to-face with him when they were virtually alone together. Now she was going to have to do it again while dozens of pairs of curious eyes looked on. It was too much to hope no one would remember that on that most ghastly of horrid nights Devlin had been clinging to her hand, making it obvious to anyone with an ounce of sense that she had been with him on the pavilion hill when he encountered his father.

It *did* help that she was going to have Aled with her, however. He had been very attentive last evening and had made her forget her annoyance over being ignored for hours on end at the church. He had taken her for a stroll outside after dinner, before darkness descended completely. He had leaned an elbow on the top of the wooden stile while she sat on it and had gazed across the meadow and told her he must have a talk with her father one day soon and then with her. That was all. He had not added any explanation or poured out his undying love for her. He had not kissed her, though she had hoped he would. It was ridiculous at her age to have been kissed only once in her life. But he had looked at her and smiled, and his smile had promised much and warmed her to her toes. Afterward, he had asked her to play her harp and had praised her and offered suggestions and had her play one section of one piece over and over until he had nodded and smiled warmly at her and declared that before it had been only very, very good, but now it was perfection.

Gwyneth felt distinctly queasy when she saw the crowd in the reception room at Ravenswood. Her eyes took in a head table at one end of the room and a number of round tables set out in the rest of it. All were covered with starched white cloths and set with matching china and crystal and silver with a vase of flowers—presumably from the greenhouses—at the center. Very few people were seated yet, however. Everyone was moving about, greeting friends and neighbors, talking in hearty tones, laughing a great deal. There was no receiving line inside the doors. It would have been a bit absurd when everyone knew almost everyone else—except Aled, of course. But the countess was close to the doors, her eldest son beside her, welcoming the guests as they arrived.

Gwyneth and Aled had become separated from the rest of her family while he had dawdled along the corridor outside, gazing upward to admire the fretwork up close to the ceiling.

"It is always a privilege to be invited inside one of England's stately houses," he had told her. "It seems that Idris came home at just the right time, bringing me with him."

After stepping into the reception room they paused to greet the countess and thank her for inviting them. Gwyneth introduced Aled. The Countess of Stratton was still beautiful, though she must be nearer fifty than forty by now. She was still elegant and gracious. But Gwyneth remembered the warmth and charm that had once clung about her like an aura. They had vanished even before she was widowed. She offered Aled her hand as he inclined his head to her.

"You are the Welsh musician who is staying with the Rhyses at Cartref," she said. "I am pleased to make your acquaintance, Mr. Morgan. But are not all Welsh people musicians?"

Aled laughed as he shook her hand. "Indeed we are, ma'am," he said. "I believe there is even a law. I am not quite sure about that, but if there is not, then there ought to be."

"Except that we do not need a law to persuade us to make music," Gwyneth said.

"True enough," Aled agreed, and the countess smiled at him.

Devlin shook his hand too and Gwyneth looked directly at him for the first time today. Inevitably she made comparisons between the two men. Aled was taller and more slender. His light brown hair was wavy and a bit unruly. He had a long, good-humored, expressive face. He was smiling now. Devlin was half a head shorter and of a more solid build, unlike his slenderness six years ago. He looked rugged, like a man who spent a great deal of his time outdoors. His dark hair was neatly combed. His face, as she had noticed yesterday, was bronzed and hard and scarred. He was not smiling, though he was behaving with perfect good breeding. But he was looking as though he would rather be anywhere else on earth than where he was.

"Stratton," Aled said. "You must be very happy to be back safe and sound in England, though you do have a bit of a scar to remember the wars by, I see."

More than a bit, Gwyneth thought. And her knees turned weak as she wondered how that slice of a saber blade could possibly have missed his eye. Or could possibly not have killed him.

"I would be a great deal happier," Devlin said, "if a few thousand other men had been able to come back too. But such is war. Your love of music is beyond question. I observed it yesterday. You were absorbed in it at the church when Gwyneth left to stroll about the green with me."

"Really?" Aled said. "Did she? I did not notice she was gone. But I am glad she *did* take the air and had some company. I do tend to lose myself in music sometimes, and that organ is as magnificent an instrument as any I have seen or heard anywhere."

Devlin transferred his gaze to Gwyneth. Perhaps she only imagined that he slightly raised his eyebrows as though he were saying to her, *He did not even notice you were gone?* "Gwyneth," he said politely. "Thank you for coming."

She smiled though her lips felt tight. And if a large number of people were looking their way, she told herself, then it was surely at Aled they were gazing. Strangers invariably attracted notice in the country, where the monotony of the prevailing sameness always threatened. She held her smile as she looked about the room, and Devlin turned away to greet someone else.

"A morose man," Aled murmured as they moved away. "It seems strange that he fought in the wars when he was heir to an earldom. And, stranger yet, he was in a *foot* regiment, Idris told me. Perhaps the joy of violence and killing meant more to him than duty to his position. But he did have younger brothers to inherit if he could not, I believe?"

"Nicholas is also a military man," she told him, quelling the urge to jump to Devlin's defense. "He is in a Guards regiment. Cavalry. And there is Owen, the youngest son. He is over there. Come. I will introduce you."

She proceeded to present him to a number of people and was more than ever thankful to have him at her side. He was a sociable man—when there was no music to distract him—and conversed easily with people who were strangers to him. Gwyneth felt speculative eyes upon her and kept smiling.

A morose man. He had not used to be. Quiet, reserved, somewhat on the serious side, yes. And lacking in the open charm and allure that his father and Nicholas had both possessed in abundance. But not *morose*. And not without a certain charm of his own.

People were taking their places at the tables. There were no name cards. Everyone could sit where they wished, except those at the head table, of course. The countess sat in the central position there, Devlin on her right, Philippa on her left. Mr. and Mrs. Edward Ware, the late earl's uncle and aunt, sat on the far side of Devlin, and Mr. and Mrs. Greenfield, the countess's parents, on Philippa's far side.

Gwyneth drew Aled to one of the tables that still had empty places and sat beside Ben Ellis after introducing the two men. She introduced him also to the other occupants of the table, Mr. George Greenfield, Miss Wexford, and Mrs. Lamb, Devlin's great-aunt.

"I am so pleased to see you back home, Ben," Gwyneth said, turning to him. "Though I was very sorry to hear about your wife."

"Thank you, Gwyneth." He smiled at her. His eyes had grown kinder, she thought, which was a strange thing to have happened after six years of warfare and a widowhood.

"You have a child," she said. "Where is she?"

"Stephanie insisted upon missing the tea in order to play with her in the nursery," he said. "She has a remarkable gift with children. Joy has been unwilling to let me out of her sight for a long time. Since my wife died, in fact. But she has taken to her new aunt. They are dancing to Steph's singing. Dancing for my daughter, I should explain, means planting her feet firmly on the floor, holding someone's hands for balance, and bouncing from the knees. And laughing gleefully."

"I look forward to seeing her," Gwyneth said. His daughter was obviously not an inconvenient piece of baggage he had been obliged to bring home with him from war. Aled was deep in conversation with Prudence Wexford, while Mr. Greenfield and Mrs. Lamb were chuckling over something with each other and footmen were bringing plates of sandwiches and dainties to the table and pouring the tea.

"Tell me about your wife," Gwyneth said to Ben.

He thought for a few moments. "How does one describe a person in just a few words?" he said. "She was a good woman, Gwyneth." He drew breath to say more but shrugged instead.

"And you loved her," she said. "I wish I could have met her."

"She spoke with a broad cockney accent," he said.

"Did she?" She smiled.

"She was a washerwoman," he told her. "Hardworking. Strong. I was her third husband. Husbands died in droves out there. And so did some wives, as it turned out. I beg your pardon. That is more than you wanted to know. She was a good woman. She was Marjorie."

"I think I would have liked her," she said. "Are you going to be Devlin's steward?"

"No," he said. "Fortunately the current steward seems to be a perfectly competent man, so I feel no obligation to stay. I am going to set up a home for my daughter and raise her there."

She had always liked Ben, Gwyneth realized. She had also unconsciously relegated him in her mind to a secondary place behind the rest of the family because he was not a Ware, though he was the son of the late earl. That had been very wrong of her. She could see and feel the kindness in him now. She could also feel the edge of defensiveness. He expected to be seen as somewhat inferior to his half brothers and sisters. He wanted her to know that he was not ashamed of who he was or of who his wife had been. And he was going to devote his life to seeing that his daughter never had to fight for respect.

"I am glad you went away with Devlin," she said. "I think he very desperately needed you at that time. Is that why you went?" She had always wondered. He had been the steward of his father's properties then, and an excellent one too, according to her father. He had not, apparently, become either an officer or an enlisted man himself.

"It was part of the reason," he said.

He did not volunteer the other part of it, and she did not ask. The conversation at the table became general at that point. But it was not hard to guess. His father had just been exposed as a philanderer. He had brought a mistress to Boscombe and Ravenswood, and everyone had guessed, if they had not already known, that she did not represent his one and only lapse into infidelity. Not when one remembered that throughout his married life he had spent a few months of the spring each year in London without the countess. And when one recalled that even before his marriage he had had at least one mistress—Ben's mother.

A while later, just when Gwyneth was beginning to feel almost relaxed, the countess got to her feet. Mr. Greenfield, her father, coughed loudly and tapped the side of his teacup with the spoon from his saucer, and everyone turned their attention toward the head table and stopped talking.

The countess thanked them all for coming to join her family in welcoming her son, the Earl of Stratton, home. She informed them that she looked forward to further such gatherings in the future. She did not add much more. And she did not mention her son by name, Gwyneth noticed, only by his title. There was polite applause.

Devlin rose to reply. He looked about at them all, his eyes pausing a moment upon her before they moved on.

"Thank you, Mother, for this lavish welcome," he said, and it was unclear whether he intended any irony. "And thank you all for coming and in such impressive numbers. I wish you to know that I am here to stay and intend to do my duty to the earldom, to Ravenswood, and to the neighborhood around it. I intend to see to it that everyone is always welcome here, during open days when the park is available to anyone who wishes to enjoy it, and during the various social events that will be arranged here. I intend to restore the annual Christmas ball and the summer fete, among other things."

There was a buzz of interest among his guests, and perhaps

some surprise too. For he certainly looked both morose—to use Aled's word—and uncomfortable, so unlike the late earl, his father, who had reveled in speech giving and in drawing smiles and laughter from his audience.

"I will *not*, however, expect my mother to do all the work of planning such events," he added. "She did it superlatively well for many years, but she has earned a rest. I will employ someone to do what she did so graciously and uncomplainingly for so long."

His words were greeted with applause.

"I am not much of a public speaker," he said. "I will end this one without further rambling. Thank you again for coming. I will do myself the honor of paying a return call upon each of you in the coming weeks."

This time the applause was a little more prolonged, and Gwyneth thought of how typical the speech was of Devlin, with its emphasis upon doing his duty—and not expecting others, most notably his mother, to do any of it for him. How very much against the grain it must be for him to promise social events at Ravenswood and visits to each of his neighbors when he probably did not even know which were friendly toward him and which might be hostile. She suspected, though, that it would not matter to him in which camp they lay. They had come here this afternoon, and therefore he would return the courtesy.

Ah, Devlin, she thought. *Perhaps you have not changed all that much after all. You are still a decent man.*

The guests began to leave, and Idris found his way to Gwyneth's side. He set an arm loosely about her shoulders and spoke in her ear.

"All right?" he asked her.

"Yes." She smiled at him. "Of course I am all right." She had not told any of them about her walk with Devlin yesterday.

His eyes searched hers before he moved away to take his leave of Devlin, who was standing near the door. She watched the two of them clasp hands and exchange a few words, and then she turned to leave the room with Aled and her parents.

Yes, of course she was all right. *Of course* she was.

D evlin went up to the nursery with Ben, a plate heaped with sandwiches, cakes, and pastries in his hand. He was so hugely relieved to have that ridiculous tea behind him and he would have been happier to retreat to his own rooms or go striding off to somewhere secluded outdoors. But he would not allow himself that luxury.

"Magnificent speech," Ben told him.

"I thought so too," Devlin said. "And who says a speech has to last longer than one minute?"

"It was its very brevity that made it so magnificent," his brother said. "It is a pity you were destined to be the earl, Dev. You would have been a very popular clergyman. No sermon longer than two minutes. You could have advertised that fact on the church board outside."

Stephanie was sitting on a large armchair over by the window in the nursery, reading a book to Joy, who was snuggled in beside her and on the brink of sleep. She brightened as soon as she saw Ben, however, and wriggled down to come toddling toward him, prattling something incomprehensible, her arms raised high. He swept her up above his head, and she pressed her palms to his cheeks, her fingers spread wide, puckered her lips, and kissed him on the lips. Then she nestled in under his chin, gathered a fistful of his neckcloth in one hand, and put her thumb into her mouth.

"It seems," Stephanie said mournfully, "that no one is interested in the ending of this very exciting story except me." She laughed and closed the book.

"Thank you for looking after her, Steph," Ben said. "You are a gem. I had better take this little girl and tuck her into her bed." Not anywhere on the nursery floor, though. He had had a child's cot set up for her in his own room, right beside his bed.

Devlin felt an unexpected twinge of envy and found himself wondering whether there would have been other children in the nursery here now if . . . But such thoughts were pointless. And then there would have been no Joy, would there?

"I brought you some food from the feast," he told his sister, striding across the room and setting the plate down on top of the book on the table beside her. He removed the linen napkin that covered it and went to perch on the window seat nearby.

"There was food left?" she said, looking at the food with a frown. "Thank you, Devlin. But you ought to know that there are more ways of showing kindness to other people than pushing food at them. Grandmama Greenfield does it all the time when we go to visit her. I believe she feels offended if I do not take the *biggest* macaroon or the *creamiest* puff pastry as she points them out to me when she offers the plate."

"You will not offend me if you do not eat," he told her. "I thought you might be hungry."

She was still sensitive about her weight, he thought. And about the possibility that other people thrust rich foods at her on the assumption that she was a glutton. Almost unwillingly he felt the old ache of love for her and the impotent longing to be able to release her from her insecurities. He had not expected this pull back to the family he had deliberately cut from his thoughts and emotions years ago. First Owen, then Pippa, now Steph.

"And I did not mean to bite your head off," she said with a sigh. "Thank you for thinking of me. How *was* the tea?"

"I think our mother had the right idea," he said. "Let them all come at once and gawk their fill. Let me face them all in one ghastly hour."

"Dev," she said. "Mama is very badly hurt."

Is, not *was.*

"By me?" He rested his forearms across his thighs and dangled his hands between his knees.

"I do not know exactly what happened," she said. "No one ever told us—Owen and me, that is. You did not when you said good-bye to us. Pippa would not after you left, though I cried and had tantrums and swore I would never speak to her again. No one else would even admit anything *was* wrong. We were told that you and Ben had left because you were young men and needed some time away on your own. *As if we were going to believe that of either one of you!* Of course it was not hard to guess what had happened, even though I was only *nine.* Papa fancied that woman, Mrs. Shaw, did he not? I saw it that day, and a few times I wanted to go and kick her in the shins and tell her to *leave my papa alone.* But I would have been banished to the nursery for a week on bread and water if I had done anything so rag-mannered. *You* presumably *did* kick her or do something just as outrageous and very public, and you got banished for years."

"Perhaps it would be best—" Devlin began.

"Though why *you* were the one who was sent away, I do not know," she said. "You were not the one misbehaving with Mrs. Shaw. Perhaps it was because Papa could not very well be banished. But oh, Dev. You took all the light with you—you and Ben both. *All* of it. Everything changed. No more balls or parties or . . . or *anything* at Ravenswood, and some people seemed to avoid us for a while. I can remember Pippa pretending not to be upset when soon after you left she learned of a birthday party for one of her so-called friends to which she had not been invited. It was downright cruel. I swore I would never, *ever* forgive you for not going to Mama when I begged you to and working something out with her and setting everything right again. Though I suppose it would have been too late for that anyway. But if only you had gone to talk it all out with her when I begged you to. I know you were hurting too, though, and we do not always think straight when we are in pain. Oh, Dev, Mama was *so* sad after you were gone. So very, very sad. I sometimes try to remember the way she used to be, but it is hard."

Devlin had been gazing at the floor between his feet, but he looked up at her now. Their mother was not the only one who had been badly hurt, he thought. "Steph," he said. "I *did* go to her room. She would not talk to me. Or see me. So I left." He paused. "But . . . the world kept turning, and here we are. Tell me about you. Tell me about the missing years. Tell me what I can do for you now."

She gazed at him for a long time before answering. Her eyes welled with tears, but she blinked them away. "I wanted you to come home," she said. "I wanted you to write. But you never came and you never wrote. I wanted to hate you. But I never could. I was lonely, Dev. I was lonely for you and for Ben and Nick. I was even lonely for Mama and Papa as they had always been, though they were here. But nothing ever stays the same, does it? I just wish I could have grown up before I had to learn that. Then Papa *died*. It was so, so horrible. And still you did not come."

"Steph," he said softly. He gripped his hands hard between his spread knees.

"And now you are back and I want you not to have changed," she said. "But you *have* changed. You do not *want* to be here. You see your life here as one of strict duty and service. I do not doubt you will perform both quite conscientiously. But I do not want you to *serve* me, Dev. I want you to *love* me as you always used to do. You more than anyone. You *look* a bit like my brother who went away. But you do not *feel* like him, and if my heart was not already broken, it would break now."

He stared at her, appalled. *What the devil had he done?*

"I never stopped loving you, Steph," he told her, "though during all those years I dared not think of you. I was all broken up. Into a million pieces. The only way I could survive was by cutting all ties, quelling all feeling, and doing my duty."

He got abruptly to his feet, drew her to hers, and wrapped his arms about her.

"I am here now," he murmured against the top of her head. "And you were always my favorite sister, Steph—coequal with Pippa."

"There *are* only the two of us, silly," she said into his shoulder. "Would you have survived, Dev, if Ben had not gone with you? Or did you quell all feeling for him too?"

They were perceptive questions. He considered them.

"Ben kept me alive," he said.

"And me too," she told him. "He *did* write in answer to my letters. And each time he told me you were alive and well. I kept all his letters."

"Forgive me?" he said. "Can you, Steph?"

"Yes," she said, drawing back her head to gaze up at him. "I can and I do. I keep seeing you now in a million pieces of pain but looking and behaving like a tough, ruthless military officer. That is what you *did*, I think, and what you *were*. It is what you still look like now."

"The scar does not help," he said.

"It actually makes you look rather dashing," she said. "Thank you for thinking about me this afternoon, Dev. For bringing me the food."

"Do you feel like getting some fresh air?" he asked her. "Down by the lake, maybe?"

"I do," she said. "May we take out a boat? Will you let me row?"

"In this chill weather?" he said. "But at least if you are at the oars I will be able to crouch down and take shelter from the wind."

"Poor Dev." She laughed with some of the glee from her childhood. "Let me go and put on something warm. Ten minutes?"

"Nine," he said. "I want to get this boat-and-rowing torture over with as soon as possible."

She laughed again.

CHAPTER SIXTEEN

L iving in the same house with the man one was expecting to marry was somewhat different from seeing him for a few hours every couple of days or so, Gwyneth was discovering.

She had seen Aled frequently during the weeks she spent in Wales in the summer, and during those times he had focused most if not all of his attention upon her. He had talked almost exclusively with her. He had taken her for walks along beaches and drives through the countryside. He had courted her, and she had felt very close to him. She had felt that she would gladly spend the rest of her life with him.

Now he spent very little time exclusively with her. It was understandable, of course. He was a guest at the home of her mother and father, and, as courtesy perhaps dictated, he spent most of his time with them and with Idris. And with her too, of course. But they were rarely alone together.

On the morning following the tea at Ravenswood, he strolled outside with Gwyneth for half an hour before suggesting that the blustery wind and autumn chill were rather unpleasant and perhaps it would be more comfortable for her if they went back inside and joined the others for coffee. After luncheon he was going into Boscombe with her father for the young people's choir practice. He was a little disappointed that Gwyneth would not be accompanying them on her harp—because it was too big and heavy to be carried back and forth to the church except for a very special occasion. But he brightened again when it occurred to him that her father would therefore be providing the accompaniment on the organ.

"I suppose you always manage perfectly well to play and conduct at the same time, Ifor," he said. "One does when there is no alternative. But maybe I can twist your arm and persuade you to let me do some of the conducting today. I particularly love working with young voices, and I know from having heard them at the eisteddfod that you have a very good choir."

They would be there for hours, Gwyneth thought. Perhaps until the children began to fidget and yawn and start pushing and shoving one another and tittering and giggling. And, she thought disloyally, she would surely feel as they did. She loved music, both as a performer and as a listener, but it did not consume her soul. It did not even consume her father's as it did Aled's. Her father knew that there needed to be a quite strict time limit upon choir practices. In the company of his guest, though, he was likely to forget that.

"But without your harp, Gwyneth," Aled said, smiling at her, "you will be able to relax and simply enjoy the singing."

"Oh, I am going to remain at home," she told him. "I have some correspondence to catch up on, and this afternoon will be a good time to do it. You and Dad will enjoy the practice better without having to worry about me." Not that they would worry. They would forget all about her, whether she was there or not.

"But your mother will not be here, Gwyn," her father reminded her. "This is her regular afternoon with her lace-making group."

"But Idris will be here in the event that fire-breathing dragons should decide to come calling," she said. "Besides, I never mind being here alone for a while, Dad. Alone with the servants, that is."

"Well, this *is* a disappointment," Aled said, sounding as though he meant it. And for a moment Gwyneth was tempted to change her mind. But he could just as easily change *his* mind, could he not, and spend the afternoon with her? It would be a good opportunity for some time alone together. The choir, after all, was her father's, not his, and this afternoon's practice was just a regular weekly event.

Those facts obviously did not occur to him.

She waved them all on their way after luncheon and turned to go back inside. *Should* she write those letters she had been meaning for a few days to get to? Or should she go for a walk or even a ride? The gift of an unexpectedly free afternoon was not to be wasted. Idris met her at the door.

"Did you know Devlin is coming this afternoon?" he asked.

Oh.

"No, I did not," she said.

"When I was leaving Ravenswood yesterday," he explained, "I reminded him of what he had just said about calling on everyone who had attended the tea within the next few weeks. Why not come to me first? I suggested, since we were once friends and I would be home alone this afternoon. He said he would."

"You were *once* friends," she said. "Was there a quarrel, then, Idris?"

"Not really," he said. "Just some sharp words when he was leaving and then a long silence. I wrote a couple of times, specifically to Dev, but it was Ben who answered both times. That is not the way you treat your friends, but why bear grudges? He is back home and seems like a different man from the one I used to know. I am curious to discover if we *are* still friends. But at the very least he is a neighbor and will be for the rest of both our lives, I daresay. We must be civil to each other."

"I will not get in your way," she told him. "I will go into the parlor and write my letters."

"I thought perhaps you had stayed home deliberately," he said. "I will not ask if you ever got over him, Gwyn. I am sure you did not. But it was a long time ago and I know you have been trying to fall for someone else. Is Aled the one?"

She shrugged. "I like him."

He shook his head. "If I thought Eluned had ever done that and said that when asked about me, I would probably go out and shoot myself," he said.

They both laughed. "Eluned has never hidden her feelings for you," she said, "nor you your feelings for her."

She decided to stay home and write her letters. *Not* because Devlin was coming—she was going to sequester herself in the parlor with the door shut—but because . . . Well, because the letters needed to be written and she had procrastinated long enough. And . . . because Devlin was coming. She hated admitting it, but not doing so would not make it any the less true, would it?

She sat at the escritoire in the parlor. There was a view through the window out over the terrace to the lawn and flower garden beyond, enclosed on three sides by bushes and a few taller trees. All of it attracted bees and butterflies. And birds, which came in large numbers to eat from the feeder and drink from the stone bowl beside it. Sometimes, indeed, it was difficult to concentrate upon one's writing, so much of nature was there to see. And hear, with bees buzzing and birds chirping and insects whirring. Perhaps in front of the window had not been the wisest place to put the desk. But today Gwyneth bent her head over her letter as soon as she had mended a pen and dipped it into the ink. Today she was going to concentrate and not look up, no matter what the distraction.

She was one paragraph into a letter to one of the friends she had made during her Season in London when she looked up. How could she not when she heard horses' hooves and then men's voices? Idris had stepped out of the house, and Devlin was telling him that he would take his horse to the stables and come right back. Gwyneth leaned sideways so she would not be seen. His arrival—*to call upon Idris*—should really be a matter of indifference to her, she told herself in some annoyance. It was just like old times, in fact. She had seen him twice—in the village, when she had strolled and talked with him for fifteen minutes or so, and yesterday at Ravenswood. They had shared a youthful flaring of romance and passion for one single day years ago—she had been *eighteen*, still little more than a child, for goodness' sake—and then it had ended. Abruptly and totally. As Idris himself had observed a short while ago, there had been a six-year silence. *Not* that she had tried writing to him herself, as her brother had apparently done.

She could not possibly still be pining for him. It would be too utterly pathetic.

She heard his boot heels on the gravel of the terrace a few minutes later and looked up again. He walked with firm, purposeful strides, very straight backed, his expression stern beneath the brim of his tall hat. Like a military officer. Or a man who was not really looking forward to the coming encounter with his former friend. What had it cost him to come home? Or was *home* quite the wrong word for what Ravenswood and his family now meant to him?

She shook her head and returned her attention to her letter.

She finished it, all three pages of it, in a heroic act of determined concentration. Perhaps she ought to have gone to the choir practice with Aled. Would he think she was not really interested in him? *Would he be right?* She let the ink dry naturally as she cleaned her pen and quelled the sudden panic she felt. Not again. Please, not again. She was *twenty-four*, perilously close to being left on the shelf. She knew a number of women who would be over the moon with happiness if they had won the notice of a man like Aled Morgan. And she *liked* him. She would even say she *loved* him if that were a word that did not frighten her to death.

There was a tap on the door and it opened. Idris stood there, Devlin behind him.

"Dev wants to pay his respects to you, Gwyn," Idris said. "He did not even realize you were here until I mentioned it just now."

She turned in her chair.

"How do you do, Gwyneth?" Devlin said, moving into the doorway while Idris stepped back. "I wanted to thank you again for coming to Ravenswood yesterday. It meant a great deal to my mother to put on a show like that. I wanted to congratulate you too. Idris has been telling me about the competitions you have won with your harp music at the . . . Well, that Welsh word I can never quite get my tongue around."

"Eisteddfod," she said. "Thank you."

"I can remember wondering the few times I heard you play when you were a girl," he said, glancing at her harp in the corner of the room, "how on earth you could know which strings to pluck and how you could possibly make music from them. But you did."

"After a lot of practice and grinding of teeth, it does become almost instinctive to pluck the right string," she said.

He hesitated. *She* hesitated.

And then she heard herself say something quite unplanned. "Would you like to hear it now?"

His eyes came to hers. "I would," he said. "If I am not interrupting something important, that is."

"I have finished my letter," she said, getting to her feet and crossing the room to her harp.

Devlin advanced farther into the room and stood watching. Idris propped a shoulder against the doorframe, folded his arms, and crossed his feet at the ankles.

She played a few simple folk melodies, first without any embellishment, then with. By the time she had finished, Devlin had taken a seat closer to her and Idris had disappeared, half closing the door behind him.

"I have always considered music undisciplined," Devlin said. "Or maybe that is the wrong word. It must be played correctly and with much concentration and practice, so it is *not* by any means undisciplined. But it is not played for the intellect and the understanding, is it?"

She did not know what reply to give him. She gave none. She stood the harp upright again but did not rise from her chair. He was frowning down at his hands—until he looked up and directly into her eyes. "It represents chaos. It bypasses thought and reason and . . . *discipline*. It speaks directly to the emotions."

"And emotions are by definition chaotic?" she asked him.

"Yes," he said without hesitation. "They are unstable. Hard to control. Impossible to master."

"Should not emotions sometimes be surrendered to?" she asked. "In a safe way? Through music and art and fine literature?" Why had she used the word *safe*?

"Is that not like a drunk thinking it safe to allow himself one drink?" he asked in return.

"No, I do not believe so," she said. "If one surrenders to the power and beauty of music and art, one is not therefore doomed to react to every experience of life with undisciplined emotion."

Are you afraid to love? She almost—ah, she *almost*—spoke the words aloud.

"Has Idris offered you tea? Or something stronger?" She got to her feet.

"Play again," he said—quite illogically in light of what he had just been saying. "You used to sing. Do you still?"

"Yes," she said.

"Can you play and sing?" he asked.

"Yes." She sat again and tilted the harp down to her shoulder. She rested her hands against the strings and thought of what she would choose. She sang the haunting lyrics of "Barbara Allen":

> 'Twas in the merry month of May
> When green buds all were swelling
> Sweet William on his death bed lay
> For love of Barbara Allen.

And so on to its sad conclusion, the rose growing from William's grave twining about the briar that grew from Barbara's. Gwyneth pressed her hands to the strings to still the vibrations.

"It does not really matter that the story is rather unbelievable, does it?" she said. "Or do you simply want to give William a swift kick for allowing himself to die of unrequited love?"

She smiled. He did not.

He sat gazing at her until his eyes narrowed slightly. "The song relies for its effect upon the raw emotions we all feel from time to time," he said. "Even the conviction that unfulfilled love might kill us. Or that it *ought* to kill us because there seems no further point in living."

"Yes," she said. And she sang a Welsh folk song—in Welsh:

Y deryn pur a'r adain las,
bydd i mi'n was dibryder.
O brysur brysia at y ferch
Lle rhois i'm serch a'm hyder

O gentle dove with wings so blue,
fly quickly to my lady.
And take to her a message true,
while in her garden shady.

Another rather sad song. Why were so many folk songs heart wrenching? But so beautiful? She did not sing the English words aloud.

She looked up just as he was swallowing. And something had happened to his eyes, though whatever it was disappeared almost immediately. Ah, she thought, he was so full of darkness. And pain? There must be pain. Why else the darkness? She had the sudden conviction that *feeling* had been suppressed in him for a long time. Perhaps since that harrowing visit he had paid here as he was leaving home more than six years ago. Now he could see emotion—*love*—only as chaos that threatened his control over his life. Ah, Devlin.

"Your competitors at the eisteddfods—*is* that the plural?" he asked.

"Eisteffodau," she said.

"Your competitors must resent you," he said. "They have no chance against you."

From almost any other man this statement would have made her suspect over-extravagant flattery. Not, somehow, from Devlin.

"I do not always win," she told him.

Idris pushed the door open again at that moment. "Our coachman has just come walking back from the village," he said. "There is some problem with one of the wheels on the carriage and Oscar Holland is mending it. Dad and Aled will wait for it, but Dad is afraid Mam might be embarrassed if she is stranded at Lady Hardington's long after all the other ladies in the lace group have left. I am going to drop the coachman back off in Boscombe and then go fetch Mam home. I daresay Lady Hardington will insist that I stop for tea before we come, though. You will be all right on your own, Gwyn?"

Now, this was strange. Why not ask her to go with him? Or Devlin? Why not send a groom to the village with the coachman and then on to bring their mother home? And why had he abandoned Devlin here fifteen minutes or so ago, when he was Idris's invited guest?

"Perfectly," she said.

"I shall do myself the honor of remaining here with Gwyneth until you return," Devlin said.

"It might be a while," Idris warned him.

"I have a while to spare," Devlin said.

Gwyneth remained mute. If she needed a chaperon in her own home to protect her from strangers and fierce-looking men, why would the Earl of Stratton be a good choice?

"Right, then. I'll dash off," Idris said, and did just that.

Leaving silence behind him.

I dris Rhys, Devlin decided, was that most ridiculous and despicable of male types, a man in love who thinks that every other man ought to be in love too. And conspires to make it happen. It was downright embarrassing, and that was an understatement.

They had talked, the two of them. More than Devlin had talked with anyone for longer than six years, in fact, including Ben. They had talked about Idris himself and his Eluned and his plans to renovate the large cottage close to the main house of Cartref, built a century or so ago as a dower house but used as a storehouse in Sir Ifor's time. After his marriage Idris would move his bride there and raise their family while he continued to manage his father's farm. It was what he loved doing, while Sir Ifor, though he was very attached to the land too, was more interested in bringing music to the church and community.

They had talked about the wars. Idris had wondered if war could sometimes be like an earthquake, with less powerful but still dangerous quakes following it just when one thought it was all over.

"Are the wars *really* at an end, Dev?" he had asked. "With Bonaparte still alive?"

"God, I hope so," Devlin had said.

"Even though you would not be involved in them any longer?" Idris had asked.

"*My brother* would be involved." Devlin had been surprised by the powerful surge of protective emotion he felt.

They had even talked about what happened six years ago, and Devlin had asked the inevitable question.

"Did I do the wrong thing, Idris?"

Idris had thought about it, heaved a great sigh, and gone to the sideboard to replenish their glasses. "Yes and no, though who am I to say, really?" he had said as he resumed his seat. "Yes, because what you did caused a great deal of trouble and suffering, Dev—for the innocent as well as the guilty. And for the truly innocent that was a great pity. I am thinking in particular of Stephanie and Owen. And Philippa too. She was . . . what? Fourteen, fifteen at the time? And she witnessed it all. All three of them might have been protected from the worst of the consequences if you had acted with a bit more tact. Not to mention Gwyn."

"And no, because . . . ?" Devlin had asked. His friend had said *yes and no* to his question.

"Sometimes people need to suffer," Idris had said. "They ought to be shaken from their complacency and out from under the house of cards they have erected over their heads with their endless lies, both those they tell and those they do not confront. They need to be shaken out of the comfort of their illusions. I did not know the truth, Dev, but an amazing number of people did. Your mother, for example, and *her* mother and father, and her brother. No one would say anything, though. No one would risk the trouble they might cause. A man must be allowed his little foibles. And why stir up trouble when life is so very pleasant as it is and everyone is so contented and the offender himself is an amiable fellow who arouses smiles and laughter and goodwill wherever he goes? I tell you, though, Dev, if I made that discovery about *my* father, I would ram his teeth down his throat even if the whole county was present to witness it."

They had sat in silence for a while.

"Dev," Idris had said then. "It was *your father* who did the wrong thing. It was on him. It was *all* on him. It is the epitome of unfairness that many people would choose the comfortable lie over the uncomfortable truth and, in this case, would brand *you* as the archvillain instead of him. We live in a topsy-turvy world. But we *are* talking about your father. Do you feel very wretched about him?"

"I do not feel anything. I do not think about him at all. Ever," Devlin said, and Idris, after staring at him for a few moments, left it at that.

They had talked a bit more about the past six years, though. About the way much had stayed the same in the neighborhood, though everything had been somehow different.

"For one thing, you and Ben were gone," Idris said. "And Nick too, of course, but that was expected and planned for, so was not in itself what upset the order of things. A bit like us all going off to school years ago and then to Oxford. This was different. All the usual big events at Ravenswood stopped, though the countess did continue entertaining on a smaller scale. The earl continued as before. He was as jovial as ever. No one turned on him or dropped his acquaintance. But . . ."

"But?" Devlin said.

"But there was a bit of a hollowness to it," Idris said. "Just because everyone *knew* while they looked at him and listened to him, I suppose. Or could no longer pretend that they did not know."

"He continued to spend the spring months in London?" Devlin asked unwillingly.

"Your mother went with him," Idris said.

That was something new. Devlin wondered why she had gone. Should she not have wanted more than ever to live apart from him? Had she gone just to keep a proprietary eye on him?

"I am sorry, Dev," Idris had said then. "It does not feel quite right telling you things like this about your own people. Even though we are friends."

"Are we?" Devlin asked. "Despite my long silence?"

"You never did write to tell me we were no longer friends," Idris told him. "Perhaps I am just slow about taking a hint. Did you know Gwyneth is here? She is writing letters in the parlor."

No. Devlin had not known that. He had assumed she was at the church with her father and Aled Morgan, listening to the choir practice. Stephanie had walked there for it, having declined Devlin's offer to take her.

Gwyneth was here? In this very house? Now?

"Come," Idris had said, setting his empty glass on the table beside him and getting to his feet. "You can pay your respects to her."

He ended up doing more than just that, of course.

CHAPTER SEVENTEEN

N one of this was good.

At least yesterday he had been prepared for her coming to that infernal tea. And somehow, seeing her there in company with Morgan, who was clearly dazzled by her, and seeing that they made a handsome couple and were glowing with an aura of what he could describe only as *romance*, had made it easier. It had enabled him to set things in perspective. *Six years had gone by.* She was just a beautiful woman he had once fancied.

Today, though, he had ended up not simply nodding politely from the parlor doorway and muttering some conventional greeting, but sitting right inside the room alone with her—*where the devil had Idris gone?*—listening to her play the harp and then singing to its accompaniment. And he had spoken the truth to her, dash it all—music was pure emotion. The sort of music she chose was emotion multiplied by ten.

He was defenseless against its onslaught. For he could not simply stand her to attention and bark out an order to her to cease and desist. He could not just ignore her music either. Or walk away without a word. He had actually asked her to sing. All he could do as the music—*and she*—attacked him from every conceivable direction was sit and suffer. He was not good at suffering. It was something he had stopped doing a long time ago—at least any suffering that was not purely physical.

And *now*. Damn and blast Idris. What the devil was he up to? That Welsh musician fellow was *courting his sister*. And she was happy about it. Morgan was, moreover, a guest in this house. Why, then, had Idris grasped the slimmest of excuses to flee the scene and leave them to their own devices, Gwyneth and him? He had done it quite deliberately too, like a damned matchmaker.

So here they were.

She got to her feet and moved out from behind the harp. "There really is no need for you to stay," she said. "The very idea that I must have a chaperon in my own home is absurd. I am twenty-four years old. And surrounded by servants both indoors and out."

"It looks as if the wind has died down out there," he said, glancing toward the window. "Would you like to go for a walk?"

She sighed. "I'll go and get ready," she said, and left him alone in the room. And it struck him that she had always been someone else's woman—or girl. For years it had been Nicholas. Now it was Morgan. For just that one day, that one glorious, disastrous day, she had been his. A long time ago. A lifetime ago. What business did he have now asking her to come walking with him? The best advice anyone could give her was to stay well away from him. He had nothing to offer except darkness.

He met her out in the hall. She was wearing what looked like a warm pelisse but no bonnet. He had donned his greatcoat and held his hat in his hand. He set it back on the hall table and opened the door for her.

Her favorite walk, he knew, was over to the east of the inner park, which was enclosed by trees and was intimate and lovely. Beyond, there was more the appearance of wildness, though the big meadow, in which the sheep were often turned loose, was carefully tended to look unspoiled but neither overgrown nor neglected. In the spring and summer it was colorful with wildflowers and waving grasses. Now the flowers were mostly gone and the grasses were beginning to take on an autumnal hue. She liked to sit on the stile, he knew. He had seen her there numerous times, either chatting and laughing with Nick or alone and reading a book. He had never been there with her himself.

She did not stop there this time. She climbed over the stile and jumped down without his assistance. He climbed over after her and they set out across the meadow, the grasses swishing against his boots. It would be misguided, he thought, to imagine that it was only warm, sunny, blue-skied days that had any real beauty. There was something appealing too about low clouds and autumn chill. Something attractive also about the short, crisp days of winter. And spring—how had she phrased it in the village a few days ago? *Spring always comes.* And it always had come. Even on the Peninsula.

They had not spoken a word since leaving the house.

They came to the five-barred gate at the far side of the meadow. Beyond were cultivated fields, already harvested for this year, and wooded hills with more farmland to the east and west of them. Cartref was more of a working farm, less of a showpiece than Ravenswood, though it was large and prosperous and the house was somewhere in size between a manor and a mansion.

Instead of standing aside for him to open the gate, she leaned her arms along the top of it and gazed off toward the hills. He stood several feet behind her, watching her, his hands clasped at his back.

This idea of a walk had probably been a colossal, uncomfortable mistake. Damn Idris! What would they do now? Turn and walk back to the house in silence?

"What happened?" she asked him. "Out there on the Peninsula. What did war do to you? What did the long silence and estrangement do to you?"

Good God. How did one answer such all-encompassing questions? Did one let the silence continue? Was there any other choice?

She turned after several moments and leaned back against the gate.

"You are filled to the brim with darkness, Devlin," she said, echoing the thought he had had earlier. "You are so terribly, terribly hurt. Was it dreadful out there?"

He licked his lips. "Violence and death are always dreadful," he said. "I am not going to talk about it, Gwyneth."

"Because it is not for the ears of a woman?" she said.

"Because it is not for *anyone's* ears," he said.

"But it is not that, is it, or not that alone, that caused the darkness?" she said. "It has not happened to Ben."

"Ben was not an officer," he said. "Or an enlisted man."

"Why did he go?" she asked.

"He had personal reasons for leaving here," he told her. "He came with me to keep me alive."

Her eyes searched his. "You do not mean just physically, do you?" she said.

"No," he said. He had not really thought about it until very recently, but he did not believe he would have lived if Ben had not been with him. Not that he would have been more reckless necessarily if he had been there alone. He would have died because he would have lacked the will to live. The presence of his brother, though there had never been anything demonstrative between them and they had rarely spoken at length on any topic of great

significance, had been the one thin thread of connection to . . . To
what? His humanness? Warmth? Family? Love?

"I cannot recall my exact words," she said after the silence had
stretched again. "I was hurting and I lashed out. But I believe I accused you of being incapable of love. Of substituting righteousness
for it. I beg your forgiveness for that. It was untrue, and I ought not
to have said it even in anger."

"We all say things in anger that we regret," he said. "We can
only move on. Put it behind us and continue with our lives."

"I know that is the accepted wisdom," she said. "We can never
go back and change the past. Therefore we must forget it and move
forward. I do not believe it. Or, rather, I believe it misses a crucial
step. Or series of steps. There can be a gap between past and present
that grows denser with darkness as time goes on. We deceive ourselves when we believe that as we move on we will forget and put
behind us what can never be forgotten or changed. Devlin, the six
years of your darkness and silence need to be brought into the light.
So that you can heal."

"What sort of nonsense is that?" he asked her, hearing the harsh-
ness in his voice. "I must admit publicly that I was wrong? I admit
no such thing. I must beg everyone's forgiveness, cry a few tears, hug
and kiss? And then light will flood in, there will be eternal sunshine,
and all will be well with the world?" He frowned at her, knew he
ought to stop there but did not. "Do you wish me to start with you?
I dragged you into that mess with me after asking you to marry me,
embarrassed you horribly, and then abandoned you. I fled and did
not return until a few days ago. I am dreadfully, abjectly sorry,
Gwyneth. I behaved like a monster. Do please forgive me. Come
and give me a hug and a kiss, and we will plan a wedding before
Christmas. And happiness for as long as we both shall live." He
spread his arms wide and gazed at her with hard mockery.

"Devlin," she whispered.

He curled his fingers into his palms and dropped his arms to his sides. "I am no longer that person you remember, Gwyneth," he said. "That person adored you and loved his family and his home and did not see any clouds on the horizon of his life. That man was a dangerous innocent, quite unprepared for what real life was about to hurl at him. I have a connection to that man. I have somehow developed from him. But I am as I am now. I will care for the needs of my family. I will make a home of Ravenswood. I will fulfill my duty both there and in the larger world as a peer of the realm. I will try to do it all with justice and fairness. I will try to be hospitable and even amiable to my neighbors. Within the next few years I will marry and set up my nursery—as is my duty. But I am not the man who kissed you down among the trees behind the pavilion and promised you the moon and the stars. At least, I assume that is what I did."

"And you will live unhappily ever after," she told him. He was not sure, because he stood some feet from her, but it seemed to him that her eyes were bright with unshed tears.

"Happiness is an *emotion*, Gwyneth," he said. "It is only women who assume that life can be lived from that unstable base. It cannot. I have lived for six years without emotions and I have been perfectly satisfied with their absence."

She surprised him then. She left the gate and came toward him and did not stop until she was against him. She pressed her face to his chest beneath his chin and wrapped her arms about his waist. His own arms came reflexively about her back and shoulders.

And . . .

Ah, hell!

His mind went to the women with whom he had lain on the Peninsula. To how they had *felt*. A variety of physical types, some taller than others or more slender or more curvaceous. Some were more passionate or more skilled than others, or more talkative, or more quietly alluring. He had enjoyed them all, and he had enjoyed making *them* enjoy *him*. It had been a pleasurable, satisfying pastime, and it had kept him sane. Or human, at least. He would be able to put names to them all if they came before him now. He had always tried to see them as persons, never simply as bodies presented for his pleasure.

But none of them, held to his body, had felt like Gwyneth. Because with them it had all been about physical satisfaction and sexual enjoyment. A shared enjoyment, yes—he could not remember a reluctant woman or one who went away unsatisfied—but no more than that. With Gwyneth it had never been just about the physical. The yearning for it, yes. But not the yearning for sexual pleasure alone. With her it had always been the longing for Gwyneth herself—for the beautiful, wild, free girl with the light of life in her eyes and music in her fingers and her voice and passion in her soul. And the lilt of her slight Welsh accent. And . . . Well. And that unique essence of her that could never be put into words.

And here she was now again in his arms. And with her the threat and the danger of everything he had felt with her before. She was wearing a thick pelisse over her dress. He was wearing his greatcoat over several layers of clothing. It did not matter. She was Gwyneth. He would know her if several layers of down blanket were added to everything else between them and he was blindfolded.

It was not a physical knowing. He had never known her in the biblical sense and did not want to. He dared not even think of it. Please . . . He dared not.

She tipped back her head after a while and looked into his face, her eyes troubled. He kept his arms about her, but he held himself rigid and kept his expression blank. He had had long practice at both. Her warmth seeped through to his body. He ignored it.

"Kiss me," she said.

He gazed into her face. Soft, parted lips, cheeks flushed with cold and perhaps something else besides, blue eyes looking very directly into his. Eyes to lose himself in.

"I have always made it a rule not to kiss other men's women," he said stiffly. "Or fornicate with them," he added for good measure.

"I am not any other man's woman," she told him.

"Morgan?" he said.

She shook her head. "Aled and I are not betrothed," she said. "He has never asked me to marry him." She closed her eyes, and he watched her inhale slowly and let the breath go before she opened them again. "I would not say yes even if he did."

No? Had he misread the signs yesterday?

She gazed at him for a few moments before half smiling and removing her arms from about his waist and dropping them to her sides.

"Let us go back to the house," she said. "Mam and Idris will probably be home soon. I am sorry, Devlin. I ought—"

But he had drawn her close again and spread one hand over the back of her head to angle it and hold it steady. She stopped talking abruptly and he kissed her.

The shock of it went through him like a shaft of pain. He had kissed one woman once in his life before now, and that had been more than six years ago. He had taken the bodies of many women for pleasure since then and given his body in return. He had never kissed any of them, though. For a kiss was not about sex, or never had been for him. A kiss was . . . personal. It was intimate.

And he was kissing Gwyneth again. Hard and fiercely. His lips ravished hers as his tongue probed her lips and her teeth and plunged into the heat of her mouth and withdrew and plunged again while he felt himself harden into arousal and knew that a kiss could *lead* to sex. It would be violent sex if he continued and if she did not stop him. But even sex without love never called for violence. *Never.* It was one cardinal rule of his that he had never broken. There had been too much violence in other aspects of his life. He let go of the fierce urge inside himself and explored her mouth more gently with his tongue, using the tip of it, feeling her shiver and arch inward against him and grip his greatcoat on either side of his waist and moan with what he recognized as desire. Even through the layers of both their clothing he could tell that she had grown hot. She must be able to feel the hardness of his arousal.

Desire engulfed him. It pounded through his whole body and throbbed in his temples. But she was Gwyneth. He withdrew his tongue into his mouth and played her lips softly with his own before drawing back his head and looking into her face.

She had been in his dreams, the only part of his consciousness he had *not* been able to control. But dreams were easy to quell once one was awake—that jumbled mass of unrelated, incomprehensible, often bizarre thoughts and images that passed through the unconscious and unwary brain when one slept. She had been there—as had all of them. His family. And sometimes he had loved her, while at other times he had hated her. Undisciplined emotions, which had been easy to squash as he awoke, for emotions have no basis in fact or reason and no place in the waking world.

He had convinced himself that he had not once thought consciously of her in all those years. Except that he could remember—at least, he *thought* it was a real memory—Ben's voice: *No one has ever doubted it, Dev. She has never doubted it.* It was when he, Devlin, had believed he was dying from the gash across his face that had filled his eyes and his mouth and nostrils with blood. He had been babbling something about letting Gwyneth know—*please, Ben, please tell her . . .* That he had always loved her, that he would love her with his dying breath.

Good God, he had forgotten that excruciating embarrassment. He wondered if Ben had forgotten. Very likely not.

She was looking a bit heavy eyed, her lips soft and moist and swollen.

"No," she said quietly. "Don't do that, Devlin."

"What?" he asked. "Kiss you? It is a bit late now, is it not? Were you lying about Morgan?"

"Don't retreat back inside yourself and rebuild that wall," she said. "Don't make yourself all hard and cold and cynical."

"If you thought that was love and romance and roses and violin music just now," he said, "you were mistaken. You asked me to kiss you, you assured me you had no commitment to your Welshman, and I accepted the invitation. It is what men do, Gwyneth. We do not need to be asked twice."

She nodded and took a step back from him. Apart from the rosiness the chill had whipped up in her cheeks, she looked pale.

"I will not ask again," she told him. "But I have long wanted to say this, Devlin, and I *will* say it now. You did the *right* thing that night. You are the only man—or woman—I know who would have had the courage to do it. I urged you to wait and confront your father privately. Probably everyone else believes that is what you ought to have done. But if you *had*, nothing would have changed. That new knowledge would have somehow been hushed up with everything else, and life would have continued as it always had been. The woman concerned would have left Boscombe quietly and without fuss, and everyone would have dutifully forgotten about her within a week."

"Would it not have been better that way?" he asked harshly.

"No," she said. "When people live in denial of the truth—sometimes large groups of them all together—they lose their . . . I am not sure of the right word. They lose something precious, something good and right and true. Their integrity, perhaps? You forced everyone to confront the truth—even those who did not know it before. You did the right thing."

"Even though it deprived you of a marriage?" he asked.

She closed her eyes briefly. "Even though," she said. "And do *not* go on to say that I could not have loved you then. I loved you with all my heart."

"Past tense," he said.

"Your words." She looked back across the meadow. The house was out of sight from here, but there were the unmistakable sounds of clopping hooves and carriage wheels coming from that direction. Someone was home.

"Love can bring only unbearable suffering, Gwyneth," he said. "I really do not know why anyone would want to risk it. Don't love me again. I wish you all the good things in the world. But don't love me."

Her expression softened, and for a fleeting moment she looked like that wild child he remembered. She smiled and her eyes danced with merriment. But only for a moment.

"Don't climb that tree, Gwyn. You will fall. Don't ride that horse bareback, Gwyn. He will toss you. Don't chase that dog, Gwyn. He will bite," she said. "Never say *don't* to me, Devlin."

And she turned to walk back across the meadow with long, almost mannish strides—and looked achingly feminine as she did so.

He fell into step beside her and found himself in an undisciplined moment realizing that he might have been married to her for five years by now if things had turned out differently at that fete. She might have been as familiar to him as the air he breathed. She might have been as dear to his heart as its beating. They might have had a couple of young children or more. Dark clouds may never have threatened their skies.

Yet that very thought jolted him back to reality and reminded him that it was never a good thing to daydream. There were *always* dark clouds. In everyone's life. No one was immune. There were no such things as eternal sunshine and fairy-tale endings and happily ever after. If it had not been that shock of knowledge of what his father was really like, then it would have been something else.

It was all in how one reacted to disaster when it hit. Perhaps that was what life was all about—the reason for it, the meaning of it. One giant classroom. One lifelong learning opportunity to divide the men from the boys and the women from the girls.

How well had he done on the test?

You did the right *thing that night. You are the only man—or woman—I know who would have had the courage to do it.*

Sometimes there was no definitive right or wrong. He would probably never know if he had done the right thing or the wrong thing that night. No one would ever know, because either answer was only opinion.

But ah, it had felt good—it *felt* good—to hear those words. From Gwyneth, one of those most deeply involved. *You did the* right *thing that night.*

"Idris and your mother are the first home," he said as the house came into sight after they had crossed back over the stile. Idris was driving the gig to the stable block.

"Well, of course they are," Gwyneth said. "Dad and Aled will be at the church until the children and young people in the choir stage some sort of mutiny."

CHAPTER EIGHTEEN

D evlin had not expected to be gone so long. He would stay
perhaps an hour with Idris, he had thought. He had *certainly*
not expected to have all his emotions wrung dry. The more fool he,
to let them come bubbling up like that, as though he had learned
nothing in six years.

He had intended to call at the village inn on his way back to
Ravenswood. And he would, by God, do it anyway, he thought,
gritting his teeth as he left Cartref behind. It was something that
needed doing, and he was not going to have wrung-out emotions
dictating his actions and driving him home to hide.

The choir practice was still on at the church, he could hear as he
rode past. Poor Steph. She would be hoarse. Though she had been a
loyal member of the choir when she was a child and must have remained loyal ever since then. He would ask her what singing meant to
her. He was terribly out of touch with his siblings' lives.

There were a few people in the taproom at the inn—all men.
They all looked a bit wary when he stepped inside the room. An

awkward silence fell. Jim Berry, the innkeeper, was behind the counter, wiping it off with a wet cloth.

"Good afternoon." Devlin included everyone in his greeting and his nod.

There was a low growl of returned pleasantries.

"What may I get you, my lord?" the innkeeper asked him.

"A glass of ale would go down nicely," Devlin said, and he stood at the counter to drink it after the tankard had been set before him, foam all but spilling over the brim. He was trying not to remember that his father had died here.

"That's a wicked scar you have there, my lord," the innkeeper said.

"I like to think it makes me look more manly," Devlin said, and everyone chose to laugh heartily, as though he had just made the joke of the week—as they had used to do almost every time his father opened his mouth. "I understand there is to be an assembly upstairs here next week, Jim."

Jim Berry had resumed his task of wiping off the counter. His hand paused midswipe and he looked warily at Devlin. "Aye, there is," he said.

"The assembly rooms are small, I remember," Devlin said. "I thought we might hold it at Ravenswood again. The ballroom there is a bit more spacious." A lot more, actually.

"Aye, that it is," the landlord agreed.

"I believe everyone pays to attend the assemblies here," Devlin said. "To cover the rental cost."

"And other things," Jim Berry said. "The orchestra. Extra hands to help. And more."

"You normally provide all the drinks?" Devlin asked.

He was aware that everyone else in the taproom was avidly listening.

"I do," the innkeeper said, his hand still motionless as it held the cloth. "I have already put in an extra order. And the missus has ordered what she will need for the food."

"The admission charge covers all those expenses?" Devlin asked.

"With a bit of profit for me and the missus," the landlord said defensively. "There is a lot of work involved, my lord. It is a business I am running here, not a charity."

"We never had to pay nothing in them days when the assemblies was at the hall," someone said from a dark corner of the room.

"You will not have to this time either," Devlin said. "Perhaps I can send some wagons here on the day, Jim, to carry everything over to the hall. I can arrange for Mrs. Berry to talk with my cook if she would like. Perhaps she can direct operations and do the cooking there. Maybe you would care to serve the drinks, with a bit of help from some of the footmen at the hall. You can make an estimate of the number of people who attend and I can pay you the full fee, just as if the assembly had been held here. What do you think?"

Jim Berry looked at him with slightly squinted eyes. "The old earl never paid me nothing," he said. "And he had the countess do all the planning. And all of you. The servants did all the cooking and serving."

Really? His father had taken away what must have been fairly lucrative business from the innkeeper without thinking to compensate him?

"Them rooms *are* a bit on the small side, though, when everyone decides to come," Jim admitted. "You would let me serve the ale and spirits, my lord? At Ravenswood? I don't have no fancy uniform to wear."

"I do not believe any of the guests would have a fit of the vapors at the sight of you as you usually look," Devlin said.

"Wear a clean apron, though, Jim," one of his other customers said.

"Will it be workable?" Devlin asked. "Or would you rather keep things as they are?"

"We can work in partnership for other assemblies too?" Jim asked, swiping again at his already clean counter.

"It sounds like a good idea to me," Devlin said. "My mother will no longer be burdened with the planning of every social event at the hall. I may hire someone to do it, or—"

"People around here would be only too happy to get back to all their old committees, my lord," Jim Berry said, cutting him off. "The way things used to be when I was little more than a lad. Everyone pitched in to plan and help and we didn't have to pay nobody to do it for us. We was a real community then."

Devlin was feeling a bit stunned. His father had taken that away from them? He had centralized almost all the social life of the neighborhood about himself? And passed on all the work to Devlin's mother? Was that *really* the way it had been? But—

"I'll talk to the missus," Jim said. "I'm not going to force nothing on her she don't like. That's not the way we work. But I think she will like going up to the hall with her food and her recipes and showing the cook there a thing or two. No offense meant, my lord."

"You had better be careful, Jim," Devlin said. "I may decide to keep her."

That drew guffaws of mirth from everyone gathered there.

"You walked into that one, Jim," someone said. "Evelyn Berry, head cook at Ravenswood Hall. Looking down her nose at lesser mortals. Including her own husband at the village inn."

The poor innkeeper was still being mercilessly teased when Devlin took his leave.

T he countess and Philippa had gone after luncheon to call upon Miss Wexford, the colonel's sister, who had declared yesterday at the tea that she would be celebrating her birthday quietly at home because at her age—she was turning fifty—she had no wish for anything louder. However, anyone was welcome to come and commiserate with her over a cup of tea.

His mother and sister were returning home just as Devlin was riding up from the village. He had to draw his horse to the side of the drive beside the ha-ha to allow the carriage to pass. He touched the brim of his hat to them but could have avoided a closer encounter. He could have continued on to the stables to unsaddle his horse and rub it down himself.

It was amazing actually to what lengths he could go to avoid his mother. Even in less than a week he had it down to a fine art. So did she. It had not always been so. He could remember her telling him not long before he left—it was probably during the height of the busy preparations for that fete—that she did not know what she would do without him. *And never put me to the test on that, Dev, my beloved boy,* she had added, laughing.

It was strange how random memories like that could pop up out of nowhere when one's guard was down.

He did not ride to the stables, weary as he was from an eventful afternoon, to say the least. He followed the carriage onto the terrace and waited while the coachman set down the steps and handed his mother out and then Philippa.

"Mother." He removed his hat. "Were you the only ones to attend Miss Wexford's non-birthday party?"

"We would have been surprised if we had been," she said. "And of course there just happened to be enough cakes and pastries baked this morning to feed everyone."

"Mother," Devlin said as they turned to climb the steps to the front doors. "May I have a word with you?"

It was probably the worst possible time. She would be weary after her visit. He was still feeling rubbed raw after what had happened at Cartref and then at the inn. He actually wanted to crawl into a hole somewhere and stay there until he had put himself back together. But his mother was looking back at him and nodding.

"Come to my sitting room in a little while," she said.

This, Devlin thought a little less than half an hour later as he knocked on the door of his mother's private sitting room, was the very last thing on earth he felt like doing. But then he did not want to be doing any of this. What he really wanted was to be back with his men and his regiment. It had suited him admirably, that life, for all its discomforts and dangers and brutality. Sometimes he thought his father had died deliberately to avenge himself upon the son who had wrecked the very satisfactory double life he had enjoyed for years by disclosing the truth of it to a large gathering of his family, friends, and neighbors. And, ultimately, to the *ton* itself. His revenge would be to force Devlin to give up his life of soldiering and return home to clean up the mess he had created.

Millicent, still his mother's dresser, opened the door. "Come in, if you please, my lord," she said. "Her ladyship is expecting you." She let herself out after Devlin had stepped inside, and she closed the door quietly behind her.

It had been his sitting room—or his den, as he had liked to call it as a boy—attached to what had been his bedchamber and dressing room. The whole suite was now his mother's. But he was immediately engulfed in a different familiarity. A faint scent of gardenia and the sight of the furniture from her old sitting room. There were the soft love seat and chair with their cheerful chintz covers, and the dark green velvet chaise longue, on which as a boy he had loved to lie when he was feverish or had the sniffles or was otherwise feeling under the weather and sorry for himself. His mother would cover him with the cozy wool blanket she had knitted herself, and he would thread his fingers through the holes and

pull it up about his neck while she laid a cool hand on his forehead
and bent to kiss his cheek and told him she would have him feeling
all better in no time at all. Words he had always trusted without the
shadow of any doubt. In those precious days his father had protected him from all ills *out there* somewhere while his mother had
held him close in a nest of warm security and love *in here.*

Childhood was a golden time for those who were loved.

She was standing by the window, but she moved away from it
as soon as he came in and she bent over the tray on the low table
before the love seat to pour two cups of tea. She put a buttered
scone and two small macaroons on a plate to hand him after she
had set his cup and saucer before the armchair. Just as she had used
to do, picking out the best of his favorites for him instead of offering him the whole plate. He had always loved macaroons. And
scones with lots of butter but no jam or cream. *You like scones with
your butter, do you, Dev?* his father had asked one day, laughing and
ruffling his hair.

He did not want these memories.

"Thank you," he said, taking his place and setting down his
plate beside his saucer. Any food would surely stick in his throat.

She sat on the love seat, her own cup and saucer cradled in her
hands. "Well, Stratton," she said.

"Well, *Mother,*" he replied.

And they had spoken volumes with just those four words. The
whole history of the past six years with its bitterness and pain and
estrangement was in them. *Stratton* and *Mother.* The silence between them was loud. No, not that. There was no suggestion of
sound. The silence was *thick.*

"Devlin—" she said.

"Mama—" They spoke together.

And they gazed ruefully at each other.

"Tell me," he said. "Why did you send me away? Why would you not even say goodbye to me when I knocked on the door of your room? Why me and not him?" He drew breath to pour out another dozen or so questions, but he stopped there.

"I desperately wished to protect you," she said. "You were still so very young even though you were twenty-two. You were still very . . . innocent. And very bewildered and hurt. I needed to get you away from here until somehow the situation had sorted itself out and things had settled down. I needed to get you to safety for a while."

"Safety." He stared at her.

"I had *no* idea," she said, closing her eyes briefly, "that you would turn to the military, and a foot regiment at that. It seemed the very worst choice for you, unlike Nicholas. I had no idea you would cut yourself off from us so completely. I never intended it to be forever, or even for very long. I never said that. If Ben had not gone with you, I might well have lost my mind."

And that was what had mattered to her? That she somehow hold on to her sanity? That she keep the peace? And therefore that she keep her son and her husband apart? Was that what the whole of her married life had been about? Somehow preserving the threads of the illusion of a happy marriage and family life?

"Refusing to see you the morning you left was pure cowardice and selfishness," she said. "Saying goodbye. I just could not do it. And afterward, when I understood how it must have seemed to you when you were at your most vulnerable, it was too late. I ran out to the stables, but you were gone. You and Ben both. I . . . thought I would die. No, that is foolish. I *wished* I could die. For some things are so nearly unbearable that life itself seems unlivable, the future unthinkable."

"Was it all my fault?" he asked her.

She set her cup and saucer down on the table. She had not touched her tea. She drew an audible breath and released it.

"You told the truth," she said. "That can never be wrong, can it? Children are taught from the cradle up that they must always tell the truth, that lies are wicked and cause only harm. And you told it out of love—for me and for your sisters and grandmothers. For very decency's sake. And out of a terrible disappointment in your father—whom you had always loved dearly. Perhaps you chose the wrong time and place. Or perhaps not. Either way, Devlin, it was not your *fault*. It was your father's. And mine."

"You blame yourself for what he did, then?" he asked her.

"Not in the way you perhaps mean." She sighed. "Only perhaps for never having the courage or the will to do myself what you did. To have the truth out in the open. To confront him. For fear of the very thing that did happen after you spoke out. A burst bubble. For it was no longer possible to pretend that we were the perfect Wares presiding with great benevolence over the neighborhood beyond our doors."

"Pretend," he said. "But you *did* know. Even before that day. Even before my outburst."

"Devlin." She looked directly at him, and her eyes were suddenly hard and her lips a thin line. "Women *always* know. They live with the knowledge. They build a world for themselves that helps them avoid the pain and humiliation of it. They make their own happiness."

"Happiness?" He frowned.

"Yes," she said. "It is what we all seek, is it not? Men are free to find it in myriad ways. Women have to make their world small enough that they can enclose it and possess it like a precious gem. Derive their happiness from it. It is what being a woman means. It is what we are *taught*."

He gazed at her, appalled, as though he were seeing her for the first time. As though he were seeing society and womanhood for the first time—as perhaps he was. Were women never free, then? Not just because they were always the property of some man— either father or husband or other male relative—but because there could never be *truth* in their lives? Not if they wished to live with a measure of peace, anyway.

"Is it what you have taught Pippa and Steph?" he asked her.

She gazed at him, her mouth partially open.

"I am sorry," he said. "That was uncalled for."

Gwyneth, he was thinking. *Gwyneth.* Was that what *she* had been taught? But his mind stuck there. He could not think about her yet. Everything was still too raw. And he was unaccustomed to dealing with feelings and what they did to him. He still resisted them with all his being, despite the cracks that were fast spreading in the impenetrable armor he had worn for six years.

She had loved him with all her heart, she had told him just a couple of hours ago. He seemed to remember that he had loved her too. With all his heart. A long, long time ago. When he had been someone else. When he had still had a heart to love with.

"Tell me what happened after I left," he said, and braced himself.

She thought about it for a while. "Nothing very much," she said. "Surprisingly little except that you and Ben were gone. She went away—that woman. I believe George saw to it. Everyone was obliging enough to behave as though nothing of any great significance had happened. Perhaps after a while they really believed it. People are good at that. And I daresay most had known of your father's little weaknesses anyway even though he had never before been indiscreet enough to bring them here."

Little weaknesses.

"He hired a new steward to take Ben's place," she said. "And all continued as before. With a few differences. I could no longer continue with all the elaborate social events I had organized here. Not without the help I had always been able to rely upon from you and Ben and Nicholas. And your father persuaded me to join him in London each spring for the Season while he busied himself with his duties in the House of Lords. Then he suffered his sudden heart seizure here and . . . and died. And you became Stratton."

Self-deception was a powerful force, he thought. Did she really believe all she said? That *nothing very much* had changed after he left? When it was as clear as day to him that *everything* and *everyone* had changed. If other people were to be believed, the very active social life that had centered upon Ravenswood and his mother's virtual withdrawal from local society had not happened because she no longer had the help of her sons. It had happened surely because she was deeply humiliated and ashamed and could not keep up the pretense. Yet she had continued to deceive herself. And she herself had changed. He could see it. Stephanie had commented on it. How must it have been for her, in a marriage with his father and unable to pretend to him that she did not know him for who and what he was?

But . . . Good God, who was he to judge? He was not a woman.

His mother did not blame him, she had told him. Let him not blame her either, then. None of it had really been her fault. She had merely been coping as best she could. The man who was to blame for the whole of it was dead.

"Mama," he said. "Can we now have done with the *Stratton* and *Mother* business? I love you." They were always the most difficult words to say, whether to a lover or to a mother. Sometimes, though, they were necessary. And in this case they were true. He might have deadened emotion in himself, but that did not preclude everything.

Not now he was back. Life here would be insupportable if he did *not* love his mother and his sisters and brothers. And he would not deceive himself and call it mere duty to those for whom he was responsible as the head of the family. He would call it what it was. Truth mattered.

It was love.

Not an emotion, but a fact upon which his behavior would be based.

"Devlin," she said. "I have never for one moment *not* loved you since I knew you were in my womb. But . . . Your tea will be cold, and it is obvious you are not going to touch either your scone or your macaroons. Will you please go away now, then? I am very, very tired."

He could see that she was close to tears.

He got to his feet and bent over her to grasp her shoulders and kiss her forehead. "I promise always to do my best to see to your comfort now that I am home," he said. "And I will never dishonor you, Mama."

She patted one of his hands.

"I must tell you before you hear it from someone else," he said, "that the village assembly planned for the assembly rooms next week is going to be held here instead. But you need do absolutely nothing about it except perhaps attend. Everything will be seen to. *Everything.*"

"Oh," she said.

"And there will be no arguments about that," he told her.

"Go away, Devlin," she said.

He went.

Chapter Nineteen

After Devlin left Cartref, Gwyneth retreated to her room to avoid her mother's questions—and to be in a safe place if her father and Aled should come home in the next little while.

She was inclined to chastise herself for having practiced self-deception. But that was not it, was it? She had never deceived herself. She had known that she loved Devlin heart and soul and for all time. The fact that she had been only eighteen at the end of it all did not diminish those facts. She had got over the terrible pain, of course. One did. She had put it behind her. Got on with her life. She had had no choice. One did not literally fade away or die of love as Sweet William had done in the song she had sung earlier. One lived on.

Any of the men whose marriage proposals she had rejected in the past six years would have made good husbands. She was fortunate to have attracted the regard of such estimable men. Aled would make a good husband, even though he would always be distracted for long stretches of time by his music. It was an honor indeed and a great compliment to have captured his notice at all. But those men and any others she might meet in the coming years were lacking in one essential component. None of them was Devlin Ware. Just as Nicholas, the beloved friend of her girlhood, had not been.

She had been trying for six long years to tell herself that she would do perfectly well without Devlin if she could merely find someone else upon whom to focus her esteem and affection, even her love. With Aled she had come very close to convincing herself that it had happened at last. He had everything to recommend him, including the respect and affection of her family both here and in Wales. With him she could embrace her rich Welsh heritage and yet reach out into the world too. With him she could move on into full adult independence, away from her parents' home. Away from Ravenswood.

But he was not Devlin.

Perhaps if Devlin had not come back . . . But he *had* come back.

Of course, Devlin was not Devlin either. Which was a head-spinning piece of nonsense. He was Devlin as he had become over a six-year retreat into cold, seemingly impenetrable darkness. When he had kissed her out in the meadow—at *her* invitation—she had been almost frightened by the barely leashed violence with which he had pressed her to him and invaded her mouth. It had been nothing like the sweet, youthful, romantic kiss of six years ago. And yet—oh, he *had* been Devlin. She had felt that long-lost man trying desperately to get out, and more than anything else in her life she had wanted to help him. To heal him.

It could not be done, of course.

Only he could heal himself.

And that realization had shattered her heart. All over again. For it was surely impossible.

He had spoken of taking a wife and having children as a *duty.*

He had not offered her the position. She would not have accepted anyway. How *could* she? He was so terribly damaged and might—probably would—remain that way for the rest of his life. She could not take that upon herself.

And yet . . . Oh, there had been that look in his eyes while she was playing her harp earlier, so fleeting that she might have imagined it. Though she did not believe she had. And—*I wish you all the good things in the world. But don't love me.* Ah yes. There had been those words too. Cold, crisp, decisive—yet surely there had been yearning behind them. The understanding that he had hurt her. The fear that he would do it all over again.

Love can bring only unbearable suffering, Gwyneth.

Which was true if one omitted the word *only.* That was not *all* love could bring. When love was at war with other powerful forces, which it had been in their case, then it seemed very easily vanquished. It seemed the weakest of all forces. But what if people got their definitions of strength and weakness backward? What if love was the one thing that always survived and could carry one through to the other side of suffering?

In front of the mirror in her dressing room she took her hair down, brushed it out, and coiled it at the back of her head again without summoning her maid. She leaned closer to the mirror to see if any of the aftereffects of that kiss still showed on her face, was satisfied with what she saw, and went back downstairs. She had heard carriage wheels crunching over gravel, and she could hear her father's voice as soon as she began to descend.

Aled came toward her, his hands outstretched for hers, a warm smile on his face.

"We practiced those poor young people until they had almost lost their voices," he told her. "But I was able to tell them at the end of it all that they are the best youth choir I have ever heard. I did not add the words *outside of Wales.* But I do believe I spoke the truth anyway. And I told them they were fortunate indeed to have the best accompanists anywhere in the world."

"But you did not add the words *outside of Wales,* did you?" Gwyneth said, setting her hands in his.

"They were not necessary," he told her, laughing. "I claim both you and Ifor for Wales. Did you get your letters written?"

"One of them," she said. "It is three pages long."

"Women are a marvel," he said. "I have to work very hard and use my largest, most sprawling handwriting to achieve six lines."

She took him into the library after dinner, on the pretext of finding their copy of the poems of William Wordsworth, which he had mentioned while they were eating. She put it into his hands and looked into his face.

"What is it?" he asked, setting the book down on a table beside him without opening it.

"I find myself embarrassed," she said, clasping her hands at her waist. "You have not actually asked me, and you have not spoken to Dad, or I would have heard about it. But I believe—"

He came to her rescue when she hesitated. "You believe correctly, Gwyneth," he said. "I do wish to marry you."

"I want to save you the embarrassment of asking and being rejected, then," she told him, wishing there were another way to say it. Something less abrupt and harsh. She supposed she could have waited for him to bring up the subject first, but it would have been unfair. "I cannot marry you, Aled. I am sorry. I like you exceedingly well."

"Ah," he said. "That dreaded word *like.* I would want more than liking from a wife. It is as well to know now that I would not have it from you. I am sorry too, Gwyneth. Am I right in believing that you did mean to have me even as recently as yesterday?"

"Sometimes love does not work," she said, "and one tries to forget it and find it with someone else. I wanted to love you, Aled. I thought I did. And the fault is *not* in you. It is in me."

"Your mother mentioned at dinner," he said, "that Idris went in person to fetch her home after the misadventure with the carriage, and that he left the Earl of Stratton here to keep you company."

"Yes," she said.

"Did I hurt you yesterday," he asked, "when I described him as a morose man?"

"You described what you saw," she said. "The wars do appear to have hardened him."

"He would not be a good husband for you, Gwyneth," he said. "There is coldness and cruelty in that man. He would kill your soul, which is full of music and light."

She half smiled and looked about the room, more shadow than light with only a single candle burning. "It is fortunate, then," she said, "that he has not offered to be my husband." Not in six years, anyway.

"I do beg your pardon," he said. "I was quite out of line in offering you advice about a man I do not know at all. I take it there is some history between you and Stratton? I appreciate your speaking with me directly in this way. It took some courage. And already I know that my main feeling when I wake up tomorrow will be relief. I am thirty-five years old. I have known and been interested in a number of beautiful women over the years, but I was never tempted to offer marriage to anyone until I met you. I had decided long ago that marriage and I would not suit, but then you tempted me. I believe my earlier decision was the right one, however, and I will feel a bit like a prisoner newly set free in the morning. I am sorry. That is not a very apt comparison."

"Yes, it is," she said, though she was not quite sure she believed what he had just said. It was possible that he was merely putting a brave face on it. She smiled at him. "Do you wish to take that book to your room, Aled? Or shall I return it to the shelf?"

"I will take it," he said, picking it up. "I want to find that poem about the daffodils—*I wandered lonely as a cloud* . . . Those are the opening words, I believe, and the only ones I can remember exactly. Except *a host of golden daffodils*."

Gwyneth picked up the candlestick and led the way back to the drawing room, where her mother was regaling her father and Idris with bits of news and gossip she had picked up from her lace-making group during the afternoon.

T he following day, Aled recalled that he had business in London that he really must attend to very soon. The wars were over and the Continent was opening up for travelers and for a resumption of cultural pursuits for all. He had been approached with a tentative invitation to do some conducting in Paris and Vienna and possibly Rome. It was something he would need to discuss in person with certain people.

It all sounded a bit vague to Gwyneth, but her parents were delighted for him. They did agree with Idris, however, that he would be missed.

"But you must stay for church on Sunday, Aled," her father said. "The choir boys—and girls—sit in the choir stalls, of course, but the rest of the youth choir always sit together in the front pews, and the hymn singing is something to gladden the heart. I can almost imagine that I am back in Wales, where the singing sometimes lifts the roof a good six inches off the church."

"There is silly you are sometimes, Ifor," Gwyneth's mother said, laughing.

But Aled did stay that extra two days and left on Monday after thanking everyone profusely for their hospitality and shaking her father's and Idris's hands warmly and kissing both Gwyneth and her mother on the cheek. Gwyneth felt something very close to grief. At any other time and under any other circumstances . . .

But no. It would always have been a mistake, and Aled deserved far better than a wife who would live to regret marrying him.

"All right, Gwyn?" Idris asked, his arm tight about her shoulders as the carriage disappeared from sight.

"Yes, of course," she said.

"Of course," he agreed.

"I thought perhaps," their mother said, frowning and looking rather intently at Gwyneth, "he might have had a word with Dad before he left. But some men are dreadful slowtops. Perhaps next summer . . ."

"No, Mam," Gwyneth said, smiling and fearing the expression looked like a grimace on her face. "No."

And she picked up the sides of her skirt and hurried inside after her father, leaving her mother staring at Idris.

Gwyneth waited for two days. She knew it was something she could not possibly do. Just last week she had told herself she would never do it even if she could. But it was also something she could not *not* do, and if that was not a head spinner, she did not know what was. If she did not do it, no one else would. *He* would not. And she was tired of always waiting and of always trying to make a life and a future for herself that could never bring her happiness or even lasting contentment. It was *so hard* being a woman. But perhaps what she ought to realize was that it was probably not easy being a man either. It was not easy being Devlin. She understood that.

It was her mother's lace-making day again and her father's day for youth choir practice. She was going to ride over to Ravenswood, Gwyneth told them at luncheon when her father asked if she wanted to come listen to the choir and perhaps play the pianoforte while he conducted. She was going to have a word with the countess to see if there was anything she could do to help with the preparations for the assembly on Friday. It was a very slim excuse and would possibly be recognized as an outright lie. Everyone knew—it had been one of the main topics of conversation for the past week— that the countess was to have nothing to do with the organizing of the assembly even though it was to be held in the ballroom at the hall.

"Well, it will be pleasant for you to have a visit, cariad," her mother said. "You have been in low spirits since Aled left."

And so here she was, Gwyneth thought as she rode up the slight slope toward Ravenswood Hall. She had left a few minutes after her mother and father, having declared that she would rather ride on such a lovely day than go with them in the carriage. The groom who sometimes accompanied her when she rode beyond her father's land had frowned when she told him she did not need him today, but he had known better than to argue. And this might be for nothing after all, she thought as she rode around to the back of the hall in order to leave her horse at the stables. She had no idea if Devlin was at home.

He was, though. He was leaning against the wooden fence that surrounded the paddock beside the stables, one booted foot propped on the bottom rung, his arms folded along the top rung. He was dressed with shocking informality in breeches and shirt and unbuttoned waistcoat. His hair was windblown and a bit in need of a cut. He was looking really quite gorgeous.

Beside him was Ben Ellis, also leaning on the fence. On his back he was carrying that contraption she had heard about. Cameron Holland and Sally, his sister, had made it between them out of an old knapsack Ben had had on the Peninsula and taken down to the smithy a week or so ago. Cameron had made a sort of metal frame to hold the bag open and firm, and Sally had cut and bound two holes at the bottom of the front of it and had folded and bound the top of it over the metal to make it warmer and more comfortable to the touch. And they had tried it out. Ben's daughter now rode everywhere with him, snug and safe inside the bag on his back, high enough to see past him and set her hands on his shoulders. There she was now, hugging his sides with her legs, bouncing and squealing as she pointed into the paddock and delivered one of her high-pitched monologues in gibberish—though one frequently repeated word was recognizable.

"Papapapapapa."

She was pointing at Owen Ware, who was dressed like Devlin and riding the horse that had been badly injured earlier in the summer when it had stepped into a particularly large rabbit hole. Owen himself had been thrown and had suffered a sprained ankle and numerous scrapes and bruises. The horse had to be put down—or so the steward and all the most senior grooms had agreed. Until, that was, Owen, in great wrath, had threatened to shoot himself if anyone shot his horse.

"If a bad sprain is a death sentence for him," he was rumored to have said, "then it must be for me too. But before I shoot myself, I'll get in a bit of practice by first shooting whoever kills my horse."

The horse had lived, though his sprain had been far worse than Owen's. Gwyneth had heard that the horse was being exercised again and Owen was going to get up on his back one day soon and gradually set him through his paces again. This was the day, it seemed. He was taking the horse from a walk to a cautious trot.

All of this Gwyneth took in with a single glance. The next moment Ben turned and Joy stared at Gwyneth over his shoulder. Devlin looked over *his* shoulder before lowering his foot to the ground and turning too. He would have come toward her, but a groom was already lifting her down from her sidesaddle and then leading her horse away into the stables.

"Good afternoon, Gwyneth," Ben called, and Joy pointed and smiled. "Ah, excuse me." Owen had ridden up to the fence farther along and was patting and running a hand along his horse's neck. Ben went to confer with him.

"Gwyneth," Devlin said. "Allow me to escort you inside to my mother. Is she expecting you? But it does not matter. She *is* at home and will be happy to see you. I must apologize for my appearance."

"I came to see you," she told him, walking toward him before he could move away from the fence.

He leaned back against it and crossed his arms defensively over his chest and his legs at the ankles. He frowned. "I am honored," he said.

"Has anyone from the committee talked with you yet?" she asked him.

"Committee?" he said. "Ah. Yes. I did have a delegation of four wait upon me this morning. Two men and two women, who claimed to be representatives of a larger committee. They were all looking mulish and determined, as though they expected to have a fight on their hands. About paying the expenses for the assembly. Is that what you were referring to?"

"Yes," she said. "They called upon everyone. They came to Cartref, but they did not ask only Mam and Dad and Idris and me. They talked with all the servants and grooms and gardeners. As well as the farm workers, I believe. They said the verdict so far had been almost unanimous."

"Everyone actually wants to pay to attend," he said. "They want to purchase their tickets from Jim Berry at the inn, as they always do."

"I hope you agreed," she said.

"I did." He gazed at her for a moment. "I am beginning to understand that my father was something of a benevolent tyrant—one of those delightful contradictions in terms. Apparently he took over every traditional social event of the neighborhood after my grandfather's time and insisted upon organizing and financing everything."

"He was very good," Gwyneth said.

"Which is exactly what the committee said," Devlin told her. "And his goodness obviously exasperated a large number of people."

"Mam and Dad have been talking about it," she said. "Apparently there used to be all sorts of committees here. They organized everything of a community nature and delegated tasks. No one had to be forced—people actually liked to volunteer. There even used to be a summer fete on the village green and the connecting streets. The maypole would be set beside the duck pond. Everyone was involved in planning and running the whole thing. Everyone shared the expenses."

"Until my father decided that Ravenswood would be a far more spacious and scenic venue," he said. "And that my mother would organize it all and he would pay for it."

"Yes," she said.

His face was looking as hard as ever. His jaw was tight. *He was a good man,* she almost added again. But she did not say it. Devlin had agreed to let everyone buy a ticket to Friday's assembly. Apparently he had invited Mr. Berry to provide and serve the beverages and Mrs. Berry to cook the food—and to do it in the kitchens here if she wished. Apparently, she *did* wish. Devlin had obviously realized, as his father seemed not to have done, that he would be hurting both the feelings of the Berrys and their income by taking the assembly right away from them. He had offered the venue but had left everything else to them, including all the profits. And now he had agreed to allow everyone to pay their way so that no one would feel beholden to him.

"Gwyneth," he said, "was it for this you came here to see me?"

"No," she said, suddenly not knowing what to do with her hand that was not holding her whip. Let it dangle at her side? Clutch the side of her riding habit? What did she usually do? She tucked it behind her back.

He gazed at her, narrow-eyed. She stared back. Joy was chattering to Owen across the fence, and he was grinning back at her and telling her he absolutely agreed with everything she said.

"Well?" Devlin said.

"I was wondering," Gwyneth said, feeling as though she had just run over from Cartref on foot and needed a few minutes to catch her breath. "No, not that. I think you ought— Not that *you* ought on your own. But that *we* ought."

"We ought to *what*?" he asked her. "Dance with each other at the assembly? I have not danced in six years."

"Not that," she said. Why had it seemed so easy when she had imagined it yesterday and last night and this morning? Well, not easy, perhaps. But at least possible. With just a bit of courage and determination. She swallowed and said it.

"Devlin, I think we ought to marry. Each other, that is."

But instead of being outraged or overjoyed or any of a dozen or more things in between those extremes, all of which she had been prepared for, he merely continued to lean back against the fence. His arms were still folded over his chest, his ankles still crossed, his eyes still narrowed, his jaw still looking like granite—and he said nothing.

"You asked me to marry you more than six years ago," she said.

"You were going to talk to Dad the next day. You went away instead. I do not remember everything you and I said before you left. I know I was upset and angry and frustrated and said things I did not mean, but I do not remember telling you I was rejecting your offer, that I no longer considered myself betrothed to you. I do not remember you asking to be let out of the commitment *you* had made. I may be wrong, but I do not think so. Is there a term limit on a betrothal that has not yet been converted into a marriage? Is there such a law?"

"You are about to sue me for breach of promise?" he asked her. It did not sound as if he was joking. Or as if he was in any way amused.

"It was never a formal engagement," she said. "I would probably lose the case."

"Well, that is a great relief," he said. Still no sign that he was joking.

"I told you last week," she said, "that I had never got over you. Or something to that effect. I have tried to feel for other men what I once felt for you. I really thought I had succeeded this time with Aled Morgan. But it has never worked. And you have not found someone else either, as Ben did. At least I assume you have not. You told me last week, in a quite impersonal way, that you would be marrying and having a family in the foreseeable future, as one of your duties as Earl of Stratton. I do not believe you had anyone in particular in mind. Why not me, then? You loved me once."

"I was another person once, a long time ago, Gwyneth," he said. "I *will* marry, for the very reason you have just stated. But not for love. It will be a business alliance. I will choose someone who clearly understands that and feels the same way about marriage as I do. That would not be possible with you."

"No, of course it would not," she agreed. "And what nonsense you speak, Devlin. As though any marriage could remain on the footing of a *business arrangement* for a lifetime. When by the very nature of its principal function, the procreation of children, it must also be an intimate relationship." Her cheeks suddenly felt uncomfortably hot.

He broke eye contact with her and glanced in the direction of his brothers. They were still talking—Joy had turned her head and set her cheek against Ben's back and fallen silent—but they were also glancing curiously Devlin's way.

"Let me go and fetch my coat from the stable," he said, turning back to her. "We need a little more privacy than we have here. It is not every day I receive a marriage proposal."

He *still* did not sound amused.

"Then take my hat and whip with you and leave them there," she said, handing them to him.

CHAPTER TWENTY

I t was not a marriage proposal," she told him. "It was a betrothal resumption suggestion."

They had been walking for several minutes, striding along as though they were late for some appointment. They were going in the direction of the poplar walk, Devlin realized, though it had not been a conscious choice. It was the first time either of them had spoken.

Betrothal resumption suggestion, for the love of God. Had it taken her all this time to dream up that one?

It was the worst suggestion he had heard since he returned to England. And the very idea that they might be betrothed because as a young man hot with lust more than six years ago he had asked her to marry him and then abandoned her the very next day was preposterous. Why the devil would she still want to marry him anyway? *He had abandoned her.* And he did not for a moment believe that she had an eye on the title or the fortune that would come with him. He had never known Gwyneth to be either ambitious or mercenary.

The devil of it was that he did need a wife. Ravenswood ought to have a countess—one who was married to the earl, that was. He ought to have sons to secure his line. And probably daughters too— just because. It had actually felt good to grow up in a home with siblings of both genders. He had not thought much about it at the time. He had just *lived* it. And he was not looking forward to Ben's leaving, though it was inevitable. They had already come to an agreement over Penallen, and Ben was in the process of purchasing it. He would have a few renovations done, and then he would move to his new home—probably sometime after Christmas, by spring at the latest. Devlin would miss him—a massive understatement. He would also miss Joy, though, a realization that took him by surprise. She somehow lit all their lives with . . . Well, with *joy.*

But . . . *Marriage with Gwyneth?* No. Absolutely not. He wanted his marriage to be the sort of business arrangement he had de-scribed to her earlier. Something controlled and sensible and dispas-sionate. An alliance, a partnership.

They were coming up on the poplar walk, and Devlin slowed his steps. It had not occurred to him until now to shorten his stride to match hers. But she had kept up with him. She was wearing rid-ing boots. He had been unconsciously listening to the skirt of her riding habit swishing against them.

The wide grassy alley stretched ahead of them, the poplars like guards on either side. A scattering of fallen leaves dotted the grass. In a few weeks a thick carpet of them would crunch underfoot. And *that* brought back childhood memories of leaf fights with Ben and Nick, and even Pippa in later years, and building mounds of leaves so that they could burrow carefully into them for the pleasure of jumping up in a rush and scattering them far and wide while whooping with exuberance or roaring ferociously. Pippa had always preferred to fall backward onto the mounds, arms spread, shrieking and giggling with fright and glee.

"It was definitely a marriage proposal," he said abruptly, breaking a long silence. "There never was a proper engagement, so there is nothing to resume. You were eighteen, a minor, and your father's permission was neither asked for nor given. As for now, I would be the poorest possible choice for you. I have nothing whatsoever to offer apart from the obvious material things."

"Then offer me those," she said.

He stopped walking. So did she.

He turned to regard her with a frown. "You covet the role of Countess of Stratton of Ravenswood Hall, then?" he asked, and he could hear the steel in his voice.

"Yes, I do." She lifted her chin. "Because you are the earl."

Oh, devil take it. He had been aware of her passionate nature when she was a girl. He had not doubted her when she told him at that infamous fete that she loved him with all her heart and had loved him in secret for many years. But he had always seen her also as an intelligent, firm-minded female who did not base her life and her happiness upon romantic drivel. Could she not see him for what he was now? Did she not understand that the old Devlin Ware was long dead and could never be resurrected? Did she have a sentimental image of herself as angel and savior, able to release him from his demons and soothe him back to his boyhood self so that they could be in love again and live blissfully ever after?

"And because you think you can unfreeze my heart," he said harshly.

"No." She tipped her head slightly to one side, and her eyes roamed over his face. "I think you will do that all on your own, Devlin."

He laughed. "There *is* no heart to thaw," he said.

She turned to walk onward, and he fell into step beside her.

"Shall we forget about marriage proposals and hearts for the moment?" she suggested after a while. "Look at how beautiful this place is, Devlin. Green and secluded, as though one had stepped off the world for a short while in order to be comforted and restored before returning. It even *smells* peaceful." She drew in an audible breath through her nose and lifted her eyes to the tops of the trees as she let it out. "Tell me about your visit to the inn last week. Everyone has been buzzing with news of it ever since. It provoked the committee that sent a delegation to you this morning. But one can never quite distinguish fact from fiction in such cases. Tell me why you went there."

"Perhaps," he said testily, "I went for a glass of ale."

"What an anticlimax that would be," she said, laughing with what sounded like genuine amusement. "Tell me."

"When you have been given much," he said, "you can hoard it, or you can share it. The just and fair thing to do is share. We were taught that as children and came to believe it. It still makes practical good sense. What have we ever done, after all—what have *I* ever done—to deserve such a home and such wealth as I have? The answer is *nothing* except to be born into the right family. And that was no choice of mine. Who knows what higher power makes such decisions? Unless it is a purely random thing. It is not fair. But much in life is unfair. It is how one deals with what one has been given that matters—whether one has been given poverty or riches or something in between. I would rather not be who I am, but it seems I am stuck with being Devlin Ware of Ravenswood, Earl of Stratton, for the rest of my life."

"And *this* explains why you went into the taproom at the village inn?" she asked him, sounding amused. "It is no wonder you needed a glass of ale."

Yes, it *did* explain why he went there.

"Ravenswood is home to my mother and brothers and sisters and me and a number of servants," he said. "It is large enough to house an army battalion. The park would be considered more than spacious enough if it were set down in the middle of a crowded city for the use and pleasure of all its citizens. I cannot in all conscience keep it entirely to myself, for my private use and that of my immediate family. You heard me at that tea last week informing our guests that the park would be open to everyone again on certain days of the week. When I learned about the upcoming assembly, I remembered that the assembly rooms above the inn have long been inadequate for the numbers who always like to attend. I went to the inn to suggest to Jim Berry that the ballroom at the hall be used again, as it apparently has not been since I went away."

"Did he raise any objection?" she asked. "Or was your suggestion more like a command?"

"A command?" he said. "No. I do not believe that is how he took it. It was not how it was intended."

"Did he ask that he be allowed to order and serve the drinks?" she asked him. "Or that Mrs. Berry be allowed to provide and prepare the food?"

"It seemed to me," he said, "that they would have everything arranged by the time I spoke with Jim, that they would have already put in orders for all the supplies they would need. I knew there was an admission charge for the assembly, to cover the rental cost, the orchestra's fee, and the refreshments. I was aware that the Berrys stood to lose financially from my offer of the ballroom at the hall.

But it was a problem easily solved—provided Jim was not offended at the very suggestion that the assembly rooms were inadequate. If he had been, I would have dropped the idea. He seemed delighted, though. He and his wife will still be in charge of the refreshments, and I think that fact is more important to them than having everyone invade the inn and fill it to bursting. I am happy because my mother will not feel obliged to have anything whatsoever to do with the planning of the event. So, is it being said that all these arrangements were forced upon the Berrys? And that I insisted they do all the work while I basked in the glory of being the grand, generous host?"

"No!" she said so emphatically that they both stopped walking again. "Everyone is amazed that you even thought of how your offer would adversely affect Mr. and Mrs. Berry. Your father never did. But everyone was also indignant to learn that you intended to pay all the expenses, even the rental fee on the assembly rooms despite the fact they were not going to be used. Your generosity made everyone feel like a charity case again. Or like dependents of the hall again."

Again? Was that how his father, with his openhanded largesse, had made everyone feel? Had he ever been told? He would have brushed off any protest, though. He would have insisted *not* upon sharing but upon *giving*, focusing all attention on his generosity and the jovial good nature with which he distributed it. But perhaps that was being a bit unfair. His father was no longer here to speak for himself. Perhaps no one had explained the effect his generosity had on their pride.

"Do you not see?" she asked him when he said nothing. "You *care*, Devlin."

"I think you ought not to refine too much upon the fact that I have offered the ballroom, which sits idle and empty in my home, for a village assembly, Gwyneth," he said. "It does not follow that I suddenly have a heart to lay at your feet."

"It is not just the offer of the ballroom," she said. "It is the fact that you care how people *feel*. I doubt that caring has ever died in you, for you are basically a *decent* man."

"Ah, that is right," he said. "I had forgotten for a moment. Whenever the French were sending their vast columns to break through the British lines, I used to call out to them to get back, to go home to their wives and mothers, because I really, really did not want to hurt them. Unfortunately, the sound of their drums and all their men chanting *Vive l'empereur* drowned out my decent voice. Or perhaps they did not understand English." Too late, he heard the bitterness, the anger in his voice. And he wondered not for the first time how many hundreds or thousands of deaths he was responsible for, either directly by his own hand or as the result of orders he had bellowed. *Fire!* He had always been hoarse after a battle—from the smoke of all the guns, yes. But mainly from yelling that one word over and over again.

They were almost at the end of the alley. The summerhouse was just ahead of them.

"I had better get you back to your horse," he said. "I will ride home with you."

"May we sit in the summerhouse for a while?" she asked, and when he looked at her he could see that she was blinking back tears.

He needed a wife. Suddenly, dizzyingly, he could not remember why she could not under any circumstances be Gwyneth.

He led the way without replying or showing that he had noticed her tears. There was a lock on the door. There was even a key somewhere—or had used to be. But the door had never been kept locked. What sort of a message would *that* send to their neighbors on open days? his father had once replied when Nicholas had asked about it. The boathouse had never been locked either. And nothing had changed, he found now. He opened the door and stood back so that she could precede him inside.

The sun had warmed the inside of the summerhouse. There was no discernible dust on the ledges or furniture. The floor was clean. There was no musty smell. The Ravenswood gardeners must clean here regularly, Gwyneth thought as she sat on one of the comfortable chairs she remembered from her girlhood, when she had used to come here sometimes with Nicholas. Devlin sat on the sofa and looked at her. His shirt was buttoned to the neck, but he was wearing no cravat or neckcloth. The shirt itself was rather untidily bunched beneath his waistcoat and hastily donned coat. His hair was still disheveled.

She tried to remember the Devlin of six years ago, the one who had kissed her down among the trees below the pavilion. But it was impossible to transpose that youthful face onto this dour man. And why would she want to? She was no longer the girl who had returned his kiss. And he was far more attractive now. A strange word, that—*attractive.* It had very little to do with looks or perfect grooming or personality. But she had not come here to analyze a word in her mind.

"I have been doing a lot of thinking," she told him. "About honesty and lies."

He sat back, crossed his legs so that his booted ankle rested on his knee, and spread one arm along the back of the sofa. It was an informal, relaxed pose, but he looked anything but relaxed. His gaze upon her was steady and steely.

"It is so easy to be dishonest and to tell lies," she said. "Even if only to ourselves." This had sounded eloquent and earnest and passionate when she had thought about it in the past few days. But something always happened between thought and speech. He would be yawning in a moment. Or just walking out, and she would be left to nurse her heart's truth in silence for the rest of her life.

"Women are raised to tell lies," she said. "Almost every parent and nurse and governess would be shocked to hear that and protest that quite the opposite is true. They teach the children under their care always to tell the truth, never to lie. But girls and women are taught to obey their fathers and then their husbands without question, to devote their lives and energies to supporting them and making their lives comfortable and never, ever doing anything to embarrass or shame them. Some boys clearly are raised to believe that the truth is something that can always be bent to suit their desires, provided it is done with discretion and brings no open shame upon themselves or their women." Oh, this was as dry as dust.

"Did you come here to advocate for *my mother*?" he asked her. "And to tell me that perhaps my father went too far in his bending of the truth?"

She sighed. "I came to advocate for myself, Devlin, and am doing a terrible job of it. Women are taught that a man must make all the first moves and we must pretend to have no thoughts or feelings or even opinions of our own. The best we can do is to use *wiles* to achieve what we want. We are never allowed simply to speak our heart's truth."

"Yet you asked me to kiss you last week," he said. "And today you asked me to marry you."

"Yes." It was downright hot here in the summerhouse. "I spent six years telling myself that I was over you. I convinced myself that with a little effort I could fall in love with someone else, or at least hold someone else in high enough regard that I could commit the rest of my life to him. It has proved not to be so. I still may marry someone else, for I do not fancy the alternative. But before that happens, I must speak the truth. It has always been you, Devlin, right back to the days when you used to come to Cartref to spend time with Idris and did not even know I existed."

"I knew," he said.

She frowned, but he did not continue. "I was very much in love with you long before the day of that fete," she said. "But I did not believe you had any interest in me. And I have never been comfortable with the idea of using *wiles.*"

"You never needed to," he said. "I was interested."

"That day," she said. "It was magical. That is not a strong enough word, but I cannot think of another. It was . . . magical."

"That is exactly the right word," he told her. "It *was* magical. Not real. Insubstantial. An illusion."

"Was it?" she asked him. "Devlin, if . . . If everything had not happened, would you have come the next day to talk with Dad? Would you then have made me a formal offer? Would we have married? Would we still be happy? Happier, maybe? Because we did not really *know* each other then, did we? Not to the depths of our souls. We would have had those years and all the years to come to grow together. Was it that *one incident* that made all the difference to our lives?"

"Yes," he said without hesitation. "It was the one thing that crashed the world and made me understand what an innocent fool I had been all my life. For *nothing* was as I had thought it. I had been living a grand illusion. A great lie. There is more honesty, Gwyneth, in an army fighting and killing for a cause no one can quite put into words than there ever was here." He made a sweeping gesture with the arm he had draped along the back of the sofa, indicating the world beyond the summerhouse.

"Was Stephanie not what you thought her?" she asked.

He looked impatiently at her. "She was a *child*."

"And a person," she said. "Your sister. Your *beloved* sister, I believe. Was Philippa not what you thought her? Or Owen or Nicholas? Or Ben?"

His eyes narrowed. "Ben is the rock upon which I have steadied myself for more than six years," he said. "He was not part of the corruption. He was the acknowledged son of a whore. There was no lying there."

"And he was the son of your father," she said. "Was *I* not what you thought me?"

He laughed harshly. "It was the other way around, Gwyneth," he said. "It was *I* who was not what I thought myself to be. I was part of the whole illusion—a Ware of Ravenswood Hall. That wonderful, perfect, benevolent, always genial family that brought happiness to all within our orbit."

"It was not all illusion," she said. "That day, for example. The day of the fete. It gave an enormous amount of enjoyment, even happiness, to a lot of people, people for whom life is often somewhat tedious. Your father and your mother made that possible, and you and your brothers and sisters helped make it happen. *Everything* was not a lie."

"To me it was," he said.

"You fought back against it by telling the truth," she reminded him. "Regardless of the consequences. You have suffered those consequences. But it was your *father* who did wrong. He suffered too in his own way, I suppose. So did your mother, who had enabled him, along with numerous other people, her own mother and father and brother among them, because that was what society expected them to do. You *told the truth*. Are you going to punish yourself for the rest of your life for that? You cannot suffer the consequences of the lies. You neither told them nor condoned them. You cannot take the burdens of the whole of your family and a large segment of polite society upon your shoulders."

"I am dead inside, Gwyneth," he said. "I can function as a living man. I can and will do my duty here. I will marry and fill the nursery here if my marriage is so blessed. But I cannot resurrect the man you remember. I cannot love you. I can only want you."

She sat back in her chair and drew a slow breath. He was looking very directly at her with those hard blue eyes, which had once gazed into hers with warm, open adoration. He *wanted* her?

"You must understand that," he said. "There is no magic, Gwyneth. No romantic love. At least, there is not for me. You *must* understand my terms if you are to marry me."

She sat very still.

"You would have a role to play as my countess," he said. "It would be an alliance, a partnership. There would be no tasks I would *expect* you to take on without even consulting you. We would discuss each and come to an agreement either way. We would remain together spring, summer, autumn, and winter. You would never have to worry about my fidelity. You would have it. I have *not* been celibate during the past six years, but I will be after my marriage—celibate, that is, apart from the conjugal relations I will have with my wife. They will be regular and frequent. I wish for children—plural. No sentiment, though. No romance. No love except for the respect and even affection I would hope would be inevitable in a relationship that by its very nature would be an intimate one."

She licked her lips. "You are asking me to marry you?" she said.

"No," he told her. "I am accepting your offer to marry me. But upon strict conditions. With no illusions, Gwyneth. If you hope that I will fall in love with you again if you can only marry me and soften me up, then think again. For your own sake. The last thing in the world I want to do is hurt you. I did love you once."

What a very foolish man he was, she thought as she gazed back at him and marveled anew at how that saber cut could have spared his eye. Thinking that for her love was all about magic and sweet, sparkly eyed romance. Love was so many things that no one, not even the greatest poets, had ever been able to define it and establish one single meaning applicable for all time. Love was . . . Well, she was *not* a poet, and she was not even going to try. Not even in her own head.

He had come home. To do his duty, he had said. To hold his family together and this home. To reach out and make life better for the community around him. He had not been obliged to offer the ballroom here for the assembly. And he certainly had not been obliged to consider the feelings—and the finances—of Mr. and Mrs. Berry. His father had never shown that sort of sensitivity. He had just told her he had not been celibate during his years on the Peninsula. She would have been surprised if he had been. But he had *told* her so that there would be truth between them. When she had arrived here earlier he had been with two of his brothers, relaxed, leaning on the fence about the paddock, enjoying their company. He wanted children. *Children*, not just the heir and perhaps the spare that most men in his social position hoped for when they married. The last thing in the world he wanted was to hurt her.

What else *but* love were all those things?

He was hard and full of darkness. That could not be denied. But oh, he was not *all* cold, hard darkness. There was love in him too. He just did not realize it, and she was not going to explain it to him. At least, she assumed he did not realize it. Maybe he had admitted to himself that he loved Stephanie. And Philippa. And perhaps—perhaps?—his mother too. Gwyneth was not going to use any sort of wiles to tease him into falling in love with her. She was not going to do anything about the love that was there inside him, all mixed up with the darkness. She was just going to allow him to discover it for himself. To discover who he really was deep down at his core. Or not.

In the meanwhile, she was simply going to love him and live her life to the full.

"I think," he said, "you would be well advised to rescind your offer, Gwyneth. You deserve more than I have to offer."

"You have everything to offer that I want," she said. *You are Devlin,* she almost added, but did not.

"Well, then," he said. "I will ride back to Cartref with you when you go, and have a word with your father. If he is at home. Today is choir practice, I believe?"

"Yes," she said. And dear God, this was real. This was *happening.* Was she making the biggest mistake of her life? No, she thought. No, she was not. For there were no illusions—on either side.

She smiled.

He did not.

She should get to her feet and lead the way back out into the cool autumn sunshine. There was much to look forward to. Including heartache. But she wanted to stay here forever. Just like this. She did not want to move and risk spoiling everything.

"I do *want* you, Gwyneth," he said.

CHAPTER TWENTY-ONE

H is eyes seemed to look straight through hers to the very heart of her, and everything inside her ached with a longing so intense she thought she might not be able to continue breathing.

"Now?" Her question hung in the silence.

"We *will* be marrying," he said. "By Christmas. I will not take your virtue and leave you."

Oh. *By Christmas?*

"There will be no way back if we make love now," he said. "Not for either of us."

"I will never want a way back," she said.

He continued to look at her for a few moments longer, his eyes still hard, not letting her in. Then he got abruptly to his feet, looking upward as he did so. There were long curtains for the windows, three of them, which could be drawn to cut out most of the sunlight on a hot day. He pulled all three across their rails until they met, and only the door facing down the long alley remained uncovered. The curtains brought little darkness, just a deeper sense of seclusion and privacy in the very unlikely event that someone should wander within sight of the summerhouse.

He turned and reached out a hand for hers. She set her own in it, and he drew her to her feet. But not directly into his arms. His hand was firm about hers. She could feel the heat from his body. His chest, his shoulders were broader, more firmly muscled than she remembered—even last week she had not been as fully aware of that as she was now. His face was that of a man who had suffered and survived but still did not fully trust anyone or anything beyond himself. He was a man afraid of love yet unable to stop loving, though he did not use that word. He called it *duty*. He was a man who wanted her but did not love her and never would. He would only *act* as though he did. Many men—many *people*—did just the opposite, professing a love their actions denied.

He looked back at her with an intensity to match her own.

"You are very beautiful, Gwyneth," he said. "Age suits you. Being a woman rather than a girl suits you."

Age suits you. Would any other man say such a thing? Sometimes his honesty was astounding. Would he say it when she was fifty? Sixty? Eighty?

He raised the hand that was not holding hers and ran the backs of his fingers—hard, strong, *calloused* fingers—down the side of her jaw to her chin. He ran the pad of his thumb lightly over her lips, sending raw need knifing through her body to tighten her breasts and throb in her womb and ache between her thighs.

He released her hand then and cupped her face with both of his hands. He lowered his head and touched his lips lightly to hers before drawing back in order to look into her eyes again. Then he opened his lips over hers, teasing them with the tip of his tongue until they parted. The kiss was light, quite unlike last week's almost violent assault. Light and unbearably . . . What? She did not have the word. It was light and nearly more than she could stand. She yearned to be closer. She yearned . . . Ah, there were no words to complete the thought.

He lifted his head again and glanced back at the sofa. "I will make it very good for you when we have all the space and comfort of a marital bed to lie upon," he said. "Since we will be creating children, God willing, and must be intimate to do so, and since we will be intimate only with each other for the rest of our lives, we might as well make it enjoyable. I will make it so for you. It is the least I can do."

"Perhaps," she said, "I will make it enjoyable for you too."

And something, for the briefest of moments, sparked in his eyes. Laughter? Desire? Both? Then it was gone. "But all we have this time," he said, "is the sofa."

"It is not," she said, and she *did* smile, "as though we will be trying to keep our distance from each other."

"True," he said.

His eyes seemed very dark suddenly, and she could have moved against him and twined her arms about his neck, but instead she raised her hands to the top button of a long line of them down the front of her riding habit and opened it, and then the next. But he nudged her hands away and did the rest of it himself, slowly and deliberately, his fingers brushing against the flesh beneath, until he could push the heavy velvet fabric of the garment off her shoulders and arms, and it fell into folds about her feet.

His eyes moved down her body, and he took her by the shoulders and sat her back on the chair before going down on one knee to pull off her riding boots one at a time and then her stockings. His hands, fingers spread wide, moved hard up the outsides of her calves and thighs and under her shift and upward until she raised her arms and he removed the one remaining garment and tossed it aside. She wore no stays. She almost never did. To her they were a contrivance from hell.

He stood and drew her to her feet again to remove the pins from her hair and send them tinkling to the floor while her hair tumbled over her shoulders and down her back in what was surely a disheveled mess.

"You used to go riding with your hair down and flowing out behind you," he said. "I used to think there was nothing in the animal kingdom to match you for wild grace and beauty."

It was still a shock that he had noticed her in those days, and that he had looked upon her not with disapproval but with admiration and perhaps some of the yearning she had felt for him.

He drew her into his arms and kissed her with more intensity than before. And her longing for him, her naked body against his fully clothed body, was even more unbearable than before.

"Beautiful beyond belief." His voice was low. "And very, very desirable."

"Devlin."

He sat on the sofa then to pull off his boots and stockings and stood to shrug out of his coat and waistcoat and draw his shirt off over his head. He unbuttoned his breeches and lowered them with his drawers and stepped out of them. And he reached for her again.

Her first impression was that she was looking at a warrior. A battle-hardened soldier, his body surely a map of all the engagements in which he had fought, from the firmly honed muscles of thighs, chest, and arms to the numerous scars and even what must have been a bullet wound below his left shoulder, really not far from his heart.

Her second impression was that he was indeed extremely attractive. He was Devlin. He had carried her heart with him when he left her that long-ago morning. He had taken it onto those battlefields with him even if she had known nothing of the battles and he had known nothing of the extra burden he carried within him, next to his own heart.

"Devlin," she said again, her voice a mere murmur of sound.

"Come." He laid her on the sofa and sat on the edge of it while moving his hands and then his mouth over her, knowing *exactly* what they were doing, arousing magic and need and that unbearable ache of longing, and making her very aware of her own inadequacy and inexperience. He was giving her the enjoyment he had promised. He was not making love to her.

Oh, but he *was*.

It was just a term—*making love. Being in love.* Just words. She raised one arm and ran her fingers through his hair and then down over his bare chest with its hard muscles and light dusting of dark hair.

This was *happening*. She did not care what he called it, or what she called it for that matter. This just *was*, and ah, Devlin. *Ah, my love.* And it did not matter that he was experienced while she was not. They were here to *enjoy*—his word. And to *love*—her word. She let passion bubble through her and out of her. She reached for him with both arms, drew him down to her, kissed him openmouthed, murmured words into his mouth, unaware that she was speaking Welsh. *"Rwy'n dy garu di"*—I love you.

He moved to lie fully over her and on top of her. He pushed her legs apart as he came, and she wrapped them about his. His weight robbed her of breath, but it did not matter. His hands came beneath her and held her steady and he came inside her with one firm, swift thrust and did not stop until he was deep. Pain and shock robbed her for a moment of what breath was left her, but it lasted *only* a moment before glory burst in to replace it. They were together. At last. Ah, at long, long last. He was Devlin. Dear God, he was *Devlin*.

He held inside her, rocking his hips slightly against hers, and he raised his head to gaze again into her eyes. His still looked very dark in the dimness of the curtained summerhouse. And still hard and inscrutable. Ah, he was locked so tight inside himself.

"I am sorry to have hurt you," he murmured. *Not* the words of a hard man.

She shook her head. "I want it all," she told him.

He moved then, withdrawing from her, thrusting inward again, and repeating the motions over and over until there was a rhythm to the enjoyment he gave, accompanied by the sounds of their labored breathing and the wetness of their coupling. Gwyneth was unable to move freely on the sofa beneath his weight, but she moved her hips and matched his rhythm with the clenching and unclenching of inner muscles. And there was surely nothing lovelier, more intimate, more raw, more nearly painful in this life. And nothing with which to compare it. His rhythm quickened and deepened after a long, wonderful while, and the yearning for something just beyond her grasp grew until it threatened to drive her to madness. Until suddenly he stopped moving and held hard inside her, and she reached and reached and . . .

And cried out.

And shattered into . . . Not into a million pieces as she had expected, but into that nameless something for which she had yearned. Something that was sweet and quiet and so . . . But the word would not come, and really, did it matter? Some things just simply *were*. She wrapped an arm about his shoulders and ran her fingers into his hair. And deep inside her she felt the hot gush of his release.

I t had not felt like enjoyment at all. It had left him feeling closer to tears than he had been since . . . when? He could not remember a time. Though yes, he could. When he had been saying goodbye to Stephanie and Owen and Philippa. And then Gwyneth. On the last Sunday in July six years ago. When he had still been human—and a virgin.

In all the time since then he had associated sex with pleasure and relaxation and . . . comfort. *Not*, damn it all to hell, with tears and a soreness in his chest and a strong urge to run away. From everyone and everything until there was no farther to run. Except . . . Ah, except that he could not run from the one person he most wished to escape. He could not run from himself.

Or from Gwyneth either.

There will be no way back if we make love now. Not for either of us, he had told her earlier. They had made love. Or had sexual relations, anyway. There was no way back. Not for her. Not for him.

They dressed in silence, their backs to each other. He waited for her to retrieve enough hairpins from the floor to pin up her hair relatively neatly. He pulled back the curtains. And then they were walking side by side back along the alley. The air felt chill and welcome after the warmth of the summerhouse.

"What did you say?" he asked her, though he was not sure he wanted to know.

"Say?"

"It sounded like Welsh," he said.

"Oh," she said. "It was nothing."

He looked sidelong at her. Gwyneth. He *knew* her now. He knew the feel of her, skin to skin, the heat of her, the taste and smell of her. And she was his, for the rest of their lives. He still could not remember why, since he needed a wife and the sooner the better, he had decided his wife would definitely not be Gwyneth Rhys. Perhaps because he would be hers for the rest of their lives, and that would be no bargain for her.

"It was *rwy'n dy garu di*," she told him.

He waited.

"I love you," she said. "That is the translation."

There were a few clouds overhead. Were they going to lose the sunshine?

"The thing is, Devlin," she said, "that I meant it then, though I did not know I was going to say it aloud, and I mean it now. And I am not going to pretend to stop feeling it or living it just because you cannot. I will try not to say it too often, because that will annoy you, just as it would annoy me if you were to keep on telling me that you cannot love me. You promised a partnership. Let us be partners, then, working together for the good of both of us, but separate persons, entitled to our own thoughts and feelings and inclinations."

"That," he said, "sounds fair enough."

. . . but separate persons.

"But faithful to each other," he said.

"Yes," she said. "Of course."

"Of course," he said softly. "But what would you do if I ever were unfaithful, Gwyneth? Would you turn a blind eye, provided I was discreet about it?"

"No," she said. "I would make a fuss. A very noisy and very public one. I would shout it from the rooftops."

"And leave me?" They had stopped walking and turned toward each other. Her head was thrown back and her eyes were flashing. "With our children?"

"Think again," she said. "Ravenswood is to be my home. It will be my children's home. *You* would be the one to leave, my lord Stratton. I would toss all your clothes and personal belongings out onto the lawn. I hope it would be raining in a great downpour."

He felt closer to laughter than he had felt since he did not know when. There was a gleam of answering laughter in her eyes.

But it was not funny. Very few women reacted as Gwyneth said she would. His mother had not. And, according to his mother, women were brought up to endure, to put personal dignity and unquestioning loyalty to their men above all else.

"I will not be a comfortable wife, Devlin," she said.

"Alas," he said, "your warning has come too late."

"I like it when you almost smile," she said, turning to walk in the direction of the stables.

He fell into step beside her. "I cannot be the man you want, Gwyneth," he said. "The one with whom you tumbled into love when you were no more than a girl. But I will never dishonor you."

She smiled dazzlingly at him a minute or two later. "I am very proud of myself," she said. "I have never made a proposal of marriage before. Nor, therefore, have I ever had one accepted before."

"I thought it was a betrothal resumption suggestion, not a proposal," he said. "I accepted on that understanding. After I have spoken with Sir Ifor, I will make you a formal offer of marriage and you will give me your answer. A man must be allowed *some* pride."

"Very well," she said, laughter in her voice. "But I will expect something extraordinary." She turned her head to look very directly into his eyes, and he was almost knocked back on his heels, so much did she resemble the old Gwyneth. Just as though all the cobwebs of six years had been blown away without a trace. She *did* know what she was getting herself into, though. It did not matter to her.

Before they reached the stable yard, someone called to them from the front of the house. It was Stephanie, waving her arms and hurrying along beside the east wing toward them, a spring in her step, her face beaming. She was on her way home from choir practice, Devlin guessed. Miss Field always released her from the schoolroom on choir days, since music was considered an important part of her education.

"Sir Ifor told me you had ridden here after luncheon to call upon Mama, Gwyneth," she cried when she was close. "I was hoping you would still be here. You have to come to the maypole dancing practice tomorrow evening."

That still happened, did it? Devlin wondered if it was still held inside Sidney Johnson's large barn every second week. And was Steph a regular attendee?

"I always love watching the dancers, Stephanie," Gwyneth said. "But I have never felt any burning desire to be a regular part of the group."

"But it is not to be maypole dancing tomorrow," Stephanie explained. "Mr. Johnson went to London this past spring and spent a couple of months there. Edwina Rutledge was there too, for her second Season in a row. She apparently came to an understanding with the second son of a viscount while she was there. She says he is very handsome, though I have not seen him myself. They both know how to *waltz*—Mr. Johnson and Edwina, that is. And they are going to teach the steps tomorrow evening to anyone who wants to learn them. The orchestra members who are going to play at the assembly on Friday will be there too. There are going to be waltzes *at the assembly.*"

"The waltz?" Gwyneth said. "I saw it performed when I was in London for a few weeks two summers ago. It was very new then, and many people considered it quite scandalous."

"Why?" Devlin asked, frowning. He had heard of the waltz, but he had never seen it performed. Was not a dance a dance?

"It is not danced in lines or sets," Stephanie told him. "The two partners dance exclusively with each other."

"I thought it was the most romantic dance I had ever seen," Gwyneth said. "Unfortunately there is a silly rule in tonnish circles in London that one may not perform it in public until one has been approved by a patroness of Almack's Club."

"You must go tomorrow, Gwyneth," Stephanie said before turning an eager face to her brother. "And you must go too, Devlin. Please, *please*? Mama will surely say no if I am the only one who wants to go. Owen will just pull a gargoyle face if I ask *him*, and Pippa never goes *anywhere*, and Ben never goes anywhere he cannot take Joy too. So it has to be you. *Please*, Dev? You will be able to waltz at the assembly, and as the sort-of host, it is probably important that you do. No one will dance with me, of course, even though Mama has said I may go, but just to see other people waltzing will be *wonderful*."

Why did Pippa not go anywhere? *Why* would no one dance with Stephanie?

The two partners dance exclusively with each other.

I thought it was the most romantic dance I had ever seen.

His sister was gazing at him with anxious eyes. And oh, how could he say no to her? How could he watch disappointment wipe that eager expression from her face? Had he really just been telling Gwyneth that he was incapable of love?

"I will take you, Steph," he said. "I will learn the steps with you. But *only* so that I may waltz with you at the assembly. If a mere brother will be an acceptable partner, that is."

"Oh, Dev," she cried, and her eyes brightened with pleasure— or was it with tears? "Will you go too, Gwyneth? I was hoping, as a last resort, to be allowed to go with *you* if I could not persuade anyone here to take me."

"I did learn the steps when I was in London," Gwyneth admitted. "I was not allowed to dance them at a ball, though, and it was all of two years ago anyway. So yes, maybe I will go to Sidney Johnson's tomorrow evening so I can remind myself. Perhaps I will even find a partner at the assembly."

"Oh, *of course* you will," Stephanie said, beaming. "Devlin will waltz with you if no one else asks, though I am sure *everyone* will. You will, will you not, Dev? There will surely be more than one waltz."

"I will waltz with Devlin if he asks me," Gwyneth said, and laughed—a sound of pure mischief.

Stephanie looked from one to the other of them, a suddenly arrested look on her face. "Where have you been?" she asked.

"Strolling along the poplar walk," he told her. "And sitting in the summerhouse for a while."

"Oh," she said, looking between them again. "Well. I must go inside and find Mama. I will see you tomorrow evening, then, Gwyneth." And she hurried off back to the front of the house.

Devlin gazed after her, a frown on his face. "The old Pippa would have been first in line to learn a new dance," he said. "She would have been fairly bouncing in excited anticipation of an upcoming assembly. I have not heard her mention this one, and Steph does not seem to think it even worthwhile to ask her to go to Johnson's tomorrow evening. She really is very badly hurt."

"Yes," Gwyneth said.

"And Stephanie is convinced no one will dance with her," he said. "She *is* only fifteen, of course. But I seem to recall that young people her age were allowed to attend the assemblies and did. Is it her weight, Gwyneth?"

"I think that may be part of it," she said.

"But she eats very sparingly," he told her.

"I have an aunt in Wales," she said, "who insists that she has only to *look* at food and her waist expands by two inches. For some people weight seems to have little to do with the amount they eat. But women often feel unattractive if they believe themselves to be fat. Or they are made to feel unattractive. Perhaps men too, though not quite as much, I believe."

"I adore her, Gwyneth," he said with a sigh—and realized that he really was allowing his tight grip upon his emotions to be loosened. But, God damn it all to hell, Pippa and Steph were his *sisters*.

"I know," she said.

"I am going to need your help," he said before realizing that he *never* needed anyone's help. But she was going to be his countess and . . . Ah, hell.

"I know," she said again.

The stable yard was deserted, Ben and Owen having long gone about their business elsewhere. Gwyneth and Devlin went inside the stables, where he saddled her horse, despite her insistence that she could do it herself, while a groom was saddling his. She put on her hat, and Devlin helped her to the sidesaddle and handed up her whip.

They rode to Cartref in a silence that was unexpectedly companionable. Though he did feel close to exhaustion, Devlin realized. It was something he had felt a number of times since his return to Ravenswood. It was surprising, really. His life on the Peninsula had been far busier, less comfortable, more strenuous, more dangerous. More full of anxiety. Though that one word gave him pause. There were numerous types of anxiety. It had been almost exclusively a physical thing when he was there. Here it was something quite different. Emotion was battering at him from all sides here, and the effort to keep it outside of himself while at the same time dealing with the issues that had caused it was fatiguing.

"Would it be better if I talked to your father tomorrow instead of now?" he asked her. "If I merely made an appointment with him today?"

"Yes," she said. "I want to have time to be looking my best for this extraordinary marriage proposal you have promised me. And I think I want you to be looking your best too. And Dad will have time to prepare some impressive speech to deliver to you. Mam will have time to rise to the occasion. Idris will have time to hide."

Was she *laughing* at him? He looked across at her. She *was*. Though not so much laughing in derision, perhaps, as bubbling with exuberance. She was feeling *happy*, God help him. And God help *her*. She was looking like the Gwyneth he remembered, though now he was the cause of that look and was not merely observing it from afar.

"I believe *extraordinary* was your word," he said.

"But I will insist upon a very special marriage proposal," she told him.

He wondered for a startled moment if she would always *tease* him. If she would refuse to allow him to take himself too seriously.

"Sir Ifor and Lady Rhys will not drive me from the door with a broom when I arrive tomorrow, then?" he asked her.

"Devlin," she said. "You are *the Earl of Stratton*. Besides which, they do not want me on their hands all their lives. Yet they know that is precisely what will happen if you will not take me."

"Ah," he said. And he felt close to laughter again. And so tired he hardly knew how to remain upright in the saddle.

CHAPTER TWENTY-TWO

I think," Sir Ifor Rhys said the following morning as he spread his linen napkin over his lap and prepared to tackle the breakfast his butler had laid before him, "Stratton is coming here this morning because he wants to beg me to let him sing solo with the choir at our Christmas concert. I will have to think of an answer to give him before he gets here. How does one say *no* very, very tactfully?"

"Da-ad!" Gwyneth protested, though she could not help laughing too.

"Number sixteen," Idris murmured.

"What was that, Idris?" Lady Rhys asked.

"Number sixteen," he said more loudly. "Dad made fifteen guesses last night. I counted. The only one he *still* has not thought of is the obvious one."

"Which is?" his mother said.

"He is coming to ask Dad if it is all right for him to be my friend again now that he has the earldom and all that," Idris said.

"But how *do* I say no tactfully?" his father asked. "No one can tell me that."

"Sometimes," Lady Rhys said, "I think I must be living in a madhouse. Gwyneth, cariad, they are just teasing. But one as bad the other they are, your father and your brother."

"Not quite, Mam," Gwyneth said, eyeing her plate with its single poached egg and slice of buttered toast and wondering if she was going to be able to eat even that modest breakfast. "Dad has made sixteen suggestions if Idris is to be believed, while Idris has made only one. Here is another from me. Perhaps Devlin is coming to ask Dad for my hand in marriage, though he does not need to since I am practically *middle-aged*."

"Number eighteen," Idris said. "And a worthy contribution, Gwyn. It is what men do regardless of necessity, though. It is what I did a few weeks ago even though Eluned is twenty-six. Luckily for me, Mr. Howell said yes after giving me a good grilling."

"How do I say *no* tactfully?" Sir Ifor asked again.

"Enough now, Ifor," his wife said. "Can't you see that Gwyneth is off her food this morning?"

Which was ridiculous really, Gwyneth thought. Yesterday *she* had proposed marriage to *Devlin*. She had actually *lain* with him, and then had lain awake half the night reliving every moment. Today was just a formality. But that was the point, was it not? Yesterday had been just the two of them, while today their families would be involved, and tomorrow . . . Well, tomorrow they would be borne inexorably onward to their wedding and their married life together. The thought had a strangely calming effect. For she had no doubts, no regrets, no second or third thoughts. No illusions either.

"I am not, Mam," she said, and took a bite of her toast. "I was just so fascinated by the conversation that I forgot to eat."

Idris patted the back of her hand.

"You have not lived with me here for twenty-four years, Gwyn," her father said, "without discovering that I like to tease. I will be ready for your young man when he comes here at ten o'clock, and I will treat him gently. It is more than thirty years since I went on a similar errand to beg your grandfather for your mother's hand, but I have not forgotten how my legs were shaking in my boots and my heart was booming in my chest and I was afraid I might forget my own name."

Gwyneth dipped her toast in the yolk of her egg and took another bite.

"But I do hope you know what you are doing, Gwyn," her father said, all signs of joking and teasing gone. "I know you took us all by surprise years ago when it turned out it was Devlin you had fallen for, not Nicholas. And then you got all caught up in that nasty situation and ended up with a broken heart. I will not belittle what you went through, but you *were* just eighteen. There is a difference between eighteen and twenty-four. A difference in maturity. Now he is back and he is a different man. There is hardness in him, maybe worse. And he has problems galore to deal with. Ravenswood has not been a happy place since that night. All of them have suffered and are still suffering, from what I see. Poor things. I feel particularly for the young ones. Their world was rocked. That is what you will be going into, Gwyn, if you say yes. Your mam and I are feeling sick at heart."

"We agreed not to say anything, though, Ifor," Lady Rhys said. "About our feelings, I mean. This is not about us, Gwyneth. It is about *you*. And when you love a man, you see him differently from the way other people do. It is not as though Dad and I dislike Devlin. We do not. We did hope with Aled, though . . . But no. No, no. Forget I mentioned his name. You see with the heart. We have been looking with the head for someone who will make you happy. The head has nothing to do with such decisions."

"*Nothing*, Bronwyn?" Sir Ifor asked.

"Nothing," she said. "My father warned me that if I married you, it would be forever music, music, music with you—and *this* from a Welshman, I might add. I knew it, but I married you anyway because my heart would not listen to my head. And I have never for a single moment been sorry. Well, perhaps once or twice when the pew in church has got to feel very hard after I have been sitting on it for a couple of hours at a stretch."

"Gwyn," Idris said, setting his napkin beside his empty plate and pushing his chair back as he got to his feet. "The quality of this conversation is rapidly deteriorating. Are you finished?"

She was surprised to see when she looked down at her plate that indeed she was. Both egg and toast were gone. She got to her feet too.

"You must not let your hearts ache over me, Mam and Dad," she said. "There is a great deal of goodness at the core of all the darkness you see in Devlin. And kindness. And love. And, if nothing else, he has a strong sense of duty and responsibility. And a deep commitment to doing what is truthful and right."

"And you hope to bring all that out of him?" her mother asked. "Oh, Gwyn."

"No," she told her mother. "As Dad just said, I am twenty-four, not eighteen. I am not going to try drawing anything out of him. I am just going to love him. And be his countess."

Idris walked upstairs with her and they stopped outside the door to her room. "All right, are you, Gwyn?" he asked.

Idris would never press questions or advice on her. He was not much of a talker at all, in fact. He never had been. He was neither a very sociable nor a greatly ambitious man. He had always wanted to work their father's large farm, and that was what he was doing—

with steady competence and hard work, out in the fields and in the barns and in the office at the back of the house. He was a kind and considerate man, and Eluned was one of the most fortunate women in the world to be marrying him. Or so believed Idris's fond sister.

It had been his signature question throughout her life—*all right, are you, Gwyn?* Or some variant of those words. Letting her know that he understood whatever turmoil life had led her into, that he was there to listen or to help if she needed him, though she had rarely taken him up on his offer. But he was a rock of stability in her life, someone she knew without any doubt she could lean upon if there was the need.

"Oh, I say," he said when she stepped forward into arms he opened reflexively, and hugged him tightly. He patted her back.

"I am *very* all right," she assured him. "Go and read your letter. I know you must be itching to do so."

He was holding it now. It had sat beside his plate through breakfast. A fat-looking letter addressed to him in Eluned's hand.

"Well," he said, "if you are sure you are *very* all right, Gwyn, I will."

He turned away to his own room, and Gwyneth let herself into hers. It was time to get ready. A comical thought, perhaps, when she was already dressed perfectly decently. And it was not even nine o'clock yet.

D evlin was feeling a bit like a Bond Street beau as he drove himself to Cartref in his curricle. He had somehow slipped out of Ravenswood without being seen by any of the family, though why he should have done his best to contrive it that way he did not quite know. They were going to find out soon enough. He just hoped they would not expect him to behave like a besotted bridegroom. And that they would not expect any great fuss over wedding plans.

And, he thought as he descended from the curricle and tossed the ribbons to one of Sir Ifor's grooms, who had been hovering in the vicinity and was clearly expecting him, he hoped the Rhyses would not expect it either. Or Gwyneth. Good God, he hoped not. But anything was possible with the volatile Welsh.

The front door was open, and the Rhys butler, behaving with far greater formality than he ever had when Devlin had used to come here as a boy, conducted him to the small parlor, announced him to Sir Ifor, the lone occupant of the room, and closed the door quietly behind him.

Sir Ifor Rhys did not prolong the interview. He did not deliver any speech, though Devlin had anticipated one. Nor did he allow Devlin to deliver the speech he had prepared with meticulous care.

"I doubt you can tell me anything about yourself that I do not already know," Sir Ifor said. "And as for your record as an officer with the Ninety-Fifth Rifles, it would seem that since you recently sold out rather than being kicked out, you must have done your duty on the Peninsula just as you always did it here and doubtless intend to do again now you are back. I fully expect that you will do your duty to my daughter too if you marry her. There is only one thing I want to know, Devlin, before I give you my blessing as well as the permission you do not need. No, two things. Would you always, from the moment of your marriage until death takes one or other of you, remain faithful to Gwyneth? And look in my eyes as you answer, if you please."

"Not from the day of my marriage, sir," Devlin told him, looking directly at him. "From the moment she says yes to my proposal. Which will be this morning, I hope."

Sir Ifor nodded. "And do you love her?" he asked. "Look in my eyes, please."

"I will honor and keep her," Devlin said carefully. "I will work in partnership with her and respect her words and opinions equally with my own. I will raise children with her, if we are so blessed, and with her I will teach them the meaning of family and respect and loyalty and honesty. I will never belittle her or deliberately embarrass her. I will never expect her to do anything simply because I have decreed that she should. As for love, sir, I can only answer honestly. I do not trust it. I am not sure I even believe in it—not romantic love anyway. It is just a word, and to my knowledge no one has ever been able to define it."

Sir Ifor nodded slowly, his lips pursed. "I think maybe you just did, son," he said. "All except for the magic." His eyes twinkled suddenly. "But maybe you have to be Welsh to experience that. We do like to live on the edge of our emotions, we Welsh."

"Dragons?" Devlin said.

"Those too. Red ones." Sir Ifor laughed and stepped closer to slap a hand on Devlin's shoulder and squeeze. "I'll go and fetch Gwyn. She is in the drawing room with her mam. You have my blessing."

And he left Devlin alone in the parlor. Where she had been writing her letter at the escritoire last week. Where she had played her harp for him and sung her melancholy folk songs, one in English, one in Welsh. He had not understood a word of the latter, but it had not mattered. The harp music, her voice, what had been behind her voice, had spoken straight to his heart. The heart he did not possess.

She stepped into the room alone a few moments later, and they stood looking at each other. She was wearing a pale green dress of fine wool, high to the neck, with long sleeves snug to her arms and a narrow skirt falling from just beneath her bosom and molding to her curves. It was totally unadorned. It did not need to be, though. She had a perfect body whether she was clothed, as she was now, or whether she was naked, as she had been in the summerhouse yesterday. Her dark hair was shining and smooth over her ears and the crown of her head and confined in a knot high at the back of her head, with wisps of ringlets feathering over her ears and neck.

"I think," she said, "that on your way home from the Peninsula you must have gone to London and stopped off on Bond Street."

"A bit overdone?" he asked her.

"You look gorgeous," she said.

"You have stolen my words," he told her. "Now how do I describe you?"

"A bit underdone?" she suggested.

"You are beautiful," he said. "Your father has given his blessing, Gwyneth. Does your mother give hers too?"

She nodded. "They are a bit anxious," she said. "But they know that for me it is you or no one. And they trust my judgment."

He marveled. She had never really known him, just as he had never really known her. They had had no relationship even though they had loved each other for years. There had been only that one day, and only parts even of that, because his wretched sense of duty had sent him to mingle with other guests at the fete too, when all he had wanted was to be with her. There had been that one set of dances at the ball and the one chaste kiss and a brief confession of their mutual love out on the hill. There had been some sort of marriage proposal—he could no longer remember just what he had said. Yet her feelings for him had apparently remained constant . . . *they know that for me it is you or no one.*

We like to live on the edge of our emotions, we Welsh.

It was more than just emotion with Gwyneth, though. There was the solid weight of something else behind it.

Love, perhaps?

"Come." He held out a hand for hers, and she came farther into the room and took it. He closed his fingers firmly about her hand and did the ridiculous thing—not quite the extraordinary gesture she had asked for, perhaps, but surely what was expected of him. He went down on one knee and looked up at her.

"Gwyneth," he said, "will you do me the great honor of marrying me?" He seemed to remember as he stopped speaking that he had had a whole speech both planned and memorized. Unfortunately, he could not recall any of it.

She was smiling down at him, her eyes twinkling with merriment and—with tears.

"Yes, Devlin," she said. "I will."

"I will do my best," he told her, "not to break your heart again." And good God, where had *that* come from? It had not been part of the speech.

She bent a little closer. "It was at least severely bruised," she told him. "But I have discovered again since your return what I always knew about you. You are incapable of breaking my heart completely because it is not in your nature to be a scoundrel. It was not you but circumstances that caused all the pain at that time. Now, today, I am utterly happy. I do expect to be happy with you. But it is not a burden I am putting upon you. I have no illusions. I do not expect more than you can give. What you can give will be enough."

Ah, devil take it, Gwyneth. How could there *not* be a burden in what she was saying? But there was not. She was not a fragile female who depended for every moment of happiness upon the man who had the charge of her. He would not even *have* the charge of her except in the strictest of legal and ecclesiastical senses. She was a person in her own right. She had a very strong sense of self. She had come to Ravenswood yesterday, had she not, to propose marriage to him? Or a betrothal resumption agreement.

"There you go again," she said. "Almost smiling."

He got to his feet and drew her into his arms. He held her close and rocked her. "Thank you, Gwyneth," he said. "I am the most fortunate of men. And why is it that I can seem to talk only in platitudes this morning?"

"Because often platitudes hold great truth," she said.

He held her away from him. "I have no ring to give you yet," he said. "Or any other jewels, though I might, I suppose, have picked something from the family heirlooms, which will be yours anyway after we marry. For your lifetime, at least. I did not bring any of them. Doing so would not have been a personal gesture. I did bring you gifts, though." He turned to the table beside her harp, where he had set two folded linen handkerchiefs before she arrived. But now he felt very foolish indeed and wished he had said nothing, or at least not called them *gifts*. It would have been better to have come empty-handed.

"Oh," she said. "*Did* you?"

"You will laugh," he warned her as he spread his hand beneath one of the handkerchiefs and turned toward her.

"Laughter is good," she told him, and leaned over his hand as he carefully turned back the fold of linen that covered four leaves, one still summer green, the others varying shades of autumn.

"I found them early this morning," he told her. "They were out on the back side of the pavilion hill. Beneath our tree."

Good God, it had seemed such a good idea at the time. But why would she want to be reminded of that night? And with a few half-dead leaves.

She was running a finger very lightly over them. She lifted her face to smile at him. "I asked for something extraordinary," she said.

"Four leaves?"

"Yes," she said. "I will press them and keep them all my life."

"You said spring always comes," he said. "We were standing on the bridge outside the village."

"Yes," she said.

He set the handkerchief down very carefully and picked up the other, which he set on her upturned hand. "I found these last evening beside the bridge," he told her. "But they seemed incomplete in themselves. So I went out to our tree this morning."

She opened the linen folds and looked down at the smooth, flat oval stone inside, resting on a pure yellow leaf. On the stone he had painted words. *"Spring always comes."*

He heard her swallow. And gulp down what could only be a sob. She looked up into his face, smiling, her eyes swimming with tears. "You could try forever, for the rest of our lives," she said. "You could spend a fortune on me. But you could never give me more precious gifts than these today, Devlin."

Which was the daftest thing he had heard in a long time. Maybe ever. But . . . What if it was true? What if spring always *did* come? As well as all the other seasons, one by one?

There was a tap on the door as she set down her second gift beside the other one. The door opened a crack.

"The champagne will be flat if you do not come soon," Lady Rhys said without actually poking her head around the door.

"Oh, Mam," Gwyneth cried. "Do come and see my treasures."

And Devlin had to endure the excruciating embarrassment of having both Lady Rhys and Sir Ifor bending over the table to look at five leaves and a painted stone while Gwyneth told them the story behind the objects.

A fabulously wealthy earl comes a-courting, he thought with an inward grimace and a fervent wish that the floor would open up and swallow him whole.

And to make matters worse, Idris had come to drape himself against the doorframe in order to wink at Devlin and then grin at him.

"Well, son," Sir Ifor said, straightening up and beaming at his future son-in-law. "It would seem that after all you must have some Welsh blood running in your veins."

B oth the gig and the carriage were on the terrace outside the front doors when Devlin returned home after drinking two glasses of champagne and eating one slice of each type of cake— five of them—Lady Rhys had baked herself that morning because she had not been able to decide which would be best to celebrate the occasion.

"Mr. Ellis is taking Miss Ellis to play with the children of Mr. and Mrs. Cox," the groom who was with the gig explained when Devlin looked at him with raised eyebrows. "I believe the younger Miss Cox has a birthday today."

Devlin nodded. The carriage, he knew, would be taking his mother and Owen to his grandparents' home for a farewell tea in honor of Owen's leaving for his first term at Oxford next week. He had been hoping they would have left already.

But they were all gathered in the hall, he discovered when he stepped inside after relinquishing his curricle to another groom, who had seen him returning and come hurrying from the stables. Stephanie was there too. She must have been granted another after-noon off from the schoolroom.

Nobody looked to be in any great hurry to leave, though. Joy, wearing one of the frilly dresses Ben had bought for her in London, an improbably large bow anchored somehow among her very short curls, was running about the hall on her little legs, giggling and occasionally shrieking. Owen was in hot pursuit, though for all the length of his legs, he never quite caught up with her but clapped his hands on empty air and roared every time he came close and missed.

"She will be tossing her luncheon if you keep that up," Ben was telling Owen while everyone else looked on, seemingly quite undismayed by the noise and the delay in their departure.

Then Owen spotted Devlin and stopped abruptly. "I say," he said. "Where are *you* off to, Dev, looking like a Bond Street beau?"

"Are you coming to Grandmama and Grandpapa's with us?" Stephanie asked.

Well. The moment was upon him, it seemed.

"I have just come from Cartref," he told them.

"Cartref?" Owen stared at him in some puzzlement. "To see Idris? Looking like that?"

"Gwyneth was here yesterday, Owen," Ben said. "Remember?"

Owen looked Devlin over again. "You went *courting*, Dev?"

"Gwyneth has done me the honor of accepting my marriage proposal," Devlin said curtly.

"I *knew* it," Stephanie cried, clasping her hands to her bosom. "I came and told you yesterday, did I not, Mama?"

"You did," their mother said. "But I did not believe you, Stephanie. I thought she was going to marry that tall, good-looking Welshman. Devlin?"

"No, Mama," he said. "She is going to marry me."

"It is the scar that did it, Mother," Ben said. "It makes Dev irresistible to the ladies. They forget the tall, good-looking ones as soon as they set eyes on that face of his."

"Devlin," his mother said again, and came toward him, her hands extended for his. "I did not see it coming, I must admit, just as I did not . . . last time." Her voice faltered for a moment. "I am very happy for you. Gwyneth will be a fine countess and a good wife."

"I know, Mama," he said, setting his hands in hers. "It was important that I choose someone who can do the job well."

Stephanie was coming toward him too, her eyes shining, her arms spread wide. Owen was grinning at him. Ben was smiling. And then—

"Look out!" Owen roared, and he dived for a large urn, which was swaying ominously on its base, and Ben swept Joy to safety and blew softly in her ear and murmured low words to comfort her loud wails of protest at having her game so rudely interrupted.

Devlin stepped back out onto the terrace five minutes later to see them all on their way. By that time his mother had learned from him that the wedding date had been set for December 23, the day before the children's Christmas party at the hall. She had announced her intention of calling upon Lady Rhys tomorrow to discuss the wedding, and Devlin had informed her that Lady Rhys intended to call upon *her* tomorrow for the same purpose.

"They can wave to each other in passing," Owen said.

Devlin had a growing suspicion that his idea of a wedding was not going to fit with anyone else's, particularly those of the three women at the heart of it all—Gwyneth, her mother, and his. His determination not to be an autocrat was to be put to an early test, it seemed.

"Devlin," Lady Rhys had said to him when he had made the remark over champagne and cakes that neither she nor his mother need worry their heads over the wedding since it was surely going to be a small and quiet event. "Weddings are for the mothers of the bride and groom. It is you and Gwyneth who need not worry your heads over the details."

Gwyneth, far from backing him up, had merely twinkled at him and said nothing.

"Is Pippa not going with you?" he asked now as Owen was handing their mother and then Stephanie into the carriage.

"No," Owen said.

"Where is she?" Devlin asked.

But his brother merely shrugged and disappeared inside the carriage.

He was going to have to go and find her, Devlin decided. This was disturbing. It must not be allowed to continue. Perhaps for everyone else the memory of how she had been at the age of fifteen had faded. For him it was as vivid as if it had been yesterday.

As it happened he did not even have to start searching. He glanced upward as he was climbing the steps back to the front doors and there she was, sitting inside the turret room at the front of the west wing, her back to him. She had not even watched her family leaving, then. He frowned as he continued on his way to his own room. He changed quickly out of his finery and went up to the turret.

CHAPTER TWENTY-THREE

The room had been warmed by the sunlight shining through all the windows, just as the summerhouse had been yesterday. Philippa was sitting on one of the deep sofas, nothing in her hands and no book or needlework or anything else beside her—just as there had been nothing out in the rose arbor a week or so ago. She turned her head only long enough to see who had come to intrude upon her privacy, and then continued gazing through the window in the direction of the lake. Devlin went to stand by the window and looked out in the same direction, though he was careful not to obstruct her view.

"I have just come back from Cartref," he said after the silence had stretched for a minute or two. "I have offered for Gwyneth and she has accepted me. I need a countess." He needed a *wife*, though he did not try to explain to himself what the difference between the two was exactly.

"I am happy for you," she said after a few beats more of silence. "I used to assume that it would be Nicholas who would marry

Gwyneth, but I think maybe it was always you with her. We heard that she was very . . . sad after you left. It was she you were with that night."

"Yes," he said.

The lake looked cold as a small cloud moved over the sun, and he wondered if it would freeze over this winter. It did sometimes. They used to go out there and skate and slide though they had always been warned to stay close to the edges, where the ice would be thickest. He and Nick—rarely Ben—had always tested those limits, of course, when there were no adults close enough to bellow at them. Or save them if they fell through. Children were often idiots by their very nature.

"You are not planning to come with Steph and me this evening?" he asked her. "She wants to learn to waltz."

"No," she said.

"Are you going to the assembly tomorrow evening?" he asked.

"I suppose I will feel obliged to," she said, "since it is to be held here. Though you are not going to be the master of ceremonies, are you?"

"No," he said. "That will be Colonel Wexford. It will not be in any way a family affair. There are committees and subcommittees planning everything. I think people are enjoying themselves. I believe they felt a bit stifled for a number of years." They had felt *condescended* to, he thought, though he did not say that aloud.

"Yes," she said. "Maybe I will *not* go."

Could this young woman with the lackluster voice possibly be the vivid, eager girl who had twirled for his approval in her new gown on the evening of that fete? The girl who had sparkled on the brink of womanhood and all it promised in the way of parties and beaux and courtship and marriage?

"There were men out on the Peninsula, both officers and those in the ranks, who cracked," he said. "Not for any discernible reason, in most cases. Some would rave, out of their minds, and have to be hauled away in a straitjacket. A few ran away. Others curled up on the ground somewhere, covered their heads with their arms, and refused to move. Any threat of punishment—a whipping for the enlisted men, court-martial in the case of the officers—had no effect whatsoever. There were no physicians for them as there were for those who were physically wounded. Their condition was considered shameful. It was attributed to cowardice or to weakness—to not being a *man*."

He paused for a moment, but she said nothing.

"They were just the few, though," he said. "There were many more who did not crack but were nevertheless shattered inside. They kept the facade of manliness. They carried on. They followed orders and did their work. They often showed great courage and were held up as an example to other men. But inside they were lost and empty. Even if there had been physicians able to treat their condition, they would not have appealed to them for help. They would have denied that anything was wrong at all."

Still the silence from behind him. Though no, she had broken it.

"As you did," she said. "And do."

Oh, hell! That was not where he had been leading. He spun around to look at her. She was gazing back, her eyes large and blue in a pale face.

"Pippa," he said. "You were fifteen. I think it was probably worse for you than for anyone else. Nicholas was able to set out for the new life he had been preparing for. Owen and Stephanie were still children. Mama was an adult with an adult's experience and maturity. You were betwixt and between any of those things. Our father was no longer a rock upon which to lean. Ben and I were both gone. I see in you what I saw in some of my men. Differently manifested, of course, but essentially the same thing. Life has been too much for you, and there has been no one to give you the help and support you need."

She was half smiling at him, a ghastly expression. She shrugged but said nothing.

"What in particular has overwhelmed you?" he asked. "Or is there no single thing?" There probably was not. And that was the whole trouble. With his men it had often been the guns. The incessant pounding of the cannons.

"Nothing," she said. "I adored Papa and then I hated him and then he died. And I was glad."

The brevity of her story, especially its ending, chilled his already cold heart. But she was not finished.

"You think you were the only one who noticed," she said, "because you were out there on the hill when he was there with that woman. I saw her at church and a few times in the village before that day, and I was afraid because she looked at him and he looked at her, mere darting glances, but I felt like vomiting though I did not understand why. And *that* day. She came to dance about the maypole while Steph and I were there and then you. And Papa stood and watched and laughed and clapped for everyone. But she was dancing for *him*, and he was there to watch *her*. Oh, they were very careful all day long, and I tried *very* hard just to enjoy myself and not even see them. I hoped and hoped she would not return for the ball, but she did, and he *danced* with her, smiling and laughing as he always did, though it was *different* with her. And then after supper he took her outside and did not come back and every minute as I danced I felt like screaming and screaming without stopping. And then . . . it started. I heard raised voices and realized one of them was yours. I knew before you came close what must have happened, and I was *glad* that at last someone else had found out and was doing something about it."

He bent over her and took her ice-cold hands in his. He drew her to her feet and into his arms. He held her tight. Good God! Where had this come from? She had *noticed* even before the day of the fete and been uneasy? Just as he had noticed when he was in London with his father? But she had denied it, just as he had, and bottled it all up inside. That bright-eyed, happy girl. Was there no end to the illusion under which this family had lived?

"The one thing we could never seem to do," he said, "was speak truth to one another. Yet we considered ourselves the happiest family in the world. Pippa! This has to change. For all of us."

"I was *glad*," she said again, her voice muffled against his neck-cloth. "But I left it all to you to deal with. I did not say anything—at the time, or when everyone was in the drawing room afterward, or when you were leaving. I only begged you to talk to Mama. I was horrified that *you* were the one being sent away and that Ben was going with you. But I did not *say* anything. I did not have the c-c-courage."

"Pippa," he murmured against the top of her head. "You were *fifteen*. For God's sake, you were still just a child. You were absolutely, totally *innocent*."

"I never did say anything," she said. "Not until— Oh, never mind. I never said anything."

"Until . . . ?" he said. "Tell me. Please tell me, Pippa."

She tipped back her head to look up at him.

"Until after the Marquess of Roath came here with James Rutledge for Easter the year I turned eighteen," she said. "The year I was supposed to go to London with Mama and Papa and make my come-out. He came with James to watch a practice of the maypole dancing. I had joined the group after my birthday. Mr. Johnson suggested that the marquess partner me for one dance, and James nudged him and waggled his eyebrows and told him I was *Lady* Philippa, daughter of the Earl of Stratton. The marquess looked at him as though he had just had the shock of his life and said something like 'Stratton? I do not dance with soiled goods, Jim.' And they both left. I heard he went away altogether a day or two after."

Devlin gazed back at her, thunderstruck. "And no one *did* anything?" he asked her. "No one knocked his teeth down his throat? He was allowed just to . . . *leave*?"

"They were in a group of men," she said. "I was in a group of women, all chatting and laughing. They did not know I had heard. I probably would not have done if he had not been so handsome and I had not fallen in love with him as soon as he walked into the barn with James. I was so . . . *ridiculous* in those days."

"What you were," he told her, "was a young lady of eighteen, ripe for love and courtship. Oh, Pippa."

They were still standing, his arms about her. She drew away then and sat back down on the sofa. He sat beside her and took one of her hands in both of his.

"A few days after that," she said, "a letter came from Ben telling us of the terrible wound to your face, though he was able to assure us that you would live and would not be blind. And I turned on Papa when I was alone with him after he had read the letter aloud at the breakfast table and told him it was all his fault. That *everything* was. It all came bursting out of me. At last. He did not deny it but actually *apologized* to me. I told him it was to *you* he ought to be apologizing. And to Ben. And he promised that he would write to both of you. I do not suppose he did, though. I told him also, and I told Mama, that I would not be going to London, that I did not want to go. And I remained firm on that even though Mama pleaded with me. What if *he* was there in London? I would not have been able to bear it. And what if everyone else there had called me *soiled goods*? Then, only days after he and Mama came home from London, where they had gone without me, Papa died. Without saying goodbye. Without giving us a chance to say goodbye to him. At least we were able to say goodbye to you and Ben. Not that it made any difference."

She turned her face into his shoulder and wept with noisy, gulping sobs.

Soiled goods. Those words stuck in Devlin's mind. *Soiled goods.* Pippa. *His sister, that bright, happy little star.* Who the devil was this Marquess of Roath? If he was still alive, *why* was he still living?

When her sobs had subsided to a few forlorn hiccups, he set a handkerchief in her hand, and she turned away to dry her eyes and blow her nose. Clouds had moved over the whole of the sky, Devlin saw, though he did not believe they were rain clouds.

"Pippa," he said. "I do not know who the Marquess of Roath is, though I *will* find out. And he will be dealt with. But . . . Are you going to allow an ill-mannered man of such low character to blight the whole of your life?"

She turned back to look at him. Her face was marred by red blotches. Her eyes were bloodshot. But the beauty that had already been blooming six years ago was still there. It just needed something to light and animate it.

"I am *not* going to London, if that is what you are about to suggest," she told him. "I do not *want* a Season."

Which was answer enough, he supposed.

"Has anyone else here ever insulted you?" he asked her. "James Rutledge, for example? Sid Johnson?"

She thought about it. "No," she admitted. "Edwina Rutledge said James sent Lord Roath away, but that was absurd. You do not send away a *marquess*, the heir to a *duke*, do you, when you are yourself only the second son of a baron and he has deigned to be your friend?"

"Yet it is just what I would expect James Rutledge to do," he told her, "from what I remember of him. I would also expect that Sid Johnson would have had a word or two to say on the matter." She had *not*, he noticed, mentioned that birthday party from which she had been excluded, according to Steph. Perhaps that had been in the early days, when everyone would still have been embarrassed about the scene Devlin had made at the fete.

"What you must remember, Pippa," he said, "is that you are the elder daughter of an earl. And the elder sister of an earl. Twenty-one years old and dazzlingly eligible. Do you think perhaps it is time you learned to waltz? At Sid Johnson's this evening, where the lesson will replace the maypole dancing practice?"

It was no solution to what ailed her, of course. He did not *know* the solution, if there was one. But sometimes all one could do to cope with life was get oneself upright and set one foot before the other to begin the journey.

Her chin lifted an inch and she gazed at him for a long while. "What time are we leaving?" she asked.

By the time the carriage from Ravenswood stopped outside Cartref to convey her to Sidney Johnson's, Gwyneth was feeling very glad of the chance to escape from home for a while. Not that she was ungrateful for the outpouring of love after Devlin took his leave, but sometimes her normally placid mother became overwhelmed by emotion, and everyone around her became the victim of it. Her father had prudently withdrawn to the church to look for some music he was convinced must be there because it was not at home. Idris had disappeared to attend to some unspecified farm business. That had left Gwyneth.

How on earth, her mother had asked her, were they going to solve the problem of Sir Ifor playing the organ at her wedding *and* at the same time escorting Gwyneth into the church as father of the bride? Oh, and *did* Gwyneth think there was any merit in suggesting a double wedding with Idris and Eluned? She answered her own question in the negative before Gwyneth could open her mouth, however, for of course Marged, Eluned's mother, already had that wedding more than half planned. And *could* there be any mother anywhere happier than she, Bronwyn Rhys, was today, with *two* children getting married and the hope of grandchildren in the foreseeable future? And *would* they have Adeline Proctor make Gwyneth's wedding clothes, or should they go up to London to a more fashionable dressmaker? But would Adeline be hurt if they did that? Oh, and *what* did Gwyneth think about . . .

And so it had gone on through the day until Gwyneth was ready to suggest to Devlin that they elope. Not that she was seriously considering it, of course, but really . . .

Sir Ifor had come home with ideas for music he would play at the wedding. He had discussed the matter at great length with himself and confirmed his own ideas and contradicted them quite indiscriminately while Idris had winked at his sister and was probably relieved that his own upcoming nuptials were no longer the full focus of his parents' attention. Today, anyway.

Gwyneth was very glad, then, that she was to have an unexpected evening out, and on her own, without her family. She was going to brush up on the steps of the waltz, and tomorrow evening she was going to dance it at the assembly—with Devlin. She did not know how that would be accomplished, but it would be. He might even think it was all his own suggestion. Oh, she did know *something* about feminine wiles.

She could hardly wait to see him again.

But it was Stephanie who came hurrying down the steps of the carriage, her arms spread wide. "I am so *happy*," she cried, folding Gwyneth in her embrace and squeezing tight. "One story at least is to have a happy ending. *May* Pippa and I be bridesmaids? It is quite all right if you say no. Who would want me anyway? But I thought I would ask. Oh, Lady Rhys. And Sir Ifor. Is this not exciting news?" She rushed up to the door to hug them too.

Gwyneth laughed while Devlin came down the steps to hand her into the carriage. She set her hand in his and felt unabashed happiness. His eyebrows were raised.

"Need I say," he said, "that my choice of bride has met with the approval of my sister?"

"I would never have guessed if you had not told me," she said.

She was surprised when she climbed into the carriage to find the elder of his sisters sitting there. "Oh," she said. "Hello, Philippa."

"I am happy for you too," Philippa said, her voice quiet and grave. "I agree with Steph. Sometimes stories really do have happy endings."

"Thank you." Gwyneth smiled at her. "Are we all going to take the assembly by storm tomorrow night with our waltzing skills?"

"Yes," Philippa said. "We are."

She looked very like Devlin at that moment, Gwyneth thought in some surprise. Serious, hard-jawed, a whole lot shut up inside herself. Gwyneth could not recall seeing her at an assembly during the past couple of years or so. She did not attend many other social functions either, except the occasional tea, when she sat beside her mother and participated very little in the general conversation. She seemed to have distanced herself from all the friends of her own age she had once had, both male and female. Yet she could not have made friends elsewhere to compensate for their loss. She had never had a come-out Season in London despite the fact that she was *Lady* Philippa Ware, daughter of an earl.

It was a very damaged family into which she was about to marry, Gwyneth thought as she took a seat facing Philippa and made room for Devlin beside her. Stephanie climbed back in and sat beside her sister. It was a daunting task she had set herself. Though perhaps not, for she had not really set any task at all. She had decided simply to love and to do it quite openly and without apology. If she was being quite disastrously naïve, then so be it.

Devlin surprised her by taking her hand in his and setting it palm down on his thigh. He kept his hand over it. She wondered if he had done it deliberately. To convince his sisters that he felt *some* regard for his betrothed, perhaps? It did not matter. She turned her head to smile at his stern profile.

Sidney Johnson and Edwina Rutledge had already taught the steps of the waltz to the regular group of maypole dancers. They were all dressed as though for a performance, Devlin was interested to find, the women in their pastel-shaded dresses, the men with shirts to match. The garlands for the women's hair were absent, however. Sidney and Edwina awaited the raw recruits, of whom there were several. And no one was to be without an experienced partner. Sidney had it all organized.

Sidney himself would dance with Philippa, Bradley Danver (Owen's friend from the vicarage) with Stephanie, Clarence Ware with Gwyneth. It was all very satisfactory to Devlin, who had agreed to come as an escort for Stephanie and had been prepared to dance with her if absolutely necessary. It was not going to be necessary, however. Everyone had a partner. Except—

"I need not be a wallflower after all, Sidney," Sally Holland, looking pretty in her peach dress, called. "Here is the Earl of Stratton cowering in the corner. Looking ferociously *military*. I can remember you once dancing about the maypole, Devlin, and doing a creditable job of it. Waltzing is far less intimidating. I will show you."

He was given no choice in the matter. She was standing before him, the blacksmith's daughter, grinning mischievously, her hand outstretched for his. The other couples had all turned their heads to watch. The fiddlers were waiting to begin playing. Devlin, it seemed, was about to learn to waltz. Which did not bode well for tomorrow evening. *Nothing* boded well for tomorrow evening actually. Gwyneth had informed him on the way here that Sir Ifor had sent a notice of their betrothal to the morning papers in London and expected that it would be published on Monday. He had also had a word with Colonel Wexford in Boscombe this afternoon, sworn him to secrecy, and asked him in his capacity as master of ceremonies at the assembly to make the announcement there.

Not that Devlin wanted to keep the betrothal a secret. Why would he? He and Gwyneth would be married soon, and actually it could not be soon enough for him. And they would be married here. It was just that . . . Well. He did not want anyone to know. Sometimes trying to understand oneself was impossible.

And they waltzed. All of them, without any great mishap except for a few minor collisions and a screech from someone as her partner trod upon her foot. They performed the steps slowly and deliberately at first, and moved more or less in a straight line along Sidney's barn, then with a bit more speed and a few modest twirls. Then the music was added, and they all somehow kept their feet beneath them and followed the rhythm and kept in time with both the fiddles and their partners. There was laughter, some of it a little self-conscious, as no one was accustomed to dancing face-to-face with the same partner for more than a few seconds at a time. And there was enjoyment.

Devlin wondered if he would waltz with Gwyneth at the assembly tomorrow. She knew the steps already, of course, and danced them gracefully with his cousin, who was smiling appreciatively at her and saying something to make her laugh.

And was that . . . *jealousy* he was feeling? *Possessiveness?*

"I tried to persuade Cameron to come tonight," Sally said. "But he seems to think waltzing would be an affront to his manhood. Men can be *so* foolish. I am glad you are more enlightened. And may I say how happy I am you have brought Stephanie and even persuaded Philippa to come? Maybe things will improve at Ravenswood now you are home. And maybe I talk too much. I am sorry."

"I will do my best," he told her.

It was all he *could* do.

Philippa was smiling uncertainly at Sidney Johnson. Stephanie was giggling. Gwyneth was laughing.

Maybe . . .

Maybe there really was such a thing as happiness. Even if only in brief bursts.

CHAPTER TWENTY-FOUR

B en was leaning on the paddock fence. Owen was exercising his horse again inside.

"He could take the horse out into the park for a ride," Ben said when Devlin came up beside him. "But he does not want to admit he is terrified."

"For the horse?" Devlin said. "I suppose he was riding neck or nothing when it happened."

"Yes, I suppose," Ben agreed. "But he was seventeen. What would you expect? He has learned a lesson, anyway, and both he and the horse have survived it."

Owen was not going to take the horse with him when he left for Oxford on Monday. He was probably feeling more melancholy over that than over saying goodbye to his family. He was accustomed to going off to school for a few months at a time, after all.

"You are looking a bit naked this morning," Devlin said. "No knapsack? No Joy?"

"Her aunts have her up in the west turret room," Ben said.

"They are pointing out to her every landmark within a five-mile radius, and she is pointing too and supplying the commentary, though no one can understand more than one word in ten of it. I believe I have an ingenious daughter who is inventing her own language. They had started a game before I left that involved a great deal of squealing and jumping on and off furniture. When I asked if I should stay, Joy had one perfectly intelligible word for me: *Go.* So I went."

"Feeling aggrieved and neglected." Devlin grinned at him.

"I have to find a good nurse for her before we move home," Ben said. "Someone of mature years who will play with her when I cannot. I have to get her a dog too. And probably a cat. What has happened to Pippa?"

"She learned to waltz last evening," Devlin told him.

"Ah," Ben said. "Well, that explains everything."

"Ben?" Devlin squinted off to the hills in the distance. "Was there ever a letter from . . . our father?"

"Yes," his brother said. "Once."

"Addressed to you?"

"One to me," Ben said. "One to you. Less than two months later news came that he was dead."

Devlin did not ask why his letter had not been delivered to him. He would have refused to take it or have torn it to shreds, its seal unbroken. But he was feeling a bit now as though there were an iron band about his chest, squeezing off the beating of his heart.

"What did you do with mine?" he asked.

"Kept it. It is in a drawer in my room with all the others," Ben told him.

Despite everything else he had needed to carry, especially after the death of his wife, Ben had kept all the old letters?

"I'll go and fetch it," Ben said, and turned away.

Owen rode up to the fence for a chat. He was excited at the prospect of university life, he admitted when Devlin asked.

"But I will look forward to Christmas too," Owen told his brother. "More than I usually do. I am awfully glad you are marrying Gwyneth, Dev. I was very afraid you were going to choose someone horribly high in the instep who would be an excellent countess and a ghastly sister-in-law. You were gone from the breakfast table when I read Nick's letter, weren't you? He is still in Paris, but he is hoping to get leave to come home for Christmas. He does not know about the wedding, of course. It will be jolly if he is here, won't it?"

"It will," Devlin agreed, and he immediately wondered how Nick would feel about Gwyneth marrying *him*.

"I'll try to live up to your example, Dev," Owen was saying. "Though it's a bit of a daunting example, you must admit. You came down from Oxford with a degree and top marks in everything."

"You do not have to live up to my example or anyone else's, Owen," Devlin told him. "And I am serious about this. You do not have to compare yourself with *anyone*, within the family or outside it. If there are some things about me or about Ben or Nick that you find admirable, well and good. It is always fine to have someone to look up to. But you can never *be* that person. You can only be yourself if you wish to be happy. That is your job as you grow up—in your case, as you come closer to completing the process during the next few years. Find who *you* are. Being Owen Ware is only part of the story. Find what *you* want to do with your life, not what I or Mama or Grandpapa believe would suit you and make you worthy of your heritage. I will always . . . I will always hold you dear as my brother, no matter what."

Good God. Where was it coming from? He hardly recognized himself these days. He was talking about Owen completing the process of growing up. When was it going to happen for him? Just a few months ago he would have said it was over and complete. But did one *ever* grow up?

Owen was grinning. "I was wondering what sort of speech you would deliver as head of the family before I left," he said. "I did not expect this. Are you going to deliver the stuffy version on Monday morning just before I hop into the post chaise?"

"The stuffiest one I can devise," Devlin said. "The one about studying your head off in some lonely garret and avoiding wine, women, and companions who would lead you astray. Ah."

Ben had returned and was holding out a bundle of letters neatly tied together with string. "I'll ride with you along the bridle path to the lake and back if you wish," Ben said, addressing Owen. "He looks a bit restless in that confined space."

"I am a bit restless too," Owen admitted. "Come on, then."

Devlin took the bundle and strode away. He went into the courtyard to sit in the rose arbor even though the wind, hardly discernible outside, was swirling a bit in there. He took shelter on the seat behind one of the trellises and pulled up the collar of his coat.

There were letters from Idris, his uncle George, Philippa, Owen, and Stephanie, all of them addressed either just to him or to both him and Ben. All of them were dated in Ben's hand—the date of their arrival, that was. Most of them had been sent during the first year. His father's letter was on top. The date Ben had recorded, more than two years ago, was actually about one week after his father's death and two weeks before the letters from the solicitor and his mother had been forced upon him.

The urge was strong to destroy the lot of them, to light the fire in his private sitting room and toss the bundle into the heart of it and watch it burn. The past was over and done with. There was no point in raking it up. Life was proceeding, and really it was not so bad. Not nearly as bad as he had anticipated, though he did wish that managing a home and a family and an earldom could be a little more like managing men under his command during a military campaign.

He knew he would not do it, though. Burn the letters unread, that was. The past must be looked into if he was to know any real peace. He took his father's letter from the bundle before tying the string about the rest of the letters again lest the wind catch them and send them fluttering in all directions. He broke the seal on the letter and then gazed off to one corner of the courtyard. Where a fortune-teller had once set up her tent and made some disturbing predictions. Some very accurate ones too, he thought, remembering for the first time in a long while.

He opened his letter and swallowed at the familiarity of the bold handwriting. His father's hand had written that. To him. Just a few weeks before his death.

Dear Devlin, he had written.

I am not sure I have ever quite understood you, my son, but I do know you. I know you well enough to understand that you are inflexible in your hostility to me and rejection of me. I know you well enough too to guess that you blame yourself for the suffering your public outburst caused your mother and your brothers and sisters and grandparents. The whole embarrassment of that incident was, of course, not your fault at all. You were right and I was wrong. I have always been a restless man and, yes, a weak man. Even the pleasures I had carved out for myself over the years since my marriage began to seem not quite exciting enough and I tried something more daring and dangerous. I got caught and suffered the consequences. You were right to expose me.

I do not ask your forgiveness, Devlin. What I did, and the consequences to my family, including you—perhaps especially you—are all on my head. I regret the consequences, but am not sure I would change much if I could go back. I choose to be honest, you see, since honesty is what you understand—and you are right. You may not believe me when I tell you that I love your mother and that I love each of my children. It is the truth, but I cannot expect you to believe me just because I say it.

I ask only that you forgive yourself, Devlin. For doing what was right. For telling the truth and not compromising with it as most people do. I am proud of you even though I know my approval can mean little if anything to you. Or my love. Forgive yourself.

I am assured by those who have heard from Ben that you are a superb military officer. I would have expected no less even though I never anticipated that life for you.

Be kind to yourself, my son.

And his signature, large, bold, unapologetic.

Stratton.

What did he *feel*? Devlin asked himself after he had folded the letter with care and restored it to the bundle, the string enclosing all the letters. In the realm of emotion, which had been dead to him for so long and had been slowly returning only recently, how did he *feel*?

He felt only one thing. Nothing extreme. Only a sort of grudging respect. His father, imperfect and aware of his own shortcomings, had ultimately been honest with the son who had seen through the illusion to the heart of a weak man. It was a bit ghastly to think of his father that way, but it was the truth. A weak man but not an evil one. One whose weaknesses were not to be in any way excused—as he himself had admitted. But he had not been abject with apology. He had not been like so many people whose sins had found them out—dreadfully sorry, but perhaps more regretful that they had been caught than of what they had done. His father did not regret his infidelities and had admitted as much to his son. But he *was* sorry for the suffering he had caused. He had claimed to love his family. *Had* he loved them? But perhaps love was no more a pure thing than evil was. Perhaps it was possible to love and to do harm to the loved one at the same time.

There was a faint headache knocking at his temples as he got to his feet and went indoors to drop off the letters in his room and fetch his greatcoat.

S ir Ifor had driven Lady Rhys to Ravenswood to call upon the Countess of Stratton. He did not go inside with her, however, weddings, in his opinion, being the exclusive preserve of the women most nearly concerned—except for the music, of course, and the important, heart-pounding matter of escorting one's daughter into the church and along the nave in order to relinquish her into the permanent care of her chosen bridegroom.

Gwyneth did not stay either, since she had been assured that wedding preparations were for mothers, and the bride did not have to worry her head over them. Her father let her off outside Mrs. Proctor's, where she was to pick up a gown that had been altered slightly for the assembly this evening. She stayed for half an hour since the former Audrey Proctor, now Audrey Davies, was visiting her mother and had her two-year-old son with her. She was within weeks of a second confinement and was lamenting the fact that it seemed forever since she had last seen her knees.

Gwyneth was a bit surprised not to hear organ music when she arrived at the church afterward, but her father was indeed in there. He was standing behind the organ bench, in conversation with the vicar and Devlin. Two of them merely smiled and raised their hands in acknowledgment of her arrival, but Devlin came striding along the nave toward her. He took her by surprise when he was close by, taking both her hands in his and squeezing them tightly.

"If your father could choose all the music he feels would be perfect for the occasion," he told her, "our wedding would be six hours long."

He was hurting her hands.

"I have spoken to the vicar about the banns," he said. "They will not need to be called just yet, of course."

She might be walking out of here with eight squashed or cracked or broken fingers. Her thumbs seemed relatively safe. His eyes were more intense than usual. Was this just wedding nerves? Second thoughts?

"I have just been walking around the churchyard," he told her.
Ah.

"I do beg your pardon," he said suddenly. He looked down at their hands and loosened his hold on hers, but only in order to set them palm to palm and clasp his own more loosely about them. He kept his eyes on their hands.

"I think," he said, his voice abrupt, his words clipped, "I have always demanded perfection of myself yet have been aware every single day that I have not achieved it. I have expected it of others and occasionally been colossally disappointed when I have not found it. I thought we were a perfect family with a perfect father and mother. But because I knew myself to be imperfect, I never felt worthy of them all. I . . . Dash it all, Gwyneth, did you have to come through the door just when you did?"

If they had not been standing in full view of her father and the Reverend Danver, she would have leaned forward and kissed him—on the mouth. "I have been collecting my gown for this evening from Mrs. Proctor," she said. "Having a skilled dressmaker so close to home makes a person very lazy. I am not an enthusiastic needle-woman, Devlin. You ought to know that about me before it is too late. I am not perfect."

"Neither was he," he said curtly. "Indeed, he was very *im*per-fect. He hurt us all. Irretrievably. But there was goodness in him too. I always believed that he had an affection for me and that he was proud of me even though I was not the son he had hoped for. I always believed he loved us *all*, including my mother. Including Ben. I could not have been entirely wrong despite the secret life he was living behind all our backs. Children know when someone is . . . not perfectly genuine. Especially someone close to them. A parent. I adored him and wanted more than anything else in the world to be like him. Funny, that, when I also always wanted to be perfect. I am going to let him go, Gwyneth. I will remember what was good about him and accept what was not. He was human. We are a bewildering species."

Did he realize that darkness was emptying out of him? Slowly but very surely. Not that she was either expecting miracles or de-pending upon them. He was as he was, and she would live with him and love him until her dying day—or his—and be ever thankful for the idealist she was about to marry, the man who wanted to be perfect but was gradually learning the painful lesson that nobody was. That nothing was. Everyone and everything was in a state of becoming. That was the terror and the wonder of life.

"We are," she said. A bewildering species, that was. "Are we not wonderful?"

He tipped his head to one side and frowned.

The other two men were descending upon them. The vicar, beaming, held out a hand for Gwyneth's.

"I am delighted indeed at your news, Gwyneth," he said. "It will be my great pleasure to officiate at the nuptial service of the Earl of Stratton and the daughter of Sir Ifor Rhys. Goodness me, how grand that sounds! My chest will be puffed out for at least a month afterward. I will be the envy of all my fellow clergymen in this county and beyond. But be assured that my lips are sealed until after the official announcement, which will be this evening at the assembly, I believe?"

He patted the hand she had placed in his and continued to beam at her while she smiled back. Devlin continued to frown.

D id I do the right thing?" Devlin asked his mother later that evening. "I intended to take a burden off your shoulders. But perhaps you feel you have been displaced. I ought to have consulted you first."

"No," she said. "You did the right thing. Planning something even as relatively simple as a village assembly is a large undertaking, and I am done with that part of my life. I could not be more delighted that you will be marrying soon. Before Christmas. Gwyneth will be a good countess. I will be happy to relinquish my duties to her."

"She will never have to do them alone, Mama," he said. "We will work together, she and I. And if any of the work becomes too onerous, then I will simply hire people to do it."

"I know you will." She inhaled audibly and let the breath out before continuing. "Devlin, he was not a bad man, your father."

"No," he agreed. "He was not." Though he had wronged her terribly. Had she loved him? It was not really his business, though. If there were demons from her past—and there *must* be—then they were his mother's to deal with.

Devlin and his mother were standing in the doorway of the ballroom, her arm drawn through his. As usual, they were somewhat early for the assembly itself, but curiosity had got the better of them even though they were not in any way responsible for seeing to it that everything was ready, that nothing had been forgotten.

They had not been near the ballroom all day, though Devlin had been aware of much coming and going in the vicinity of the west wing. Committees had apparently spawned other committees during the past week, and everything had been taken care of, rather to the consternation of Richards and Mrs. Padgett, the butler and housekeeper here. Everything had been cleaned and polished and shined without any of the Ravenswood staff being involved. Fresh candles had been set in the grand candelabra overhead and in the wall sconces. Autumn flowers and leaves and ribbons and bows in varying shades of orange and peach and brown had sprouted everywhere, including about three sides of the orchestra dais.

Long tables had been set up all along the far wall, making inaccessible all the French windows except the one in the middle. The tables had been covered with white linen cloths and an impressive display of smaller cloths that had been fashioned of fine lace—probably made and loaned by various women of the neighborhood. Mrs. Berry, the landlady from the inn, with the help of the food-serving committee, was covering them with heaping plates of dainties, both savory and sweet, and not forgetting piles of plates and linen napkins. They all looked happy, even excited. Jim Berry's tavern—a banner had been erected with those exact words written on it in large letters—had been set up just inside the open doors into the dining room. Jim himself, puffed out with pride, it seemed to Devlin, was behind a long bar, organizing his bottles and taps and glasses, while the eager-looking liquor-serving committee prepared to help him pour drinks and pull mugs of ale and carry around trays of drinks to those who did not wish to crowd the bar. The musicians were tuning their instruments, watched by Colonel Wexford, who, as master of ceremonies, looked as though he considered himself personally responsible for the music.

The old assemblies, organized by his mother and staffed by the family's servants, had always been perfection itself. But . . . there was a certain spirit here tonight that was difficult to define but was unmistakable. It was a community coming together to share their efforts and enjoy one another.

Guests were beginning to arrive, and two members of the ticket committee were taking their places behind a small table just inside the doors. One of them, a son of one of Devlin's tenant farmers, grinned cheerily at him and held out a hand.

"Tickets, please, my lord," he said.

Devlin produced two and handed them over while the young man laughed. He led his mother inside.

"I think," she said, "that maybe this is going to be a happier place, Devlin."

Happier than *what*?

She did not explain. She did not need to. She felt it too, then.

CHAPTER TWENTY-FIVE

G wyneth did not always attend the village assemblies, partly because they were so crowded and finding enough space in which to dance was difficult, and partly because conversation was nearly impossible as everyone tried to talk above everyone else and the musicians tried to play loudly enough to be heard above the din. There really had seemed little point in attending.

Tonight, however, she was enjoying herself enormously. There was space in which to dance, and the high ceiling and the sheer size of the ballroom absorbed enough sound that conversation was possible without the speaker having to bellow or the listeners having to cup hands about their ears. Tonight she was enjoying the assembly because everyone else was too, and enjoyment was infectious. No one had complained several years ago when the Ravenswood ballroom was no longer available for the assemblies. Some claimed that the old assembly rooms were more cozy anyway, and others rejoiced because they had the assemblies back to themselves and really there was nothing to compare with Jim Berry's ale and Mrs. Berry's miniature sausage rolls and meat pasties.

Yet now, tonight, they had the best of both worlds—the spacious ballroom with all its architectural splendor *and* an entertainment they had organized for themselves and financed independently, without any interference from the earl. They also had Jim Berry's ale and Mrs. Berry's cooking, which seemed to have multiplied in both quantity and variety from her usual efforts.

More people than ever had come, drawn perhaps by the promise of more space, or perhaps by simple curiosity. By this time most of them had seen the Earl of Stratton since his return. A few had even spoken to him or been close enough to hear him speak to someone else. Almost all had been shocked by the changes in him. There was that nasty facial scar for one thing. But there was also a hardness, a darkness, a severity to him that had not been there before, though he had always been a serious young man. He had developed size and muscle since they saw him last too. He moved with a military firmness of stride and bearing. He was surely as different from his father as it was possible for a man to be—which, some whispered, was not a bad thing, though one could not help but like the poor late earl, who had always had a smile and a handshake and some jovial remark for everyone.

There was also something puzzling about the present earl, in the estimation of many villagers. For so far his behavior seemed somewhat at variance with his looks. He had opened the park on certain regular days of the week again for their leisure, for example. There was to be a Christmas ball again and a summer fete at Ravenswood. And there was this assembly, held in the ballroom again at his invitation, but *not* as a demonstration of the largesse of the lord of the manor. The earl had allowed them to do all the organizing themselves and all the financing too. Neither he nor his mother had interfered in the smallest of ways. There had even been a bet on about it at the tavern.

Gwyneth had heard all the talk and gossip during the week, for miraculously word of her betrothal had *not* leaked out and no one, therefore, felt it necessary to guard their tongue in her hearing. But tonight it would be announced officially, and tonight her happily-ever-after would begin. Not that there was really any such thing, of course. She was not ignorant enough to imagine there was. But sometimes surely one could be excused for dreaming that it was there just waiting to be grasped. No! That it was *here* and already in one's grasp. There *was* such a thing as happiness, and it would be silly not to enjoy it when one felt it rather than shy away from it for fear it would not last.

She was happy, and had been happy ever since she had realized out at the summerhouse that Devlin would marry her. Maybe she was being foolish, but there was room in life for foolishness too. Wisdom was not always the best guide to living.

She danced the opening set of country dances with Sidney Johnson, the second with James Rutledge. Devlin danced with Ariel Wexford and Barbara Rutledge. His brothers and sisters danced too, Gwyneth was happy to see, though Stephanie danced only the first set—with Idris. She wondered when the first waltz would be and whether there would be *only* one. She wondered when the announcement of her betrothal would be made. She wondered when Devlin would dance with her, for *surely he would*. Most of all, though, she relaxed into the pleasure of the evening and enjoyed herself. For tonight she was *happy*.

The announcement was made after the second set. Colonel Wexford climbed to the orchestra dais and called for silence. It did not come immediately. Most people were quite content to assume he was announcing the next set and were more interested in continuing their conversations than in hearing what the next dance was to be. He raised his arms. There were a few halfhearted shushing noises. And then he used his parade-ground voice and silence fell instantly, followed by a few titters of amusement, for the colonel was known as a soft-spoken, mild-mannered gentleman.

"I am fortunate indeed to have been invited to be master of ceremonies for this of all assemblies," he said. "I have a particularly happy and important announcement to make. It concerns the betrothal and imminent nuptials—before Christmas, actually, and right in our own village—of two young persons very well known to all of us here."

He had a sense of the dramatic. He paused, just long enough for a buzz of anticipation to swell and fall away to an even denser silence than before.

"Our own Miss Gwyneth Rhys, daughter of Sir Idris and Lady Rhys, is to be the bride," the colonel said, singling Gwyneth out among the crowd and nodding and smiling in her direction. "And an outstandingly lovely bride she will be too."

The buzz rose again, louder than before, but it was quickly shushed to silence.

"And the fortunate bridegroom-to-be who has won her hand and her heart," the colonel continued, "is our very own Devlin Ware, Earl of Stratton. I am sure—"

Very few people heard what he was sure about. Voices rose all around the ballroom. Everyone in Gwyneth's vicinity turned toward her. All seemed to be smiling. Several were speaking. A few squeezed her shoulder or tapped her arm. Someone whistled piercingly. Someone else began applauding and soon almost everyone joined in. There were a few more whistles. Gwyneth's cheeks were feeling decidedly hot. She was smiling, she realized. And laughing.

The orchestra played a decisive chord, and Colonel Wexford used his parade-ground voice again to restore a semblance of silence.

"Some of our young people, led by our maypole dancers," he said, "have been learning the steps of the waltz. You have never heard of it? Neither had I until a few days ago. It is a German dance that has been taking London by storm in the last couple of years. It is said by some to be scandalous. By others it is said to be the best invention since the wheel. I will leave you to be the judge. Two of those young people are our newly betrothed couple. If you will clear the floor enough to give them room, ladies and gentlemen, they will demonstrate it for us now. And if others wish to join them after a minute or two, we will be happy to see you as well. My lord Stratton?" He looked off to his left. "Your partner awaits you over there." He gestured in Gwyneth's direction.

What?

Oh dear. *Oh. Dear.*

The ballroom floor suddenly looked vast and empty as people moved back, and Devlin, perhaps with a flair for the dramatic himself, came striding across it, though he looked more like a soldier on his way to face a firing party than a man about to claim his partner for the next dance. His face was downright grim, his scar more noticeable than usual. He was also looking terribly handsome in a plain black evening coat and breeches, with silver embroidered waistcoat and crisp white linen and stockings.

Gwyneth smiled at him, and there was an audible sigh from those around them as he reached out a hand for hers and bowed over it.

"Was this your idea?" he murmured.

"No." She laughed.

"I am about to make a prize ass of myself," he told her. "I hope I do not also tread upon your feet, Gwyneth."

"I shall try not to scream," she assured him.

He led her out onto the alarmingly empty floor. There was more than one gasp from the onlookers as he set one hand behind her waist and she set a hand on his shoulder and he clasped her free hand and held it on a level with her other shoulder. There was a decorous space between them, but it seemed to Gwyneth that it sizzled and was really no space at all.

The orchestra played a chord, and a moment later Devlin and Gwyneth were waltzing.

She had waltzed with Clarence Ware last evening. He had danced correctly and competently but without any flair at all. Devlin had danced with Sally Holland, another of the maypole dancers, who had looked thoroughly at ease with the steps. Devlin had kept up with her, looking very grim as he did so. How he would lead without the assistance of a reasonably experienced partner was another matter.

But he did very well indeed.

He danced with his eyes upon Gwyneth's. But while it was quite obvious that at first neither really saw the other but concentrated upon remembering the steps from last evening and fitting them to the orchestra's playing, soon everything flowed naturally. She trusted him to lead her through the loops and twirls that made the waltz so exhilarating to dance and so lovely to watch, and he clearly trusted her to follow his lead without getting her feet all tangled up with his. How those four feet knew quite where to place themselves and how to stay in harmony with one another she did not know. But it was best not to think. If she did, she would surely think herself into one misstep after another.

They waltzed, and she knew herself to be surrounded by family and friends and neighbors, all of whom would sustain her through the rest of her life. They waltzed, and she knew herself to be in the arms of the man with whom she would live that life. Her own particular family would be at the heart of the larger family and community. She could hardly wait . . . But she did not have to wait. Her happiness was not a future thing. It was *now*. It was *here*.

She smiled at him, aware that they were no longer alone on the dance floor. Philippa was here too with Sidney Johnson, Stephanie with Bradley Danver. And there were others.

She smiled at Devlin, and he . . . Oh, other people watching him would doubtless talk afterward about how fierce and dour he had looked, so inappropriately for the occasion. But other people could not see into his eyes. Deep into them. She could, and from the depths of his darkness he smiled at her.

Fanciful thoughts?

Perhaps.

But she knew that he smiled.

"It is not a warm summer night, alas," he said just before the music ended. "You wore a warm cloak here?"

"I did," she said.

"Go and fetch it, then?" he said. "And meet me on the terrace outside?"

"Two minutes," she told him.

I t was not to be as easy as that, of course.

Far more than two minutes passed.

As soon as the music ended noise erupted in the form of applause and even cheers, to Devlin's great embarrassment. And the dance floor disappeared around them as people crowded onto it, most of them trying to cluster about him and Gwyneth. Many wanted to shake their hands and congratulate them and wish them well. Others wanted to commend them and the other dancers on the way they had waltzed. A few wished to thank Devlin for making the ballroom available for the assembly. Others wished to express their delight that Gwyneth would be remaining among them and would not after all be going off to live permanently in Wales. A surprising number wished to tell Devlin how happy they were that he had come home—and that he had chosen one of their own as his bride.

Colonel Wexford announced the next set and suggested that the gentlemen lead their partners out to form the lines for it. But since he chose not to use his military colonel's voice again to restore order and move things along, he was largely ignored for a good ten minutes.

But finally those who wished to dance again asserted themselves, and Gwyneth was able to slip away, followed soon after by Devlin. He met her on the terrace outside a couple of minutes after that, while music played merrily inside the ballroom and large numbers of people danced.

She was wearing a dark cloak, the wide hood drawn up over her head. The sky was clear and the moon and stars were doing their best to light up the darkness. But it was not nearly as bright a night as the one that must be in both their memories had been. And the moon was not in a position to be beaming across the lake.

"It is chilly," he said, taking her hand in his.

"The ballroom is stuffy," she said. "The air feels good."

He was warm inside his greatcoat. Through her glove her hand felt warm too.

They walked in silence to the pavilion hill and up it to stand before the stone pillars and look outward over the river and the village and the dark shape of the lake off to their right. He thought of his father inside the pavilion six years ago and felt a twinge of sadness that he was gone forever. That they had not said goodbye. He wondered briefly what had happened to the woman who had called herself Mrs. Shaw. He thought of all the women he had known on the Peninsula, with some of whom he had slept. He thought of Ben's mother.

"Do you think one grows more tolerant as one gets older?" he asked.

"Not necessarily," she said. "Only if one is the sort of person whose heart is always open."

Well. That did not apply to him, did it?

He had not brought her here, though, to stand on this spot, remembering, and gazing out upon a landscape that was not clearly visible despite the moonlight. These were not the memories he wished to arouse, perhaps even relive. He led her around the pavilion and down among the trees. It was quite dark down there, but they did not have far to go, and he had come here very recently to find the leaves he had wanted. He turned her and set her back to the tree where they had stood that night. He traced the shape of her face with his fingertips, pushing them beneath her hood. Her arms came about his waist and drew him closer.

He kissed her, teasing her lips with his own, the inside of her mouth with his tongue. He feathered kisses over her eyelids and temples, down over her cheeks to her jaw and chin, and he kissed her mouth again. She kissed him back, her mouth growing hotter, her breath more audible. His body was pressed to hers, all the heaviness of their clothing between them.

"I long to have a bed at your back," he murmured against her lips, "and nothing between us but skin."

"Mmm," she said.

He wanted to impregnate her and watch her womb swell. He wanted to make a family with her and raise them with her and play with them and enjoy them. He wanted . . .

He touched his forehead to hers. He had brought her here to say something to her.

"Gwyneth," he said. "I can say the words if it is important to you to hear them. I will even mean them in an impersonal sort of way. I just cannot *feel* them."

"It is important to me," she said, and he closed his eyes. Not that he could really see her anyway.

"I love you," he said. "I honor you and I . . . I want you. I want you as my countess and my companion and lover. I want to have children with you. I came here to remember. I did it on my own a day or two ago. But I needed you here with me. Not to remember *what* happened but how it *felt*. I can remember love. I can remember the euphoria and the hope and the . . . trust. I can remember being in love. I believe I can offer you almost all I could offer when I was able to love. And I will do my best. I will even remember to tell you from time to time that I love you, and I will not be lying. But I am not that young man any longer."

Was he sounding as idiotic as he felt? She was laughing softly, and her hands had found his face to cup it between her palms.

"Devlin," she said. "Love is not a *feeling*. It can reveal itself in feelings. It can bring intense happiness and the depths of despair. But it is *not* a feeling. It is not a belief or action either, though it can show itself in both. It is . . . But there I am stumped, of course, for the word itself means nothing, and what it represents cannot be confined within words at all. I did not even know you very well six years ago, even though I had been in love with you for at least six years before that. But I am very sure that you love far more deeply and compassionately now than you did then. Including me. You love me more now than you did then. If that word does not suit you, then let it go from your vocabulary. It is not important. It is just a word."

He gazed into her face, though he could see it only very dimly. As it seemed he could see everything. Very dimly. He had left behind the controlled, disciplined outlook upon life he had adopted in the Peninsula. It had worked well for him there, but it could not be applied here. Here he had felt all asea since his return, unable to go back, unwilling to go forward. *Afraid* to go forward. Unable to see anything clearly.

He sighed. "Unfortunately we need words," he said. "I am not sure we would do very well without them. I do love you, Gwyneth. I have the strange feeling you are the air I breathe. Help me?"

"Always." She brought his face closer and spoke against his lips. "*Always*, Devlin. But only if you will help me. Not in any dependent way, but in the way that we will always be better together than separate—two independent wholes choosing to act together. I love you too. I love you, I love you."

And she kissed him.

He relaxed his weight against her, pinning her to the tree. And he was aware of a greater darkness as a cloud must have moved across the face of the moon. But the darkness, he realized at the same moment, was *out there.* It was no longer *in here.* In here was all light and trust and eagerness to move forward with his life and his duties and responsibilities. Perhaps even with love.

"Say that phrase again," he said. "That Welsh phrase."

"*Rwy'n dy garu di?*" she asked.

"Yes," he said. "That one."

"*Rwy'n dy garu di,*" she said. *I love you.*

Chapter Twenty-Six

It very rarely snowed for Christmas. It might not happen this year, but it was certainly snowing on December 23. It was no major storm. The snow did not fall in such quantities that it blanketed the countryside and obliterated distinguishing features, including roads and ditches. It did not make travel impossible or even very dangerous provided one kept in mind that it could be a bit slippery underfoot if one was not paying attention to how one stepped.

It was, in fact, a white Christmas.

It turned bare branches to silver and white lace. It settled softly upon grass and rooftops. It looked, as it floated downward, like balls of cotton.

It was surely, Gwyneth thought as she gazed from the window of her bedchamber, every bride's dream of a perfect wedding day.

And the snow had been kind enough to come at just the right time. During the past few days guests had been traveling. Some of the Wares who lived a considerable distance from Ravenswood Hall had come to stay there. Her uncle and aunt and cousins had come from Wales to stay here, as well as Idris's Eluned with her parents and brother. Owen Ware had come home from Oxford yesterday, his first term at an end.

And Major Nicholas Ware had arrived at Ravenswood almost on his brother's heels. He was home on a month's leave.

The four brothers had come to Cartref last evening. It was not Devlin, however, who had swept Gwyneth off her feet and swung her in a full circle before setting her back down and grinning at her, his arms still about her.

"Gwyn!" Nicholas had said. "Just look at you. You are as lovely as ever. But no, that is not right. You are *lovelier*! But you are a faithless wench nonetheless. You could not wait any longer for me, could you, but had to go and betroth yourself to my own *brother*? You have shattered my heart."

And just look at him! He was broad chested and solid with muscle about the arms and thighs. His hair was shorter and blonder than it had used to be, his face more weathered. There was a hardness to his jaw and a military set to his shoulders. He looked fit and dangerous—and had entered the room with a slight limp. He was ten times more gorgeous than he had been as a boy, if that was possible. Gwyneth suspected he had even grown an inch or two.

"It was like this, Nick," she had said, patting the sides of his arms in an invitation to let her go. "I was twenty-four years old and a veritable spinster. When Devlin offered for me, I thought it might be my last chance, and I took it."

She had met Devlin's eyes beyond Nick's shoulder and known they were both remembering that actually *she* was the one who had asked *him*.

"Shall I challenge him to pistols at dawn?" Nicholas had asked her, still grinning—still with all the old charm. The attention of everyone in the room was riveted upon him. What, heaven help them all, must he look like in his scarlet regimentals?

"Better not," she had said, patting his arms a little more briskly. "I need him intact and in church at eleven tomorrow."

"And I need my two younger brothers intact and in the pew behind me on either side of our mother," Devlin had said. "Ben will be beside me, making sure I do not lose Gwyneth's ring. Or drop it."

"He does not trust us to do it, Nick," Owen had said.

Gwyneth had proceeded to introduce Nicholas and Owen to the Welsh contingent, and both had shaken hands and made conversation with all the famed Ware charm. Ben had smiled at everyone—he had already met them all—and Devlin had taken Gwyneth's hand in his, raised it to his lips, and looked at her with that smile no one else would see because it was in his eyes but not on the rest of his face.

Now it was their wedding day—at last! How could Idris and Eluned bear to wait until the spring? Their wedding was planned for March 1—St. David's Day—in Wales. "Drowning in daffodils, Gwyn," Idris had explained when she had asked why that particular date. "And reaffirming my Welsh identity. I was born there, remember. And once a Welshman, always a Welshman, as Dad is fond of saying."

It was her wedding day and there was snow coming down and it was Christmas. Almost Christmas, anyway. There would be a wedding breakfast at Ravenswood after the nuptials, and the children's party tomorrow afternoon, at which she would perform her first official duty as Countess of Stratton, helping organize games and hand out gifts. She would host the event with Devlin. Christmas Day would be celebrated with both families here at Cartref. And on Boxing Day there would be a grand Christmas ball at Ravenswood, the first in six years, at which she would perform her second official duty and stand with her husband in the receiving line to greet their guests.

Her husband!

Sometimes she still felt that she needed to pinch herself to be sure all this was real. But what if it was not? Would she want to know? She had not pinched herself yet.

This was a moment of quiet reflection. A short while ago her dressing room had been crowded as her maid dressed her hair and everyone else handed the maid needed items or commented upon how gorgeous Gwyneth looked and how clever it was of her to have aimed for simplicity when most brides wanted to look as fussy as it was possible to look.

"It is because Gwyneth is perfectly beautiful as she is and does not need adornment," her Welsh aunt had said, beaming at her.

"Do you think I will weep when Ifor brings her into the church?" Gwyneth's mother had asked.

"Yes!" everyone had chorused, except the maid, who had merely smiled.

"Well, I will not, then," her mother had said. "Just to spite you all. Come to see Gwyn, have you, Eluned? And your mam too? Yes, yes, we can make room for two more."

But they had not stayed after exclaiming over how lovely Gwyneth looked and kissing her cheek without touching any of her curls. It was time for them to leave for the church, and Eluned's father had told them they must be down within one minute or else.

"Mind you, Gwyneth," Eluned had said, laughing. "I have never yet discovered what exactly Dad means when he says *or else.* It is all meaningless bluster, I daresay."

It had been time for Gwyneth's aunt to go to church too. And time for the two bridesmaids to go and get ready themselves, especially as the third bridesmaid had just arrived. Gwyneth's maid had gone with them to help with their hair. Her mother had gone to make sure Sir Ifor was still in possession of his sanity, and an extra linen handkerchief in the event that she would need it herself.

And Gwyneth had been left alone for a few minutes to watch the snow fall and to savor the realization that this was her wedding day. Her and Devlin's. And she was ready.

Both her mother and Mrs. Proctor had been dubious about her choice of a wedding gown. But she had persisted, and Mrs. Proctor had outdone herself. It was of fine white wool, long sleeved, high to the neck, and falling almost straight from under her bosom. It appeared unadorned, but it shimmered with a smattering of sequins, which were otherwise almost invisible. Just yesterday the Countess of Stratton, who later today would be the *dowager* countess, had presented her with an heirloom brooch in the form of a spray of flowers, the largest of which had always reminded her of the star of Bethlehem, she had told Gwyneth. It was pinned to the dress now, just below the shoulder, the one splash of color on the dress itself.

Spread across her bed was the cloak she would wear, for it was winter and a dress, even with long sleeves, would not be warm enough. The cloak was a bright scarlet velvet and bordered up the sides and around the wide hood with a thick white lamb's wool.

She was not alone for long.

"Everyone who should have left for church has done so," her mother said, coming into Gwyneth's bedchamber after tapping on the door. "Dad is downstairs pacing like a caged dragon."

"I suppose," Gwyneth said, turning from the window with a smile, "he is worried about the music as much as he is about leading me down the aisle."

Her bridesmaids came into the room at that moment. Philippa

was dressed in her pale pink gown with matching cloak. Stephanie was in pale peach. And Joy, in Stephanie's arms and sucking her thumb, still obviously not quite sure she was not going to make a fuss about her father bringing her here and then leaving her alone with her aunts, looked like a shimmering snowflake in white. The bow in her hair must be almost as large as her head.

"Oh," Gwyneth said. "All three of you look *beautiful*." She wagged a finger at Stephanie, who had made the derisive puffing sound with the lips that was characteristic of her. "I said all *three* of you." Philippa's hair had been elaborately styled. Stephanie's was in its usual heavy braids wrapped about her head.

"Sir Ifor is complaining that his cravat is a size too small," Philippa said.

Stephanie clucked her tongue. "He says that every time we have a special concert," she said. "When we were in Wales for the eisteddfod, he said it was *three* sizes too small."

Joy wriggled to get down and went to pat the wool on Gwyneth's cloak and run her hand over it.

Idris poked his head about the door. "I say," he said. "Everyone is looking as fine as fivepence in here. Is there a *person* inside all those frills over there? It has white shoes. Ah, it is Joy Ellis. All right, Gwyn?"

"All right." She smiled at him.

"Ready, then, Mam?" he asked. "It is time we were on our way. We had better get on ahead of the bride."

Her mother hurried toward her and hugged her wordlessly before leaving the room.

"And time we followed," Gwyneth said. Philippa crossed the room to help her on with her cloak and arrange the hood becomingly at her back.

"I am *so* glad happiness is returning," she said. "Oh, you look . . . stunning, Gwyneth. Does she not, Steph? Just wait until Dev sees her!"

Stephanie was taking Joy by the hand.

It was her wedding day, Gwyneth thought as she went downstairs and her father stopped his pacing to gaze up at her with eyes that were suspiciously bright.

"Oh, Gwyn, fach," he said. "I am speechless. *Speechless* I am." And it seemed he was too after speaking those few words.

She kissed his cheek, squeezed his hand, and turned to the door, which the butler was holding open.

The church choristers and some extras from the youth choir were squeezed into the choir stalls and onto a row of chairs that had been placed in front of them on each side. The church pews were packed with invited guests. There were even a few people standing at the back and along the sides, Devlin saw with one quick glance back. He had no idea what time it was. Still before eleven? After? Right on?

Did all bridegrooms at this point feel sick with fear that the bride had changed her mind and would simply not show up? Did it ever happen? But even if it never had before, there was always a first for everything, was there not?

"Did you feel like this before *your* wedding?" he murmured to Ben, who was sitting beside him on the front pew. It was probably not the best thing to ask. He had had the suspicion yesterday and this morning that his brother was a bit melancholy. Dash it all, it was not quite a year since his wife died, even though it seemed more like a decade. Did it seem so to Ben?

"Nervous, do you mean?" Ben asked. "No. When I married Marjorie, she went with me to the chaplain, if you remember. She had to. I had her firmly by the hand, and Joy was well on the way in her. I was not going to take no for an answer."

"I do not believe she was reluctant," Devlin said.

"Only because of the fact that I was the son of an earl," Ben said. "Daft woman."

But he spoke with a fondness that almost brought tears to Devlin's eyes.

And then the vicar, clad in his full vestments, came from the vestry and strode along the nave to the back of the church, where there seemed to be an extra flurry of activity, and a few moments later Idris appeared, escorting Lady Rhys to the front pew across from Devlin's. She smiled at him before seating herself, and Idris winked.

She must be coming, then. Good God, his bride must be coming.

The vicar returned along the nave. Philippa and Stephanie, looking exceedingly pretty, followed him, side by side, Joy between them, clinging to a hand of each, so frilled and flounced that she looked like a snowflake winking and glittering in the sun. When they stopped walking, she bounced a few times on her feet and then spotted Ben.

"Papapapapapa," she cried, and dashed toward him, her arms raised, her hair ribbon somewhat askew. He scooped her up and she looked behind him over his shoulder and pointed to Devlin's mother in the next pew. "Grandmama," she said quite distinctly. "Owen."

But Devlin's attention was fixed on the back of the church as the congregation rose to its feet. A single note sounded from the pianoforte beside the organ, and the choir began to sing, unaccompanied.

Blest be the tie that binds
Our hearts in Christian love
The fellowship of kindred minds
Is like to that above

The first verse was sung by the treble voices alone, in perfect unison with one another. The following verses were sung by the whole choir in three-part harmony. But Devlin was only partially aware of how exquisite they sounded and how carefully the music and the words had been chosen—and rehearsed. For his bride was approaching on the arm of her father, and she had never looked more startlingly beautiful. Like a bright piece of Christmas, with all its promise of love and hope and peace.

But she was not *like* anything at all. She was Gwyneth. Unique and vivid and lovely. His wild child grown to womanhood. And his bride. His love.

She was smiling at him.

While he, like an idiot, was blinking back tears. He was almost not aware that he was also smiling, turned to face her as she came along the nave, and facing too his family and hers and their neighbors and friends from miles around.

There was a faint *aah* of sound from the congregation quite apart from the music of the choir. But whether it was for the beauty of the bride or the fact that the bridegroom's face was lit with love and happiness was not at all clear.

And then she was beside him and taking off her gloves to hand to Stephanie while Pippa was removing her cloak and draping it over her own arm. There was a gasp from those people gathered there as Gwyneth was revealed in all the figure-hugging, slightly shimmering simplicity of her white dress. She set her hand in her father's again, and he transferred it to Devlin's.

They turned to face the Reverend Danver, and Devlin swallowed against what felt like a lump in his throat. The wedding was beginning.

"Dearly beloved," the vicar said moments after the last note of the opening hymn had died away.

Feeling had been ruthlessly suppressed for many long years. It had been denied, fought against, explained away for several months since then. He had admitted to facts—the fact of love—but not to feeling, which was long gone. Which could never be resurrected. Denial could be a powerful force.

But now feeling came back in a wave of emotion.

Love was not a feeling, she had told him. No, it was not just feeling, though by God it could be felt. It was not anything that could be confined to the body or the mind or the spirit. It was not something to be understood or explained. Or owned. But whatever it was, suddenly it was fairly bursting from him.

He loved Gwyneth Rhys. He had loved her since he was a boy and she had seemed as unattainable as the wind. Or the sun.

More than that, though, he *loved*.

He was not just an observer of this life. He was a participant in it. And he wanted *all* it had to offer—every day, every experience, every pain and pleasure, every feeling from this moment until he took his dying breath. With Gwyneth. Had he told her she was the air he breathed? He thought he had. But he had not fully understood what he had meant until this moment. The air he breathed was *love*.

"I do," he said when prompted by the vicar.

"I do," she said.

He took the ring from Ben's steady hand—Joy was bouncing on his other arm and chuckling at something Owen must be doing—and slid it onto Gwyneth's finger. Symbol of eternal commitment. Of eternal love. He looked up into her eyes when it was in place.

And they were husband and wife, and he was leading her off to the vestry to sign the register and make it all official and final. Ben and Philippa witnessed their signatures and Ben hugged Gwyneth and shook Devlin's hand firmly while Pippa helped her on with her cloak and passed her the gloves Stephanie had held through the service. The vicar shook both their hands.

And then they were making their way back along the nave, her arm drawn through his. Through the open church doors he could see that it was still snowing. Sir Ifor was playing a glorious anthem on the organ. The church bells were ringing. A group of villagers were gathered on the village green, smiling and waving, perhaps even cheering. Owen and Nick and Idris and the Welsh cousins were preparing to launch an ambush in the space between the church doors and the carriage, which was all decked out with holly and ivy and ribbons and bows. Flower petals—from the Ravenswood hothouses, no doubt—rained down on their heads with the snowflakes.

Gwyneth was laughing and clinging to his hand. Devlin was laughing too and helping her into the carriage before arranging her cloak about her feet and climbing in after her.

"Well, my lady Stratton."

"Well, my lord Stratton." She looked at him with shining eyes.

"Gwyneth." He took her right hand in his right while he wrapped his left arm about her shoulders.

"At least have the decency to wait until the door has been

closed." It was Idris calling out to them, his hands cupped about his mouth.

"Yes, Dev," Owen called. "Remember that I am only eighteen."

The congregation was spilling out of the church.

"To the devil with them," Devlin said, smiling at his bride as he drew her closer and kissed her on the mouth.

There were a few piercing whistles. The organ was still playing inside the church. The bells were still pealing. The carriage door slammed shut. The carriage rocked into motion, and the unholy din of the expected pots and pans and other paraphernalia tied beneath the carriage drowned out all other sound.

Devlin lifted his head and looked at his bride. She looked back. And they both laughed.

"I love you," he mouthed to her.

"I know," she mouthed back.

As the carriage rumbled over the bridge on its way back to Ravenswood, he kissed her again. What else was there to do, after all?